CHOOSING LOVE

WELCOME TO HARDY FALLS

BETSY HORVATH

VARIOUS MINDED BOOKS

Various Minded Books
PO Box 792
Quakertown, PA 18951
Email: admin@variousmindedbooks.com
www.variousmindedbooks.com

Publisher's Note: This is a work of fiction. Names, characters, places, and incidents are a product of the author's imagination. Locales and public names are sometimes used for atmospheric purposes. Any resemblance to actual people, living or dead, or to businesses, companies, events, institutions, or locales is entirely coincidental.

Choosing Love / Betsy Horvath. -- 1st ed.
ISBN 978-1-943725-11-3

DEDICATION

For my mother, Lorraine, and my dear friend, Christine

Gone too soon. Missed so much.

1
____

"I'm sorry, Jenny. I'm so, so sorry."

Jenny Kline stared into the tear-filled brown eyes of the woman sitting across the table from her and tried to resist the urge to pinch herself. There was no point. This whole conversation might seem like a dream, but she knew she wasn't asleep.

She really was sitting in a worn booth at the Sunnyside Diner in downtown Hardy Falls, Pennsylvania. She really was having breakfast with Missy Leon, her friend and boss, while a chilly late-March rain pounded against the diner's big plate glass windows and turned the morning outside to steel gray. She really was smelling bacon and eggs and coffee, as Mr. and Mrs. Bunson and their staff served the local crowd that was bustling in and out of the rain on the way to work on a Monday. And she really was...

"Did you just say you're firing me?" she asked, wanting to confirm she'd heard her friend correctly. Maybe Missy had said, "I have to *hire* you." Although that didn't make any sense because Jenny had been working with Missy for a long time now. Almost nine years. Even when Jenny still lived with her ex-boyfriend, Stefan, in his townhouse near the university a few miles away, she'd worked for Missy's housecleaning business. She'd assumed they'd gotten even closer once she'd finally ditched the bastard and moved home.

"I'm sorry," Missy repeated and reached across the linoleum tabletop to grab Jenny's hand. "I don't have a choice. I just can't pay you anymore."

Jenny pulled her hand away.

"I thought everything was good! What happened to all the money?" Okay, that wasn't exactly tactful, but she was honestly stunned. As far as she knew, the business had been chugging right along. They'd certainly been working hard enough between the housecleaning and the catering work Missy had insisted they start doing last year. In fact, they'd gotten so busy that Jenny hadn't been able to get out to her art studio in weeks.

Missy sat back in her seat. Her round face was still blotchy from tears, but there was a harder light in her eyes now.

"I'm not sure that's any of your business," she said flatly.

Jenny drew in a sharp breath, the slap-down unexpected. *Ouch. That hurt.*

Because, yes, technically Missy owned the housecleaning service and was Jenny's boss. And Missy had been the one to cut the deal with Mr. Foster, the caterer, so they could both earn some extra money. Jenny had happily tagged along. Technically, Jenny was a freelancer. But it never felt that way. She might not have been especially interested in all of the business stuff Missy tried to show her—she had enough trouble with her own taxes, thank you—but in everything else she'd considered herself to be kind of a partner. She'd thought she and Missy were a team.

Wrong again.

"Sorry," she managed.

"God." Missy ran her hands through her thick mass of curly, brown hair.

"Here you go, loves." A matronly waitress came up to the

table holding two thick white ceramic plates. She slid them across the table before stepping back and studying them with sharp eyes partially hidden by large glasses. "Everything okay?"

Jenny forced a smile for the older woman. "Yes, thanks, Mrs. Dorinsky. We're good." She'd worked at the Sunnyside through high school and a couple of years after graduation, so she still knew everyone on the staff. Which meant they all felt free to be up in her business.

Mrs. Dorinsky looked skeptical, but she nodded and headed off, sturdy black sneakers squeaking, to get orders from the four old men who'd just settled at a nearby table. It looked like Albert Cromwell, Harry Newman, Joe Horton, and Martin Scanner were right on time today.

Jenny turned her attention back to Missy.

"You don't need to tell me," she apologized. "I'm sorry I was snarky."

"It's okay." Missy avoided eye contact and looked out the window at the rain. "Buster's been borrowing money from the business for over a year." The words came out in a rush.

"What?" Jenny gaped at the other woman, shocked again. "Really?"

Darren "Buster" Leon was Missy's husband. The two had dated in high school and gotten married a year or two after graduation mostly, Jenny knew, because Teagan, their now thirteen-year-old son, had been on the way. Jenny actually liked Buster, although sometimes the man could be pretty damned dense.

"Yeah." Missy sighed and turned to look at her. "He needed cash to pay for parts and taxes and stuff like that at his shop." Buster owned a motorcycle repair shop on the other side of town. "He always paid it back before—he just needed it when his accounts receivable got behind, so he could keep the cash flow working."

"Okay," Jenny said, although she honestly knew nothing

about accounting and was happy to keep it that way. "If he was paying it back, then—"

"I said *before*," Missy interrupted and picked at the ridged metal strapping running around the edge of the tabletop. "His shop hasn't been doing so well, and then he got stiffed on a really big job so he couldn't pay me back, and he needed more to keep going. It all kind of snowballed."

"Wow." Jenny couldn't think of anything else to say because Missy normally wasn't this stupid.

She tried not to let her thoughts show on her face, but she must have failed because the look her friend shot her was defensive.

"He's my husband," Missy said shortly. "His business pays our mortgage."

"No, I know." Jenny tried to soothe, although she wanted to point out that it was total bullshit. Obviously Missy's business was the one bringing in the cash or Buster wouldn't have needed to borrow it all the damned time, and he would have been able to repay what he *had* borrowed.

On the other hand, finding out what had been going on sure explained a heck of a lot. Not only had Missy hooked them up with the caterer, but she'd also been adding more and more properties to their housecleaning list over the past couple of months. Jenny had been surprised when her friend had refused to discuss the need for another cleaner to handle the expanding workload, but now it was clear why.

Shoving her scrambled eggs around on her plate, she frowned at Missy. "So, what? You're thinking you're going to just do everything yourself? That's impossible." They were overwhelmed as it was.

Missy fiddled with her own food. "Buster's going to help me," she said.

Jenny couldn't control her snort of disbelief. "Oh, *right*." Buster wasn't exactly known for his cleanliness.

"He *will*," Missy insisted, frowning at her. "This is our business, and he knows we need to make it work." She shrugged. "Until he gets the motorcycle shop turned around, anyway."

Like that will happen.

"So he thinks he's going to able to do both?" Jenny asked, feeling even more skeptical. Easy going Buster Leon was far better at coasting along than multitasking.

"We'll find a way to make it work," Missy maintained. "It will just take a little juggling."

"If you say so."

Jenny didn't want to argue anymore, but she had a crystal clear picture of how this was all going to go down.

Last fall, Missy had taken on the contract to clean Dr. and Mrs. Black's huge McMansion after the couple had fired yet another cleaning service. Mrs. Black wanted what she wanted when she wanted it with no excuses—especially when she was hosting one of her many charity fundraisers.

On top of that, Ms. Gregory, the town librarian, had just hired them to clean some of her business properties. The old lady was a real estate mogul and a shark who put up with zero shit. Between the two of them, Missy was going to have her hands full and then some.

"I could help you for a while for free," Jenny offered. She might be angry and, yes, hurt, but this woman had been one of the most important people in her life for a long time. She wasn't going to let her drown merely because she was pissed off.

Missy shook her head and her curls bounced, the fluorescent lighting catching the red highlights in the brown. "No, but thanks for that." She smiled slightly. "I'm not saying it wouldn't help, but Buster and I have to figure out a way to handle this on our own. You wouldn't be able to work for free forever."

Well, that was true. Jenny was living with her mother at the moment, but she still had expenses and debt, and she really,

really, *really* wanted to be able to afford her own place soon. As much as she loved her mother, Jackie Kline wasn't always the easiest person in the whole world to get along with. It probably came from being the police chief. You think you're in charge of everything.

"I could ask Mr. Foster to give me more hours," she said, considering her options. For the most part, they'd only been working with the man when he handled Mrs. Black's events, but he certainly had more clients. He could probably use her, and the work would be flexible.

Missy shifted and looked even more uncomfortable. "Um... about that."

Uh-oh. That doesn't sound good.

Jenny frowned at her. "What?"

"He asked me to tell you that, uh," Missy cleared her throat, "he doesn't need you anymore."

Jenny sat back. "He's firing me, too?"

"I guess."

She tried to understand. "Well, why? I ran my feet off for that man." Mrs. Black's fundraisers were killers.

Missy's big brown eyes pleaded for understanding. "You spilled champagne on Mayor Truelove's new dress at the fundraiser on Friday. She complained to him."

Jenny gasped, outraged. "That was her own damned fault! She couldn't wait a freaking second, like a civilized person, for me to hand her a flute. No, she has to try to grab it. And because she's been having the nail salon put on artificial talons that make her look like a bird of prey, she couldn't get a grip, and the glass slipped, and she knocked the tray." Champagne had poured down the new mayor's fancy sequined evening dress. But Mayor Truelove had laughed it off, shook her bright blond bouffant-styled hair, and said it didn't matter. And then apparently she'd run right to Mr. Foster! The snake!

"I guess she thinks you could have caught it. And the dress

is ruined. It was expensive."

"Oh, right. I'll bet she couldn't wait to tell Foster what happened," Jenny muttered. Mayor Margo Truelove had it in for the Kline family these days. In the last election, some people—including, Jenny knew, the four old reprobates currently yukking it up over at the other table—had written Jenny's mother's name on their ballots, even though Jackie Kline did not want to be mayor and was not running.

It didn't matter. Margo became convinced that Jackie wanted her job. The woman couldn't even acknowledge that the only reason she'd beaten the incumbent mayor in the first place was because the write-ins had split the race three ways. No, now Margo spent her days figuring out ways to assert her dominance.

"Mr. Foster can't afford to have Margo angry at him," Missy continued. "She's holding a lot of town events now. Besides, she's good friends with Mrs. Black and you know how much business he does with the Blacks. He didn't have a choice but to agree to fire you."

"Right." Jenny resisted throwing her fork across the room because, with her luck, she'd spear somebody. "So what you're saying is that I've lost both of my jobs today."

Missy bit her lip. "I'm so sorry, Jenny. But you'll find something."

Jenny looked at her friend. "Yeah?" she demanded sarcastically. "Like what?"

Missy was quiet for a moment, obviously struggling to come up with something.

"Well," she said at last, "you have all of that waitressing experience. Maybe the Bunsons need someone to work here at the Sunnyside? Or maybe Hannah needs someone at the Country Time?"

Well, *yeah*, Hannah *had* needed someone at the Country Time Bar and Grill. Past tense. In fact, she'd asked Jenny if she wanted to come on board as a waitress because she'd decided to open her local tavern hangout earlier for lunch service. Jenny's younger sister Josie, a marketing guru and Hannah's best friend, had been urging her to open the place earlier for a while now, but Hannah had been afraid of the risk. Now that she had an investor fund to help finance the business, she was even more paranoid about taking chances.

But for whatever reason, Hannah had finally decided to give lunch service a try. Since Jenny had helped out at the Country Time before, she'd asked her to think about making it more official.

Jenny had declined the offer because Hannah couldn't give her enough hours to replace the income she made with Missy and Mr. Foster. And Jenny hadn't wanted to cut back on her hours working with Missy because, you know, they were a team.

Surprise, surprise.

Although, to be fair, another big reason Jenny had declined Hannah's offer was because Josie was usually at the Country Time. Her sister had moved back to town and hooked up with Mateo Guerrero, the tavern's sexy cook / bartender / dishwasher. It was bad enough that being with Josie and Hannah always made Jenny feel like a complete outsider. She didn't think she'd be able to handle watching Josie snuggle up with Mat day in and day out on top of it.

Especially since Jenny had kind of been hoping to snuggle up with Mat herself.

So, yeah. She'd said no, and Hannah had hired other people for the lunch service starting the first week of April.

"And you have your painting," Missy continued, blissfully unaware of her thoughts.

"Yes." Jenny always had her painting. Always had her dream hovering just at the edge of the horizon. Just out of reach.

"It's nice to have a hobby," Missy said, smiling and chattering away. "It will give you something to do while you look for another job. I wish I had something I could do like that. Take my mind off things. If I have downtime, I just watch television."

Jenny held onto her patience. "It's not a hobby," she reminded her friend. "It's more than that."

"Oh, no. I know." Missy seemed to realize she'd made a misstep. "No, you're doing good. And you're even selling things now that your paintings are hanging at the Country Time." Hannah had decided to feature local artists and had taken on a few of Jenny's paintings. "People are starting to know who you are. So maybe this is a good thing. You'll have time to concentrate on that before you have to be tied down with a real job again."

"Sure."

Her art WAS a real job.

It was just a real job that didn't pay any money at the moment.

Missy opened her mouth and closed it again. Her face made it clear that she didn't know what else to say.

That was wrong, Jenny thought. It shouldn't be like this between her and Missy.

"It's okay," she said, making herself smile at her friend. "I'll work it out."

"I know you will," Missy nodded and then shifted to gather up her purse. "I'm sorry, but I have to take off and head over to the Walsh's house." She rooted around for money.

"Um, have fun?" Jenny said.

"Right." Missy wrinkled her nose. She threw some bills on the table and grabbed the muffin off her plate. "I've got this, but you'll take it up to pay, right?" They hadn't gotten the check yet, but they both knew the menu inside and out at the Sunnyside.

"Okay." Jenny wanted to protest about her friend picking up the tab, but she stayed quiet when she remembered she didn't have a job anymore. Missy slid out of the booth and stood for a moment, looking down at her.

"I really am sorry," she said.

"I know," Jenny assured her. And she did.

Missy hesitated, then turned and left. Jenny watched her go out the door and step into the heavy rain. After another minute or two, Missy's little car pulled out onto Main Street and drove away.

The shock was wearing off a little bit, and now all she wanted to do was cry.

"Everything okay, honey? Missy left without finishing her breakfast and you haven't eaten a thing."

Jenny looked up to meet Mrs. Dorinsky's concerned pale eyes behind her dark-framed glasses.

"It's fine, Mrs. D." She hesitated. "I don't suppose there are any openings here, are there?"

"No, dear. The Bunsons have been having a bit of a rough time of it since that restaurant with 24-hour service opened out on the highway. We can't compete." Mrs. Dorinsky's plain face creased. "Are you sure you're okay?"

Jenny smiled. "I'm sure. You can just bring the check." She hesitated. "Does Mrs. B. have some extra muffins around? I wanted to get six or so to take down to mom at the police department."

Better make an effort to sweeten her mother's mood, since it didn't look like she'd be moving out of the house any time soon.

"Of course, dear," Mrs. Dorinsky smiled. "I'll get them for you." She bustled away and returned a few minutes later with a white box.

"Here are six. And the check."

Jenny thanked her, took the box up to the register to pay the bill, said hello to a beaming Mrs. Bunson, waved at the four old men at the table and a few other people she knew, then headed outside. She got drenched immediately.

Well, this sure was a hell of a way to start the day.

2

Not much ticked off the genial Mrs. Bunson, but taking up a parking space at the Sunnyside when you weren't eating there definitely topped the list, so Jenny drove from the diner to the police station instead of walking. It took longer to move her little pickup truck than it would have to simply walk the four blocks, but today it was definitely the drier option. Plus, she wouldn't get an angry phone call later if Mrs. B. noticed her vehicle was still in the lot.

After she parked her truck again, this time between the squat brick police station and the bigger, fancier borough hall, Jenny turned off the engine and sat, tapping her fingers on the steering wheel. The bakery box of fresh-baked muffins made the cramped cab smell like heaven.

She knew her mother would appreciate the muffins, but that was about it. Jackie wouldn't like hearing that her older daughter was suddenly and completely unemployed.

Jenny had been working with Missy because, up until the last few months, the housecleaning job had been intense but not all-consuming. Before the cleaning schedule had gotten out of control, and before the catering gig with Mr. Foster had come up, she'd been able to structure her days pretty much as she'd seen fit. That meant she could paint. As far as Jenny was concerned, that made the work perfect.

Her mother disagreed, to put it mildly. Jackie thought Jenny was being foolish and wasting her time, and she said as much on a regular basis. Now she'd feel vindicated. The phrase "I told you so" was bound to get tossed around.

Jenny drummed her fingers on the steering wheel. She didn't *have* to tell her mother what had happened, of course. She was almost thirty-two freaking years old, and she sure as hell did not have to run to her mommy whenever there was a problem. She could look after herself.

But Jackie would find out sooner or later. Heck, she might already know some of it. Jenny wouldn't have put it past Margo Truelove to prance over from the mayor's office specifically to tell Jackie that she'd gotten Foster to fire her daughter, delighted to have flexed her power to such effect. And besides, as soon as people found out Missy was working with Buster now instead of Jenny, the gossip would start.

No, her mother would hear everything eventually, so it would be better if Jenny told her before the rumor mill got a hold of it. At least that way Jackie would only be pissed off that she'd been fired from both of her jobs and not because she'd lied or tried to keep it a secret.

As if anything could be kept a secret in Hardy Falls.

With a resigned sigh, Jenny grabbed the box of muffins and her purse, opened the driver's door, and sprinted through the rain to the glass double doors engraved with "Hardy Falls Police Department." She pushed them open and stepped into the small entry vestibule.

As the doors slapped shut behind her, she shook herself like a wet dog and then walked over to a long, rectangular window next to a security door. The frameless window had a metal drawer underneath that looked like a bank drive-through and a red button on the side with an index card saying you should "press for service" taped to the wall above it. Jenny hit the call button.

"Yes?" The voice that came through the speaker on the metal drawer was tinny, but still smooth and controlled. "Can I help you?"

"I'm the one who can help you," Jenny said. "I brought breakfast."

"Jenny?" There were sounds of a struggle, and then Suzy Griffith was at the window's thick bulletproof glass, smiling back at her. "Come on in."

The security door buzzed open. Jenny walked through to the reception area and pulled the taller and hugely pregnant Suzy into a one-armed hug.

"Suzy!" She laughed because hugging the station's receptionist was a little hard these days. "How is the hellion?"

The other woman's dark eyes sparkled in a pretty face that was all honey-brown skin and deep dimples framed in close-cropped black hair. "The kid is ready to pop." She took a step back and rubbed her protruding stomach with one hand. "Or maybe that's just me. I'm ready to see my baby."

Jenny held up the bakery box and shook it. "This will make it all better. Muffins from the Sunnyside." Knight's Bakery in town could do many things well, but Mrs. Bunson rocked the muffins. "I'm sure the chief won't mind if you have one."

"You are my hero." Suzy waddled back to her desk and collapsed into her chair with a sigh. "Gotta sit down. My back is killing me today."

Jenny frowned with quick concern. "You shouldn't be working."

Suzy shrugged. "I feel okay. Just a little unwieldy. The kid's not due for another couple of weeks anyway, and I'll go nuts if I'm stuck at home." She ran her hands over her stomach then scowled at the phone when it rang at her elbow. "Sorry." She picked up the receiver and answered.

"Hey, hobbit. What are you doing here?" a lazy male voice said.

Jenny squeezed her eyes shut for an instant.

Of course *he* would be there. She should have known. It was just her luck today.

Police Officer Harry Newman III. Grandson of one of the old men she'd left back at the Sunnyside Diner, and one of the few people in Hardy Falls she actively tried to avoid if it was at all possible.

Smoothing out her expression, she turned deliberately and looked at the man lounging in the hallway that led back to the squad room.

He made an impact, she could admit that much. His dark uniform shirt was unbuttoned at the neck to expose a bit of white T-shirt underneath, his arms were crossed over his broad chest, his long legs were crossed at the heel. His black police-issue shoes gleamed with polish, his golden-brown hair sparkled in the fluorescent lights overhead, and his eyes, more green than blue, glinted with undisguised amusement behind ridiculously long lashes.

The first time she'd met him when he'd joined the department three or four years ago, she'd about swallowed her tongue despite the fact she'd been living with Stefan at the time. But that had been before she'd gotten to know him and found out how annoying he could be.

"I told you not to call me that," she reminded him coolly. Once upon a time, she'd made the mistake of saying that she thought of herself as the "hobbit in the middle" of the three Kline kids because her older brother, Jordan, and her younger sister, Josie, were both so much taller than she was. Harry heard, and he never forgot anything.

He smirked, obviously unrepentant.

"If the shire fits," he said, shrugging.

Jenny tried not to growl.

"You're an ass," she assured him.

He shrugged again, but his eyes were laser-focused on the white box she held. "Is that food?"

"No." She resisted the urge to clutch the box to her chest, which would not have done the muffins any favors.

"You're lying. I can smell it from here." Putting his nose in the air like a wolf, he sniffed then grinned. "Hot damn. Muffins." Straightening, he reached out and gestured with his hand. "Give."

"No." Jenny swung around, putting her back to him to protect the baked goods. "I need to see my mother, and I might need a bribe."

Suzy, who was still on the phone, looked up at her with huge, soulful eyes.

"Exceptions made for the pregnant woman, of course," Jenny amended and slipped open the box to put a random muffin on Suzy's desk. The receptionist gave her a broad smile.

Harry had tried to circle around her, but she spun away again before he could make a grab for the box. She looked at him over her shoulder and saw him scowling, hands on hips.

"Why do you have to be so mean? And why do you need a bribe? What did you do this time?" he demanded.

Jenny knew she shouldn't let him irritate her. She really shouldn't. But...

"Nothing," she snapped. "I didn't do anything, there's nothing wrong, and even if there is, it's none of your business."

She immediately cursed herself because now he would know that something was indeed wrong. Before he could press her further, she turned back to Suzy. The other woman had hung up the phone and was watching the two of them like a spectator at a tennis match, one hand cupped protectively over her belly.

Crap.

"Is the chief busy?" Jenny demanded.

Suzy's big eyes widened, but she smiled. "Well, nobody's in there yelling at her at the moment."

Jenny nodded sharply, then marched to the closed office door on the other side of the reception area. A sign on the wall read, "Jacqueline Kline, Chief of Police." The smell of old coffee coming from a huge machine bubbling in the break room next door was potent enough to knock out the faint of heart, and she wondered if that was where Harry had been heading before he'd decided to stop and harass her. Or maybe he'd just heard her voice and thought he'd grace her with his presence.

She raised her hand to knock on the door and couldn't stop herself from glancing back at him. Sure enough, he was watching her, but his expression was thoughtful and without any of the usual cynical amusement. It occurred to Jenny that a focused Harry Newman was even more attractive than the normal smirking one.

Shaking off the thought, she knocked. When the call came to enter, she pushed open the door. Stepping into the little office, she closed the door behind her and smiled at her mother.

"Hey," she said.

"Jenny!" Jackie Kline, slender with sharp blue eyes under short black hair just starting to turn silver at the edges, settled back in her chair and grinned. "I thought I heard you out there. This is a surprise."

"Yeah." Jenny sank into one of the visitor's chairs.

Jackie was quiet for a moment.

"Uh-oh," she said.

"Nothing bad," Jenny assured her quickly. "Look, I brought you muffins." She put the box on her mother's desk. "From the Sunnyside, so you know they're good."

"Muffins? Really?" Distracted, Jackie opened the box and looked inside. "I'm a cop, and you don't bring me donuts?"

"Ha ha. You know you like muffins better."

"True." Jackie picked out one and put it on the desk on top of one of the napkins Mrs. Bunson had provided. She picked off part of the crown and popped it into her mouth. "Good," she mumbled around the crumbs. "Want one?"

"No." Jenny shook her head. "I just had breakfast."

"Did you give one to Suzy?"

"Do you think I'm crazy? Of course I gave one to Suzy."

"And Harry?"

"No," Jenny said shortly. "Harry doesn't deserve one."

"Hmmm." Jackie pulled off another bit and tossed it into her mouth, watching Jenny as she chewed. "What did you do?" she asked after she'd swallowed.

Jenny's irritation flared again. "Why does everyone think *I* did something?" she demanded. "Maybe something was done to me."

Her mother's eyes sharpened. "And was something done to you?"

Jenny shifted in her seat. "Sort of."

"Jenny."

Jenny shifted again.

"I'm handling it. I'm only here to try and beat the gossip," she said. "I didn't want you to be blindsided."

Jackie settled back and watched her steadily. "I think you'd better spill it."

Jenny didn't *want* to "spill it." But at this point she kind of had to.

Drawing herself up, she cleared her throat.

"Okay. So, I didn't tell you this before, but at the Blacks' party on Friday, when I was working with the caterer, I sort of, um, spilled champagne all over Margo Truelove, our town's beloved new mayor."

Jackie closed her eyes.

"And she was wearing an evening gown."

Jackie winced.

"And I think it was expensive."

Her mother's sigh was heartfelt and deep.

"And *why* didn't you tell me this before?" she asked, eyes still closed. "You know that woman has gone insane as far as I'm concerned."

"Because Margo said it was okay. She said it was a mistake, and mistakes happen, and the gown didn't cost that much."

"And you believed her?"

Now Jenny winced. "I guess." She'd forgotten about it, to tell the truth. "But then today I found out that she went to Mr. Foster yesterday and told him to fire me and so he…is. Firing me, that is."

Jackie's eyes snapped open.

"Say what now?"

"Mom," Jenny warned, leery of the expression on Jackie's face. "Don't do anything stupid. I wouldn't have even told you about it except you know as well as I do that Margo is going to wait for an opportunity to come over here and make snide comments and throw her weight around—"

"She's got enough of it," Jackie muttered.

"—so I didn't want you to be caught by surprise."

"Well, thanks for that, but if that old biddy—"

"That old biddy is the mayor and has power in the town council for some reason I will never understand. And she still basically runs the Chamber of Commerce." Margo had been head of the town's Chamber of Commerce for years before she was elected mayor. Her roots ran deep. "Don't pick a fight, okay? She can make your life a living hell."

"She already makes my life a living hell," Jackie grumbled. She leaned forward and jammed about half of the muffin she'd been picking at into her mouth, chewing violently and swallowing with some effort. "I won't have her hurting you," she warned.

Jenny shrugged, resigned. "I did spill the champagne on her. I lost the whole tray of flutes, and it made a mess. Mr. Foster has the right to fire me. He would have fired any of the other girls—he didn't single me out. I remember when Kayla, one of the college kids, dropped a tray of canapés on Mrs. Black's dress. She didn't even get to finish out the evening."

Jackie's scowl was ferocious. "I still don't like it, and I'm going to make sure I let Foster know."

"It's his business, so he has the right to run it the way he sees fit."

Jackie was silent for a moment. She took another, more manageable bite of what was left of the muffin. "At least it was just a part-time job, and you were only working for him once or twice a month," she said when she was done chewing. "With as much work as you and Missy have in the cleaning business, you won't even miss the money."

"Yeah," Jenny said. *This was the harder part.* "About that. There's something else you should probably know before the rumors start flying."

Jackie went still. "Do tell," she said softly. It was not a suggestion.

"Um...I'm not going to be working with Missy anymore."

Jackie blinked.

"Excuse me? Did you get another job?"

"No." Jenny fidgeted and wished the office was large enough to pace. "Missy's, uh, having financial problems, so she can't pay me." She figured her mother didn't need to know about the situation with Buster.

Jackie's eyes were steady on hers. "So, are you telling me that you lost *both* of your jobs?"

Jenny shrugged.

"And, since you weren't considered a W-2 employee in either job, you can't even get unemployment?"

Jenny had really hoped her mother wouldn't figure that part out so quickly.

"Yeah."

"Jennifer Marie Kline, I told you it wasn't a good idea for you to work this way," her mother's voice snapped. "Forget the extra taxes—"

"That Missy helped me pay," Jenny pointed out.

"You need a real job with real benefits. You're thirty-two years old, for God's sake, and now that you've finally gotten your head out of your butt as far as that loser Stefan is concerned, you need to be moving forward and planning for the future!"

Jenny's stomach clenched. Here it was. The conversation she'd been dreading. The argument they always seemed to have.

"I—"

She was interrupted by a knock on the door. Harry stuck his head into the office without waiting for a response.

"Chief," he said, sounding urgent. "We've got a situation out here."

"What is it?" Jackie asked as she got to her feet and moved quickly around the desk.

"Suzy."

"Suzy?" Her mother's face morphed from disapproval to concern as she followed Harry out into the reception area. Worried, Jenny went after them.

Suzy was sitting at her desk. She was panting. Her face was sweaty, and her hands were on the mound of her stomach. Her dark eyes were wild when she looked at Jackie.

"I was getting up to go to the bathroom, and...and..." she gestured. There was a puddle of liquid on the floor near her chair.

"You peed yourself?" Jenny asked, confused.

Suzy's scowl was sudden and deep. "No!" She shut her eyes. "Oh, man."

For a moment Jenny still didn't get it. Then she did, and her mouth dropped open.

"Your water broke? Is that what that is?"

"Yes!" Suzy yelled, panting harder. "I'm not sure this little bugger is going to take his time," she told Jackie and winced. "I thought I was just having back spasms, but maybe I've been in labor? Now the contractions are coming pretty hard and fast. Oh, man." She breathed hard. "Crap. Shit. My first one was in a hurry, too."

Jackie ignored the puddle on the floor and crouched next to Suzy. She put her hands on her stomach before she nodded.

"Yeah, I think you're right."

"Holy shit." Suzy swallowed. "Holy shit, I'm having a baby."

Jackie grinned at her. "Yes, you are." She got to her feet and turned to Harry. "Call Tony, will you? He was heading to Pocono Summit for some training today. Tell him to meet us at the hospital."

Looking a bit shell-shocked, Harry ran to do as he was told.

"But the hospital's forty minutes away," Suzy wailed, even as she gasped through the next contraction. "The baby wasn't supposed to come yet. This is too early. He wasn't due for two weeks! We don't have a baby sitter for Marley today after daycare!"

"Babies have their own schedules. I'll call your mother from the car." Jackie gently helped Suzy to her feet.

"I'll call the ambulance," Jenny said, trying to be helpful. But her mother shook her head.

"No point. We'll lose more time waiting for them to show up. I'll get her there."

"But what if the baby comes before we get there?" Suzy

wailed. "Marley was fast. The second is supposed to come even faster!"

"Well, then I'll have to dust off my midwife skills," Jackie told her with admirable calm as she steered her toward the hallway. Jenny ran into the break room and got the coat she assumed was Suzy's. She draped it over the pregnant woman's shoulders to try to protect her from the rain.

"Can I do anything?" she asked.

"Maybe answer the phones?" her mother said, obviously distracted. "Help Harry?"

"Sure."

Okay. She could answer phones. Harry could fend for himself.

"But I was supposed to get drugs this time!" Suzy wailed and then panted again as she waddled and dripped fluid down the hallway to the employee entrance. Jenny followed, feeling helpless. "They were going to give me an epidural this time! They promised!"

"I'm sorry, sweetie. We'll see where you're at when you get to the hospital." Jackie tried to soothe her and usher her down the hall and past the squad room and the holding cells.

"It's not fair! I didn't even know I was in labor!"

Jenny put her hand over her mouth to smother her laugh because she was pretty sure Suzy wouldn't appreciate it. "Do you have a bag packed?" she asked.

"Yes!" Suzy turned her head, and her crazed eyes latched onto Jenny. "I have everything packed. Tony laughed at me because he thought I was jumping the gun. But it's at home!" Big tears rolled down her face. "It's at home, and I can't get it, and I wore a skirt, and now I'm dripping everywhere!"

Jenny helped her mother maneuver Suzy through the employee entrance at the end of the hallway. "We'll get it," she promised.

"Tony's on it," Harry said from a safe distance away. "He's

going right by the house. He'll pick up the bag and meet you at the hospital."

"Okay." Suzy clung to the doorframe when Jackie tried to pull her outside. "I'm having a baby," she said. And then she smiled.

"Yes, you are." Jenny reached up to kiss Suzy on the cheek and then peeled the other woman's fingers from the doorframe.

Jackie helped the receptionist, who wouldn't be pregnant too much longer, through the door. Harry hustled after them. A minute later, Jenny heard the sirens.

Baby Griffith was coming in hot.

Harry came back inside, and for a moment they just stood staring at each other.

"Holy shit," he said, running his hands through his hair until it was a rumpled mess. "Holy *shit!*" He pointed at the floor. "And what the hell is that?"

Jenny turned and saw that Suzy had left a wet trail the length of the police station.

"Want to help me clean up amniotic fluid?" she asked.

Harry went pale.

"Oh, *hell* no!"

"Wimp."

3

Jenny followed Harry to the doorway of the squad room and stood with her hands on her hips, glaring at him as he sat down at one of the four desks clustered in the center of the space. He ignored her and picked up the phone receiver, glanced at the computer screen, and punched out a number.

"You know, I don't even really work here," she pointed out.

Harry waved her away and started talking to whomever it was he had called.

"Just because I've been cleaning houses for a living doesn't mean I want to clean the police station, too. If it's anybody's job, it's yours."

He ignored her. From what she could hear of the conversation, he was contacting the part-time police officers to help provide coverage since Tony would be out of action for a while.

She *guessed* that was important.

Muttering under her breath because of *course* she would clean up the damned floor, Jenny took off her coat and hung it on a hook before heading to the utility closet to get a mop and bucket. After she filled the bucket with water, she hauled it out and started mopping.

The phone rang, but Harry yelled that he would get it, so she kept working.

By the time she made her way back to the squad room, she could hear that he was talking to Suzy's mother, who'd gotten Jackie's call and seemed to be freaking out because her daughter was on the way to the hospital.

"Yes, Mrs. Brennan. Yes, ma'am. The chief will drive very safely, ma'am. Yes, I know it's a long way." He paused. "No, ma'am. I swear you don't need me to take you in the police cruiser. Just meet them at the hospital, like the chief said when she called. Don't even worry about intercepting them."

Jenny grinned as she mopped, listening to him calm the woman down. She couldn't blame Mrs. Brennan for being nervous, though. Under the same circumstances, her own mother would have been a wreck, trying to boss everyone around.

Her smile faded. When Josie and Mat had kids, that's the way it would go. Jackie would be simultaneously over the moon and as protective as a mother bear.

Maybe if things had gone differently with her and Stefan, she'd be pregnant by now and—

"Done?"

Jenny jerked back to reality, only to see Harry standing in the doorway of the squad room watching her. He was keeping a safe distance away from the bucket, though.

"Almost." She frowned at him, irritated for no good reason.

Out in the main open space, the phone on the receptionist's desk rang again, and Jenny jumped.

"I need to forward the phones to dispatch," Harry muttered. "I'll get it."

She scowled at him when he turned away. "I'll answer it this time," she snapped and propped the mop up against the wall. Her mother had asked *her* to answer the damned phones.

"You don't—"

"I said I'll get it!"

Pushing him aside, she strode over to one of the desks and picked up the phone. She didn't know a lot about how the station's antiquated system worked, but she took a guess and pushed the button next to a red, blinking light. To her surprise, it connected.

"Hardy Falls Police Department."

"He-...hello?" The voice was elderly and frail.

"Yes." Jenny sat down on the chair at the desk. "Who is this?" She looked at the caller ID and blinked. "Mrs. Brady?"

Vera Brady was 92 and still lived alone in a farmhouse at the foot of a mountain.

"Yes." Mrs. Brady took a quavering breath and then let it out. "Is this Jackie? It sounds like Jackie."

"No, Mrs. Brady. This is Jenny. I'm Jackie's daughter."

"Jenny. I know you. And your sister and brother." Another breath.

Harry had followed Jenny, and now he made an impatient gesture, wanting to know what was going on. She waved her hand at him. "What's wrong, Mrs. Brady? I can tell there's something wrong."

"I...I fell, dear."

"Oh, no." Jenny thought of the little lady who looked like a stiff breeze could knock her over. "Don't move, Mrs. Brady," she said urgently.

"I...can't, honey."

"Hold on." Heart pounding, Jenny looked up at Harry, who was already shrugging into his coat. He glanced at her with green-blue eyes that did not hold even a hint of humor.

"What happened?" Concise. In control.

"Mrs. Brady fell," Jenny told him. "I don't think she can get up."

Harry nodded. "Tell her I'm on my way," he instructed. "I'll be there in five minutes. Less, if possible."

"The ambulance—"

"I'll call them from the car."

"Her door is probably locked."

"I'll get in." And then he was gone.

"Harry's on the way, Mrs. Brady," she told the woman. "Officer Harry Newman. He'll be there soon. And he'll call the ambulance."

"Oh, that's good, dear." Already there was less tension in the fragile voice. "He's such a good boy. He's been here before, so he knows where the key is."

"Good." Jenny swallowed her emotions and forced herself to concentrate. Harry would be there soon, but the ambulance could take a few minutes longer if it was in another part of the county. Then there'd be the ride to the hospital, which, as her mother had pointed out, was pretty far away. "What happened, Mrs. Brady?"

"Oh, don't you have to go do something else, dear?" The sweet old lady sounded concerned. "I don't want to keep you."

"It's okay. Don't worry about it. I'll stay on the phone with you until Officer Harry gets there." Jenny was in the back of the building and couldn't see what was going on up front. But she was afraid if she tried to put Mrs. Brady on hold, she'd lose her, so everyone else was just going to have to wait.

"That's nice, dear. I fell in the kitchen. I lost my balance."

"That's too bad," Jenny said. She wasn't sure if talking was good for Mrs. Brady or not, but she thought she remembered something about concussions and not falling asleep.

"I had mice in the furnace last year, and Officer Harry came to help me. Such a nice boy." The voice was drifting away, becoming fainter.

"Mrs. Brady!" Jenny said, urgency making her blood pump. "You stay with me now. Don't you leave me. Officer Harry will be there in just a minute."

"Can't move, but I think I might have broken my leg." Mrs. Brady sounded petulant. "Hurts like a son of a bitch."

Jenny bit back a laugh at the unexpected language. "Well, you shouldn't move anyway."

"Just one bloody step between the living room and the kitchen, but it did me in. Lucky I didn't hit my head. But I carry my phone with me. My children told me I needed to carry my phone..."

Mrs. Brady's voice started drifting again.

Jenny stayed on the line with the elderly lady, trying to get her to talk until, after a few minutes that seemed to last an eternity, she heard faint sirens in the background. Then there was the noise of a door opening and a deep male voice, muffled because the phone receiver was likely against Mrs. Brady's cheek.

"Well, you certainly have gotten yourself in a mess, haven't you?" she heard Harry say. He sounded gentler than Jenny had ever heard him before.

"I'm so glad you're here, Harry." Mrs. Brady started to cry, and Jenny wished she could hug the old lady and tell her it would be okay.

There were some more muffled noises, and then Harry's voice came over the phone line.

"Okay, I've got this. I told the chief what was going on, and the ambulance will be here in a few minutes."

"Good," Jenny said. Mrs. Brady really should have called 911, and the ambulance would have been notified even sooner. But the emergency service number hadn't been available in their area for very long, and the older people forgot it existed. Plus, 911 operators were strangers, not townspeople, and the ambulance service covered the whole region, so they were strangers, too. "Is she okay?" she asked and held her breath.

"She took a good tumble, didn't you, sweetheart?" Harry said, and again she heard the care in his voice when he addressed the old lady. "I think she broke her leg and maybe her hip. But we'll get her all fixed up."

"Okay." Jenny started to breathe again.

"I'm hanging up now. See you soon."

"All right." They hung up, and Jenny went to deal with the rest of the mopping, trying to keep her mind off of what was happening to a woman she'd known her whole life.

Once she'd finished, emptied the bucket, and put away the supplies, she headed back out to the reception desk in the main area. There wasn't anyone waiting for service at the window—thank God—so she swapped out Suzy's wet chair for another. She settled herself behind the desk and clasped her hands together on the wooden top.

And suddenly little old Jenny Kline was in charge of the entire Hardy Falls Police Department.

Eeep.

Jenny looked around the room. The coffee maker had shut off automatically, so it was deathly quiet except for the faint hum of the computer, and the purr of the copy machine tucked away in a corner.

Really, really quiet.

Mommy?

Jenny chewed on her bottom lip, not entirely sure if she should stay or go. Harry had talked about transferring calls to dispatch, but he hadn't done it before he left, and she hadn't thought to ask how it worked. If the technical gods smiled upon her, she *might* be able to figure out what to do. Except the technical gods rarely smiled upon her. And wouldn't it be special if she broke the police department phone system while she was here alone?

No. It would not.

Sighing, Jenny got her purse from where she'd dropped it in her mother's office, and pulled out her cell phone on the way back to the receptionist's desk. She was going to have to call her mother to ask for help. That's assuming Jackie wasn't too busy assisting the doctor in the delivery room.

Chief Kline could be a little bit of a control freak.

Sitting back behind the desk, Jenny hesitated with her finger poised over the speed dial number.

She didn't want to leave, which was stupid considering she didn't have the slightest clue what she was doing. But if the phone line had been forwarded earlier, she wouldn't have answered the call when it rang, and sweet Mrs. Brady would have been stuck talking to a stranger. What if another little old lady called the station by mistake before someone got back?

Jenny stared at her phone.

On the other hand, surely they'd had this kind of situation before. Suzy wasn't freaking nailed to her desk.

"You're overthinking this," she told herself.

Before she could decide what to do, her cell phone rang in her hand and scared the crap out of her. The ring tone wailed the "Immigrant Song" by Led Zeppelin.

There was no little old lady on the other end of the line this time—it was her mother.

"Hi," Jenny said when she answered. "Everything okay?"

"Baby Griffith is in a hell of a hurry, but at least they're in a room at the hospital and not in my squad car on the side of the road," Jackie said. "Sounds like Suzy's sister has Marley, so Mr. and Mrs. Brennan are on the way. Tony came flying in a few minutes ago. He looked like he was going to faint when the nurse ushered him into the delivery room. I could hear Suzy yelling at him from out in the hall." She chuckled. "I'll be heading back to the station soon."

"Okay." Jenny tried not to sound relieved, but she knew she'd failed when her mother laughed again.

"Don't worry. Harry told me what's happening with Mrs. Brady. The ambulance is there, and they're getting her ready to head to the hospital, so he'll be back as soon as he locks up. But I forgot to switch the phones to dispatch, and it sounds like he did, too. Usually Suzy takes care of that kind of thing." Her mother sighed. "I'm going to miss the hell out of that woman. I always do when she's out. Anyway, I'll tell you what to do, and you can lock the front door so people don't wander in to pay tickets or whatever."

"I'm going to stay for a while," Jenny said before she thought better of it. "I can answer the phones and help, like you said."

Jackie was quiet on the other end of the line, and Jenny could tell she was surprised by the offer.

"I honestly didn't mean for you to stay," she said. "I wasn't thinking right when I left."

It was nice to hear that her mother could be as fallible as the next person.

"It's okay," Jenny assured her. "I want to do it."

"Do you think you can handle it?" Doubt was evident in Jackie's voice.

Jenny tried not to be hurt by such a clear lack of confidence.

"Sure," she said. "It's just answering phones. I know how to talk on phones. But I will lock the front door since I don't know that part. Harry will be here soon, anyway." She wasn't exactly sure why she was pushing. She should just transfer the damned calls and be done with it.

"I don't think you know what you're getting yourself into," Jackie said after another moment. "But okay. Listen to the callers complain and take messages. Either Harry or I will get back to them as soon as we can. And call one of us right away if something comes up that you can't handle." She paused again. "Are you—"

"I'll be fine," Jenny said with as much assurance as she could muster. "All is well here. Drive safely and tell Suzy I said good luck."

"All right. And...thank you, honey."

"Sure."

As she clicked off her cell phone, Jenny wondered why the hell she'd done what she'd just done.

"You are the biggest idiot," she said out loud. Who in their right mind volunteered to listen to people argue and complain?

Maybe she'd done it because it would be nice to feel needed, even for a little while. Especially today.

At that moment the phone rang. After the silence in the station, it made her jump a mile. Thank God the call turned out to be just a telemarketer trying to sell her toner for the copier. Jenny dealt with it by hanging up on him and felt a lot better about things.

"See? Nothing to it."

Then she remembered the front door and what her mother had said about locking it. She pulled out some paper and wrote a quick note to say they were closed, then grabbed the tape dispenser and trotted out into the entry vestibule.

It wasn't until the inner security door "snicked" shut behind her that she remembered it was self-closing.

And self-locking. You needed a code to get back into the main area.

A code she did not have.

Which meant she had just locked herself out.

"Are you kidding me?" she demanded of the heavens. "Are you freaking kidding me? For Christ's sake!" Could this day get any worse?

Yes, she could get out of the front door. But her coat, purse, and cell phone were all inside, along with the keys to her truck.

All going outside would do was get her wet. She'd still have to wait around until someone let her back into the station.

Standing at the transaction window, she looked over at the receptionist's desk and put her hands on the thick glass, feeling like a puppy at the shelter. She could see her cell phone on the desk, her purse next to it.

So close. So close and yet so far.

A few long minutes later, the question about whether or not the day could get any worse was answered with a resounding "yes" when Harry Newman, hair so wet it looked almost black under the lights, came striding into the reception area from the hallway. He stopped, obviously puzzled, and looked around the empty space before he spotted Jenny standing on the other side of the window. He stared at her, then grinned.

Jenny closed her eyes because, *really?*

Harry's voice came over the intercom. "I'm sorry. Can I help you?"

When Jenny opened her eyes, she saw him standing at the desk, watching her with definite amusement. She punched at the button on her side of the intercom.

"Just open the goddamned door," she snarled.

Nothing happened for a moment. She was just about to walk outside, rain be damned, because he was so obviously playing with her. Then the buzzer sounded, and she heard the security door unlatch. She quickly pulled it open and marched in before the asshole could change his mind. Stopping in front of the receptionist's desk, she glared at him, hands on her hips.

"Thanks," she spat.

Obviously unfazed, Harry cocked his head. "That didn't sound very sincere."

"Go to hell," she snapped before she thought better of it.

"That's better." He nodded. "Just out of curiosity, why were you out there?"

"Mom thought I should lock the front door, and I forgot this door closed on its own until it was too late," she muttered, stomping around the desk and dropping into the chair. When the phone rang, she practically jumped at it, glad to have an excuse to stop talking to him.

It was Mr. Looper, a gentle older man she knew from her time working at the Sunnyside since he'd been living in town forever. Apparently some loose dogs were running around his house, and he thought they belonged to his neighbor. He wanted the police to go talk to the neighbor because Dazzle, Mr. Looper's Chihuahua, was frightened.

Jenny made soothing noises and took careful notes, assuring Mr. Looper she'd pass on the information. When she hung up the phone, Harry had his hip propped on the desk, arms crossed.

"What?"

He rolled his eyes, green in this light, to the ceiling. "I was just waiting for you to get off the phone so I could forward the office line," he explained patiently. "I locked the front door while you were talking."

"I had a sign—"

"I know. I saw it and taped it up." He gestured with his chin to the tape dispenser sitting nearby.

"Oh. Good." Jenny felt jittery, and she didn't exactly know why. This might be the first time that she and Harry had actually been alone together. "You don't have to forward the phones yet," she said. "I told my mother I'd stay and answer them for a while," she told him.

Harry's surprise was evident before he smoothed his expression.

"Really?"

"Yes, really. Why is it such a shock to everyone that I want to help?" she demanded.

He shrugged. "Because you've never shown any interest in doing it before."

That gave her some pause, but at least he didn't say it was because she was stupid or couldn't manage things. She looked down at the phone on the desk and ran her finger along the edge of the silver receiver.

"I was just thinking it was nice that Mrs. Brady got through to someone she knew," she tried to explain. "Maybe it made her feel better."

"I think it did." Harry nodded. "She was crying when I came in, clutching her phone like it was a lifeline. Thank God she carries the receiver around with her."

"How bad is she?" Jenny asked. Concern for the sweet old lady moved through her all over again. "Will she be able to come home?"

Harry's mouth tightened. "I don't know. But honestly, she probably shouldn't be living alone anymore anyway. I've been stopping by to see her now and then when I can, and I've tried to get her to consider assisted living, but she doesn't want to leave her house. I can't blame her, but I think her daughters have had enough."

"Oh."

Learning that Harry had apparently been going to see Mrs. Brady on what seemed to be a routine basis left Jenny at a loss for words. It was something her mother would do for someone she was worried about, but Jenny never would have guessed that Harry would show as much concern.

She was saved from continuing the conversation when the phone rang. Soon she was busy trying to convince Mrs. Cahill that it wasn't against the law for the Main Street Dress Your Best store to have a secret sale and only invite certain people to participate.

When she finally hung up the phone, after assuring the woman she'd let her mother know about the issue, Harry was gone.

4
___

A little more than an hour later, Jackie was back from the hospital, and baby Griffith had already made his grand entrance. Anthony Jr., or "Speedy" as his father was calling him, had launched himself impatiently into the world right after Jenny had spoken with her mother.

Once she'd handed over all of the phone messages she'd collected, Jenny lingered in Jackie's office and studied the photos of the event on her mother's phone. Most of the pictures showcased a sleepy newborn with a thick thatch of black hair who seemed pretty pleased with himself and the uproar he'd caused. In one, Suzy, sweaty but grinning, held the baby close while Tony beamed at them like they'd made the sun come up that morning.

Harry, who'd gone to his desk to get something, breezed back into the office, holding some papers.

"I think Speedy's already in charge," he commented when he saw what Jenny was looking at. He gave Jackie the paperwork and leaned forward to grab a muffin from the box still on her desk. Jenny couldn't exactly yell at him for that since she'd already eaten the one Suzy had left behind.

"Probably," Jackie agreed. "At least he's okay, even though he's a little early. But now Tony's going to be out for three weeks on paternity leave, and Suzy will be out at least twelve. We'd better figure out how we're going to handle things."

Harry swallowed a large chunk of the muffin and went around the desk to hunch over Jackie's shoulder so they could both see her computer screen. Soon, they were muttering darkly about schedules and vacations and other things.

Since she couldn't do anything to help, Jenny left them to it and went back out to the receptionist's desk.

She felt at loose ends, but she wasn't quite sure why. Really, this had nothing much to do with her except that she liked Suzy and Tony, and she was glad they'd had a safe delivery and a healthy baby.

Maybe it has something to do with the fact you just lost both of your jobs today, dumbass.

Could be.

The phone rang, and it was for Harry, so she got up and knocked on her mother's office door to interrupt them. As Harry left to take the call in the squad room, Jackie sat back in her chair and pinned Jenny with her sharp blue eyes.

"Can you stay longer?" she asked as she pulled the white bakery box toward her and took out one of the remaining muffins. "You're doing a good job out there."

Jenny blinked, surprised. "Really?" It was nice to hear after the day she'd had.

Her mother spread another napkin on the desk and started picking the paper sleeve off the muffin.

"Harry said you handled Mrs. Brady very well this morning, and that helped her stay calm until he could get there. The phone messages you took are detailed and tell us everything we need to know about the problem. Anyway, if you think you can give me a couple more hours, I'd appreciate it. I'll make sure you get paid."

"Oh. Okay." Jenny was stunned. She thought this might be the first time she and her mother had talked about work without fighting.

And getting paid would be nice.

"Thanks." Jackie sighed and pulled the muffin apart and stuffed a chunk in her mouth.

Harry came back and made his way around the desk again, his presence seeming to suck all of the available air out of the office.

Even more at a loss for some reason, Jenny went back out to the reception area and sat behind Suzy's desk. Where she was doing a good job. Apparently.

Who knew?

The phones were perversely silent, and she started to fidget. She wasn't used to sitting around waiting. All of the jobs she'd had required her to be constantly on her feet and on the move. And dealing with the phone calls had kept her from thinking about her own problems.

She didn't want to think about her own problems.

Maybe Harry would come out soon, and she could fight with him again.

Suzy's computer was on, but the screen was dark until Jenny accidentally bumped the mouse. Then it lit, showing an array of strange programs.

Foot tapping, Jenny considered the fingerprints she could see on the screen now. Then she got up and walked quickly to the closet where the cleaning supplies were housed.

Cleaning, she could do.

After retrieving a spray bottle of cleanser and some paper towels, she went back to the desk and cleared off the top before methodically wiping everything down. The small task helped her settle. As she worked, she listened to the rumble of her mother's and Harry's voices coming from the office, reminding her that she wasn't alone.

She shouldn't be here. She should be at home, working in the garden shed she'd converted into an art studio when she'd left Stefan and moved back into her mother's house. Jackie had let her move the tools originally stored there to the garage so that she could have her own space. At the time, Jenny had hoped the gesture meant her mother understood how much painting meant to her. Then she'd made the mistake of telling her that she wouldn't be looking for a "real" job and would continue working with Missy. It had...not gone well.

Jenny shook off the memory of the ensuing argument and her own hurt. She had no right to take offense at her mother's concerns. After all, Jenny was the one who'd crawled back home with her tail between her legs when she finally realized all of the things people had been trying to tell her about Stefan were true. Jackie had welcomed her with no judgment and open arms, just as she had later when Josie came home after losing her job in Manhattan. No questions asked, and no doubts they'd be welcomed. Jenny was nothing but grateful and had precious little room for complaint.

That didn't mean she wanted to stay in her mother's house forever, though.

The phone rang—thank God—and she quickly put down the cleaning supplies to answer it. Unfortunately, it wasn't much of a distraction—just someone wanting the date of the Bigfoot Parade.

After passing on the information, she hung up and took Suzy's keyboard out of the tray to put it on the now sparkling desktop, so she could clean it, too. She tried to focus on getting all of the crud out from between the keys, but the chore did nothing to stop her thoughts.

Her mother and her sister both thought she should call her painting a hobby and get that mythical "real" job. Jenny wasn't quite sure what work they thought she'd be qualified to do other than what she'd been doing, but she could understand why they were concerned. It wasn't like she'd been swimming with success.

"Maybe they're right. Maybe I am wasting my time," she murmured to the keyboard. "It's just...I can see it."

The dream.

The dream she'd had since she was a little girl. Her aunt had given her a box of colored pencils and a sketch pad from a real art store for her birthday. They'd been the only gifts she'd paid any attention to that year and, alone in her bedroom, she'd spent hours drawing until the sketch pad was full, the pencils were broken, and she'd begged her mother for more.

She'd drawn everything she could think of—superheroes and dragons and people and planets. She'd drawn until she'd gotten good enough that some of the kids at school had actually bought a few of the pictures with their lunch money. And the dream had been born. The dream that she could do this thing she loved forever.

The dream hadn't died over the years, it had just gotten stronger.

Nobody else could see it, though. Not even Missy.

Jenny sighed and set aside the now-clean keyboard. She definitely didn't want to think about her friend...boss...friend... and what had happened at breakfast. Not now.

Her cell phone rang, and she grabbed it, answering without checking the ID.

"Hey," a familiar voice said with customary abruptness. "Got a second?"

"June!" Jenny grinned.

June Esperanza worked for Hannah Frederickson at the Country Time Bar and Grill—had been there ever since Jenny was a teenager. The older woman's main job theoretically was head waitress, but she could fill just about any role in the place if she had to. Jenny thought June could probably move mountains.

"How's it going?" Jenny asked her now.

"Super." June's voice was dry. "Listen, I'm sorry to bother you, but I have a big favor to ask."

"Sure."

"Hannah had to go home sick, and we're short staffed. We're getting kind of busy again, especially now that the weather's warmer, so it's a problem."

"Crap." Jenny frowned with concern. "Has Hannah been working too hard?"

"Probably. But she'll be okay soon," June said cryptically.

Hannah worked too much, especially now. Seven months ago, Hannah's uncle—and accountant—George, had run off with all of the Country Time's money, leaving Hannah flailing around and desperate for cash. At the same time, Pat Murphy, who owned and ran the bowling alley next door to the Country Time, had renovated his restaurant and reopened it with resounding success, stealing most of Hannah's customers in the process.

Now Hannah was in a fight for her business life, which was why Jenny's sister, Josie, had been trying to get her to branch out with things like opening for lunch. But it wasn't easy, and the situation had only been made more difficult when they'd found out that Pat's restaurant was being run by his goddaughter, Louise Weber.

Jenny didn't know Louise very well. The other woman was a couple years younger than she was and had been a year behind Josie and Hannah in school. But as far as she knew, Josie, Hannah, and Louise had all been good friends back in the day. Hannah had even made sure Louise got a job at the Country Time when she'd been forced to leave college. Louise had worked there as a waitress for about five years before she'd been caught having sex with Hannah's boyfriend, Sam, in her car in the Country Time parking lot.

Caught by Jenny's mother, as a matter of fact, who'd charged them both with indecent exposure.

Louise had left town immediately after that. She'd stayed away for two years until Pat brought her back last November to run his bowling alley restaurant.

Fortunately, Hannah had realized the love of her life was not Sam, but the guy who'd been working as her bartender—Sam's younger brother, Deacon. Once she'd fallen for Deacon, she kicked Sam to the curb and never looked back.

Jenny rubbed her eyes. Jesus Christ, but Hardy Falls was a freaking soap opera.

"Anyway," June continued, "Grace is coming in later, but she has classes she can't miss, and Mary Alice is out of town. We have the new kids we hired, of course, but they haven't officially started yet. Think you could give us a few hours to get through the dinner rush? Then Deacon can stay with Hannah for a bit before he heads back, and I'll take care of the bar."

"Sure, I can come over," Jenny said, making a quick decision. She might be a little uncomfortable being around Josie and Mat, but working would keep her mind occupied a little while longer. And it would be nice to do something she understood.

It would be nice to get paid, too.

"Thanks." June sounded relieved. "I'll let Deacon know."

After June told her when to show up and disconnected, Jenny sat contemplating the ironies of life for a moment.

The next few hours passed quickly enough until she went into her mother's office around four to let her know she was leaving.

"I appreciate you pitching in like this," Jackie said.

Jenny shrugged helplessly. "I'm glad I could."

"Me, too." Her mother toyed with a pen and studied her with those eyes that saw too much. "I want to say something," she said after a few moments, "but I don't want you to get worked up about it. It's just a question, okay?"

Jenny felt herself stiffen. "Okay," she said warily.

"We're going to need a temp to replace Suzy while she's out on maternity leave."

"I was guessing."

"Would you like to try it?"

Jenny opened her mouth, closed it, and opened it again. "What?"

"You heard me." Jackie threw the pen on the desk and sat back in her chair, swiveling back and forth. "You did good today. Temping here would give you a chance to see if this kind of work is something you'd like."

"I'm a waitress or a house cleaner. I've never worked in an office." *And I'm an artist. I paint. Don't forget the painting.*

Jackie shrugged. "So this experience might give you another option. Or let you know that it's completely off the table."

True, but...

"I'm not sure I can work with you," Jenny told her honestly.

Jackie's smile was broad. "Ditto, sweetie. That's why this will be probationary. It works out, great. It doesn't, I'll give the temp agency a call. But you seem to be good on the phone, and you know the people of Hardy Falls. They're comfortable with you. I called Mrs. Brady's older daughter to check on her, and she said her mother was so grateful that you talked to her while she waited for Harry."

"That's nice," Jenny said absently, her mind completely scrambled. She had never expected this. Not in a million years. Maybe her mother had early Alzheimer's like Calvin Hardy's mother. "Do you seriously think the town council will let you hire your daughter?" she asked. "Remember that the mayor isn't exactly fond of me."

Jackie's mouth firmed. "You'll be a temp, and I'll deal with

Margo Truelove. It helps that you don't have blue streaks in your hair anymore."

Jenny put a hand to her hair self-consciously. She'd added the blue streaks last year, but let them grow out over the winter, so now her hair was back to its normal dark brown.

Normal, she knew, would be better for the police station. And her mother.

"Can I think about it?" she asked.

Jackie nodded. "Just don't take too long."

Still stunned, Jenny left the office and went to collect her things at the desk.

Her friend had fired her, and her mother had offered her a job. Seriously. What the hell?

She had obviously stepped through the looking glass and hadn't even realized it.

5

The windshield wipers of her pickup truck slapped against the rain as Jenny merged from the Hardy Falls business district onto the highway running past the town. She drove by the Murphy Lanes Bowling Center with its giant bowling pin sign out at the road shining like a beacon in the murky afternoon, then turned into the parking lot of the Country Time Bar and Grill next door, where the neon beer ads splashed colors on the wet pavement like impressionist paintings.

She saw that there where actually cars and trucks in the lot today, which was good, considering the bad weather and the fact that it was still early. Back when Pat had first reopened his renovated restaurant at the bowling alley, he had threatened to tow any vehicles in his lot belonging to people who left their cars at Murphy Lanes and walked over to the Country Time. Up until then, the league bowlers had been Hannah's best customers, habitually venturing over to the Country Time to eat and drink after they'd finished their games.

But people tended to follow the path of least resistance, and it was a pain in the ass to move your car a few hundred feet without a good reason. Once the convenient restaurant and bar at the bowling alley had been improved with the renovation, a lot of the bowlers had stopped coming into the Country Time.

Jenny just hoped the strategies Josie was talking Hannah into implementing to attract more and different customers would pay off. She loved this old place, and she loved the girl who ran it. She wanted her to succeed.

Jenny drove her pickup around the square brick building and parked next to a little car she knew belonged to June. Jumping out of her truck, she ran through the pelting rain to the back door, pulled it open, and walked into the kitchen. Then she came to an abrupt stop when she saw an unfamiliar sandy-haired young man standing at the fryer.

Who the hell was he? He wasn't one of the cooks.

The kid batted his hand in front of his face when steam rose up, noticed her, and grinned.

"Help you?" he asked cheerfully.

Before Jenny could answer, June Esperanza, dark haired and leggy, pushed through the door from the taproom and slapped two slips of paper on the pickup counter.

Jenny frowned, distracted from the stranger at the fryer.

Since she'd been trying to avoid the Country Time, she hadn't actually seen June in a little while. The other woman looked...different somehow. It took Jenny a minute before it finally dawned on her that June's face was a little fuller, her body a bit softer around the middle. And were there strands of...silver in her dark hair? What the hell?

Of course, there was no way in *hell* Jenny would say anything. She didn't have a death wish.

"Hi, Jenny. Thanks for coming. Everything okay, Drew?" June asked the kid at the fryer.

"Sure." He grinned at her. "I've worked in lots of other places, you know. This is nothing."

"Yeah, yeah. Mat will be here in a few minutes, so you won't be alone long."

Drew wisely decided not to argue, just shrugged, and took the order slips.

Jenny jerked her thumb toward him. "New cook?" she asked June, and then paused as another thought struck her. "Please don't tell me Kevin quit."

Kevin Barbet was the Country Time's third cook, along with Mat and Hannah, and the big man was one of Jenny's favorite people in the whole world. He had a broad smile that lit up his round face the color of dark chocolate, and his voice held the music of his native Haiti. Someday Jenny wanted to paint him as she saw him, dancing around the kitchen from task to task, moving to the beat of an internal drummer, wearing his usually splattered chef's apron.

"Of course he didn't quit, don't be ridiculous," June told her. "It's just not his night to work. Drew's the cook for the lunch crowd. We wanted him to come in and learn what the hell to do."

"You really don't have to worry. I worked in the country club kitchen for almost a year before I left," Drew said genially as he flipped burgers. "Just saying."

"Does this place freaking look like a country club?" June demanded, and turned. "Put away your things and come to the bar," she said to Jenny. "I don't want to leave it alone for long. There's a uniform shirt for you in Hannah's office." She pushed open the door and walked out of the kitchen.

Obediently, Jenny hung up her coat, stowed away her purse, quickly changed into the royal blue Country Time polo shirt, and went out to the taproom.

It was nice to see customers sitting around the bar and at some of the small tables scattered about. The familiar old oak paneling on the walls gleamed gold in the lamplight, with the occasional streaks of color cast by stained glass lanterns hanging over the tables. In some ways, the place looked exactly as it had for the last hundred years.

But in other ways, it was different. The new burger toppings bar gleamed in stainless steel glory in one corner, across from a little area that was set up as a stage so live bands could come in and play on the weekends. Hanging on the walls were matted and framed photographs that June had taken of the town and townspeople. The paintings Jenny herself had contributed were there, as well—colorful scenes from in and around Hardy Falls to add some "pop" amid all the wood tones.

June was behind the old oak and maple bar that dominated the space, a big mirror behind it reflecting the room. Glass shelves holding bottles of all shapes and sizes ran up to the ceiling and were lit from below with changing LED strips, so the bottles glowed eerily in colored, indirect light. Those shelves were new—Jenny remembered Josie telling her that she'd talked Hannah into upgrading earlier that year. A huge flat-screen television hung to the side, currently tuned to a baseball game no one could hear over the country music blaring from hidden speakers, but a few people were watching it anyway.

As Jenny walked behind the bar, June filled a glass from one of the beer taps and slid it to a guy sitting on one of the barstools. Jenny recognized him, but she realized she didn't know most of the other people in the room. It was strange.

"You're getting more tourist traffic," she said quietly to June as she walked up beside her to grab an order pad from the stack on the shelf.

June shrugged. "Some. I guess that website deal Josie set up is working. Hannah hates blogging, but she does it every now and then. I sold another picture yesterday." She looked almost baffled. Nobody had known about June's hobby of taking photographs until Hannah had mentioned wanting to display work by local artists. June was still uncomfortable talking about it. She'd been shocked the first time one of her photos had sold.

"That's great." Jenny tried to sound supportive and excited, but she couldn't help comparing her own efforts to June's. The other woman had certainly sold a lot more photographs than Jenny had sold paintings. Of course, the paintings were a lot more expensive.

"Yeah, whatever." June shook her head and turned to face her. "Sorry to call you in like this at the last minute. It's just that you know the place already, and it's only for a few hours, so I didn't want to contact the temp service or try to get one of the new kids if I didn't have to. Thanks for giving us the time."

"It's okay." Jenny cleared her throat. "So, um, you like the new people you hired, huh?" She tried to sound casual but didn't think she pulled it off.

June gave her a sharp look. "Wait." She went off to serve some people who'd just walked up to the bar.

It was probably a waste of time to even bring it up, Jenny thought, but she guessed it couldn't hurt to ask. After all, June was right—she *did* know the Country Time. Working here would be safe and easy, even if she did have to come in contact with Mat and Josie all the time or didn't get enough hours and had to work several jobs. Kevin had three.

"What happened?" June demanded when she got back.

"I'm surprised you haven't already heard," Jenny countered.

"I've been busy," June said. "Talk."

Shrugging, Jenny told her. It wasn't like it was a secret. Sooner or later, the whole town would figure out she wasn't working with Missy or Mr. Foster anymore.

"Shit." June frowned, hands on hips. "Sorry to say this, but I do like the newbs. We hired two good kids to waitress and told Grace and Mary Alice we'd give them more hours, too. I don't want to dick anyone around at this point."

"It's okay," Jenny said, feeling glum but not surprised. That would have been too simple.

June crossed her arms. "Hell, we don't even know for sure that we'll get enough business to keep them—this whole thing might crash and burn. But it sucks we can't take you on. I know you were Hannah's first choice."

"Thanks," Jenny smiled, although hearing it only made her feel worse if that was possible. Shaking it off, she straightened her shoulders and slipped on her professional smile. "Okay, enough of all that. What are the specials?"

June told her, and Jenny went out to the tables.

There would be turnover eventually, she reminded herself as she took the orders for a group of college students. The Country Time had been a close-knit little group up until now, but it was bound to be different as it expanded. Turnover happened in the hospitality business. People came, people went. You got attached, and then they moved on. Something might open up for her later.

Jenny pushed through the swinging kitchen door to deliver the food orders and ran right up against a big reminder of why she'd turned down Hannah in the first place, and why it probably wouldn't be a good idea for her to work at the Country Time, regardless. Because now the new kid, Drew, wasn't the only person standing at the fryer contemplating chicken wings.

Mat.

Mateo Guerrero was a big, handsome, well-built man with dark, shaggy hair and even darker eyes—the kind you just wanted to stare into. He stood with his hands on his lean hips in a way that drew her attention to the breadth of his shoulders, the strength of his biceps, and the muscled length of his legs.

She'd managed to avoid him for weeks, so the impact of seeing him again was like a punch to the gut. Suddenly she was swamped by all of the emotions she'd been keeping bottled up since he'd chosen her younger sister.

He saw her and grinned, oblivious as always. "Hey."

Jenny did her best to smile and put the order slips on the pickup counter.

"Hi there," she said. "Where's Josie?" Ever since Josie and Mat had hooked up, you rarely saw one of them without the other.

"She'll be here in a couple of minutes. June said you were going to handle the tables until Grace comes in later. Thanks for that."

"Sure."

The awkwardness between them was her fault, she knew. Mat had never lied to her about his intentions, and although he'd definitely had some interest in her before Josie had moved back to town, she knew now that it would have only been sex for him. Probably a one-night stand. She'd wanted more, longed for a nice guy after Stefan, and thought Mat was it. She'd been wrong. Mat was nice, but he wasn't the man for her. He'd been clear, and she'd ignored the hints.

It was humiliating.

"So, you have a new young apprentice, huh?" she asked him, gesturing at Drew and trying to put the conversation on an easier footing.

Mat grinned at the younger man at his side.

"I'll teach him all I know."

"I keep telling them that I already know stuff. And mostly he's been teaching me how to run the dishwasher," Drew argued good-naturedly. "But it beats working as the overnight clerk at a hotel like at my last job." He snickered. "Although I did find out some interesting stuff working there."

That made Mat roll his eyes for some reason.

"I'm glad Hannah finally decided to open for lunch," Jenny said to Mat.

He shrugged. "Josie pushed for it for months, but it was a big decision, and Hannah's paranoid about losing money from the investor fund. We had lots of staff meetings while she talked and talked and *talked* about the pros and cons until I wanted to stab out my ears. But now more than ever she needs the business to be successful, so it finally pushed her over the edge."

"Oh." Jenny frowned, concerned because there was something here she wasn't getting. "Is there another problem? Is that why she went home sick?" As far as Jenny knew, they hadn't found Hannah's reprobate uncle George yet. She hoped the old bastard hadn't caused any more issues.

"Nah," Mat said, smiling easily. "I just meant that she can't keep things going forever the way she's going."

"Right." Jenny gave him another smile and headed back out to the taproom, but she knew she was still missing something. Like he was keeping a secret.

It annoyed her. She was used to knowing everything that happened at the Country Time.

Putting those thoughts aside, she held up her order pad and smiled down at a couple who told her they were from Cleveland on their way to New York. They hadn't known what they wanted when she'd stopped by before because there were "so many choices."

"Have you decided what you want?" she asked as she let her smile widen. "How about an ostrich burger? Bison? Sweet potato fries?"

Josie had gotten Hannah to expand the menu. Someday Jenny was going to have to try a bison burger. She'd pass on the ostrich.

The woman tittered and ordered a salad, but her husband did indeed ask for the bison burger, albeit with onion rings instead of the sweet potato fries.

"Only one adventure at a time," he told Jenny.

"I love those pictures," the woman said, admiring some of June's photographs hanging on the wall over their table.

"They're great, aren't they?" Jenny agreed because they were. June had quite an eye for composition, and you could tell that she loved her subjects.

"Oh, yes. The paintings are nice, too. Look at that one." She pointed at one Jenny called "Sunrise on the Mountain." She'd chosen to hang it here because the colors vibrated with energy, and she'd thought it would stand out against the wood paneling. "It looks like one of Emma's, doesn't it?" the woman continued, gesturing to her husband.

"It sure does," he chuckled. "But her stuff is a little more abstract. Our daughter," he told Jenny. "She's five." He frowned. "But I don't think that one is done with finger paints."

Thanks to years of practice, Jenny kept her smile in place and took their orders. On her way back to the kitchen, she glanced at the painting in question. Maybe it was too immature. She should bring in something else.

Still frowning, she pushed open the door to the kitchen and saw that Mat and Drew had been joined by a very familiar woman. She stood next to Mat with her arm draped around his waist and her dark hair swinging back as she smiled up at him with her blue, Kline family eyes.

"Josie!" Jenny's frown instantly morphed into a grin at the sight of her little sister. They talked and texted almost every day, but she hadn't actually seen her in a while. It was the big downside to trying to avoid the Country Time and Mat.

"Jenny!" Josie turned and leaped forward to give her a hug. "Thanks so much for coming in. I would have tried to wait tables, but we both know how that would have gone." Her sister had many, many talents, but waiting tables was not one of them. "I'm going to help cook instead," she told Mat as she walked back to him.

Mat frowned down at her. "No, you are not. You're almost as bad at cooking as you are at waiting tables."

"Oh, pumpkin pie," Josie cooed and tickled under his chin. "You're here to make sure I don't go astray."

Mat laughed, a deep and sexy sound, and Jenny headed back out to the taproom.

She was glad her sister was happy, but *Jesus*. All that sweetness was pretty damned annoying.

To be fair, Josie and Mat had endured their share of troubles, she reminded herself as she got some drinks at the bar. Their journey hadn't been a bed of roses. Jenny could remember Josie crying her eyes out because Mat had been an idiot and shoved her away.

But he'd gotten his head out of his ass and apologized. He'd told her he loved her. He'd come for her, chosen her.

Jenny wondered what that felt like.

Customer traffic picked up as it got later, and more of the factories and other businesses let out. Jenny was glad. She was kept busy moving from table to table and making sure the toppings bar was stocked. Once the early bowling leagues finished, a few members wandered in wearing their bright bowling shirts. Not nearly as many as there used to be, but some. Music pounded through the speakers, and the television was set to a sports channel. Milo Grant wandered in wearing his Mets baseball cap and was roundly booed by the guys at the bar. A normal evening.

Around six, Albert Cromwell, Joe Horton, and Martin Scanner came in and took their accustomed table in a corner. They liked to be able to people-watch from the sidelines.

"Where's Harry Senior?" she asked when she walked over to them. Officer Harry Newman's grandfather was almost always with the group.

"He'll be along in a minute," Albert told her. "His woman don't let him leave right away some nights."

"Maybe she wants him to stay with her instead of going out with you," Jenny suggested.

The old men laughed uproariously.

"Nah, she wants him out of the house so she can watch television in peace," Joe told her. "He gets in her way."

Jenny studied them. "Then why do they stay together?" she asked.

The three looked at her with expressions of open astonishment.

"Because they're married," Albert said.

As far as the men were concerned, that apparently explained it.

When she went into the kitchen, she saw Mat steal a kiss from Josie as he set her up at the dishwasher.

Jenny knew that was what she wanted. Not really Mat specifically—not now that he was with Josie—but she wanted what he and her sister had. What Hannah had with Deacon Black. What June had with Calvin Hardy.

With all due respect to Mr. and Mrs. Newman, she wanted more.

6

Harry had finished his shift at the police station and was on his way home to his apartment over Knight's Bakery when he came across a couple having a loud argument in front of Miss Clara's Bridal Salon. Miss Clara, the put-together forty-something who owned the store, spotted him driving by and flagged him down because the altercation was disturbing her customers.

The fight was actually about a wedding dress, and the couple arguing was Mindy Monroe and Travis Bickle, who'd only gotten engaged a few weeks ago. It was a shame, but at least he was able to help the kids calm down. He didn't even need to cite them once they'd apologized to Miss Clara and she'd accepted.

Still, it made a guy wonder if anybody could just be happy these days.

After he left the bridal shop, Harry found himself driving through the town in the steady rain instead of heading directly to his apartment. Soon he was on the road that wound around the lake in Hardy Falls Park, where the Fallside Restaurant perched on the rocks near the waterfalls that had given the town its name. In the dreary, rainy afternoon, the white fairy lights that wrapped around the restaurant and surrounding trees glistened and reflected like tiny sparks of life.

Tony and Suzy sure were happy, Harry thought. He'd talked to his fellow officer on the phone a little while ago, and you could practically hear hearts floating out of the other man's mouth. Then Harry's cell had been bombed by pictures—thirty of them—of a sleeping newborn and his three-year-old sister.

It would be a bit of an adjustment to cover for Tony while he was out on paternity leave, but that was okay. Harry was used to adjusting. He'd done it his whole life.

For example, it had been a big adjustment to have Jenny Kline in his personal space for most of the day today. Even though he'd been working for her mother for a few years now, he tried not to have too much contact with Jenny if he could help it. He'd never understood his reaction to her—it should have been hard-working Josie who appealed to him the most. It didn't make any sense that Jenny was the one he found fascinating, especially because she seemed to be just drifting her way through life.

Sort of like Harry's own mother and father.

He shook his head sharply and told himself not to go there.

But thinking about Junior and Daisy brought to mind Harry's grandparents—the people who'd actually raised him.

He should let them know about Vera Brady. The old lady was a friend of theirs, so they'd want to know about her fall. It would also give him a good excuse to go check up on them. He tried not to make it obvious since his grandfather had gotten a little touchy about his "hovering."

There was cell service in this area, so he used the voice control on his phone to dial the familiar number.

"Hello, boy," his grandfather answered, probably recognizing his number on the caller ID.

"Hey, Pops. I was hoping you'd be there. I thought I'd come by and visit for a few minutes."

His grandfather tended to go out to the Country Time for dinner with his friends most nights. It gave his grandmother a little space and got the old man out of the house and talking to people. He also got a dinner that was actually edible, which couldn't be overrated.

"Haven't headed out yet. I was just going to call you."

Harry's senses went on high alert. "You were?"

"Yeah." His grandfather's voice sounded heavy.

"I'll be there in a few minutes."

Gut churning, he turned his Jeep Wrangler around in the Fallside's parking lot and headed back to town.

Whatever it was the old man wanted to talk about, it was probably *not* a good thing.

About fifteen minutes later, he pulled into the driveway of his grandparents' small, neat ranch house. Harry hadn't grown up in this quiet Hardy Falls neighborhood. His grandparents had lived in a big, rambling farmhouse outside of Friendsville until about five years ago when it had become too much for them. That's where they'd lived when his grandfather had somehow talked Junior into giving them custody.

Harry had been eight years old and used to Los Angeles, cold hotel rooms, and lots of cereal. He'd been right on the cusp of heading into violence and addiction when he'd moved in with them. But even though he'd rebelled some once he felt safer, he hadn't been stupid enough to push to go back to his old life. Staying in one place where there were safe neighbor-hoods and beautiful mountains, not traveling from place to place with a third-rate rock band well past its prime, going to school, and being able to have new clothes and home-cooked meals, well, it had all been new and frightening and wonderful.

Pulling his phone out of the holder on his dashboard, he called the house. Even though his grandfather had insisted many times that he should just knock on the door, Harry still called first so he wouldn't scare his grandmother. The phone rang only once before his grandfather answered.

"You there?"

"Hi, Pops," Harry said.

"Well, come on in. Don't be a goddamned idiot."

"Roger that."

The rain had backed off a little but was still falling. Harry ignored it as he climbed out of the Jeep and jogged up to the front door. It opened before he could knock, and a lean banty-rooster of a man stood on the threshold with his hands on his hips.

"Good to see you, boy," he said. "Glad you could stop by."

"What did—"

"Harry Three! Come here and give me a hug!" His grand-mother's voice came from the living room down the hall, loud over the television that was always on. She'd called him "Harry Three" since he'd started living with them, and usually called his grandfather "Harry One" when they were all together. Otherwise, she claimed, she got too confused about who it was she was talking to.

"Better get going," his grandfather grumbled.

Harry wanted to push—wanted to insist the old man tell him what the hell was going on—but he knew it would just be a waste of breath. His grandfather wouldn't say anything until he was damned good and ready.

Shaking his head, he walked into the living room and smiled at his grandmother, who was sitting in her recliner, then leaned down to hug her and give her a kiss on one soft cheek. Esther Newman, a round woman who was even shorter than her husband, kissed him and beamed, knitting needles indus-triously clicking away without a pause.

He could clearly remember how she'd knitted him his first hat and mittens, back when he'd just come to live with them. At the time, Harry hadn't known what to do with the gifts. He hadn't wanted to wear dumb old-lady shit, but he'd been afraid that he'd get shipped back to his father if he didn't do exactly what they said, so he'd tried to seem grateful.

Originally, he'd thought he would pretend to lose them at school, but he never did. He'd discovered it made him feel good to wear things that someone had cared enough to make for him, even when the other kids teased him.

After a while, he'd realized his grandparents weren't going to send him back to Junior, not even when he'd raised some serious hell as he'd gotten older. But he still had the hat and mittens somewhere in his dresser at home.

"Hi, Grandma," he said and put a hand on the back of her chair. "How are you?"

"Oh, I'm fine, honey," she told him, brown eyes sparkling under her halo of thick white hair. "There were so many shows on today that I didn't know what to watch first. Not like some days when there's not a thing on I want to see."

"That's great," Harry said as enthusiastically as he could.

"Are you hungry?" she asked him anxiously. "I could make you something."

"I'm good, Grandma," Harry lied. "I ate at work." He might have been raised on Esther's cooking, but that didn't mean he wanted to continue the acquaintance. There was a reason his grandfather went out every night he could.

"Good choice," the old man muttered, sitting in his own recliner next to his wife's.

Harry found his customary spot on the sofa and tried to ignore the game show blaring on the television.

"I have to tell you about Vera Brady," he said to them. "She fell and broke her leg and hip. It was pretty bad."

"Oh, no!" His grandmother dropped her knitting and put her hands to her mouth, eyes wide and wet with sudden tears.

His grandfather sighed and shook his head. "Shit. What happened?"

"She tripped or lost her balance. I don't know which."

"I guess it doesn't matter what it was," his grandfather said heavily. "We'll go see her once she's settled."

"I think she'd like that."

"Is that enough? We should do something for her," Esther said, her hands still on her face.

"She's okay, Grandma," Harry told her gently. "Her daughters are here. You don't have to do anything at all."

"I'll still send her a card," his grandmother insisted.

"That would be nice." He hesitated. "She'll be at rehab for a while, and then I think she might have to go into assisted living," he said carefully. "Or maybe she'll move in with one of her daughters."

"Oh, no." His grandmother looked sad. "Vera's going to miss her mountain."

His grandfather reached over and patted her hand. "She doesn't have a nice setup like we do here, honey," he reminded her. "This house isn't old, and we have lots of neighbors keeping an eye on us. Hell, one of them is even a contractor, and Noah is happy to help any time we have trouble. We're fine."

Which was why Harry hadn't had "the talk" with them yet about their living situation. The older Harry Newman was still spry and healthy for an eighty-something-year-old. As long as the old man could keep things going, Harry figured they were better off where they were. And, of course, Harry would be there for them, too. He could even move back to live with them if it came to that. He didn't *want* to do it, but he would for them.

"Is there any good news?" his grandmother asked him. "Or was it all bad today?"

"Suzy had her baby."

"Oh!" she exclaimed. "Already? He's early, isn't he?"

"A little." Harry wasn't exactly sure, to be honest, but he thought he remembered Suzy saying something about it when Chief Kline was trying to get her to the hospital. "They're all okay." He pulled out his phone and showed his grandparents the pictures Tony had sent. They oohed and aahed and made kissy noises through all thirty of them.

"Guess Tony's off for a while then," his grandfather said, once he'd settled back in his chair.

"Yes. But we'll work it out."

They chatted a few more minutes. His grandfather still didn't mention what he'd wanted to talk to him about, and it occurred to Harry a little belatedly that the old man might not want to say anything in front of Esther. Acting on instinct, he got to his feet.

"Well, I'd better be heading out," he said.

"Oh, no—" his grandmother protested, but he bent and kissed her cheek again.

"I'll have to be back on duty soon enough since Tony's out, Grandma," he reminded her.

"Let the boy go home," his grandfather said and, as Harry had expected, got to his feet as well. "I'm going to head down to the Country Time for a bit. Can you give me a lift?" he asked him. "Albert will give me a ride home."

"Sure, Pops."

"Don't you dare stay out too late," Esther scolded her husband. "You're not as young as you used to be."

Harry smiled at his grandmother's familiar complaint and drifted to the front door while his grandparents said goodbye. His grandfather followed him out, then closed and locked the door behind them and set the alarm Harry had insisted they install. They walked together through the still falling rain to the Wrangler parked in the driveway.

"What—" Harry started.

"Let's go," his grandfather said and easily swung up into the passenger seat, even though the Jeep was raised for off-roading.

Frowning, Harry walked around and got in the driver's side. Soon they were heading down the residential street and back through the town of Hardy Falls.

Harry wasn't surprised when his grandfather didn't say anything right away, but as they drove past the Sunnyside Diner, its big windows gleaming through the rain in the gathering darkness, the old man finally stirred.

"Don't suppose you saw Jenny Kline today," he asked.

Harry blinked at the unexpected question.

"Yeah, she was at the station. Why?" he asked suspiciously.

His grandfather shrugged. "No reason. She was with Missy at the Sunnyside this morning, and she seemed upset, is all. Gladys Dorinsky was waiting tables, and she said neither of them ate their breakfast. I just wondered if there was a problem."

Harry frowned as he pulled to a stop at the traffic light.

He realized that he'd never actually found out why Jenny had shown up at the police station today. What with Suzy going into labor and then Mrs. Brady's fall, it had slipped his mind. But his grandfather was right—there was definitely something wrong.

"I'll find out," he assured him.

"No, no, it's the girl's business. I was just wondering. She's been through a lot, so I hope it's nothing bad. On the other hand, I expect her mama will get it all straightened out, whatever it is. That Jackie Kline's got a lot of moxie. Reason why I wrote her name in on the ballot for mayor this last election."

"Yeah, she was thrilled about that." Jackie had been royally pissed off, actually, since she didn't want to be mayor, and it was causing a lot of problems now that Margo thought she did.

His grandfather grinned unrepentantly in the dim light but remained quiet as Harry got onto the highway, driving past

Murphy Lanes to turn into the Country Time's parking lot. The bowling alley was busy, but the Country Time had a reasonable number of cars, too, and Harry was glad. Hannah needed as much business as she could get to make up for all of the money her uncle had stolen.

It burned his ass that they hadn't been able to find the guy. Still couldn't find him. The last anyone had heard, he was in Vegas, but he seemed to have disappeared off the face of the earth since then.

Harry found a parking spot relatively close to the front door and turned off the engine before facing his grandfather.

"Okay, talk," he said firmly because enough was enough. "What happened? I'm guessing Junior called again."

It wasn't too much of a reach. The only reason his grandfather would be acting this strangely was if he'd heard from Harry's father.

The old man sat, staring out the windshield for a moment.

"Yeah," he said, his voice heavy. "He called."

"He wanted money."

"Sure. That's the only reason he ever calls."

"You going to give it to him?"

"No," his grandfather said. "Of course not."

"Good."

His grandparents wired Junior cash sometimes, but not nearly as often as they had before Harry had turned eighteen. It was why Junior still called them. Harry wondered if it was also why his grandfather gave in every now and then—so they would hear from their son once in a while.

"It's just hard," the old man said, staring out the window. "It's hard to know that he is who he is because of us."

"No," Harry said with confidence. "He's the way he is because of the choices he's made."

Which was why Harry was determined not to do the same things his father had. He'd almost fallen into the trap his first year of college, nearly thrown everything away. But then he'd talked to his grandfather and gotten his head out of his ass.

"Where is he?" Harry asked, just out of idle curiosity. Where Junior lived had ceased to matter to him a long time ago.

"Still in California. Around Los Angeles, I believe."

Harry nodded. "Is she with him?" His mother came and went as she pleased, but the two still collided regularly.

"No." His grandfather sighed heavily. "Sounds like she hooked up with a drummer in another band or something. Your father didn't seem to care—I think he has a new girlfriend."

"Jesus Christ." Junior and Daisy both had to be getting near fifty. "They need to grow the fuck up."

"I know." His grandfather's voice sounded old in the darkness. "They were so young when they took off and not much older when they had you—"

"Don't you dare make excuses for them." Harry heard the hardness in his own voice and took a deep breath to try to pull himself back together. "Sorry, sir," he apologized. Regardless of his own thoughts on the matter, he would *not* disrespect the man who'd raised him and had been the only real father he'd ever known.

His grandfather shook his head. "No, you're right, boy. But it's hard."

"I know." Harry couldn't imagine how it felt.

The old man stirred in his seat and looked over at him for the first time since he'd gotten in the Jeep. "And I'm the one who's sorry."

"Absolutely no need."

"We'll have to agree to disagree there." He paused. "I haven't told your grandmother I heard from him yet. Just didn't have the heart."

"Probably better not."

As hard as things were for his grandfather, they were hell on his grandmother.

"I wouldn't have told you either, but I thought I'd give you a heads-up. He sounded a little more desperate than usual, and he's already tried with me a couple of times. He might try to call you."

"He never contacts me."

"That's something anyway." The old man sat for a moment longer, then gave him a one-armed hug and opened the passenger door. "Thanks for the ride."

"Any time."

"Coming in?"

"Not now."

His grandfather nodded and slammed the door shut, then headed toward the warm lights of the Country Time.

Harry watched him go.

Suddenly he couldn't face going back to his empty apartment quite yet. One drink wouldn't hurt anything.

Pocketing his keys, Harry got out and followed his grandfather.

7

———

Inside the Country Time, Harry paused to let his eyes adjust to the dimmer light. He was happy to see that the number of vehicles in the parking lot seemed to be a fair indication of the number of people actually in the place for a change. Hannah hadn't put parking restrictions in place like Pat had, although Harry privately thought she should, as was her right.

When he'd asked her about it, she'd told him she believed some of the people who took up a spot and walked over to the bowling alley would come back into the Country Time when they were done bowling, so it was worth the irritation. But sometimes when Harry happened to come in, the taproom was fairly empty even though the lot was full.

Tonight it was busy. Not packed by any means—not what it used to be—but people sat at the tables and around the bar, a comfortable crowd for a Friday night. Some of the patrons even wore bowling shirts, so maybe Hannah's decision was right after all. Country music played, and the television at the bar was tuned to a Phillies game since the season had just started. More than a few people who were sitting at the bar drinking beer were yelling at the screen. One or two were yelling at Milo

Grant, who was wearing his damned Mets cap and looking more than a little smug.

Business as usual. No problems here.

As expected, Harry spotted his grandfather jammed into a corner with his friends, Albert, Martin, and Joe, at their normal table. He walked over to the four old men and smiled at them.

"Change your mind?" his grandfather asked, cocking an eyebrow.

"Thought I might as well grab a burger and a beer," he told him. "Seemed stupid to go home and nuke something when I was right here."

"That's always my opinion," Joe agreed with a grin.

"Come sit down." Albert gestured and moved as if to get up and grab another chair.

"Nah." Harry waved his hand, stopping him. "That's too much of a squeeze. Don't upset yourselves. I'm just going to go sit at the bar." He loved these guys, but he knew his grandfather would want to vent to his friends. And, frankly, Harry wanted to be alone.

"You sure?" Martin asked. "It's not a problem."

"I'm sure. I'll sit and watch the game for a while." When he looked over at the bar again, he was a little surprised to see June was behind it, pulling taps and joking with some of the customers. "Where's Deacon? Did he finally take a night off?"

It was unusual these days to walk into the Country Time and *not* find Deacon Black tending the bar. Lord knew the man had always worked hard, but now that he'd finally gotten Hannah to take a chance on him in both their personal lives and with the business—had even convinced her to agree to marry him—well, he was practically obsessed.

Harry understood. If a woman like Hannah ever decided he was worth the effort, he'd be manic, too.

For some reason, Jenny Kline's image flowed into his mind. Smiling at him. Reaching for him.

At that moment, the kitchen door opened, and, as if he'd conjured her with his thoughts, Jenny herself walked out into the taproom. She was wearing a blue Country Time polo shirt and expertly balancing a tray full of plates of food on her shoulder. The light from the lamps in the room glinted in her dark hair where it was pulled back into a bouncing ponytail and warmed her skin to a golden glow.

She didn't see him standing there. Instead, she moved straight to a group of tables that had been pushed together and smiled down at the college kids huddled around them as she handed out their food.

"What's Jenny doing here?" Harry asked absently as he watched her. He'd always loved watching her move. Energy and grace all wrapped in one hell of a tight little package.

"June said Hannah went home sick, and they asked Jenny to pitch in," Joe said. "Deacon went with Hannah to make sure she settled down, so he should be back soon. Oh, hey, there he is."

The man in question walked in from the kitchen and slid behind the bar, then fell into conversation with June. His polo shirt was strained to capacity across his broad shoulders when he folded his arms and scowled at the older woman.

Harry was only two years younger than Deacon, but he didn't know the other man very well. Deacon had lived in Hardy Falls when he was younger, and Harry had been in a different school district. Since they'd both headed out of the area as soon as high school was over, they'd never really run into each other until they'd both moved back. But, Harry liked what he knew of the bartender.

Deacon turned to point at something on the glass shelves of bottles behind the bar, and the light from the television reflected on his skull. He had a pronounced receding hairline and kept what he had left brutally short.

Almost without thought, Harry ran a hand through his own hair.

All there.

That was a relief. Maybe he wouldn't inherit his grandfather's baldness after all. Junior had, but unless something had changed since the last time he'd seen the man twelve years ago, his father shaved his head anyway to show off the tattoo on his skull.

Harry saw that Jenny had finished serving the college kids and was now at the bar listening to June and Deacon—her empty tray clasped to her chest.

She had a really nice chest. And the rear view wasn't bad either.

Hmmm.

He became aware of the silence from the table beside him and turned to find all four old men watching him and smirking.

"What?" he demanded.

"Yeah," Albert said, his grin widening to show his pink gums. His dentures hurt, so he tended not to put them in all the time. In spite of that, he was very popular with the elderly women of Hardy Falls and never lacked for female companionship, the acknowledged Don Juan of the group. "Why don't you just head on over to the bar, boy. Watch a game. Or something."

The other men chuckled.

Shit.

Harry refused to react. He just nodded and left them.

By the time he made his way to the bar, Jenny had gone back to the kitchen with June, which was both a relief and a disappointment. He tried to shake it off and shifted past the other customers to perch on a stool out of the way. It wasn't a surprise when a moment later, Deacon turned from serving someone and nodded at him. The man always seemed to know what was happening in his domain.

The kitchen door pushed open, and Jenny strode out, but

again, she didn't seem to see Harry, so he watched her walk to the other side of the room to take orders. She laughed at something one of the customers said, shaking her head as she scribbled on her order pad, then fluidly turned to talk to a person at another table.

"Hey, Harry. What can I get you?" Deacon's question finally pulled Harry's attention away from Jenny, and he ordered one of the craft beers they had on tap. Deacon came back a minute later, holding a tall glass filled with golden liquid complete with a flawless head of foam on top.

"How's Hannah?" Harry asked as Deacon put down a paper coaster and set the glass on it. "Martin said she went home sick."

The other man's professional smile morphed into a frown of worry. "She's okay. Stubborn as a mule, but okay. She had an upset stomach and was tossing her cookies in the ladies' room, but I still had to practically drag her out of here. I hope she actually stays home to rest and doesn't get it into her thick head to drive back later."

Harry knew Deacon was right to be concerned that Hannah would ignore common sense. This bar had been in her family for generations, and she was determined to make it succeed. It was a difficult task after her uncle had stolen all of her money.

Deacon started to turn away again, then hesitated.

"I don't suppose you've heard any more about George?"

"No." Harry hated like hell that he couldn't give him good news. Or any news, really. "We have a warrant out for his arrest, but so far no word. He's vanished into the ether."

Deacon sighed. "That's what I thought."

"Sorry."

The other man shrugged and smiled a little. "We'll be okay. Josie's got Hannah on board with most of her ideas, so we're figuring it out, I guess. I don't know if you heard, but we're going to start opening for lunch service next week."

"Really? That's huge." It also meant a lot of money and commitment on Hannah's part.

"Yeah." Deacon glanced around the taproom. "This is a good place. I like it the way it is. But I guess everything changes, doesn't it?"

"It does."

For a moment, Deacon's face appeared even harsher than normal, and he looked like the soldier Harry knew he had been. "It kills me, you know? George did this to Hannah, and I can't make it right. I can't do anything. She trusted him to help her, and he shit all over her. He's her fucking uncle! Her mother was his baby sister! What kind of an uncle steals all of his own niece's money?"

"He probably thought Hannah would just cut and run." Because it's what George himself would have done.

Deacon shook his head. "He should have known better. Anyone else would have realized that Hannah would pick up the pieces and try to keep things going, no matter what. But George doesn't know her at all. Or care."

"No."

The bartender left to wait on some other customers, and Harry took a long drink of the beer in his glass.

It was always a surprise, he thought, when you found out that someone who should have had your back was just out for themselves. At least Hannah had Deacon and Josie and the rest of the town behind her.

And he'd had his grandparents, he reminded himself. He hadn't been alone either.

"Harry?"

He'd been so involved in his own thoughts, in the memories stirred up by the news that his father had called, that he started at the sound of Jenny's voice behind him.

Trying to pretend he hadn't just jumped like a rabbit, he grinned as he swiveled on the stool to face her.

"Hey."

She returned his smile. "I didn't know you were here." She glanced toward the little table in the corner where his grandfather and the rest of the posse were probably watching them. "Did you come with Harry Senior?"

"I brought him and thought I'd have a beer."

Harry realized he was having trouble focusing. In the mellow light of the bar, her skin was flawless, her eyes were huge, and her mouth was soft. He wanted to bite it.

The breath he'd taken choked on the way out.

Keep it together, Newman.

Jenny's smile turned a little confused when he didn't say anything else, and she shrugged.

"I'd better go get these drinks before the customers think I've forgotten them."

He nodded, and she went behind the bar, grabbed some glasses, and started pulling taps.

Oh yeah. He'd always liked the way Jenny Kline moved. There was something almost feline in the roll of her hips as she went from task to task.

He had a sudden, inexplicable urge to go up behind her, crowd her into the bar, grab her hips, and yank her close to him, to run his mouth all over that smooth, taut body.

Harry forced himself to look away and took another long, long drink of his beer.

Jesus H. Christ, man. What the hell are you even thinking?

For one thing, Jenny had never indicated that she was interested in him. Maybe he'd caught a glimpse of something hot in her eyes once or twice, but it had quickly faded. He sincerely doubted she focused on him the way he did on her.

For another, if he lost his mind and made a move even close to what he was imagining, Jenny would cut his off his dick. And then her mother would cut off the rest of his body parts. Slowly.

A group of boisterous young guys who, based on the logos on their sweatshirts, were from the track team at the local university, bellied up to the bar next to him, crowding him. A few of them recognized him and greeted him with cheerful good humor, but Harry wasn't in the mood to talk. He trusted Deacon to deal with the ones he knew for a fact were underage, so he slipped off the stool and found an empty table tucked back in a corner near the new little stage. It also had the advantage of being out of the line of sight of his grandfather.

Of course Jenny, efficient waitress that she was, tracked him down a minute later.

"I thought you might have left," she said. Her smile was as professional as Deacon's. For some reason, seeing it made Harry want to prod her, push her until that fake facade cracked, and her magnificent blue eyes snapped at him. He often had that urge when Jenny was around.

"I thought I'd get something to eat, but then the whole university decided to descend," he told her, trying to rein in his inner asshole for once. He was rewarded when she gifted him with a more natural smile.

"I don't think it's the whole university—but enough of them to make this a big night for Hannah." She held up her order pad, pencil poised. "What can I get you?"

How about you?

The words rushed through his thoughts and almost burst out of his mouth before he choked them back.

Seriously, what the hell? Yes, he'd always been attracted to her, but his control was titanium. He *never* had to fight with himself like this. But tonight, all he wanted to do was haul her somewhere private and wrap himself up in those wickedly perfect legs of hers. Jenny might be short, might call herself a "hobbit," but she was all kinds of fine as far as he was concerned.

He must have stared at her a little too long because Jenny's brilliant smile dimmed, and color bloomed in her face. She took in a deep breath that made her breasts—pretty, full, breasts—press against her plain blue polo shirt.

Before he could move some blood back up to his brain to speak, the front doors burst open, and another pack of college kids strode in. They called loudly to their friends at the bar, who then hooted back until Deacon scowled at them and told them all to "shut the hell up."

The interruption was enough to break the mood. Harry was glad.

Jenny cleared her throat and turned her attention back to him. "So? Decided?" she demanded, pencil poised in a way that told him he'd better be careful or she'd stab him with it.

With a mental reminder to himself that she really would cut off his dick if he made the wrong move, Harry ordered a random burger without looking at the menu that was on the table.

"Anything else?" That shallow smile he hated was back, but he didn't push her again. "Ostrich burger? Bison? Sweet potato fries?"

"I'll stick with cow for now. But, sure, I guess I'll try the fries." He ordered another draft of beer, and she escaped to the kitchen.

She wasn't running away, he thought as he watched her leave, but it was close.

A minute later, she was back in the taproom, drawing his beer. She delivered it and took away his now empty glass before he could stop her.

Harry took a sip of his beer to hide a smile. The liquid was cold and smooth on his dry throat.

Well, now. She was rattled.

He decided that he was okay with that.

8

Harry drank his beer, sat in the shadowed corner, and watched Jenny glide around the taproom. She laughed with the old men and bowlers, talked to other townspeople, helped a couple who were probably tourists, refilled the popular toppings bar, and didn't pay him the slightest bit of attention. When he realized he was staring at her like a stalker and being just a little creepy, he finally forced himself to look away.

Contemplating the crowd at the bar, he idly wondered why Deacon and Hannah weren't married yet. They'd been engaged since December and were already living together. Marriage might not be in the cards for Harry, but it was obvious those two were over the moon about each other. He couldn't imagine either of them wanting a big wedding, and he was sure Hannah wasn't insisting on a custom-made dress she couldn't afford, like Mindy Monroe at the dress shop earlier. What was the hold up?

Seeing Deacon deal with the college kids and other customers at the bar, it was hard to believe the same man always wore a puppy dog expression when he gazed at Hannah.

It was so freaking sweet it even made Chief Kline look like she wanted to coo. Worse, Hannah gazed at him the exact same way. It was nauseating.

If you factored in June and her fiancé, Calvin Hardy, the long-lost lovers who'd reunited after fifteen years, and then added Jenny's sister Josie and her new lover, Mat Guerrero, well, the Country Time was basically just one big ol' sugar shack. A guy could get diabetes simply walking into the place.

"Here you go."

Goddamn it!

Jenny must have noticed him jump this time because he saw her hide a smile as she slid a plate in front of him— a plate that held a juicy burger and strange orange fries.

"Don't forget the toppings bar," she said, turning away.

"Hey, Jenny," June called, walking up to the table and blocking her retreat. "Hi, Harry."

He nodded and smiled. He liked June a lot. He liked how you always knew where you stood with her. She did *not* suffer fools gladly. Or anybody else for that matter.

"Take a break," she told Jenny. "You've been running around like a nut since you got here."

Jenny stubbornly crossed her arms. "What about you?" she demanded, because the woman never seemed to be able to just *do* something without an argument.

"I'll go after you're back." June frowned at her. "Grace sent a text that she's not going to be here until nine. Normally that wouldn't matter since Deacon's got the bar now. But we're busier than we have been in a while, so we should probably have two servers on deck. Do you think you can stay that long?"

Jenny let her hands drop and shrugged. "Sure."

June's look of relief transformed into a scowl when she focused on a different part of the room. "Christ, there's Margo Truelove. I didn't think she came in here anymore." She looked down at Harry. "Don't arrest me."

"Only if you get violent," he assured her.

"Yeah, well, I can't promise anything. That woman chaps my ass." June held up her order pad, plastered a fake smile on her face, and marched over to the table where the freshman mayor of Hardy Falls sat with a member of the town council.

"I'm glad June's taking that one," Jenny said darkly. "I'm not sure what I would have said if I'd had to do it."

Surprised, Harry looked at her and saw that her mouth was tight, and her blue eyes were sparking.

God, he loved it when she sparked.

"Why don't you sit down for a minute," he said impulsively, patting the seatback of the chair next to him.

"I'm okay," she snapped, because...Jenny.

"You must be tired. Like June said, take a load off. Unless you're starving and want to go get food."

Jenny hesitated, looked at the kitchen door for a moment, then shook her head and dropped into the chair. "Thanks."

This close, he could feel the warmth of her body and thought he caught the light scent of her skin under the heavier smells of beer and fried food.

"Eat your burger before it gets cold," she ordered.

"You should eat, too. Do you want half?"

"No. I'll grab something light in the kitchen," she said, but she made no move to get up.

"I don't want to eat in front of you."

"I don't care."

"Well, I do." There were some things his grandparents had drilled into him, and that was one of them.

Jenny rolled her eyes. "At least try the fries." She pointed at his plate. "They're good."

He didn't feel like arguing anymore, so Harry picked up one of the weird fries, bit into it, and chewed contemplatively before putting the uneaten half back on his plate.

"Yeah, no."

"Cretin," Jenny sniffed and turned up her nose. "I like them."

"You want them?" he asked, moving his plate so she could reach better.

"No," she said, at the same time she stole one of the fries. He tried not to stare when she slipped it between her moist, plump lips.

Jesus H. Christ.

"I can't believe you don't like these," she said after she stole another one.

Harry shook his head to get it back in the game, then shrugged.

"They're orange," he said. "It's not right. And I'm glad I stuck with the regular, old-fashioned beef burger instead of pterodactyl or whatever." He wasn't sure what was weirder— that Jenny's younger sister had convinced Hannah to put things like ostrich burgers on her menu or the fact that such things actually existed in this world.

"I think they're good. And healthy." Obviously giving up any pretense of a fight, she spread a napkin on the table and put a whole handful of fries on it.

"Healthy. Sure."

Harry felt an electric current running between them, right below the surface. He thought Jenny might feel it, too. She didn't move closer. But she didn't leave either.

Since she was eating now, and he needed to give himself something else to think about, he picked up the burger. Ditching the thought of getting up for toppings, he took a huge bite. They ate companionably, and the music and rumble of conversation around them made it seem like they were isolated in the shadows.

Why had Jenny come into the police station that morning saying that she might need a bribe?

"My grandfather said that he saw you and Missy at the

diner this morning," Harry said casually, not entirely sure why he was pushing since it was none of his business. "He said you looked upset."

"So?" She ate another fry.

"And then you came running into the police station right afterward. With a whole box of muffins. Because you thought you might need to bribe your mother."

Jenny glared at him. "Do you ever forget anything?"

"No." Although sometimes he wished he could. "What's wrong?"

Jenny ignored him a little longer, then sighed and slumped back in her chair. "Well, it's not like it's a secret. The whole town's going to know soon." She met his eyes. "Missy told me this morning that she can't afford to keep me on."

"Oh. That sucks." Harry knew that Jenny didn't only work for Missy—the two women were friends. "Were you an employee or freelance?"

"Freelance."

He considered that angle. "So, no unemployment then, huh?"

Jenny shook her head.

Yeah. Sucked.

"But you work for the caterer guy who handles the Blacks' swanky parties, right? Maybe he can use you more?" Deacon's parents were highfliers as far as the town of Hardy Falls was concerned. Which was why they wanted nothing to do with Deacon and were all about his older brother, Sam, the lawyer.

Jenny sighed again. "Apparently, our beloved Mayor Truelove has some issues with me because I accidentally spilled champagne on her dress at the last party." She shot a hot look in the mayor's direction. "It spilled because she was reaching for the flute like a vulture, I might add. It wasn't my fault. But she complained to Mr. Foster, and now he doesn't want me to work for him anymore."

Harry raised his eyebrows. "Wow. You got fired from both of your jobs this morning?"

Jenny ate more fries.

"Jesus." No doubt about it, Jenny Kline had really had a shit day. He gestured around the room. "You going to work here, then?" Hannah and the Klines were tight. "Deacon said they're opening for lunch. They must need people."

Jenny slumped further. "They asked me if I wanted to when they were hiring, but I didn't need another job then, so I said no, and they got other people."

Again, sucked.

Harry tried to think of something useful to say and came up empty. Issuing platitudes was really not his thing. He was more of a "slap them in cuffs" kind of guy.

Goddamn it, now he had an image of Jenny cuffed to his bed in his mind. *Jesus.*

"Maybe this is a chance for you to do something different," he said, not really aware of what he was saying because that image wasn't going away. "You could go to school."

Jenny groaned and leaned her head back, which served to expose the long, graceful line of her neck.

"God, I don't want to go to school."

"You should take Suzy's job while she's out," Harry said and immediately wanted to punch himself in the face. The last thing he needed was for Jenny to be around all day, every day. But he couldn't seem to shut up. "I know it'd be temporary, but it would be an income."

She straightened and blinked at him. "Have you been talking to my mother?"

Now he was confused.

"No. I mean, yes, of course I talk to her all the time, but..." He shook his head to clear it because the woman was making him nuts. "What?"

"It's just that she basically said the same thing. I mean, she suggested I take Suzy's job. I think she wants to tempt me to the dark side, so I'll start working in an office."

"God forbid," Harry said, although part of him wondered why that was a problem. Jenny had been great on the phones today, and she was obviously good with people. She even knew a little bit about how the station functioned, thanks to her mother. This way, she wouldn't be stuck working as a waitress or a housekeeper for a while. It seemed like a win-win. "You going to do it?"

"I don't know." She looked at him from under her lashes. "What do you think?"

He thought he should tell her to stay far away. He was on day shift for the next few months, which meant that if Jenny came to work as the receptionist, he'd be around her day in and day out. He was pretty sure that wouldn't be a good idea. In fact, there were some pretty awesome reasons to steer clear of her.

But...what was life without a little risk?

The wild, reckless eighteen-year-old he'd once been raised his head for the first time in years.

"I think," he said, remembering his conversation with Deacon at the bar, "that everything changes. Maybe you should take a chance."

She studied him, and he saw the light in her eyes, a wildness to match his own. Then she pushed herself to her feet.

"June's getting busy. I'd better get back to work."

Harry watched her go.

9

Jenny moved among the tables in the Country Time taproom and tried to focus on what she was doing rather than on Police Officer Harry Newman III.

Normally the man seemed to live to irritate her, but today, just now, he'd been...nice. He'd even appeared interested in her problems and tried to give her some career advice—although it was obvious he didn't have a clue what to say.

Then she thought about the way he'd looked at her, watched her, and decided that maybe "nice" wasn't exactly the right word.

"Hot" might be closer to the mark.

"Smoking" could also apply.

It was unsettling and exciting all at the same time, and it made it hard to remember who'd actually ordered the ostrich burger.

A little later, Jenny came out of the kitchen and saw the table Harry had been sitting at was empty. He must have left when she'd been busy serving other people. She didn't know why she found that so disappointing.

He'd left a good tip, though.

She bussed the table, took Harry's tip money to the communal jar, and surveyed the room to make sure everyone was doing okay. June was talking to Harry's grandfather and the other three old men with him, laughing at something one of them had said, the ponytail of her dark hair streaming down her back.

As Jenny watched, the front door opened, and Calvin Hardy, June's fiancé, came walking in. There'd been no news of a wedding date yet for Calvin and June, or for Hannah and Deacon, which was strange considering both couples were stupid in love.

Calvin, a strongly built man with dark hair threaded with silver and equally dark eyes that could see right through a person, spotted June and immediately went to her. He wrapped his arms around her from behind and spread his hands on her belly as he bent to kiss her neck. When June turned in his arms and met his mouth with her own, the old men at the table erupted in cheers and whistles.

Jenny turned away and went to check on a couple who'd been studying the menu, then took their orders to the kitchen. She handed the slips of paper to Mat, who was standing next to Drew at the grill, but didn't bother trying to talk to him since the big stainless steel dishwasher was running and the noise drowned out all other sounds. Josie stood in front of the machine, frowning in concentration. She had on thick yellow gloves that encased her arms up the elbow, and her face was bright red from the steam.

When the wash cycle finished, Josie pulled out the rack of now sanitized plates and shoved them down the counter to finish drying, then went back to the prep sink to rinse glassware and load them into other racks.

Jenny hated running the dishwasher, but Josie had told her she didn't mind it.

"When I try to wait on tables or cook, well, let's just say it's ugly," her sister had admitted. "But now that I know I have to scrape food off the plates before I put them in so I don't break the dishwasher again, it's right up my alley."

We all have skills.

As Jenny started filling her tray with completed food orders, she saw Mat leave the grill and go to stand behind Josie. He dropped a kiss on her sister's neck as Calvin had done with June, right where her T-shirt was pulled aside by the chef's apron she wore over it. Then he added a dirty frying pan to the pile at the sink behind her back.

Josie noticed and scowled at him before spotting Jenny at the pickup counter.

"He thinks he can be sneaky now that he doesn't need to impress me anymore," she complained.

"Honey, I impress you every damned day," Mat said, exaggerating his slight Texas drawl with a laugh and patting Josie's behind before going back to the grill.

Josie shrugged. "Okay. He does."

Jenny grinned at her sister, but her smile evaporated as soon she headed back out to the taproom to deliver the food.

"Have you heard from Hannah?" she asked Deacon when she stopped behind the bar to get ice for a customer.

He shook his head. "No. I think she's actually down for the count this time."

"I hope you don't get whatever she has."

For some reason, that statement made him smile. It was luminous, lighting up his hard face. At that moment, he appeared almost beautiful.

"I think it's only a matter of time."

Shaking her head, Jenny went back to the tables.

These people were all so much in love it was sickening.

From listening to the customers, Jenny learned that Pat had two events at the bowling alley today, and the restaurant over there was packed, so that was probably why the Country Time was as busy as it was. Jenny didn't care. She was glad to be working instead of thinking about what had happened and worrying about the future. But soon enough she turned around to see Grace Cooper rushing into the taproom. June stopped on her way to the kitchen to talk to the girl, and Jenny walked over to join them.

"Thanks for coming in, Jenny," Grace said as she grabbed an order pad from the stack. "Sorry I'm so late. I was just telling June that I had to work with my cohort to get ready for a presentation on Monday."

"That's my idea of hell," June stated unequivocally and continued on to the kitchen.

"You're going for an English degree. Why do you have to make presentations?" Jenny asked. She'd always imagined that English majors sat in libraries writing incomprehensible papers about the anxiety levels in *Hamlet* or something like that.

"You'd be surprised." Grace grinned at her, teeth flashing against her mocha-colored skin. "But it's good practice for when I go for my Ph.D."

Jenny wondered if Grace's parents knew about her plans. Mr. and Mrs. Cooper owned the grocery store in town, and as far as she knew, they were not made of money. Graduate school was expensive.

"At least you're thinking ahead," she said diplomatically. Good thing somebody was.

Grace rolled her dark eyes. "I've been questioning my decision ever since I started working with this bunch of whiny babies. My other classes aren't nearly as bad." She looked out at the taproom. "Everything okay here?"

"Yup. Busier than I thought it would be. Two parties over at Murphy Lanes."

"Oh, good. Mary Alice will be happy we have so much business," Grace said.

Jenny was surprised.

"Mary Alice? Don't you mean Hannah?" she asked, wondering why a server would care more than the owner.

Grace waved that away. "Oh, sure. Hannah will be happy, too, but Mary Alice is very, um, committed now that she and her boyfriend put money into Hannah's investor fund."

Jenny frowned. "She knows that it's still Hannah's business, right?" she asked cautiously because you never could tell with Mary Alice.

Grace shrugged and headed out to take care of a group of bowlers who'd just wandered in.

June walked out of the kitchen with a loaded tray.

"I think we'll be good now, Jenny," she said. "Anything we need to know?"

Jenny brought her up to date on the tables she'd been handling, and June nodded.

"Got it. Thanks again. I don't know what we would have done without you."

"No problem."

"Just mark down your hours, and I'll make sure you get paid."

That would be nice.

Jenny said goodbye to Deacon and Grace at the bar as she tossed aside her order pad, then hesitated, wishing she could just duck out the front door. But even if she didn't need to get her coat and purse from the back, she knew it would be more trouble than it was worth to try and avoid her sister. If she slipped away like Harry, Josie would let her have it later.

So she took a deep breath, pushed open the kitchen door, and walked into the heat and thick smells of the kitchen. She came to a stop at the sight of Mat and Josie engaged in a passionate embrace in front of the dishwasher.

"Jesus. No wonder June's so keen to keep you two out of the storage closet," she said.

Josie came up for air, looking even rosier and more disheveled than before.

"June is only concerned because she and Calvin want to use the storage closet themselves," she said.

"Ask me about how I caught Deacon and Hannah sometime," Mat added. "I saw far more of Deacon Black than I ever wanted to." He shuddered, his lips swollen from the kiss, and the color riding high on his cheekbones.

Drew, the only one who seemed to actually be working, barked out a laugh as he flipped a burger on the grill.

"I think I'll pass." Jenny said her goodbyes, got her stuff, and made her escape out the back door where the rain had softened but was no less steady.

Yeah, it was definitely a good thing that she wouldn't be working at the Country Time regularly, she decided. Talk about feeling out of place. Not to mention the problem she'd have getting into the supply closet if she needed anything.

Making her way to her little pickup, she climbed in and sat behind the wheel for a moment, watching the rain bead on her windshield. Harry might be right. Her mother might be right. This whole situation might be an opportunity to make a change. Assuming she wanted to.

Jenny started up the truck and drove home through the wet spring darkness.

10

On the other side of town, Jenny turned her pickup down a quiet street and then into the driveway of the two-story house she'd always thought screamed '70s. Not Brady Bunch '70s—it wasn't that cool. Just plain old suburban '70s.

As a teenager, Jenny had thought it was the ugliest house on the planet, with its fake brick front and the old-fashioned bay window blocked by rhododendron bushes that bloomed whenever they felt like it. But since her mother owned it, it would always be someplace she could call home. She knew Josie felt the same way. Jordan might be another matter, but who cared about him?

Parking in front of the garage, she jogged through the rain to the front door. It wasn't that much of a surprise to see the house was dark inside since her mother often worked far past the end of her shift. Jackie loved their little town, and more, felt responsible for it.

Jenny guessed she appreciated the devotion. Although it would make her even happier if it turned out that the reason her mom wasn't home yet was because she was out having a good time with friends. Assuming they hadn't all drifted away over the years.

Not that Jenny had room to talk.

She let herself into the silent house and walked through to the kitchen, pulling blinds and turning on lights as she went. Then she took a minute to make herself a sandwich, because the muffin she'd had for lunch and Harry's sweet potato fries really weren't cutting it, and carried her makeshift meal upstairs to her bedroom.

Slipping off her shoes, she put the plate with her sandwich on the nightstand and crawled onto the bed to sit cross-legged with her back against the headboard.

What a hell of a day.

For the first time since breakfast, Jenny felt the weight of what had happened—and the deep hurt she'd been keeping bottled up.

Missy had *fired* her. Fired *her*.

There was a valid reason, she reminded herself. It wasn't like Missy had fired her because she didn't like her anymore. She couldn't pay her. It would have been a hell of a lot worse if she'd kept her mouth shut and then stiffed her. And she'd obviously been torn up about having to do it.

But...

Jenny guessed it was the shock that bothered her the most. It was like she'd been blindsided, like something she'd assumed to be true had turned out to be nothing but an illusion.

Missy had been her boss, but Jenny considered her to be a friend, too. When Stefan had shown his true colors, Missy had been the person she'd told first—not her mother, not her sister. Missy had been the one who'd convinced her not to put up with his shit anymore.

It was a rude awakening to find out that Missy was putting up with *Buster's* shit without telling anyone, without telling

Jenny, when she had to know Jenny would have her back. To find out that when Jenny had thought they were a team, Missy had walled herself off and blocked her out?

Yeah. A shock.

On the other hand, Jenny hadn't noticed anything was wrong, and she prided herself on noticing everything. What kind of a friend did that make her? Maybe Missy hadn't said anything because she'd been waiting for Jenny to ask.

She sighed and curled up in a ball on the bed, eyes tightly closed. Not much to do about it now, she guessed.

She probably should text Missy or call her or something. Make the first move. Try to work things out. At least try to see things from Missy's point of view.

But Jenny didn't think she was that good of a person. Not tonight anyway. Maybe tomorrow.

Sighing, she opened her eyes and looked around the room that had been hers for as long as she could remember. Jackie's bedroom was on the first floor, but Jordan, Jenny, and Josie had always slept upstairs. It had given them the privacy they'd craved as they'd gotten older, and Jackie had claimed that sleeping on the first floor made it easier to catch them when they tried to sneak out.

Jenny could attest to that, although she knew for a fact that Jordan had managed to slip away more than once without getting caught. But he'd had a tree right outside his bedroom window while Jenny's and Josie's rooms were in the front overlooking the street, so he'd had an advantage.

Contemplating her space, she realized how little had changed since she'd moved back into it. Artwork still decorated the walls—some new, some old, all hers. Her childhood bed and other furniture were scarred from years of use. The carpeting was old, but the curtains on her single bedroom window were relatively new. Her aunt had made them before she and Jenny's uncle had moved to Harrisburg for his work.

Jenny never let herself dwell much on the fact that she'd had to move home again because it was freaking depressing. Josie had moved back home, too, but only for a little while. Her sister had been fired from her job in Manhattan about six months ago, but now she was already getting on with her life and had moved in with the man of her dreams. Jenny was still here. Always freaking here. Treading water.

Sighing, she sat up and boosted herself off the bed. Pacing over to the window, she stared down at the street below, watching the occasional car drive past the house, headlights reflecting on the wet pavement.

Maybe, she thought, Harry and her mother were both right. Maybe this whole mess was a chance to do something new. Make a change.

What could it hurt to take her mother up on her unexpected offer of the temporary job at the police station? It would be different, and that might be exactly what she needed.

If she was tied down to an office job, would she still be able to paint?

Jenny snorted.

"Oh, right," she muttered. "Like you've been so freaking productive anyway. And it's not like you've got people clamoring for your work. Or even wanting to give you a chance."

Regardless of the dream she'd clung to since childhood, the fact was that since leaving Stefan she'd applied at lots of co-op galleries, tried for grants in the fine arts, and contacted as many professional gallery owners as she could find. They'd all either turned her down or never gotten back to her at all.

Yes, she had paintings hanging at the Country Time. But she'd only sold two. She'd talked to the owner of Hardy Furniture about hanging her pieces in their showroom, as well as a local real estate agent to see if he'd like to use her paintings when he staged houses.

Nothing. Looked like the great Stefan Daaz might have

been right after all when he'd told her that her stuff wouldn't sell.

She could try to set up an online store, but she had no clue how to do it. Josie would help, but Jenny wasn't sure she wanted to ask her sister. It would be just one more example of her own ignorance.

So what could it hurt to give working at the police station a try? Even though she'd never done anything like this before, look at how Josie had jumped into the unknown and been rewarded with friends, the business, and a man who loved her beyond measure.

What if she screwed up?

And that, Jenny realized suddenly, was the main reason she was hesitating. The fear of failing, and, more importantly, the fear of failing Jackie. After all, this was the first time Jenny could remember her mother telling her she'd done a good job at something.

"Well, if you can't handle it, then you'll go be a waitress."

Her mother would be disappointed, but then again, what else was new? As for the painting...

"I can do both," she assured herself. "If I can clean and waitress and paint, I can do this. Hell, I'll be sitting down for once. I'll have so much energy I won't know what to do with myself."

She turned from the window and looked around the room again. She was nervous, but for the first time in a long time, she could feel a spark inside. The spark of a new beginning, a new path. Just "new."

And, maybe, just maybe, some of the excitement that was sparking was because she'd also be working with a certain police officer she'd been trying to avoid. The thought of how Harry had watched her at the Country Time when he thought she didn't notice made her shiver.

If working with Mat would have been difficult, how awkward would it be to have sexy time feelings for a co-worker right under her mother's nose?

Did she care?

Jenny still hadn't come up with an answer to that question when Jackie came home about an hour later.

"You're really late. Everything okay?" she asked her mother when she met her in the kitchen. She leaned against the counter and watched Jackie get out what she'd need to make a sandwich for herself.

"Oh, sure. Just had to get things done, and I got backed up being away all morning with Suzy. At least Curtis can pick up more hours. He's going to cover overnight with Carly, so I won't have to go back."

"That's good. What about Harry?" Jenny asked with what she hoped was extreme nonchalance.

"He's on day shift for a while. I'm hoping he won't have to change."

Confirming that Jenny would be running into him all the time if she covered for Suzy.

"I'll definitely have to juggle schedules, though," her mother continued as she slathered mayo and mustard on bread, then added meat and cheese. "Damn the town council for not letting me hire another full-time officer. Actually, with the way the area's growing, we should probably hire more. The regional and state police help cover, but sometimes it can take a while for them to get here." She held out the bags of cold cuts and shook it slightly. "Want a sandwich?"

"Oh." Jenny winced. "Sorry. I already have one. I should have made you something for dinner."

"No problem." Jackie took her sandwich over to the old kitchen table and sat in one of the straight wooden chairs, then took a huge bite. "Did you have time to think about what I said about the job?" she asked around the food as she chewed.

"Yes." Jenny straightened. "I'm going to take you up on it."

She half expected her mother to jump for joy, but Jackie just chewed and studied her for a moment.

"And you've thought about this?" she asked after she swallowed. "I don't want you taking the job just because I thought it would be a good idea."

"No. I think I need to see what happens."

"And your painting?" her mother asked, because she knew her.

"It's not like I've been getting a lot done lately." Jenny shrugged. "No reason why I can't do both."

"That's what I've always thought," Jackie said, leaning forward. "There is no reason why you can't have some financial security at the same time you work on what you want to do."

Jenny sincerely hoped that was the case.

"Am I in?" she asked.

Jackie smiled. "If you think you can start tomorrow, we'll do that, and I'll clear it through the town council."

Jenny drew in a deep breath. "Okay."

It felt so...final. Like a door closing. But maybe the door was opening instead. What the hell did she know?

She could do this.

Jackie held up a finger. "Probationary, you understand. We've never worked together, so we'll have to see how you do. If everything seems to be going okay, we'll set you up to cover Suzy's entire leave and increase the hourly rate."

Jenny felt her stomach clutch and roll. "I won't let you down."

Her mother grinned. "Welcome to the Hardy Falls Police Department."

11

The next morning, Jenny and her mother carpooled to the police station. Since the position to cover the front desk while Suzy was on maternity leave had been approved months ago, Jackie was certain it wouldn't be a problem to get Jenny set up as a temporary employee. No worries. Piece of cake.

"Famous last words," Jenny muttered as they cruised through town in the chief's Ford Explorer, enjoying the sunshine that hadn't put in much of an appearance this spring. It felt strange not to be driving herself, but her mother had wanted them to go in together since Jenny didn't have a keycard yet.

"It'll be fine," Jackie insisted, turning onto the main drag of Hardy Falls. "And today, you'll be able to see what's really involved in the job before you get too far into the thing."

"I saw it yesterday. I won't change my mind," Jenny assured her.

Jackie looked unconvinced.

Since her mother theoretically started work at nine, they didn't pull into the police station's parking lot until almost eight-thirty. Practically sleeping in. Tomorrow—assuming there was a tomorrow—Jenny would have to be there by eight, so she'd be on her own.

She just hoped she'd be able to figure out what to wear without any maternal input. It had been odd to have to think about choosing something appropriate—in her other jobs, she'd either worn a uniform or not cared.

At least her mother had only made her change clothes once.

Jackie parked the Explorer and led Jenny to the employee entrance.

"Once I get you set up, you'll have your own keycard," she said as she swiped hers and pulled the door open. "I'll make sure you get it before we leave."

Before they could step into the building, a woman wearing in a creased police uniform walked out, then stopped and grinned at them.

"Hi, chief," she said. "Hi, Jenny."

Jenny smiled at Officer Carly Hu. The other woman was slightly older than she was and only a little taller. But despite her somewhat delicate appearance, Carly was a good cop who could take you down and mess you up if that's what she had to do. She also had a loving bear of a husband, two adorable kids, and a ranch house a few miles away in Beaver Run.

"Hey," Jenny greeted her. "Mom said you were on graveyard. How's that going?"

Carly rolled dark, bloodshot eyes. "Hate it. Always have, always will."

"Why are you just leaving now?" Jackie demanded, letting the door close so the alarm wouldn't go off. "You should have been off shift over an hour ago."

Carly's grin widened. "No problems for me, but I was making sure our boy Harry had some backup. He gets himself into trouble when he's left alone."

Jackie sighed. "What happened?"

The other woman laughed. "He'll tell you, I'm sure. And before I forget, Curtis did good last night. He was so starched and pressed he put me to shame. I felt like I should be looking for another job."

"Don't you dare."

Carly laughed again and jerked her head toward Jenny. "Bring your child to work day?"

Jenny flipped her off.

Now Jackie was the one rolling her eyes. "Jenny's going to help us out while Suzy's on maternity leave. Answering phones. Getting coffee."

Jenny frowned at her mother. "You never said anything about getting coffee."

Carly's grin was wide and sunny. "You could not pay me to answer those phones," she said. "You'll be praying for the times they ask you to get coffee."

Uh-oh. That sounded ominous.

"Really?"

"Don't scare her before she even starts," Jackie warned.

"I won't," Carly promised. But Jenny thought she heard her mutter "sucker" as she sauntered off toward her car.

Jackie swiped her card to open the door again, and they went into the station. Going directly to the squad room, her mother headed for Harry's desk, leaving Jenny to trail behind.

He was sitting, typing on his computer, his hair mussed instead of in its normal order. When he looked up and saw Jenny, the expression in his blue-green eyes was unreadable.

"Jenny needs a job, and we need a receptionist, so she'll be working here," Jackie said abruptly. "Now, what the hell is going on?"

Before Harry could respond, a sudden, shrill, female scream echoed from the direction of the holding cells.

"Jesus Christ!" Jenny put her hand on her heart so it wouldn't jump out and bounce around the room.

"You keep away from me, you two-timing hussy!" she heard a woman shriek.

"It's your fault, you bitch!" another female voice yelled.

There were the sounds of scuffling.

"Hey!" Harry shouted loudly, making Jenny jump again. "Shut it, you two!"

The noise subsided.

Jackie's only response to the commotion was a slight narrowing of her eyes.

"Harry?" she prodded gently.

"Lola Peters and Birdie Nelson," he told her. Then he looked at Jenny and raised an eyebrow.

She'd always hated it when he did that. She hated that he *could* do that. Who the hell could raise only one eyebrow? It wasn't normal. She crossed her arms and glared at him because "Nice Harry" seemed to be gone, and "Irritating Harry" was back.

"It's okay. She'll be signing the normal agreements since she's covering for Suzy." Jackie gestured toward the cells where they could hear raised voices again. "Explain."

Harry nodded and pulled a little notepad from his shirt pocket, opening it to read the notes he'd written.

"Apparently at seven o'clock this morning, Lola Peters and her sister Birdie Nelson both decided to go to the Sunnyside Diner for breakfast. Neither of them knew the other would be there."

"Oh, Jesus Christ," Jackie moved forward and sat on the edge of Harry's desk. "They haven't spoken to each other since they got into that big fight over Albert Cromwell on Valentine's Day."

Albert had arrived at the Valentine's Day dance with his date, Birdie Nelson. Unfortunately, her sister, Lola Peters, had been under the impression and *she* and Albert were dating.

The two sisters had gotten into a knock-down, drag-out fight and basically trashed the Grange Hall.

Jenny had seen it. It had been epic.

"Yeah," Harry said dryly. "Apparently, Albert broke up with Birdie after she and Lola caused such a commotion at the dance."

"Goddamn it!" Jackie groaned.

"According to Mrs. Bunson at the Sunnyside, when Lola and Birdie saw each other, Birdie went for her sister. Much screaming ensued, although fortunately Albert, Joe, Martin, and my grandfather hadn't shown up for their regular breakfast date yet. The Bunsons tried to get the ladies to take the fight elsewhere, but it didn't work. Eventually, Mr. Bunson and one of the busboys dragged them down here."

Since Lola and Birdie were both in their eighties, it probably hadn't been too hard. They couldn't weigh much more than 100 pounds together.

"They should have called you to come deal with it," Jackie said, frowning.

"Mrs. B. called to tell me they were on the way. I think they were just desperate to get them out of the diner as soon as possible," Harry said, running a hand through his hair and mussing it further. "Lola and Birdie were pretty upset. They tried to go for Mr. Bunson and, uh, me."

"Did they hurt you?" Jackie asked.

"Well, not for lack of trying," Harry admitted. "And they have bony knees, let me tell you." When he looked at the chief again, there was a sparkle of amusement in his eyes. "I had to defend my masculinity, chief. So I put them in the holding cells to calm down until you got in."

"I'm surprised they let you do that."

"They didn't exactly *let* me," Harry corrected. "But Carly was here finishing some paperwork, and Mr. Bunson was extremely motivated to see them behind bars, so he and his busboy helped. Between the four of us, we managed to get them under control."

"Christ." Jackie sounded tired. "I don't want to charge them, but if they keep causing public disturbances, I'm going to have to. I don't know what the big deal is about Albert, anyway. They don't need to fight over him like this."

"I'm pretty sure they fight like this because they're sisters," Harry said.

"That's no excuse." Jackie turned to Jenny. "You and Josie wouldn't act this way over a man, would you?"

Jenny thought about Mat. Then she met Harry's eyes over her mother's head and cleared her throat.

"Of course not."

"Hmmm." Jackie looked suspicious but shrugged it off. "Well, I'd better go talk to the old fools," she said and pushed to her feet.

"I tried to remind them that Joe and Martin are both currently single," Harry told her. "One for each. And, I never really asked, but I'm pretty sure both of those guys are continent, too. Albert always said that was his big selling point."

Jackie barked out a laugh. "I'll have to set them all up on blind dates." Shaking her head, she turned to leave and then seemed to remember Jenny.

"Can you show Jenny the phones and email and other systems?" she asked Harry. "We'll introduce her to the wonderful world of paperwork later, but first I have to get her set up as an actual employee."

"No problem."

Jackie left, and Harry got to his feet, walking around his desk to lean back against it, hands braced on either side of his lean hips.

"So, you decided to go for it?"

Jenny shrugged. "Like you said. This is a chance for me to

do something different. And getting paid sounded like a good idea."

He cocked his head. "Think the mayor's going to have a problem?"

Jenny shrugged again and made a face. "I don't know. You'll have to ask my mother about that one, Officer Newman. This is her big idea."

Harry laughed a little, and his smile glowed in eyes that looked more green than blue in this light.

"Well, welcome to the dark side," he said.

Jenny swallowed.

"Thanks." She sounded breathless, even to her own ears.

"Let's go—"

He was interrupted by female voices shouting.

"Goddamn it, Birdie! Stop it!" Jackie's voice was sharp and loud. "Harry! Get back here!"

Harry responded immediately, pulling out his Taser and running the short distance to the holding cells.

Jenny started to follow but then stopped. What could she do to help? Speak sternly?

Still, her mother might be in trouble. The only thing that kept Jenny from freaking out was the fact that Jackie had been talking to two women in their eighties who were approximately the size of twigs.

Harry had pulled his Taser.

She realized she was shaking. Of course, she knew that all police officers carried weapons. She'd just never thought about the fact that they'd need to *use* them every once in a while.

"Goddamn it."

At the sound of Jackie's voice, Jenny bolted into the hallway, watching wide-eyed as her mother emerged from the area where the holding cells were located and marched out to reception, one hand holding the other high against her chest. Harry followed, carrying a steel case.

"What happened?" Jenny demanded, falling into step behind them.

"Freaking Birdie Nelson bit me," Jackie growled, striding into her office. With Harry and Jenny following, she settled in her chair on the other side of her desk and held up her hand. There were distinct tooth prints on the side of it. Some were so deep they were bleeding.

"Holy cow!" Jenny stared. "What did you do to her?"

Birdie Nelson was a very prim and proper elderly woman. It was inconceivable that she would just...bite someone.

"I didn't freaking do anything to her," Jackie said, scowling darkly. "She was trying to get to her sister, and I got in her way. Stubborn old woman."

Harry opened the case he'd been carrying, which turned out to be a first aid kit, and pulled out astringent and bandages. He doused Jackie's hand, and she hissed, closing her eyes for a moment.

"We're charging them," she told him. "I don't care if they're a hundred years old."

He nodded. "Got it, chief."

"Let them make their phone calls and get their kids in here. We'll arraign them for disturbing the peace and get them the highest fine we can. If the kids complain, we'll throw in assaulting a police officer and anything else I can think of."

"All right." Harry bandaged Jackie's hand with an efficiency that spoke of long practice. "You're going to have to go get this checked out. Nothing nastier than a human bite wound."

"Don't I freaking know it." Her mother looked supremely pissed then seemed to realize Jenny was standing there. "Well?" she barked. "Are the phones off forwarding yet?"

Jenny jumped. "I'll do it now."

"Both of you get to work." Jackie's frown was thunderous. "I'll wait to see if their kids show up so we can have a little chat, then I'll head to the goddamned clinic."

Harry picked up the first aid case and followed Jenny out of the office. He shut the door behind them at Jackie's barked order, then turned and grinned down at Jenny.

"Welcome aboard," he said. "I'll help you turn on the phone system and show you a few other things."

Jenny went with him to the front desk and tried to pay attention to what he was doing. After he'd left to go back to the squad room, she sat, head reeling, looking at the complicated phone system and the radio and the computer. She started to hyperventilate.

Maybe this hadn't been such a good idea after all.

12

The phones started ringing almost as soon as forwarding was disabled, and for the next hour or so Jenny found herself taking a deep dive into the insanity that was Hardy Falls. She tried to be as helpful as she could, although it was a little hard to hear the callers once Lola Peters's son and Birdie Nelson's two daughters descended on the station, and the shouting started again. It got pretty loud until Jackie threatened to lock them all up.

By the time everyone was finally sorted out and gone, Jenny had decided that Albert Cromwell needed a chastity belt. How a sweet old man who'd apparently been devastated when his wife Mabel died of breast cancer had become such a chick magnet was beyond her.

After the Peters and Nelson crews left, Jackie stomped out to go to the clinic to have someone look at the bite wound on her hand.

And then...peace.

"Ahhhhh." Jenny sighed and settled back in her chair, eyes closed.

"Changed your mind about working here yet?"

She opened her eyes and swiveled to see Harry lounging in the hallway opening, watching her.

It dawned on her that they were alone.

"No," she said and gestured toward the miraculously quiet telephone. "But these people are nuts."

He grinned, and his eyes twinkled appealingly. "You're just figuring that out?"

She looked at him with pity. "Honey, I have been a waitress in and around this town since high school. I know exactly who lives here."

Harry laughed and walked forward to perch on her desk. "Well, in that case, I'll show you how to accept payments from the fine citizens who come in to pay tickets or whatever in person at the window. And I'll even give you the code for the security door so you won't get locked out again."

Jenny glanced at the rectangular reception window and straightened.

"Grreeeaaat."

She was surprised when he turned out to be a patient teacher, and, although the program to discharge tickets and other fines was complicated, she got the hang of it after the third time through.

Of course, a good reason for her lack of focus was because Harry was sitting next to her, his big body crowding hers at the desk, his arm brushing hers when he pointed at the computer screen to show her something or other.

It really messed with her ability to concentrate.

When he finally walked away, she had to breathe deeply for several minutes to calm down.

Frankly, her reaction to him was starting to worry her. Please, God, do not let her make a fool out of herself again just because a man seemed to be a decent human being.

Straightening her shoulders, she got up, unlocked the front door, and opened up the lobby for business.

A few minutes later, Jackie came marching back in from the clinic, her bitten hand wrapped in a large white bandage and a scowl on her lean features.

"How's the hand?" Jenny asked.

"Hurts like a son of a bitch, but at least my tetanus shot is up to date. I swear to Christ, I want to track down Birdie Nelson and fine her all over again. I'll be in my office cursing at the computer."

True to her word, she strode into her office and slammed the door shut behind her.

Harry left the station to do a quick drive through the town. The phones kept Jenny occupied, and so did her mother, who eventually came out of hiding to "teach" her how to use the department's scheduling program. The experience was...interesting.

Jenny decided she'd ask Harry to show her the system again once he got back.

Jackie didn't argue when Jenny told her she was going out to get some lunch. When she got back from the diner, she found her mother was barricaded in her office, and Harry was still missing.

Working from her notes, Jenny managed to disengage the phone forwarding system and unlock the front door again without incident.

Ta-da!

She was trying to see if she could figure out the scheduling thingy by herself when the call button buzzed from the lobby and scared the hell out of her.

"Crap." Hand on her heart, she took a deep breath. The buzzer came again, lasting longer this time, as if someone was leaning on it.

"Are you getting that?" Jackie's muffled voice shouted from her office.

"Yes." *No. I'm just going to let it buzz forever. Sheesh.*

Jenny pressed the intercom button on her desk. "Can I help you?" she asked politely, channeling her inner Suzy.

"Yeah. I want to, um, like, kind of pay a ticket," came a surly, young voice.

Batter up. Time to see if Harry's training had stuck.

Jenny went to the window and saw a sulky teenager on the other side. When she smiled at him, he simply glared at her.

"So, can you, like, do it or what?" he demanded.

Jenny drew in a deep breath. "Of course."

Trying to remember Harry's instructions, she took his money through the payment drawer and even managed to print up a receipt.

"I wasn't even doin' nothin' wrong," the kid whined, pocketing the receipt. "I was just tryin' to get home to do my homework."

Jenny refrained from comment and just gave him another professional smile. He didn't even bother looking at her as he turned and sauntered out the door to an old, gold Buick parked at the curb.

"He was doing seventy-six in a thirty-five mile per hour zone at eleven o'clock on a Sunday night, and since it was raining, he was damned lucky he didn't hydroplane," came Harry's voice from behind her. "That must have been some homework."

Jenny turned to see him standing at her desk, and she tried to control her jolt of pleasure that he was back.

"How was patrol?" she asked as she walked over. Maybe her hips swayed a little bit more than normal, but she tried to keep them in check.

Harry watched her move toward him, eyes heating for a second before he blinked and turned away to tap some papers he'd laid on her desk.

"Parking tickets. I'll show you how to enter them."

"Oh. Right."

Telling herself not to get distracted, Jenny slid back into her chair. Harry leaned over her to show her how to put the new tickets into the system and double-checked to make sure she'd discharged the kid's paid ticket correctly. When he bent to point out something on the computer screen, she was all too aware of the strength of his body so close to her own. Their eyes met, and she knew he was feeling the spark between them, just like she was.

"Do you have time to show me the scheduling system?" she asked, her voice husky.

His eyes latched on to her mouth, then he pulled away and glanced at Jackie's office door before turning his attention back to her. "Sure. I have to catch up on a few things first, but I'll do it as soon as I can."

Jenny straightened in her chair, his reminder of her mother's presence subtle, but there. She'd better remember she was here to do a job, not play flirty eyes.

"No, it's okay," she said quickly. "The chief gave me the basics. Let me see if I can figure it out. I'll ask you if I have any questions."

Instead of being grateful for the out, Harry frowned down at her.

"I said I'd do it."

Jenny wasn't sure if it was a promise or a threat, but she didn't have time to ask because he abruptly turned on his heel and marched off to the squad room.

Shaking her head, she pushed the mouse to wake up the computer and dove into the wonders of the scheduling program.

She was trying to resist the urge to pull out her hair when she was interrupted by another buzz from the lobby. It was followed, with barely a pause, by a hard knock on the reception window's security glass.

Surprised, Jenny looked up and saw Margo Truelove standing at the window, glaring in at her.

Oh, boy.

The mayor gestured imperiously.

"Let me in," she said, the words muffled by the thick glass.

A part of her—a small, petty part—wanted to engage the intercom and politely ask her to repeat herself, just to irritate her. Then she remembered Margo could make Jackie's life a living hell. Sighing, she buzzed her in.

Margo swept into the room as if she was walking onto a stage. Her coat of fake—well, Jenny hoped it was fake—fur swirled around her booted feet, and a cute little hat with, of all things, a sprig of fake roses on the side, perched on her stiff golden curls.

"Hello, Jenny dear." Scarlet lips pursed, Margo considered her. "I was talking to the head of town finance, and he told me you'd been hired to work here."

Jenny hoped her smile didn't look forced.

"Suzy had her baby," she said, holding it together for her mother's sake. "The chief needed someone to answer phones."

Margo's shark eyes sharpened. "You mean, your mother," she said sweetly, as she unbuttoned her coat to reveal a rose-colored skirt suit.

Jenny stiffened in spite of her best intentions. "I meant the police chief," she corrected quietly.

Margo's smile showed perfect white teeth. "Well, I'm not entirely sure you're qualified to hold this position, dear," she said. Saccharine dripped from her words. "After all, you clean houses and wait on tables for a living. We have certain standards we need to maintain here in the Hardy Falls Police Department. This position is the first level of contact with our citizens. We can't put someone in here simply due to nepotism." Her gaze moved over Jenny's simple blouse and slacks with insulting slowness.

"I am perfectly capable of doing this job," Jenny said through gritted teeth, ordering herself not to react.

"Problem?"

Jackie's voice came from the office door behind her, and Jenny felt her spine relax a little bit. The chief did *not* sound pleased.

Margo smiled over Jenny's head.

"Good afternoon, Jackie," she cooed. "I came to see if the rumors were true."

"Rumors?" Jackie's voice was like ice, and she moved forward until she could lean a hip against Jenny's desk.

"That you'd gone ahead and hired your daughter without town council approval," Margo elaborated.

"The town council doesn't oversee me." When Jenny looked up, she saw her mother was smiling. It was a very scary smile. "And neither does the mayor. I cleared the temporary position to cover Suzy's maternity leave months ago."

Margo waved those points away. "I wouldn't dream of trying to oversee the police department. There needs to be a separation of power so you operate independently." She paused. "It just seems...odd...that you installed your unemployed, unqualified daughter in a position without going through the due diligence of interviewing other candidates."

Jackie was going to say something she'd regret, Jenny could see it in her face. She surreptitiously reached over to pinch her mother's leg.

Jackie turned her glare on her just as Harry walked in from the squad room, frowning down at some papers he was holding. He looked up, saw them all around the desk, and stopped short.

"Harry!" Margo turned with flair and stretched out her hands to him, obviously expecting him to take them. Since he was on the other side of the room, he didn't, but he did smile at the older woman.

"Mayor Truelove."

Margo simpered and practically melted.

Jenny couldn't blame the woman. Under the fluorescent lighting, Harry's light brown hair sparkled with streaks of blond, while the charcoal color of his uniform intensified the color of his eyes. No doubt about it, Harry Newman III was one heck of a good looking guy. Margo Truelove might be almost thirty years his senior, but she obviously still appreciated the sight of a good-looking man.

As Harry put the papers he'd been holding on Jenny's desk, he looked at Jackie, and his smile quickly faded.

"Something going on, chief?" he asked her.

Jackie crossed her arms over her chest.

"Mayor Truelove was just sharing her opinion about me hiring Jenny. She thinks I bypassed some sort of procedure or something."

"I was merely pointing out that the interview process had not been followed," Margo protested. "And since the chief didn't go through a placement firm, there has been no vetting. This position is the face of the department." She let it go at that, but the implication was clear—she did not feel Jenny could be that face.

Under the desk, Jenny clenched her hands into such tight fists that her nails gouged the palms of her hands, but she kept her professional smile firmly on her face. This woman was *not* going to make her lose her cool. That would only prove her point.

Harry shifted until he stood face to face with the mayor. Jenny saw him glance at Jackie then smile at the mayor again with a nearly imperceptible tightening of his shoulders.

"It's good of you to be concerned, mayor," he said, charm oozing. "But I'm sure that Jenny will be a valuable asset to the department."

Margo batted her eyelashes at him, laser-focused, as if he

was the only other person in the room. "Do you really think so?" she asked, as a hand fluttered to her ample bosom.

To his credit, Harry didn't back up or run away.

"I do," Harry said firmly. "Besides, this is probationary. Suzy went a little early, and Jenny was kind enough to step in. We're all just trying it out. You don't have to be concerned."

Margo looked away, hand pressed to her lips now. "I do worry, you know," she said, her voice catching. "I worry about this town. I love this town." She looked at Jackie with damp, pleading eyes. "I'm sorry, Chief Kline. I didn't mean to question your decision or your authority. I'm just want everything to be the best it can be here in Hardy Falls. After our last mayor, I feel like it's my duty."

Jackie tucked her thumbs in her belt and rocked back on her heels.

"Sure," she said.

"Well, we'll see then," Margo said as she beamed at Jenny like she was the sun shining down on them all. "Everyone deserves a chance to move into a different situation. I'm glad that your mother saw fit to give you this opportunity, Jenny, and I hope you'll learn a lot as you work here in our little police department."

Jenny wasn't sure she trusted herself to speak, so she merely nodded.

"I really wasn't questioning you," Margo lied to Jackie. "I'm glad we had this talk. I feel so much better."

"That's wonderful," Jackie said dryly.

Margo smiled at Harry again. "Thank you so much for the reassurance."

"Of course," Harry said smoothly.

"Well, I'll just be off." She dimpled at Harry and swept out the door with the same dramatic flair she'd used to sweep in.

Nobody spoke until the security door locked behind the

mayor's robust form, and they heard the beep of the front door closing a moment later.

"And this," Jackie said to the room at large, "is why I will never give that woman the code to get into this place. If finance does, and she can come and go as she pleases, I'll go over to the borough hall and shoot those responsible." She looked at Harry. "And are we proud of ourselves?" she asked him.

Jenny couldn't control her laughter, but she put her hands over her mouth to try and keep it contained. Harry glared at her.

"Hey, I did that for you, you know." He rolled his shoulders. "I feel like I need a shower. She creeps me out. I wish Tony would come back. Margo likes him better."

"She likes anything young and male." Jackie's stern expression broke out into a grin. "Thanks, kid," she said, knocking a fist against Harry's broad shoulder. "I was about to kill her."

Harry ran a hand through his hair, rumpling it. "Yeah, I kind of got that impression." His eyes turned cold. "She's over-reaching. She's not the boss of you."

Jackie sighed. "No, but she thinks she is. And she's got enough clout with the town council that she usually can get her way." She started back to her office, then stopped and turned to Jenny. "I really do think you're good at this job," she told her. "Yes, there are things you'll need to learn, but I wouldn't put anyone at this desk unless I was sure they could handle it."

"Thanks." That meant a lot. Margo might have said that she loved Hardy Falls, but Jackie really did. "I won't let you down."

Jackie nodded and walked into her office, closing the door behind her. Jenny looked at Harry.

"What?" he demanded with ill-temper.

"Just promise you'll only use your powers for good," she said.

"Christ." An intriguing bronze color flooded his cheekbones, but his eyes were devilish when he smiled at her. "Don't worry. It's all good," he said, lips twisting wickedly.

Jenny gulped, and his smile broadened. He turned and went back down the hallway.

She stared after him. Then she stared at the papers he'd left without giving her a clue what she was supposed to do with them.

"Hey!"

Harry came sauntering back a few minutes later, holding two bottles of water. He gave her one and showed her what to do with the incident reports he'd put on her desk. Then he reviewed the scheduling program with her until she thought she finally understood it.

Jenny's keycard arrived along with the employment paper-work, delivered by a sunny little college intern and not the mayor. Jenny's mother stayed in her office and did not go postal on anyone. All was well with the world.

The calm lasted until Bethany Clark, one of the part-time police officers, came bouncing in to start her shift. Perky and young, she looked like a cheerleader with her blond hair and blue eyes as she flirted outrageously with Harry. Jenny couldn't help but notice that Harry did not seem to mind.

She was saved from witnessing more of the dance when her mother tracked her down and told her she'd take her home. Jenny jumped at the chance to leave, glad she'd have her own transportation from now on.

A few minutes later, her first day officially working for the Hardy Falls Police Department was over.

After her mother dumped her off at the house and drove away—heading back to finish the rest of her own shift—Jenny dragged herself upstairs and fell face down across her bed.

"Holy cow."

13

Even though she really, *really* tried to do everything right the next morning, Jenny managed to freeze up the entire scheduling program fifteen minutes after she sat down at her desk for her second official day of work.

Harry was in the office, but her trust that he'd be able to fix things quickly faded when he just stood beside her chair and frowned at the screen, rubbing his chin thoughtfully.

"What did you do?" he asked after a moment.

"How should I know? I only tried to input some changes the chief left for me." Jenny cast a frantic look at her mother's closed office door. "Just make it work before she finds out!"

It was only eight-thirty, and Jackie shouldn't have even been there yet, but of course, she was. Even better, she was locked down in her office pulling together reports for a review meeting she was having with the town council the following Monday. Considering the Margo Truelove situation, Jackie had told Jenny she wanted to "make goddamn sure" everything she presented was "fucking perfect." Which had put her in one *hell* of a mood.

"Make it work? How? By waving my magic wand?" Harry asked blandly. "My last name's Newman, not Potter."

"Whatever." Panicking, Jenny grabbed onto his uniform shirt sleeve without thinking. "Do something. I'm begging you."

He looked down at her hand, and she realized she was clutching him, could feel the strength of his forearm under the material of his shirt. She hastily pulled back. Harry's eyes were suddenly intensely blue, and her breath caught.

"Begging me?" he asked silkily.

"If that's what works." Her voice sounded lower than normal.

He held her gaze for a moment longer, then turned back to the computer screen.

"I guess I could reboot the system."

Jenny drew in a shuddering breath that had nothing to do with stupid computers and everything to do with the man who was leaning over her and typing on her keyboard. The heat of his body wrapped around her as she drew in the scent of his soap and aftershave and skin.

"Let me move so you can sit in the chair," she croaked.

"Nah. I've got it." He pressed a few more keys then straightened. "Let's see what that did."

Stressed for more reasons than she cared to think about, Jenny stared at the computer screen and willed it to come back to life. To her unending relief, it did, and a few minutes later the scheduling system was up and running again.

"Oh, thank God," she went limp.

Harry moved away, taking his warmth with him.

"If it makes you feel any better, you did fine entering payments and discharging fines from the window transactions," he said.

"Thanks." The irony that the only computer system she seemed to be able to use was the one that was the most arcane and complicated was not lost on her.

Abruptly, her mother's office door slammed open, and Jackie came striding out. Her eyes were snapping, and her face was drawn into a sneer of disgust.

Jenny straightened to attention, figuring her mother had found out what she'd done to the computer, and the ax was about to fall. But instead, Jackie glared at Harry.

"I'm going out on patrol for a few damned hours," she snarled. "Got a problem with that?"

Harry held up his hands like she had a gun on him. "Have fun?"

"Fun." Jackie growled the word. "More fun than freaking spreadsheets, that's for goddamned sure." She turned and stalked down the hall toward the back door.

Harry and Jenny looked at each other.

"Well, I wasn't going to stop her," he said.

Jenny shook her head. "Me either." The words were heartfelt and true.

He cocked his head. "I don't have much on my plate at the moment, and the chief's apparently handling morning patrol. Want to get lunch at the Sunnyside later if we can?

She blinked. "Together?"

He raised that damned eyebrow. "We both need to eat, right?"

"Sure. Okay."

He nodded. "Good. If there's a call, I won't be able to make it, but otherwise I'll catch you in a bit." He headed back to the squad room.

Jenny turned to her computer.

No big deal. Just lunch with a coworker. Happens all the time. Not like it's a date or anything.

Except it sort of felt like a date.

Jackie came back from patrol in a better frame of mind, but her good mood abruptly disintegrated when she remembered she had to leave almost at once for a court appearance.

Whatever lunch would, or would not, have been, didn't matter because it ended up getting canceled anyway. Harry got called out right before noon to deal with two people having a shouting match over the last croissant at the bakery. From there, he went directly to the Cooper Grocery Store to pick up Paris Boone for public intoxication and disorderly conduct.

Zeke Cooper, Grace Cooper's father, had subdued the fashionable society matron after she started throwing toilet paper rolls at another customer's head. Apparently, the other customer, a kid from the university, had cut in front of her at the deli.

All of which meant Jenny did not have lunch with Harry at the Sunnyside, date or otherwise.

Harry had just put Paris in one of the holding cells to sleep it off when Jackie got back from court.

"How did it go?" Jenny asked as her mother stomped past her desk.

"Peachy." The look on Jackie's face said it had been anything but. "The judge didn't believe me when I told him the guy was a flight risk and set a 'reasonable' bail. Which means I'll be looking for the asshole again once he skips town. I'll be in my office."

"Okay." Jenny watched Jackie march into her office and winced when the door shut with more force than was strictly necessary.

Honestly, she'd never understood why her mother wanted to be the chief of police in the first place, and working here hadn't made it any clearer.

On the other hand, Jenny could certainly see why she'd had to sign a confidentiality agreement yesterday. She was finding out more about the people in Hardy Falls than she'd ever really wanted to know.

Around four o'clock, she heard male voices echoing from the squad room and knew, thanks to the scheduling program, that Officer Curtis Perez had come on to relieve Harry. Jenny was just glad Bethany wasn't on shift again.

Footsteps rang in the hallway as Curtis walked toward her, grinning, his black eyes twinkling. She watched him move with appreciation because the man was definitely worth noticing. He had skin the color of burnished bronze, close-cropped hair as black as his eyes, and a neatly trimmed vandyke beard. He looked exactly like what he was—a man who knew precisely where he stood with the female of the species.

Curtis stopped next to her desk and grinned down at her, crossing his arms in a pose that showed off his biceps. It was enough to give a girl the vapors.

"Hey, you." She returned the smile. "I haven't seen you around lately."

"I've been working graveyard." He grimaced. "Sucks, but it's a paycheck. Heard you were here. I guess you finally caved in and begged your mama to let you into the station so you could see more of me, right?"

"Oh, right." Jenny openly laughed at him. She'd never been one of his conquests. Curtis might be the sweetest guy on the planet when he wasn't making a move, but Jenny knew a player when she saw one. She'd had enough of that kind of man to last a lifetime.

"Look." Curtis put a hip on her desk, all buff and sexy in his uniform. "Carly has to leave early tonight, so I'll be on until Harry shows up again at six tomorrow morning. How about you and me meet at the diner and have some breakfast before you start work?" He winked at her. "Might give the rumor mill something to talk about."

"Yeah, I don't think so." Jenny frowned at him. "And what do you mean you're on until six tomorrow? That's over twelve hours. You'll be exhausted."

"That's what I told him," Harry said from the hall. She looked around Curtis to see him leaning against the wall, his arms and ankles crossed, his expression enigmatic, and his attention focused solely on Jenny.

Talk about the vapors.

Curtis scowled at him. "And I told you that I'll be fine. Hell, I need as many hours as I can get. If I don't get more time here soon, I'm going to have to find another job."

Harry sighed. "I know. The chief's working on it, but..." he trailed off.

"Mayor Truelove." Still frowning, Curtis stood up again. "Don't know why that woman hates me so much."

"You're in good company," Jenny assured him. "She hates me, too."

"Yeah?" His expression instantly morphed into a wicked grin, and he winked at her. "Guess I feel better now." He shot a glance at Harry, and his smile widened for some reason. "Better get to it."

"Be there in a minute," Harry said without shifting his stare away from Jenny. Curtis chuckled and moved past him and down the hall.

"What?" Jenny demanded when Harry remained silent.

"The chief has a policy prohibiting fraternization between employees," he said unexpectedly.

Jenny blinked at him. *Well, that had come out of nowhere.*

"Huh?" she said.

"You heard me. Chief Kline has a strict policy about employees getting involved romantically, especially for a casual fling. Makes it damned hard to run an effective police department if there's a lot of interpersonal drama getting everyone's head all screwed up, so she makes sure everyone knows it can't happen. The only exception is Tony and Suzy, and that's because they were already married when the old chief hired them. Even it's a problem when they're fighting."

Jenny tried to understand what he was saying and why he was saying it.

"Okay." She folded her arms over her chest and leaned back in her chair. "And this involves me, how?"

"Because you're an employee now," he said. "So you might want to wait until that's no longer the case before you jump all over Perez."

"I was not aware that I was jumping all over Curtis." She tried to keep her voice calm in the face of the anger she could feel rolling off him in waves. She wasn't afraid of him. That he was so worked up because another man had flirted with her was...interesting.

Harry's face hardened. "I thought I was going to have to book you two a room," he said, disapproval evident in the stiff way he was holding himself. He looked like he wanted to grab her and shake her. Or something.

When he didn't move to get any closer, she got up and walked to him, instead. Harry watched her draw near with a concentration that was a touch all its own.

"Oh yeah?" she challenged softly, suddenly feeling reckless and wild. "If I was all over Curtis, then what do you call what you and I have been doing these last couple of days?"

She saw him breathe in deeply and felt a kick of triumph.

"I have no idea what you're talking about. I'm working with you. I'm training you. That's all."

She moved close enough that she was almost touching his body with her own. Definitely invading his personal space. Leaning forward, she whispered, "Liar."

"You're imagining things." His eyes were that brilliant blue again, his chest moving more rapidly than normal.

The thrill of his response ran through her like an electric current. She forgot where she was, forgot that the phone might ring at any moment, that her mother was in an office a few yards away, that Curtis was right down the hall. All that mattered was the man in front of her.

"Maybe Curtis isn't the only player in this department," she murmured, unable to stop herself from goading him, prodding him, pushing him to see if she could make him lose that composure he wore like a shield. She didn't know why she was doing it, she just knew that she was compelled to see what was underneath—see who he really was, not the facade he presented to the world. "I saw how you acted with Bethany. You let her flutter around you like a butterfly. You were eating it up."

Her own words caused a shiver of doubt to run down her spine because they were true. Harry had been amused by Bethany, but he'd seemed to enjoy the attention, too. She'd seen that look on Stefan's face far too often.

Frowning a little, she started to draw away, but Harry reached out and grabbed her arms.

"I don't think so," he snarled, moving in closer, and crowding her into the shadows of the hallway. "What are you trying to say, Jenny?" he growled at her, his voice so low it was almost a vibration.

"Nothing." She didn't know what she was doing, why she'd started this with him. "If you want Bethany, that's your problem, but don't think I'm doing the same thing."

He moved into her. "I'm not playing," he murmured. "Not with Bethany. Not with anyone. I am totally and completely..." he leaned even closer, "...focused."

Jenny stared at him, her breath short, pulse racing.

Despite the dim light, she could see his eyes were hot, narrowed slits of blue—no longer calm, no longer remote. His breath came as fast as her own, his nostrils flared in his sharp-boned face.

She felt more alive than she had in years.

Instead of trying to escape, she found herself shifting until the equipment on his duty belt dug into her stomach. The rise and fall of his chest brushed against her breasts.

"Yeah," she whispered. "You think you're such a tough guy? You think there's nothing between us?"

"There is nothing," he murmured agreement, close enough that the warmth of his coffee-scented breath caressed her face.

"Prove it."

Then, she smirked.

And he pulled her up on her toes and slammed his mouth over hers.

It was a kiss, and more than a kiss. He took her lips in an almost desperate urgency, the taste of him exploding on her tongue. She wrapped her arms around his neck and dug her fingers into his hair to yank him closer as their lips moved and their teeth clashed.

It was a kiss as much about temper as it was about need, and Jenny didn't care. She grabbed Harry's hair and pulled, felt his hands, big and hot and slightly rough, work their way under the blouse she was wearing to find her skin. He took the kiss deeper, shoved her further into the corner at the door to the hallway, and pressed her up against the wall. She wrapped a leg around his hips to hold him in place and writhed against him.

It had been so long. So long since she'd felt like this.

Maybe she'd never felt like this.

Who knew Police Officer Harry Newman III would be the catalyst?

His mouth opened over hers, and she responded, mating with his lips, his tongue, drowning in the sensations of his body under her hands, the smell of his skin, the firm strength of his shoulders.

Then, suddenly, he thrust her back.

Gasping, she stared into his face and dug her short nails into his neck.

"We can't do this," he croaked.

"Later." She panted, trying to reach for his mouth again, but he wouldn't let her. "After we leave for the day."

"No." The word was so harsh that she winced. Then she got angry.

"Why?" she demanded. She wasn't alone here. He wanted this as much as she did. "We can do what we want outside the office."

"It's inappropriate behavior," he said, the formal words a distinct contrast to the fire still burning in his eyes. "If the chief finds out, we'll both end up out of a job."

"Inappropriate behavior?" Smiling a little, she let herself run her mouth over his jaw, a little bristly at the end of the day. She wondered idly if she was going to have to explain stubble burn.

"Jenny." He groaned and wrenched himself away from her hold, stepping back so that they no longer touched. She shivered in the sudden cold. "Curtis could come out at any moment. Your *mother* could come out at any moment."

That got through to her because she knew he was right, and she shivered again. Some of what he'd said earlier came back to her through the fog of arousal.

"No fraternization between coworkers?" she asked.

He shook his head. "None. Strict policy."

"I'm only here temporarily."

"You still work here now, and you'll always be my boss's daughter."

"Oh." So that was the real problem then. She felt herself deflate. "I get it. More trouble than I'm worth."

Goddamn it.

"I didn't say that."

She stared at him, confused and so turned on she couldn't think straight. Harry didn't seem much better. In fact, he looked ravished— lips swollen, pupils shot, his body obviously hard and aroused.

She took a step toward him.

The harsh buzz coming over the intercom system at her desk was shocking. Jenny jumped a mile and spun around, heart pounding.

"You should get that," Harry said as the buzz came again. Before she could argue, he strode quickly away.

Jenny stared after him until the buzzer sounded a third time. Then she hastily straightened her clothes and her hair and raced to the reception window before her mother came out of her office, demanding to know what the hell was going on.

More shaken than she cared to admit—by the encounter and the way things had gotten out of hand so quickly—Jenny forced a smile and got back to work.

After she'd helped an elderly woman at the window pay a parking ticket, she scrabbled back to her desk, collapsed in her chair, and buried her face in her hands.

Now what?

14

H*e couldn't talk to anybody yet or he'd give himself away.*

Instead of going back to his desk, Harry took a detour to the men's room and locked himself in one of the stalls. With the droning exhaust fan blanketing him in white noise, he focused on getting himself under control. Hands on his hips, he stood with his head down, eyes closed, and breathed deeply as he'd taught himself to do whenever the emotions he kept locked up inside threatened to escape the leash.

She'd tasted sweet, as if she'd been drinking sugar. Her lips had been soft, but firm under his mouth. He'd wanted to yank her against him, mold her body to his, and devour her.

Using all of the strength of will at his disposal, he desperately tried to calm down, but most of his blood had headed south and didn't seem inclined to come back north to his brain any time soon. His lips still tingled from the kiss, and his body was raging hard.

He could still taste her.

He hadn't felt like this since he was eighteen years old.

A part of him—the mature, sensible, *intelligent* part—knew this situation was bad. Very, very bad.

Yes, he'd been finding himself more and more drawn to Jenny Kline, but now, holy fuck, he'd kissed her in the middle of the police station while he was on duty. Like he'd told her, it was more than insane, it was inappropriate beyond measure. He didn't *do* that kind of thing.

"Don't shit where you eat, boy," his grandfather had once told him. That saying had served Harry well, even when he'd been in situations where the policy about office dating wasn't nearly as clear-cut as Chief Kline's. He'd seen too many people get screwed up by sloppy emotional entanglements with coworkers—Hannah and Deacon at the Country Time were definitely the exception, not the rule.

And if Jenny's mother had caught him making out with her daughter when he was supposed to be working, getting fired for violating department policy would have been the least of his worries.

Jenny had smelled like flowers and burned like fire.

Yeah, the sensible part of himself knew he couldn't go there.

But then there was the *other* part. The part that sometimes wanted to rip off his uniform and burn it along with all the rules he'd used to structure his life. The part that had gotten so out of control in his first year of college that his grandfather had wanted to pull him out of school. The part that had been a boy who lived in cheap hotel rooms with no restrictions or supervision. The part that wasn't "Officer Harry Newman," but "Trip," as he used to be known before he'd told his grandfather he wanted to go by his given name as a way to show the old man respect.

That part didn't want to hear about anything sensible or intelligent. That part wanted to march out to the reception desk, grab Jenny Kline, and haul her outside like a caveman. Wanted to drag her to his apartment and let the fire burn.

Which would impress Jenny's mother no end.

Jenny's mother, who was his boss. And would remain his boss until he left or got kicked out. And would always be Jenny's mother, no matter where Jenny worked or didn't work.

He took a deep breath. Then another.

"This is ridiculous," he muttered quietly under the noise of the fan, so his voice wouldn't carry. "This is not you. You're not like this anymore." His career and his reputation were on the line. He was the senior officer in the Hardy Falls police department, charged with setting an example for the other people who worked there and the rest of the town. The chief had been putting him forward more and more in the last year. She'd been grooming him to assume more responsibility and setting him up so he'd be able to head a department of his own whenever he decided to leave hers.

Jackie trusted him.

But, the voice of the reckless part of himself whispered, *she doesn't own you.*

Jenny was right about that. The chief couldn't control his whole life, and she didn't want to. This was a job and nothing more. And Jenny wouldn't be working here long—only twelve weeks or so.

Yes, it would look bad on a whole lot of levels if he pursued her now, but there was nothing to say that he couldn't later, after Suzy was back. The chief might not like it if Jenny hooked up with him after she was done with this job, but she probably wouldn't be all that pissed off.

"If you want her, just wait a little bit," he told himself. "Don't be an idiot. You don't have to risk everything."

Too bad that the boy—the one who sometimes compelled Harry to go up into the mountains just so he could yell at the top of his lungs where nobody could hear him, the one who'd been hustling other kids at the arcade at seven and stealing beer by the time he was eight—didn't want to wait. Didn't want to be sensible. Didn't want to be intelligent.

The fire had been building ever since Harry had come to Hardy Falls, and it was well and truly lit now. The taste of Jenny was in his mouth, and the feel of her was on his skin.

"Wait," he told himself. "It's only a few weeks. Wait."

He didn't *want* to wait.

But he would.

15

Jenny didn't know if she was relieved or disappointed when Curtis came out to drop off some paperwork later and told her Harry was gone. Maybe a little bit of both.

The man had well and truly knocked her on her ass.

"He practically ran out of here," Curtis said, his dark eyes gleaming with curiosity. "What set him off?"

Jenny ignored the question and took the papers he handed her.

She left the station as soon as possible and thanked God she'd been able to escape before Jackie came out of her office. Her mother always saw right through her.

Jenny wasn't sure what she would have seen in this case. Probably just confusion.

Once she was sitting in the safety of her pickup truck in the parking lot behind the building, she gripped the steering wheel with both hands and banged her forehead on it several times.

Was she insane? Had she lost her freaking mind? What if her mother had caught her kissing Harry? Because he was right about that part—Jackie Kline ran a tight ship. She'd often told

Jenny that she didn't want any interpersonal drama interfering with work at her police station. Distracted cops are cops who didn't pay attention to what they're doing. Distracted cops became dead cops.

Jackie couldn't control everything, but she did what she could to mitigate the risk. And at the moment, Jenny was an employee obligated to follow all of the same rules as the rest of them. Maybe more obligated.

Harry was tall and strong, not whipcord lean like Stefan. He was filled out and tight with muscle under her fingers. His mouth had been hot and wild on hers. For a moment, just a moment, she'd forgotten everything.

Jenny drew in a deep breath.

She wished she knew what Harry was thinking. How much did he regret what happened between them? What would he do the next time he saw her? She couldn't exactly avoid him like she'd been avoiding Mat.

What if he confronted her for basically instigating the kiss? What if he told her mother that she'd seduced him?

Okay, that wasn't likely, if for no other reason than he wouldn't want Jackie to know about his "inappropriate behavior."

What would Jenny do if Harry decided he wanted more and pinned her against a filing cabinet to kiss her again, took her mouth the way he had in the hallway, his hands on her hips pulling her closer, and...

This was not helping.

Especially since, despite everything, she really *wanted* Harry to pin her against the filing cabinet. To hell with the consequences.

Jenny wasn't sure what that said about her.

One kiss. It had only been one kiss. What would happen if it went further?

Well, it couldn't go any further. Okay, it *could*—they were both consenting adults, after all. But as long as she was working at the police station, it would be a very, very bad idea to get involved with Police Officer Harry Newman III. It might be a bad idea period, chemistry or no chemistry.

As she'd learned in the past, chemistry wasn't nearly enough to base a relationship on.

"Get over yourself, Jenny," she muttered as she turned the key to start up the truck. "Relationship? It was a kiss. Putting the cart *way* in front of the horse there." She had a tendency to do that kind of thing. Hence...Stefan.

Yes, she and Harry were obviously attracted to each other, but that didn't mean anything. She didn't know his deal, but it had been a really long time since she'd had that kind of contact with a man. She'd been primed. They'd both been angry, and the fire between them had ignited. Simple as that. Didn't mean anything—not to him, not to her. And it definitely didn't mean there'd be anything else between them in the future, besides maybe some awkwardness.

Jenny grimaced.

Actually, there'd probably be a lot of awkwardness the next time they saw each other. No matter what happened, there was a distinct possibility that her time at the police station would be uncomfortable for a while. Even if they worked things out— which they would, of course—Jenny was very much afraid that all she'd be able to do whenever Harry was around was look at him and remember how he'd felt against her, how he'd tasted. Worse, she'd always have to remind herself not to reach out to feel and taste him again.

Shit.

How the hell was she supposed to deal with him for the next few weeks?

She'd have to find a way. Her mother had given her a chance. She'd trusted her and defended her to Margo Truelove.

Jenny couldn't screw that up, no matter how tempting Harry was.

Shit.

Feeling glum, she shoved the pickup into gear and drove out of the parking lot.

16

Jenny wasn't exactly shocked when she didn't get much sleep that night. But it sucked because when the alarm went off the next morning, she was exhausted from tossing and turning and staring at her bedroom ceiling while her mind whirled.

A long, long hot shower and a vat of coffee made her feel at least a little bit human again, and, after spending some time carefully picking out something appropriate to wear, she headed out to the police station to start day three, well, four.

It didn't occur to her until she was in the parking lot that she and Harry would be alone for an hour before her mother came on shift, unless Jackie got there early again today. And, even though her mother undoubtedly *would* get in early, there were still bound to be at least a little time she'd have to deal with him. Crap.

"Let the awkwardness begin," she muttered to herself.

Too bad running away wasn't an option. Especially since she doubted Harry would agree to pin her up against a filing cabinet.

Damn it.

Looking into the rearview mirror, she glared at herself and tried to drum up her mojo.

"If this situation needs to be handled, you *will* handle it. If things are awkward and tense, they'll just be awkward and tense. You will *not* jump him. You are a professional, and you will behave like one. Right? Damn right."

Nodding decisively, she got out of the pickup and marched to the employee entrance with determination. She swiped her keycard with almost violent intensity, walked into the police station, and...

She was alone.

The squad room was empty. So were the holding cells, the file room, the break room, and the reception area.

Unless Harry was hiding in the men's room or under his desk, he wasn't there. He must have gone out on a call or something.

Jenny felt a little deflated. Then she frowned and went out to the reception area to start her day.

Her mother arrived at the station about a half-hour later.

"How's it going?" Jackie asked as she strolled into the room. "I didn't get any calls for help, so I'm assuming you were okay."

"A few phone messages already." Jenny handed over the slips. "Mr. Looper said the wild dogs are circling his property now and behaving like a wolf pack. And Mrs. Cahill wants to talk to you about her latest parking ticket because she says there's not enough handicapped parking at Hardy Hair, which is why she was parked illegally."

Jackie grunted and took the pink slips.

"Harry looked into those 'wild dogs' that Hector Looper keeps yapping about—hah! Get it?"

Jenny rolled her eyes, and her mother smirked.

"Turns out they belong to his neighbor and consist of three golden retrievers who like to run around in their own fenced-in yard. The only thing they'll do to him or his Chihuahua is lick them to death. And Betty Cahill is about as handicapped as I am. Anything else?"

"No. I got the schedule updated and put in a few incident reports." Jenny cleared her throat. "Harry hasn't been here. Is he out on patrol or something?"

Jackie frowned at her. "You didn't see him before he left?" She shrugged. "Well, he must have wanted to get an early start to beat the traffic, and he'd already given the emergency dispatch the okay to route calls to me. Since Tony never made it out to Mount Pocono because of the baby, we still had funds to send someone for extra training. Harry volunteered, so he'll be out there today and tomorrow. I guess I should have told you, but I forgot."

"Oh." Jenny blinked. "It wasn't on the schedule," she said casually.

Exactly when had Harry volunteered?

"No, it was a last minute thing. He called me last night. Apparently, he was in contact with them and got in."

"Lucky," Jenny managed through gritted teeth.

"Yeah, although tomorrow was supposed to be his day off, and he's on deck all weekend. Did you remember that I'm heading out to see Uncle Bill and Aunt Noreen in Harrisburg after work on Friday?"

"Of course, I remembered. Even if I'd ignored the fact that you were trying to pack everything in the house last night, I'm an ace at the scheduling program now." Jenny patted the side of her computer screen, forcing herself to act normally.

"Right." Jackie sighed. "Why the hell did they have to move so far away? It's like planning for a safari every time we try to see each other."

The complaint was a familiar one. Jenny's mother hated the fact that her brother Bill and his wife Noreen had moved at the beginning of the year. Jackie's parents, Jenny's grandparents, had cut Jackie off when she'd gotten pregnant with Jordan. But

Bill had never turned his back on his sister. Since he'd moved, Jackie missed having her big brother around. Jenny could relate. She missed her own big brother, although she and Jordan hadn't been nearly as close.

She crossed her arms and raised her eyebrows at her mother. "It's only about two or three hours away, not across the country for Pete's sake," she pointed out. "Maybe Uncle Bill moved because he works for the state? And moving to the capital got him a promotion and a raise? And maybe Aunt Noreen found a better paying job in a bigger school district? And neither of them are getting any younger, so maybe they need to save for retirement? Think that could be it?"

"Yeah, yeah, yeah." Jackie slapped the phone message slips against her thigh. "Whatever. Now I have to go work on that goddamned report for the goddamned town council."

"It's not finished yet?" Jenny couldn't help tweaking her mother.

"Well, it *would* be if everybody in this freaking town would just leave me the hell alone. Say your prayers for a quiet day, so I can get this bitch out of my life until Monday. Call if you need me." She strode into her office.

Jenny turned back to the computer and took a deep breath. The anger, which she'd banked during the conversation with her mother, flared up again.

"Police Officer Harry Newman III is a freaking coward," she muttered.

She'd come in. *He'd* run. So apparently her sleepless night had been a complete waste of time. Harry was going to deal with their unexpected kiss in the hallway just like a typical man—he was going to avoid it, ignore it, and hope it went away.

Well, good. Better than good. Now they weren't going to have to suffer through an uncomfortable conversation, and Jenny wasn't going to have to worry about Harry slamming her against a filing cabinet as they groped each other, overcome by lust. Or vice versa.

She tried to type a memo her mother had left for her but stopped when she realized she was jabbing the keys on the keyboard so viciously she was hurting her fingers.

This was fine. She didn't like complications, and she didn't have time for cowards. Not anymore.

"Damn straight."

It turned out that Jackie did not get her quiet day on either Thursday or Friday, much to her disgust. Jenny was glad, though. Being busy gave her less time to brood. Harry hadn't been in the office again when she'd sailed in on Friday morning. But he had left her a case report to put into the system, which proved he'd been in at some point to catch up on paperwork.

It took all of Jenny's control not to shred the notes and leave them scattered on his desk.

Such a *man*. Why clear the air when you could evade the situation?

Jenny scowled at the copy machine she was currently trying to use, and then took a deep breath.

Okay, she admitted, that wasn't exactly fair.

Harry wasn't the only one evading. For one thing, if Jenny had wanted to press the issue, she could have found him—Hardy Falls wasn't *that* big. And she herself had been avoiding Missy, hadn't she? She hadn't called or texted her friend in days, which was basically unheard of.

But the thing with Missy was different, she assured herself stomping back to her desk. She just needed a little time to get settled and figure out what she was going to say before she opened that can of worms. Then she'd track her down, and they'd deal with it like two adult women.

Harry obviously never planned to address those moments in the hallway.

Well, good. Because she didn't want to address them either. Not now. If he wanted to pretend they hadn't happened, she'd do that, too.

The emergency tone came from Jackie's radio in her office, and a minute later, her mother strode out, cursing up a storm.

"What is it?" Jenny asked.

"Fender bender. I'll be back." Jackie scowled. "Who the hell let Harry leave for two days anyway?" Grumbling, she walked out of the reception area.

Jenny shook her head in reluctant sympathy. With Harry gone, her mother had to take all the calls requiring a local police presence. She could have called in the state police or someone else, of course—either Bethany or Curtis would have been more than happy for the extra hours—but Jackie hadn't wanted to rock the boat before her presentation to the town council on Monday.

Her presentation that *still* wasn't finished.

By the time Jenny was ready to close down the office on Friday afternoon, she was pretty darned glad to be going home for the weekend, and even more delighted to say goodbye to her grizzly bear of a mother.

As she headed out to the parking lot, she thought about how strange it felt to know she'd have two days off in a row for a change. It made her realize how often she and Missy had worked on the weekends these last few months, either cleaning or serving food at a party.

So that was one advantage of working as a receptionist, she guessed. She didn't have to worry about being called into work unexpectedly.

"Yay," she muttered as she unlocked her pickup and got in. "I'm an office worker now. The only thing I'm missing is a beige cubicle."

Unaccountably depressed, she started up the truck and drove home.

S aturday morning, Jenny woke up determined to get some work done. Real work. *Painting* work.

It was the weekend, her mother had left for two days, and Jenny had no other demands on her time. She should be able to bust out some good stuff.

It bothered her that she hadn't even set foot in her studio since she'd started working at the police station, and that was damned well going to change. She was freaking going to be freaking productive today.

After pulling on some crappy old clothes and equally ancient sneakers, Jenny grabbed a mug of coffee and stepped out into the early spring morning where it was, for once, only drizzling.

She paused at the edge of the back deck and drew in a deep breath of the crisp, fresh air before letting it out again in a puff of steam. It was pretty cold at the moment, but she knew warmer weather was on the way. Daffodils and crocuses bloomed in her mother's garden along with the weeds, and leaves were budding on the trees. It was only a matter of time.

Jenny could tell it wouldn't be long before the mountains were covered with the young, bright greens of new life.

"And then...pollenageddon," she said, and made her way down the wooden stairs off the back deck, then squelched across the muddy yard to the large wooden shed she'd taken over as her artist's studio. Unlocking the door, she turned on the lights and stepped inside before turning up the electric heater a little bit.

That heater, as well as the air conditioning unit mounted in one wall, existed because her mother had intended to use this space as a "she shed" for some unknown reason. Like Jackie had time to do anything even remotely crafty. That was probably why it had been full of tools and other junk, and Jackie hadn't complained too much about giving it up when Jenny moved home a year and a half ago.

Toeing off her now muddy shoes at the door, Jenny went directly to the easel sitting in the middle of the crowded room, turned so no one could see the painting on it from either the door or the studio's single window. She wasn't a diva or anything, but she never liked anyone to see what she was working on until it was finished and as perfect as she could make it. She'd learned that the hard way with Stefan.

Walking around the easel, she studied her current work in progress. It was a landscape, bright and vibrant—a stylized depiction of the main street of Hardy Falls in the winter. Jenny sipped coffee and considered it, twisting her head this way and that to see it from all angles.

She thought it looked okay. Maybe it was what some people would call "primitive," but to her, it was just cheerful. Didn't people need a little cheer in their lives these days? And it wasn't shallow or kitchy, she assured herself. See? The dark shadows there...the garishness in that corner...not everything was perfect. Not even Hardy Falls. She'd wanted to show that, too, and was happy with the little bit of foreboding she was layering in around the edges.

It sure as hell didn't look like a five-year-old's finger painting.

After taking another hit of coffee, Jenny put her mug on the workbench and began to gather her supplies from the shelves above and below it. She set up her brushes, squeezed paint onto the large wooden palette, and then mixed the colors with her knife. The smell of turpentine and linseed oil settled her like nothing else ever could.

This was her place.

No computers. No phones. No copiers or faxes or files. No angry townspeople or impatient mothers or cops with sexy mouths. She knew what she was doing here. She was *Jenny* here.

"These paintings might not sell," she said out loud, "but they're mine and I like them."

On the other hand, she needed *some* of them to sell. The world would not pay her bills simply because she was *Jenny*. She wasn't a freaking Kardashian.

Failure was not an option.

She got to work.

A little later, Jenny admitted that maybe it was just *slightly* possible she'd put too much pressure on herself with that whole failure not being an option thing because any creativity she might have felt had quickly withered on the vine. When she realized she'd been stretched out on the studio's old, comfortable sofa for the last half hour playing a game on her phone instead of standing at her easel, she decided she might as well give up.

"There's always tomorrow," she assured herself with a sigh and scraped the unused paints off her palette before closing up the studio and going back to the house.

As penance for her sins, she threw herself into cleaning, a

job she hated. When you cleaned other people's places for a living, the last thing you wanted to do was clean your own.

But after everything in the house was shipshape from top to bottom, Jenny found herself hovering in the kitchen, at a loss.

She wasn't in the mood to call someone and see if they wanted to go to dinner or the movies, so she headed to the living room to flip through channels and probably get frustrated. She'd just flopped in an armchair and grabbed the remote when her cell phone rang. It was Josie.

"Hey," Jenny answered, throwing the remote on an end table.

"Hey, Jenny!" Josie's voice was bright and happy. "How are you? Enjoying your alone time?"

"Oh yeah. It's great." Jenny felt the almost overwhelming urge to spill her guts and tell Josie all about her make-out session with Harry in the hallway at the police station and his subsequent avoidance of her. But she didn't. A girl had to have *some* pride. "What's up?" she asked. Even though they texted each other a lot, a phone call usually meant something was going on, especially since she'd just seen Josie on Monday.

"Um, I was wondering if you were doing anything tonight?"

Jenny frowned and straightened in the chair. Josie sounded tentative, which was definitely not like her.

"No...," she said slowly. "Is something wrong?"

"No, no. I was just wondering if you could swing by the Country Time when you had a minute."

"Oh." That request brought on a new concern. "Is Hannah sick? Does she need me to work?"

If Hannah was out again, especially on a Saturday night, they might as well check for the zombie apocalypse. It had happened last fall when a bad flu was going around, but even then, the girl had dragged herself into the Country Time until she'd finally been forced to give up and leave. She'd ended up in the emergency room that time.

"No, she's fine," Josie assured her. "She just wants to talk to you."

"Okay." Jenny frowned, trying to figure out what that might mean. "Did one of the new servers quit already? Because I'm kind of committed to the police station for a while."

She'd promised her mother, and she wouldn't let her down. Even if there was an opening at the Country Time, she couldn't leave now, no matter how complicated things got with Harry.

"No." Josie sounded strange. "Just...come over, okay? We'll explain it then."

"Okay." *Curiouser and curiouser.* "Let me get changed and I'll be there in a few."

"Great. See you then."

Jenny clicked off the phone and, still frowning, got up to get ready.

18

At the end of his shift at the police station on Saturday afternoon, Harry tried to take advantage of a few quiet moments to finish some of his paperwork before he had to clock out for the day. He'd hoped to be further ahead, but that sure hadn't happened. Turned out that Bethany, who'd been on the shift with him, had needed a lot more babysitting than he'd expected, so he was still catching up. It was frustrating as hell.

Well, he'd just have to finish what he could and leave the rest until tomorrow. He was meeting some of the middle schoolers at the bowling alley arcade for a pinball tournament in a couple of hours, and he couldn't be late.

At least Bethany was gone now, and Bert, another part-timer working this evening, had headed out to do a drive through town. Harry finally had the squad room to himself.

He really should be focusing on writing up the witness statements he'd taken at a minor traffic accident they'd dealt with earlier in the day, not thinking about Jenny Kline.

Her body was strong and slender, and it had wrapped around him. Her curves fit his hands as if they'd been made for him. Her mouth was hot as an open flame.

Harry settled back in his chair and rubbed his eyes, trying to dispel the erotic images flooding his brain. They'd been haunting him ever since the kiss in the hallway. Messing with his thinking, even when he'd been trying to concentrate on training.

Jesus.

So much for assuming he'd calm down if he spent some time away from the office.

"Get your head back in gear, genius," he ordered himself and made an effort to direct his thoughts to his paperwork with a spectacular lack of success.

"Stay focused, Newman," he muttered. "Think about the work. Think about the job. Think about the promotion. Not the boss's daughter."

And her mouth...

God, what a fucking mess.

He should have just manned up and talked to Jenny. Made sure she knew they couldn't do anything else. At least, not right now. That would have been the intelligent, *mature* thing to do.

But when he'd gotten back to his apartment after tasting her, holding her, he'd known he couldn't trust himself to do the intelligent, mature thing. Not when his first impulse, the irresponsible impulse, was still the strongest—to grab her and drag her off to see where the thing between them would go. Ditch the job, deal with the fallout, and go for it.

Just wait. Wait, wait, wait.

But he didn't *want* to wait. He wanted to pounce. And that was the reason why he'd made himself scarce—to give them both time to breathe.

Christ, he hoped that when they were back in the office on Monday, enough time would have passed for him to be able to deal with her like an adult, not a caveman. It wasn't looking good, but he couldn't abandon the chief again, especially since she had that meeting with the town council.

Anyway, Jenny was probably pissed off at him by now, which would help. Even if she wasn't, she had to know as well as he did that their timing was all screwed up.

And just because he was having trouble battling his more reckless urges didn't mean she was feeling the same way.

Just wait.

But what if their timing was never right?

Harry's cell phone rang. He grabbed it off his desk like a lifeline, then frowned. It was his personal phone, not the one he carried for work, so he had expected it to be his grandfather. But he didn't recognize the number displayed by caller ID and the area code wasn't local.

It was probably a sales call, but he'd also been putting out feelers to try to find Hannah's uncle, George. Maybe someone had gotten hold of this number instead of the work one. He clicked to answer.

"Newman."

"Hello, boy."

Harry froze and jolted upright in his chair. The lingering lustful thoughts he'd been having about Jenny immediately washed away in a flood of ice at the sound of the voice that was older, but no less familiar.

His father.

Harry almost hung up—almost clicked off the phone—but he knew if he did that, Junior would probably just call Harry's grandfather again and upset him. He couldn't let that happen, so he drew on his years of training and pulled himself together.

"What do you want?" he asked harshly, even though he knew perfectly well what it had to be. This must be about money. His grandfather had to be right about Junior being desperate because otherwise the man would never have contacted Harry. Junior hadn't called him since he'd become a police officer over six years ago. The question was: Why now?

"How you doing, Trip?" Junior sounded jovial, using Harry's

childhood nickname as if he had the right. "It's been a hell of a long time, hasn't it? Sorry about that. I've been meaning to call you, but, well, you know. Life."

Junior didn't sound drunk, but Harry knew that could be an illusion. His father held his liquor well…until he didn't. The man could go from happy drunk to angry drunk in a finger snap.

On the other hand, there was a manic energy to his voice that wasn't exactly normal. Maybe he was hopped up on something else. Junior was always worse when he was on something other than alcohol.

A big hand cracking down.

"Quit whining about fucking food!"

"You still haven't told me what you want," Harry said, holding on to his self-control with both hands.

"Why, just to talk." Another false laugh. "Been what? A year?"

Six.

"I don't have time to talk," Harry told him. "I'm at work."

"God. Still can't believe you're a cop, boy." Junior sounded honestly disappointed. "You could have gone places. Hit the road like your old man."

Harry could feel his icy wall of composure cracking. He had to find out what Junior wanted and get him the hell off the phone.

"If you don't tell me why you called, I'm hanging up now," he said with as much coolness as he could manage.

Junior seemed to realize he was serious.

"Well, here's the thing, boy," he said. His voice was still jolly, but strain had joined the manic undertone. "Mason, the drummer? He got himself in a mess and dragged the rest of us into it with him. Fucking idiot."

Harry had no clue who his father was talking about, and he didn't give a shit. He crossed his free arm over his chest and kept his eyes on the white wall in front of him. It grounded him to see all the notices pinned to the corkboard, to feel the crisp fabric of the uniform he was wearing, and to know that he was no longer the kid he'd once been.

"If we don't get it straightened out, there are some people who aren't going to like it," Junior continued. "What we get for bringing in someone we don't know."

He was lying.

Suspicion wound through Harry. He'd been a cop for far too long to deny his instincts, and he had the added advantage of personal experience with Junior's dishonesty. What he didn't know was what was behind it this time. Yeah, his father wanted money, like he always did, but Harry had a feeling this time it was for more than beer and hotel rooms.

"I know you've already been in contact with Pops, and he turned you down when you asked for money," he said. "I don't know what you think I'm going to do for you. Even you're not stupid enough to think I'll wire you cash." Which was why his father had never bothered calling him before.

"Yeah, okay, the old man told me he wouldn't send me anything, but I know they have more money than God. I just need a little help." Junior's voice turned into a whine. "It's hard out here, boy. You don't know what it's like. Everything's so goddamned expensive in L.A., and the clubs don't pay much. The last manager ran out with our cash and then Mason…look, if they help me one more time, I'll be able to get my feet under me. I have a real opportunity, a real chance, if I can just clean up this mess. Just talk to him for me, okay? The old man listens to you. A little cash, and I'll be able to really go places."

Unbelievable. Junior obviously didn't have access to his remaining brain cells if he thought anyone would fall for that line of bullshit.

"Seems to me you've had your chances," Harry said without emotion. "More chances than anybody else would expect."

"I know I'm a fuckup. But this is what I've been waiting for. You talk to them, okay? Just one more time."

If they'd been in the same room, Harry knew he'd be watching Junior's eyes jittering around, sliding away from his, never making contact. He'd seen it countless times in countless perps and addicts. His father, he suspected, was both.

"Why would you think I'd do anything for you?" he asked. That was actually the biggest surprise of the conversation thus far.

The flat statement seemed to knock Junior back for a moment.

"Well, because I'm your father," he said, sounding genuinely shocked.

"You ceased to have any importance to me years ago," Harry told him honestly and decided that no matter what Junior was into now, it was time to end it. "Don't call me again, and stop calling my grandparents. Stop asking them for money. You're upsetting them, and I won't stand around and let it happen anymore." He'd let it go on for way too long.

"Come on," Junior griped. "None of you get it. The old man keeps complaining that I'm wasting my life, but he doesn't have a clue. I get some help, get out of this hole, and I'm golden."

The manic undertone intensified. Harry had a bad feeling the reason why his father needed money so urgently was far worse than a drummer in debt because of some amplifiers.

If there even was a drummer at all. Or a band.

He sat back as the thought took root.

God.

"There isn't even a band anymore, is there?" he said slowly, realization dawning. "Everything's been a lie, hasn't it?" He wasn't exactly sure why it was a surprise, but it was.

"What? Don't be a fucking idiot." Junior's voice was wet with desperation. "Of course there's a band. The Blood Insects. You know that. Skinny and Norm and Mason and—"

"Shut up, you lying sack of shit." Harry's anger made his voice a slap. He knew deep in his gut that he was right. It all made perfect sense. "When did the Blood Insects finally give up?" he demanded. "How long have you been trying to scam the old man, you piece of garbage?"

"It doesn't matter, does it?" Junior snarled, his tone changing in an instant. "What matters is I have a problem, it's fucking serious, and I need to deal with it. But if I get a little cash to take care of things, I'm gold. Of all the times for the old man to turn me off. He owes me! But he likes you. He always did. That's why he took you in. You need to—"

"No," Harry said. "I don't."

He clicked off the phone.

It rang again. Harry blocked the number and threw the device on his desk, breathing as hard as if he'd run a marathon. Closing his eyes, he struggled to get himself under control.

It had been a mistake to let his grandfather handle this situation by himself, Harry could see that now. No matter how much the old man protested, he should have stepped in a lot sooner. His grandfather was tough, but he was too close to the situation, and he held too much unwarranted guilt. Junior had been playing him for far longer than he should have been allowed to.

Harry heard the employee door "beep," which meant Bert was back. A minute later, the other cop walked in wearing a broad grin. Harry forced himself to shut his emotions down until he could get out of there.

Somehow he managed to shove the conversation with his father to the back of his mind. Somehow he was able to talk to Bert and finish what he needed to do—although he couldn't be sure what he said or did. Somehow he held it together until he could leave.

At last, at last, at last, he was alone in the parking lot in his

Jeep Wrangler. He gripped the steering wheel with such force his hands ached.

What had Junior done? Who did he owe money to? The situation had to be bad.

It didn't matter, Harry told himself. It didn't matter if Junior was in trouble, if he was desperate, if he owed money to other scum like himself. It didn't matter if he was using drugs or selling them. It just didn't matter. Junior had lost the right for it to matter a long, long time ago.

For a moment, Harry thought about calling his grandfather and letting him know what had happened, then decided against it.

Hearing about Junior would upset the old man, and if he found out about all the lies Junior had been telling, he'd be beside himself and probably assume even more guilt. Hell, he might even cave in and give Junior what he wanted.

There was the risk that his grandfather would give in anyway, of course, but Harry didn't think so. If there'd been even the slightest chance, Junior would never have risked calling him.

Starting up the Jeep, he pulled out of his parking spot with so much force he left skid marks.

"It doesn't matter," he repeated out loud as he drove. "Junior made his bed, and he can fucking lay in it."

Harry tried to let it go, but as he made his way through town to his apartment, the anger he'd spent a lifetime learning to suppress built up inside him like a volcano ready to blow.

He shouldn't have stayed out of it. He should have forced his grandfather to let him take care of things—the old man's pride be damned. It would never have gotten to this point if he'd stepped in sooner. He could have reached out to the Los Angeles Police Department and had them pick Junior up. Hell, Harry could have flown out to Los Angeles, found Junior himself, and had a "discussion" with the man—one that wouldn't be misunderstood.

But up until now, Harry had just been grateful that his grandfather was dealing with it.

He parked the Jeep in the little lot for tenants behind the bakery and jogged up the stairs to his second floor apartment.

Normally the first thing he did when he got home was strip out of his uniform and change into casual clothes. Today he walked through to the kitchen part of the open space and pulled a bottle of Jack Daniel's someone had given him out of one of the cabinets. He poured himself a healthy slug and downed it without pausing. The alcohol hit his system like a bomb.

Harry usually didn't drink much, not since he'd gotten his head out of his ass after that first year of college. Not since he'd realized he was well on the way to ending up exactly like his father and mother.

Daisy, his mother, drank as much as Junior and was probably into just as much shit, but at least she wasn't likely to contact either Harry or his grandparents. Which showed nothing but common sense on her part.

Harry poured himself another drink and walked around the kitchen island to stand at the big living room window, staring down at the main street of Hardy Falls.

A few minutes later, the alarm on his phone went off, reminding him that he needed to get ready and head out to the bowling alley.

He knew he shouldn't go. It was not a good time, not a good time at all. He should just stay in and brood and get drunk for once. He figured he deserved it.

But he'd made a promise. If he didn't show up, he'd disappoint Danny and Lucio and the other kids. They'd all been looking forward to tonight, even though they'd pretend it was no big deal. Besides, if you blew the trust of kids at their age, sometimes you couldn't get it back. Especially if the kids in question already had good reasons not to trust most of the adults in their lives.

Harry made himself walk away from the window and put the half-full glass of Jack down on the counter, then went to get changed.

Twenty minutes later, he was at the bowling alley. He'd beat the kids there, but they'd start showing up soon.

Harry knew he shouldn't, knew it was a really bad idea, but he headed to the bar anyway. One more drink, he told himself. Just to loosen up. To forget. To make sure the volcano stayed capped.

19

About a half-hour after getting Josie's phone call, Jenny turned her pickup from the highway into the Country Time's parking lot and was happy to see there were some other vehicles scattered around. She parked in an out-of-the-way spot facing the bowling alley and got out, taking a moment to stretch her back a little bit.

She closed her eyes and breathed deeply, enjoying the fresh chill of the late March wind after the chemical smells of the cleansers she'd been using at the house. There was even a hint of snow in the air. If it fell, the ski resorts would be happy—this season had been all about the rain and freezing rain. Well, except for the hellacious blizzard they'd had at the end of October when Josie had been driving home from Manhattan.

Jenny knew some people were glad it had been a warmer winter, but she was with the ski resorts in wishing for snow. She'd much rather drive in that than the slop they'd been getting, and if it fell overnight tonight she could go out in the morning and take some pictures. She loved recording the lights and shadows of the ice and snow so she could try to capture the effects in her paintings.

She opened her eyes.

She'd get some work done tomorrow, she assured herself, as she headed to the Country Time's antique entry doors with their leaded stained glass insets. She was still getting used to her new schedule. Today had just been a warm up.

Opening one of the doors, she stepped into the comforting warmth of the taproom and stood for a moment looking around. There was no sign of either Josie or Hannah, just Mary Alice taking orders at the tables and Deacon serving customers at the bar.

Deacon looked up and shot her a grin, then jerked his thumb toward the kitchen.

She waved in acknowledgment and walked across the room, calling out a greeting to Albert, Martin, Joe, and Harry Senior when she spotted the old men gathered around their usual table in the corner. When she pushed into the heat and steam of the kitchen, she saw Josie, Hannah, and June standing and talking together near the very popular supply closet while Kevin, the chef, danced between the grill and the fryers. He grinned at her, a brilliant flash of white.

"How you doin', Jenny?" he called, his voice deep and filled with the rhythm of Creole.

"Fine." She went to hug him, but he held up huge hands and backed away.

"*Non, non.* I'm all greasy because my boss made me clean this bitch of a fryer again," he said and laughed his booming laugh.

"You know you love it," Hannah told him and ran to Jenny, her ponytail a swing of wavy brown hair. Grinning, she gripped Jenny in a hard hug, rocking back and forth, and then forcibly dragged her over to the other women. Whatever had been wrong with Hannah on Monday, it sure hadn't affected her strength any.

As with June, it had been a little while since Jenny had actually seen Hannah, and again, as with June, she noticed some unexpected changes. Hannah's face, normally striking and angular, seemed decidedly rounder, and so did her body. Looked like both women had put on a little weight in the past few months.

Is that what automatically happened when you were in a happy relationship? If so, it explained why she herself had lost more than a few pounds in the time she'd been with Stefan.

She didn't say any of that out loud, of course. But Hannah seemed to read her mind because her smile deepened as she stepped back, hazel eyes sparkling.

It was impossible to do anything but smile in return.

"You're so happy," Jenny said to her. "I'm glad." To be filled with that much joy would be well worth a rounder stomach.

"In spite of all the business crap, I'm delirious," Hannah agreed. She shot June a glance. "That's why we wanted to talk to you."

Jenny raised her eyebrows at that, but before she could say anything, Josie came and hugged her, and, to her shock, June hugged her as well. June wasn't normally the touchy-feely type.

When they were done, all three women just stood, staring at her and grinning like idiots.

It was creepy.

Jenny glanced surreptitiously around the kitchen to see if there was something she'd missed that might give her a clue about what was going on. But no, it looked like it always did. Same grill and dishwasher. Same fryers. Same Kevin moving to the beat of his internal drummer as he went from burgers to wings to fries.

She turned back to the women.

"What?" she demanded. "I feel like I'm on a prank video. Did you win the lottery or something?" Granted, winning the lottery would be awesome.

"Almost," Hannah giggled and slapped her hands to either side of her face.

June rolled her eyes, but she was still smiling, and that in itself was kind of frightening. June never beamed like a ray of freaking sunshine unless she was looking at Calvin.

Jenny tried to think of what might be making them all act like this.

"Did you...kill Pat?" she asked at last. Yeah, the bowling alley owner was making Hannah's life difficult, but she hoped the Three Musketeers hadn't gone to any extremes. Not that she would have put it past any of them.

"No." Hannah covered her eyes with her hands and began laughing uncontrollably.

"Josie," Jenny turned to her sister. "I'm begging you."

Josie elbowed Hannah in her side. "Just tell her already. She's gonna blow."

Hannah looked at Jenny through her fingers. "I'm pregnant," she whispered.

Jenny stared at her. "What? What?" She jumped forward and grabbed Hannah's shoulders. "What? That's awesome!"

Josie elbowed June this time. "And..."

"And I'm pregnant, too," June muttered, but she was still smiling.

Jenny stared at the other woman. "You have got to be kidding me."

June shrugged and shook her head, and, as her glossy dark hair spilled over her shoulders, a few random streaks of silver caught the light. "Nope. Well and truly knocked up."

"Holy shit!" Jenny gasped and reached for June next, hugging her hard. "Holy *shit!*"

"Yeah. Tell me about it."

Jenny gaped from one woman to the next, then back again. She couldn't believe it. But then she could. But then she couldn't. Both of them? At the same time?

"I can't believe it," she finally said.

"Neither could we," Hannah said, laughing and crying all at once.

"When...? How far along...? What...?"

"We're both at about 18 weeks. More or less," Hannah told her. "We found out in December."

Wow. *Literally* at the same time.

"Looks like they're both due sometime in August," Josie put in.

Jenny turned to her sister. "Did you know?" she demanded.

Josie nodded, her own smile broad, and her sweet oval face flushed with happiness. "Yes, but nobody else did until just now. Hannah and June started telling people today."

"Did you tell Mom?" Jenny asked, smiling as her mind spun. "She's going to be over the moon."

"She was," Josie assured her. "I told her at Christmas, in case we needed emergency backup or something. I should have said nobody else knew except her. Well, and Mat knew, of course. And Ms. Gregory. But nobody else. Hannah and June wanted to wait to tell everyone until they were further along."

Jenny felt a little hitch in her stomach when she realized she was the only one in the family who hadn't been told, except for her brother Jordan. Then she shoved the feeling aside because it was stupid.

"Are you okay?" she asked Hannah with sudden concern when she remembered the other woman had gone home sick a few days ago.

"We're fine," Hannah assured her and put her hands on her stomach. "June's morning sickness is basically over. I've been getting really tired and still having nausea, but nothing unusual."

"It's because you don't rest enough," Josie told her sternly.

Hannah rolled her eyes. "That's what the doctors say." She looked at Jenny. "Everybody wants me to back off."

"Yeah, no shit, sherlock," Josie scolded her. "You *know* you have to be careful."

Hannah pouted. "Yeah, yeah."

"I thought you said nothing was wrong?" Jenny prodded because she felt like she was missing something. Again.

Hannah grimaced. "I'm not going to shout it from the rooftops or anything, but I have endometriosis, so I'm kind of at risk. Keep that to yourself, okay?"

"And they say I'm at risk because I'm old," June put in. "Keep that to yourself, too. Nobody will figure out I'm old unless someone blabs." She frowned. "Although now that I can't dye my hair, it's only a matter of time before people figure it out."

"Are you telling me you both have risky pregnancies, but you've both been working like lunatics here? Are you insane?" Jenny shouted at them.

"Thank you." Josie crossed her arms and nodded her head firmly in agreement, even as she frowned at the other two women. "Which is why they should both cut back on their hours."

Hannah thrust out her bottom lip.

"I can still do stuff."

"Just because you can doesn't mean you should," Josie pointed out.

"My ankles are starting to swell, and I feel like a beached whale already," June said. "But Ronnie isn't going to pay for himself, so I need to earn my keep. I'll work it out."

"Ronnie might not pay for himself, but Calvin will definitely pay for him and support you," Josie told her. "You *know* that man is crazy about you, and he's going to marry you for God's sake. So *let* him take care of a few things and stop being so goddamned independent!"

June waved it off.

"Ronnie?" Jenny was so confused. She didn't like not

knowing what was going on. She *always* knew what was going on.

"Ronnie," June said and pointed at her own stomach. "Peanut," she said and pointed at Hannah's.

"Do you know what they are?" Jenny asked, forgetting about her confusion in her excitement. "Boy? Girl? Boy and girl? Twins? Triplets?"

June's scowl was fierce.

"Shut up about twins or freaking triplets," she growled.

Hannah's shoulders shook with barely suppressed giggles. "We're trying not to find out the sexes of the babies. I didn't want to know, and neither did Calvin, so Deacon and June let it slide. But there's only one bun in the oven for each of us."

"Praise Jesus," June sighed.

Josie and Hannah gave up and started laughing.

Jenny shook her head and tried to keep her thoughts from rattling around like loose change.

"I'm really happy for you guys," she said once Hannah and Josie had calmed down. And she really was. "Thank you for telling me." *Finally*.

"It was time," Hannah said candidly. "Now that I'm going to have to change my routine, and we're both starting to show and everything, we decided to let everyone else know what was going on. We wanted to wait as long as we could to make sure things were okay before the rest of the town found out."

"Mary Alice is thrilled," June added dryly. "She's going to start knitting."

"Does Mary Alice knit?" Jenny asked.

"Apparently."

"And Kevin's going to coach Deacon and Calvin on how to be a father, aren't you, Kevin?" Hannah called over to the chef.

"Sure, boss lady." He grinned at her, but a shadow passed over his face. "I tell them everything I know." He went back to work.

"I wish we could get his wife and kids here," Josie said quietly. "He misses them."

Kevin's family was still in Haiti, waiting while he worked on getting them visas so they could join him.

"We told Albert and his crew when they came in, and Albert said he considered himself to be a great-grandfather now. Joe and Martin and Harry agreed." Hannah teared up and sniffed. "That was so nice."

Imagining the older Harry Newman as a great-grandfather had Jenny wondering if the younger Officer Harry Newman had an ex-wife and some little Newmans of his own hiding in the woodwork. Maybe he'd left them behind when he'd moved to Hardy Falls. Or maybe he had an ex-fiancée like the one they'd discovered Mat had left behind in Texas.

Shaking it off, she smiled at the two mothers-to-be.

"You're not going to be hormonal all the time now, are you?" she asked them.

"No," Hannah sobbed.

"Me either," June said, but when Jenny looked, she saw the other woman's dark eyes were damp.

A hormonal June would be...interesting.

Josie rolled her eyes. "Show her the pictures," she instructed.

Both women whipped out carefully folded ultrasound images. Jenny was happy that she could actually make out the silhouettes of the babies for once, although not their gender bits (yes, she looked). Sometimes proud parents showed her ultrasounds, and she had no idea what she was supposed to be seeing. She guessed that was one advantage of not being told about the pregnancies until Hannah and June were this far along—she didn't have to lie.

The two women smiled fatuously at their respective ultrasounds.

"I'm going to frame mine and put it up in my office," Hannah told her.

"I think I'll frame mine, too, but I won't put it up until after the work on the apartment is finished," June agreed. "Noah's starting work soon, and when he's done, we'll have lots of room for Ronnie *and* pictures of Ronnie."

So, *that* was the reason Ms. Gregory was expanding the apartment over her garage. Jenny had known the work on June's apartment was going to happen, but she hadn't known why. She'd assumed it was because Calvin was moving in. Looked like he wouldn't be the only one.

She could also admit that it was a surprise to see June's pupils practically transforming into little hearts as she talked about bringing home a baby. Hannah, yes. June, not so much. And yet, the other woman's face was flushed with love and delight.

Ah, how the mighty have fallen. Josie was bound to be next.

There was that hitch again.

Regardless of whether or not they should, Hannah and June both said they needed to get back to work. Josie went with Hannah to her office to talk to her about something, but more likely to make sure the other woman sat down.

Jenny kissed them all goodbye, and then stood for a moment after they left, feeling at a loss.

"You wanna help me with the fryer?" Kevin asked, grinning good-naturedly.

"Not really," Jenny replied honestly.

"Ah, the women always leave me and now I will be stuck with Mat when he finally gets in. But," Kevin's smile was bright and sharp, "if Mat is here, Josie will run the dishwasher, no? Then I'll be able to get him to do the messy work."

Jenny laughed in spite of her unsettled mood. "Always thinking."

He raised a spatula in salute and went back to flipping burgers, singing a Neil Diamond song that had nothing whatsoever to do with whatever was playing over the sound system. Shaking her head, Jenny went back to the taproom.

Deacon was polishing glasses behind the bar, the customers under control for the moment. She slipped up beside him and gave him a kiss on his cheek.

"Congratulations, daddy."

His hard face broke into a grin so bright it practically lit up the room. "Can't believe it."

"I'll bet."

He looked around and then leaned toward her. "Did Hannah show you the ultrasound?"

"Yeah."

He frowned. "Did she look okay to you?"

Jenny was confused. "Hannah?"

"No. Peanut. The baby."

Oh. "I thought you didn't know if the baby was a girl or a boy."

"I don't know for sure." Deacon shook his head. "Hannah doesn't want to know, so the technician doesn't say. But I think she's a girl. Did she look okay? Hannah said she looked okay, and the doctor keeps saying she looks okay, and Kevin said she looked okay, but he doesn't remember if he saw ultrasounds of his kids in Haiti. Did you think she looked okay?"

Awwww. The big lug.

Jenny smiled at him. "She looks beautiful. Wonderful. Miraculous."

His eyes were blue sunbeams. "She is. Miraculous. And beautiful. I just worry, you know?"

She patted his arm. "I know. But Peanut is doing fine."

He nodded and sniffed, then straightened abruptly and blinked. "Uh, you want anything?"

"No thanks. I'm heading out."

He nodded again, then gave her a tight hug before moving off to wait on some people who'd come up to the bar.

She waved again at the four old men still sitting at their table but didn't stop as she headed for the front door. Before she made it safely outside, Mary Alice Norton took a break from waiting on tables to whirl up next to her, an order pad clutched to her chest in her big workman-like hands.

"Oh hi, Jenny!" Her eyes, blue and slightly protuberant, beamed with exuberant good cheer, and her soft brown hair was a fuzzy halo where it had escaped from its tie.

"Hi, Mary Alice." Jenny returned the other woman's smile.

"Did they tell you? About the babies?" Mary Alice asked, almost jumping up and down in excitement.

Jenny's smile deepened. "They did. And they said you were going to knit something."

"Oh, I've already been knitting booties. I knew it was just a matter of time. But now I have to start on sweaters for the winter. And Halloween costumes."

"Well...good?" Jenny said hesitantly. She wasn't entirely sure what Mary Alice's idea of a knitted Halloween costume for an infant would be.

"I wanted to tell you that someone was looking at one of your paintings when I came on at four. He had to leave, but he looked at it for a long time. That one." She pointed at "Sunrise on the Mountain," the same one the couple from Cleveland had talked about.

"What did he say?" Jenny asked, not able to stop herself.

"Well, he said something about 'primitive,' I think," Mary Alice told her helpfully, beaming her sunny, crazed smile. "He didn't want to buy it, but maybe he'll change his mind and come back."

"Maybe," Jenny agreed weakly.

"Oh, I have to go," Mary Alice said. "Talk to you later!" She took off to wait on a couple who had just sat down at one of the tables.

Jenny stood for a moment looking after her, then turned to the painting again.

She would definitely replace it. Maybe she'd paint something new that was more in line with what people seemed to want.

Abstract sells. Modern sells. This crap doesn't.

Stefan's voice.

Jenny walked through the taproom and out into the cold air. Some snow was falling, light and soft.

She got into her truck but didn't start the engine, just sat and stared out her windshield at the lights of the bowling alley, backlit by the neon signs flashing at the Country Time behind her.

She wasn't entirely sure how she felt at the moment.

Happy for Hannah and Deacon, June and Calvin. Beyond delighted. Ecstatic. Worried. Loving.

Hurt.

It was silly to feel hurt that they hadn't told her. They'd had some very, very good reasons to keep the news to themselves until things were further along. And they hadn't told the staff either or the customers or the town. It wasn't like she'd even *seen* them in the last couple of months.

But Josie had known. Their mother had known. Neither of them had said anything.

And rightly so. It wasn't their news to share, and they were one hundred percent correct to keep their mouths shut. Which meant it made absolutely no sense for Jenny to feel this way. To feel...shut out. Isolated.

God, she needed to talk to someone. Not gossip, *talk*. Talk to someone about everything that had been happening in her life. The pregnancies. The job. The doubts. Harry.

That was part of it, she thought. Seeing Josie and Hannah

and June—they really were the Three Musketeers and Jenny... wasn't.

She hadn't called or texted Missy because she wanted to take a little time, but now she longed to see her. There were other people she could talk to, of course, but no one that close, and she didn't want to complain about Missy behind her back. It was bad enough she'd had to tell her mother what had happened between them.

Jenny sighed and stared out at the bowling alley. The parking lot on the other side of the thin strip of grass was busy, and as she watched, a group of people walked up to the big glass entryway, their kids running ahead.

She wondered how Pat would react when he found out June was pregnant. Pat and June had dated before Calvin came back to town, and the bowling alley owner was still upset that June had chosen the other man over him.

Putting her key in the ignition, she paused when she remembered that one of the leagues Missy and Buster were part of bowled in the afternoon on Saturdays. They might very well be over there now.

Jenny chewed her lip.

It couldn't hurt to go look, could it? This might be a chance to talk to Missy and try to clear the air between them. Maybe figure out how to rebuild something Jenny had always assumed was rock solid.

Or should she just wait for Missy to come to her?

Jenny liked that idea better—but what if it never happened? Then she and Missy would just drift apart. That had happened more than once over the years.

Josie and Hannah had fought. But they'd never turned away from each other.

Jenny and Missy had been friends too well and for too long to let it end like this.

She pocketed her keys and got out of the truck.

20

Jenny knew it was wrong, but it seemed stupid to move her truck when she was only going to be at the bowling alley a few minutes, half-hour tops. Missy and Buster might not even be there. If Missy happened to be in the mood to talk, then Jenny would, of course, move her vehicle. But Pat's place was crowded, and she was parked out of the way. Hannah would forgive her.

"Yeah, you can rationalize anything, can't you, Jenny?" she muttered to herself as she walked across the narrow strip of grass and up the slight hill to the bowling alley's big glass front doors.

Pushing one open, she found herself in the light and noise of the lobby. Classic rock music pounded over the speakers, while pins and balls crashed out in the lanes. In a large space off to the side, the arcade blinked with lights and rang with a cacophony of musical chimes and noises from a variety of games.

She glanced in as she passed, then stopped abruptly in the arched opening.

Why Police Officer Harry Newman III, as she lived and breathed.

Looked like he hadn't vanished into a puff of smoke after all. No, he was standing in front of one of the pinball machines, obviously engrossed in what he was doing, scowl intense as he worked the flippers with rapid precision.

He had good hands.

And just that quickly, Jenny was thinking about the other things he could do with those hands. Unable to stop herself, she watched him sway from side to side in front of the machine, thrusting into it as he willed the ball to do what he wanted.

Good lord, but the man had an ass on him.

Jenny drew in a deep breath and tried to stop staring at that ass, but it was impossible when he clenched it and thrust again.

Don't think about the thrusting.

There was a sudden shout, and she realized that in her fascination with Harry's ass, she hadn't noticed the group of kids gathered around him. They appeared to be mostly boys, probably around twelve years old. Some of them she knew, some she didn't. Many of the ones she recognized came from less than ideal living situations. Harry was probably doing some sort of community outreach—her mother was big on her officers getting out to the local schools and businesses.

Whatever had happened at the machine had caused the kids to yell loudly enough to raise the roof. One of the boys she didn't recognize hooted in triumph and raised clenched fists to the ceiling, his dark hair a mop of curls against his olive skin. Jenny didn't play pinball much, but she guessed that this was a multiplayer game, and the kid had just won.

She fully expected Harry to smile at the boy to acknowledge his defeat and back away. Maybe tousle the kid's hair.

Instead, she was shocked when he grabbed the pinball machine on each side and shook it so violently that he would have lifted it off the ground if it hadn't been bolted to the floor.

What the hell?

"Dude." The boy who'd lifted his fists let them drop, dark eyes wide in his thin face.

Not pausing to think about it, Jenny moved quickly to Harry's side and grabbed his arm, feeling the tension and bunched muscles under her fingers.

"There you are," she said brightly. "What did that poor machine do? Lose your balls?"

Oops. Unfortunate joke there, Jenny. Kids.

The kids gathered around Harry smirked. A couple cackled loudly, and she remembered they were likely middle schoolers. If she'd made a fart joke, she'd have been golden.

Harry looked at her, and she was even more taken aback when she saw his face. His eyes were stormy, the expression in them something she'd never seen before. It was as if someone else was inhabiting Harry's body, prowling behind those eyes. Feral. An energy just barely contained.

This man wasn't in control. And Harry always was in control. *Always.*

Except when he'd kissed her in the hallway at the police station.

As if he'd read her mind, his eyes dipped to her mouth, his lips quirking in a sensual smile Jenny felt run all through her body. Her breath shuddered, but she couldn't make herself look away.

"Harry?" She said his name a little hesitantly, really not sure what was going on. There was the smell of alcohol on his breath, and that was unusual, too, but at least his eyes weren't bleary. They were alert and fixed on her.

Drawing in a deep breath, Jenny forced herself to break the eye contact and look at the kids, who'd gone silent and were staring at them. They might not know what was happening either, but they could tell there was something.

Harry seemed to realize it, too.

"Good job, Lucio," he finally said to the kid with the dark

hair. His voice was deeper than normal, but there was a smile on his face now.

Although Lucio grinned, Jenny saw wariness in his big, dark eyes.

"Take that, copper," he said.

"Did you tilt the machine?" a boy with red hair and freckles asked. "You said you'd give me a rematch. If the machine tilted, Mr. Murphy's gonna be pissed."

He looked like he wasn't sure whether he wanted that to happen or not. Probably the excitement of watching two adults yell at each other was outweighed by the fear of being caught in the crossfire.

Jenny could relate. Even though Harry wasn't looking at her at the moment, she still felt like a rabbit caught in a predator's trap.

Letting go of his arm, she took a step away, and his focus snapped back to her in an instant.

A wolf.

"The machine is fine," Harry told the red-haired kid, "but a rematch will have to wait. I have to go."

The kids looked between Harry and Jenny and snickered.

"There's been a break in the case," Jenny explained quickly, trying to sound like all of the cop shows she'd ever watched on television. "We need Harry at the police station."

When Harry caught her eye this time, his full mouth curved in a smile.

"Right. A break. We'd better go."

Before she could protest, he grabbed her arm and dragged her with him out of the arcade and through the lobby. She had to trot to keep up as he propelled her around the building to where she saw he'd parked his big Jeep Wrangler.

She told herself she let him get away with dragging her around like this because she wanted to make sure he could drive before she let him leave. And maybe she could get him to tell her what the hell was going on, why he was acting so strange.

But deep inside, she knew those were just excuses. The strength of him, the heat of him, the way he watched her as if she was the only thing in the room...she wanted more of that. And the part of her that *hated* being trapped behind a desk all day rose to the surface as she ran along with him.

When they were at the Jeep, Harry looked at her through slitted eyes and maneuvered her until she was trapped, his body was crowding her, his hands flat against the vehicle on either side of her head thanks to the difference in their heights. The bowling alley parking lot might be busy, but they were alone in this corner, deep in shadows as the afternoon sun dropped behind the trees at the edge of the lot.

Jenny tried to read Harry's expression, but she was having a hard time focusing with his body so close to hers. Without her being aware of it, her hands had found their way to his biceps straining against the material of the T-shirt he wore.

It was cold outside as the light snow that had been falling became steadier, but she didn't feel it, and it didn't seem like Harry did either.

"Did you have a coat?" she asked, the innocuous question just popping out before she thought about it.

He shook his head once, the dark blond strands of his hair falling across his forehead. She curled her hands into his arms so she wouldn't reach up and push them back.

"You said this wasn't going to happen," she reminded him, because she wasn't stupid. It was clear where this was going. "You said it would put your career in jeopardy."

"I know." His voice was deep and quiet. "It might."

He was standing so close that her breasts brushed his chest with every breath she took. Her nipples peaked, rubbing against the material of her bra, her breathing became even more ragged. It was everything she could do not move even closer and press into him.

"You ran away," she accused, her voice so husky she barely recognized it. "Ran away like a little boy."

Harry leaned forward enough to run his face through her hair.

"I was being intelligent and mature," he whispered into her ear. She shuddered at the sensation, shuddered again when he gave her earlobe a sharp nip. She felt the bite all the way down her spine, between her thighs, felt herself growing hotter and wetter. Jesus, but the man was dangerous.

"You were a coward," she persisted, taunting him when it would have been far, far wiser to push him back. He would have let her go if she'd asked. But she didn't want to ask. She didn't want to be sensible and intelligent and mature. Maybe Harry didn't really want that either.

Reaching up, she bit his bottom lip, daring him to retaliate.

Challenge accepted.

Suddenly there wasn't any space at all between them. She was crushed into his hard body, his mouth on hers. Hot and wet and open, he devoured her with lips and teeth and tongue. Jenny shuddered and devoured him in turn, burning for him.

Harry's lower body pushed hers into the side of the Jeep. He was heavy, pure muscle over solid bone, his arousal more than evident. Jenny ripped her lips away from his to gasp for air.

"Harry!"

His big hands fisted in her hair, and he tilted her head, then bent his head and bit her in the place between her neck and shoulder, sucking her skin up against his teeth.

Marking her.

Jenny gripped his wide shoulders, the shock electric in a way that traveled all the way to her core. Dimly she realized he'd shoved his thigh between her legs and she was riding it, unable to help herself.

It was the sound of voices coming from the bowling alley's loading dock nearby that finally pulled her out of the haze of desire enough to realize where they were.

She finally understood what had driven Louise Weber to jump Sam Black in the parking lot of the Country Time. And she also knew that, whatever was going on inside Harry's head at the moment, he would hate himself if he lost control here.

He'd hate her, too.

She tried to pull away, but he slammed his mouth over hers again and sucked at her lips and tongue.

"Harry," she said when he finally let her talk. "We can't do this here."

Still, she couldn't stop herself from wrapping her arms around his neck, the heat between her thighs pulsing as she rubbed against him.

He didn't respond, just bent toward her mouth again.

Somehow she found the strength to wind her hands through his hair and tug his head back.

"We're in a parking lot," she reminded him. "We can't do this here. Do you want Bert to catch us the way my mother caught Louise and Sam?"

That was enough to make him pause, his eyes glittering through his lashes. He didn't back away, but he drew in a deep, unsteady breath. Then another. After a moment, he looked around, and she saw him come back to himself a bit.

"Sorry," he said, his voice was like gravel. "Jumped you."

Now she tugged his hair in frustration.

"I am on board for this development, in case you hadn't noticed," she pointed out.

He glanced down at his thigh between her legs, and his mouth quirked wickedly. Jenny had a really hard time not biting it again.

"Yeah. I see."

She heard more voices, and this time it sounded like they

were coming their way. Harry looked up over the roof of the Wrangler for a moment, but he didn't let her go. She heard laughter, some kids asking for ice cream, and the banging of doors. Once the car had started and, presumably, driven off, he met her eyes again.

"Come home with me," he said.

Now that he wasn't kissing her and scrambling her brain cells, Jenny was, unfortunately, able to think.

"You were pretty clear about what you wanted on Wednesday," she said. "And this wasn't it." In spite of everything, she couldn't seem to let go of him, couldn't stop herself from moving on him. He just felt too damned good to push away.

His mouth, that wildly wicked mouth, was firm and a little swollen from their kisses, his jaw hard, as if he was having to restrain himself from just tossing her in the back seat of the vehicle and taking off.

"I changed my mind," he said.

"Are you drunk?" she asked with equal bluntness. As much as she wanted this—and she *so* did—she had too much hard won self-respect to go with him if he didn't know what he was doing.

"I'm not drunk," he said and leaned forward to trace over her cheekbone with his lips before pulling back again. "I've had a few drinks, but I'm not drunk."

"You're not yourself," she said. "I don't know what happened, but this isn't you."

"Oh, this is me." His smile was faint. "Maybe I just decided I didn't like waiting after all."

Jenny didn't like waiting either. She carded her fingers through his hair, enjoying the texture against her palms. He kept it short, but long enough that she could still enjoy the silky weight of it.

She wondered how it would feel against her skin in other places.

Jenny drew in a breath at the sudden spike of arousal. Harry's eyes narrowed, and his nostrils flared, as if he was scenting her readiness. His erection grew between their bodies, but he didn't seem to care, his attention centered on her face.

Still…

Something inside her clenched. "What about tomorrow?" she asked.

"We'll let tomorrow take care of itself." His mouth slanted over hers again, powerful, giving and taking. His tongue mated with hers until she joined in its dance. She gripped his hair again, but this time it was to pull him closer, not push him away.

When he broke the kiss, they were both panting.

"Maybe I was right. Maybe this isn't a good idea," he said. "But at the moment, I just can't give a shit. What about you?"

There was the sound of more voices coming their way.

Jenny's eyes locked with Harry's.

Pure, electric heat.

Hunger ratcheted even higher. The urge to take and be taken. No, not an urge. That was too mild a word. The demand. The need.

This might be the stupidest thing she'd ever done in her life, but at that moment, Jenny couldn't find it inside herself to care.

"I don't give a shit either," she told him.

Harry smiled.

"Get in."

21

Harry knew this was a mistake. He *knew* it. But, like he'd told Jenny, right now he didn't care. All that mattered was that the one woman who'd made him crazy since the day he'd met her was sliding into the Jeep next to him. That she'd said "yes." All that mattered was sinking into her and forgetting for a few minutes where he'd come from and who he was.

In the past, any woman would have done. But now, for whatever reason, it seemed like he could only see Jenny. As soon as she'd shown up tonight, everything inside him—all of that restless force, all of the anger, all of the need to *take*—had focused on her.

He'd deal with the consequences tomorrow.

There were always consequences.

Shoving the thought away, he jumped behind the steering wheel and started the Jeep with a rush of the motor. A thought occurred to him.

"Where's your truck?" Some dim, responsible part of his mind was still active, and he knew he couldn't let Pat tow her pickup.

"At the Country Time," Jenny said. Ignoring the seatbelt,

which was all kinds of illegal, she pressed her body against his side as much as she could with the gear stick in the way. "It's fine. Hurry."

There was an urgency in her voice that echoed his own as she ran a hand up his chest and pressed a wet kiss against his neck with just the hint of teeth.

Harry wondered if his jeans would be strong enough to contain his hard-on.

"I thought you were worried about me being able to drive," he gasped, the urge to take her right then almost overwhelming.

"Sorry." She lifted her mouth, but he clamped a hand on her thigh to keep her in place when she started to move away. He slid his hand between her legs, and she jerked, her hand balled in his T-shirt.

"Hurry," she repeated.

He threw the Jeep in gear and bolted out of the parking spot.

Harry had never been quite so glad that his apartment was in the center of town, because it meant it only took them about five minutes to get there from the bowling alley. He was also glad they didn't run into a lot of traffic because although he might not be drunk, he definitely wasn't thinking very clearly. Especially not with the softness of Jenny's breast pressed against his side, branding him.

At last, he whipped the Jeep into the tenant parking lot behind the bakery and barely remembered to turn off the engine before reaching for her again, hauling her closer and kissing her. She seemed as desperate as he was as she wound her arms around his neck, her body slim and strong, her mouth hot. The taste of her was sweet and spicy, and he lost himself in it until she shoved him away to gasp for air.

"Inside," she panted.

Because it would suck if one of the other tenants caught

them, Harry didn't argue. He jumped out and ran around the hood to find Jenny already standing beside the Wrangler. She giggled, and he yanked her against him and kissed her, her mouth curving on his. She grabbed his ass.

Growling at her, feeling wildly young and free and out of control, he tugged her over to the tenant's entrance and practically shoved her through the door.

Jenny obviously didn't care because she turned to him and slanted her mouth across his when he joined her in the vestibule.

"Which floor," she panted.

"Second." He was going to lose the ability to speak in a minute. Too much of his blood had left his brain and gone straight to his dick.

Thank Christ she didn't say anything else, just sprinted up the stairs ahead of him. He pulled her to a halt in front of his apartment door, somehow got out his keys out, unlocked it, then propelled her inside.

She whirled into him, threw her arms around his neck. He stumbled at the unexpected assault, and the weight of their bodies slammed the door shut behind them.

"Oh, thank God," she whispered. "I've been wanting to get you alone since the police station." She kissed him, eating at his mouth with a desperation that mirrored his own.

Harry wished she hadn't mentioned the police station, but the mundane realities of what he was doing stood no chance against the lust boiling through his system.

He wrestled her back a moment later, his harder than it had ever been. He wasn't going to last if she kept touching him. She knew it too, the witch—he could see it sparkling in those blue eyes of hers, her pupils huge and black with desire.

"Keep your hands to yourself," he growled.

She raised her eyebrows. "Make me." It was a challenge. Harry felt the sharpness of his own answering grin.

"Okay."

Before she could stop him, he whirled her around until she faced the door and, holding her hands above her head with one of his own, sent the other wandering down the graceful sweep of her back to cup and mold her butt. She looked at him over her shoulder, a lock of dark hair falling over her eyes. Her face was flushed, her lips swollen.

He felt his desire for her kick up another impossible notch.

"Kinky." But her smile said she wasn't bothered by it.

Harry had always considered himself a flexible partner in bed, but this situation, seeing her helpless against the door, well, it flipped a few switches that didn't exactly need flipping.

Jenny, a part of him murmured. *It's because it's Jenny.*

"Keep your hands on the door." His voice was so guttural he barely recognized it himself.

When she did what he asked, he felt the jolt of hunger run through him.

"Don't move," he ordered.

The look she threw over her shoulder this time was disobedient and flippant and sexy as hell.

"Or what? You'll cuff me?" Her voice was a throaty purr, and she sounded...intrigued.

"Would you like that?" he murmured against her ear.

She rolled her hips back against him in a wordless response.

He grabbed her hips, and she groaned but stayed where she was. Sliding his hands up under her T-shirt, he stroked over the silky warmth of her skin then closed them over her breasts. They filled his palms, her nipples tight under her bra. He plucked at them, rolled them.

"God, get my shirt off now," she demanded.

Harry bit back an unexpected laugh.

"I'm in charge here, ma'am," he said in his best police officer voice.

The shudder she couldn't control was even more interest-ing. But since getting her shirt off was exactly what he wanted, he moved quickly to yank it up and off. Then he unclipped her bra and let her move her hands so he could peel it off and toss it on the floor with her shirt.

Finally, he was touching her breasts again, this time skin to skin, the warm weight of them burning his palms, her skin soft and smooth, the hard tips pressed between his fingers.

His body tightened with pure need.

"Harry!" she gasped, writhing against him. "Let me turn around."

He ignored her and ran his teeth over her neck and shoulder then shoved his erection into her.

"I need to touch you," Jenny protested, head thrown back.

He indulged in tasting the line of her neck, but he wanted her to touch him, too, so he pulled away and let her turn while he ripped off his own T-shirt. When he pulled her back against him, they both shuddered as her bare breasts rubbed against his chest.

He kissed her, demanding entrance to her mouth. She opened for him at once, her tongue dancing with his, her arms around his neck, and her hands in his hair. It took several long moments before he could let them breathe.

"Bed," she gasped.

For one wild moment, he considered just lowering her to the floor where they stood and taking her there, but he obeyed and tugged her after him to the bedroom. They tumbled together onto his bed, unmade from that morning because, hell, he hadn't thought he'd be having company tonight. Jenny didn't seem to care. She just reached up to him, her dark hair spilling over his cream comforter.

"I want you on top of me," she said.

"Hell." He lowered his head and put his mouth on one of

her breasts, took the nipple between his teeth and tugging gently while his tongue laved it.

"Harry!" She arched her back off the bed and grabbed his head in both hands, holding him to her.

He ignored her demand and let the pebbled tip fall away then, before she could complain, turned his attention to its twin, moving one of his hands to play with the other so it wouldn't be neglected.

Her nails scraped his shoulders and back, deep enough to hurt. The twinge of pain was erotic because he knew she didn't have a clue she was doing it.

Unable to wait any longer, he drew back and unfastened her jeans, then worked them off her hips and down her legs. When she realized what he was doing, she tried to help, and they ended up laughing as the clothing got hopelessly tangled. Her laughter only increased when they realized they'd forgotten to take off her shoes.

Finally, pants, panties, and shoes were gone and scattered on the floor.

Eyes still alight with humor, Jenny lay looking at him, hand up at her mouth as if she thought she shouldn't be smiling but couldn't stop.

God, she was beautiful, Harry thought. She was short, yes, and some might have found her curves a little slight, but he thought they were perfect. *She* was perfect. Especially now that she was here in his bed, grinning at him.

"Got a thing for socks?" she asked mischievously, and he realized they were all she was wearing.

"What if I do?" he asked, running his hands up her calves to her thighs. With a little persuasion, she let her legs fall open, let him see what her dark curls hid.

Jenny's small, perfect breasts rose and fell rapidly with her breathing.

"Harry," she whispered.

"Wait," he murmured. "I have to get rid of your socks."

Slowly, oh so slowly, he drew off the first one and threw it on the floor, then, because he couldn't help himself, ran his hand up her arch. She laughed, crunching and pulling her foot away from him.

"It tickles."

Harry had never laughed this much with a lover. Hadn't really known he could. Most of the women he'd been with had been intent on the goal, and that had been fine with him. Jenny was different.

Maybe she'd always been different. Maybe a part of him had always known that she would be. Maybe that was why he'd tried to stay away from her.

Her smile faded as she looked at him.

"What's wrong?"

Another difference. She saw things nobody else ever had.

Not sure how comfortable he was with that, he shook his head and bent down to kiss her foot, up her leg, moving his hand back to the firm roundness of her breast.

"Harry!"

He stroked and squeezed her as he kissed his way to the sensitive crease of her thigh. He drew in a deep breath, scenting her arousal, and when he looked up, saw her head was back, her fists clenched.

He smiled and flicked his tongue along the skin just below her navel. She bucked off the bed again and glared at him.

"Don't tease," she threatened.

Harry smiled. And, pushing her legs farther apart, teased her some more. Jenny cried out, and he almost came right then from the fluid, rolling motions of her body—the way she gripped his head tightly and made her demands as he feasted on her sweetness. He held her in place as she writhed under his mouth, the sounds she was making sexy as hell. She was close to her climax. He could feel it. Hear it.

And he couldn't wait any longer.

She cried out when he ripped himself away from her and got to his feet. Ignoring her protests, he stripped out of his jeans, underwear, and sneakers, desire making him so clumsy he almost emasculated himself pulling down the zipper.

Trembling with the force of his need, he stood and watched her looking at him. The weight of her eyes moving from his head to his feet and back again practically brought him to his knees.

Then she smiled, and her eyes fell to where his erection jutted out proudly.

"Well, hello there."

For some reason, the teasing words broke the spell. He pulled open the nightstand drawer with such force that he almost dumped it, but managed to find a condom, opened the package, and rolled it on. When he chanced a look at her again, she was pouting.

"I wanted to do that."

"Next time."

He didn't even know what he was saying as he lowered himself over her, moving his legs between hers. Her skin was smooth and satiny against the roughness of his, her hands grasping his arms as she urged him forward.

He kissed her, and she wrapped her arms around his neck, her mouth hot and demanding.

She whimpered a little when he pulled back, then let out a low cry when he ran his fingers through the wetness of her opening, pushed in, testing her readiness. Then he braced and guided himself into her. Her inner muscles were tight and hot and clamped down on him in a way that was perfection.

He almost embarrassed himself—almost lost it after a single stroke—but he gritted his teeth and managed to hold on even when Jenny made noises that threatened to push him over the edge. She was wet and slick and wild under him, and he urged her to put her legs around his waist. Her fingernails dug into his back again, and his control shattered.

He thrust into her deep, then pulled back and did it again and again and again, bending to catch her cries with his mouth as she clawed at him.

He was balanced on the edge, struggling not to lose it, but thank Christ Jenny went over, her body taut with pleasure, eyes closed. Harry finally gave in and felt his entire body explode.

22

Jenny came back to her senses when Harry shifted and left the bed, presumably to clean himself up in the bathroom. Feeling deliciously used and sated, she kept her eyes closed and rolled onto her side, enjoying the way her body was loose and achy in all the right places. It had been a long, long time since she'd felt this way. In fact, she wasn't sure she'd *ever* felt this way before. Not even at the beginning with Stefan.

Harry came back and lay on the bed beside her, moving into her space and pulling her on top of him. Still not opening her eyes, Jenny smiled and snuggled up against him, pillowing her head on his arm, her hand flat on his chest. His heart thudded under her palm, his hair-roughened skin rising and falling as he breathed.

Neither of them spoke for several long minutes, the quiet room peaceful around them after the intensity of their lovemaking. Then, gradually, reality began to intrude.

Damn it.

Jenny really tried not to think, but it was a lost cause. Now that her raging hormones had receded—okay, *mostly* receded— it finally occurred to her that, for a man who'd been pretty determined a few days ago that nothing would happen between them, Harry sure had changed his mind in a hurry.

Why?

With a sigh, she opened her eyes and shifted back a little bit so she could see his face. The sun had set while they'd been getting busy, but there was still enough ambient light coming in through the bedroom window to illuminate him lying beside her, his free arm folded behind his head as he stared up at the ceiling.

"So, that happened," she said after a moment.

"Yeah."

Jenny didn't want to have this conversation curled up against him like a kitten. Pushing away, she sat cross-legged on the big bed, tucking the edge of the now extremely mussed comforter around her body to cover herself. She didn't know why she bothered since he'd definitely seen all there was to see a few minutes ago, but it made her feel more in control.

Harry turned his head to look at her, frowning.

"What are you doing?" he asked.

"We need to talk," she said. That should have been obvious.

His frown deepened. "About what?"

About the state of the economy, jackass. What do you think?

Jenny somehow managed to hold on to her patience.

"Why did you suddenly change your mind about us getting together?"

"I didn't change my mind."

Her hold on her patience tightened to a death grip.

"Oh, right. On Wednesday you were *very* clear that this—" she waved her hand between the two of them, "could not and would not happen. You even ran away for two days so you wouldn't have to deal with me. The only thing you didn't do was hire a skywriter to spell it out.

Hmmm. Her grip on her patience might not be as strong as she'd thought.

Harry pulled himself up to sit across from her, mimicking her cross-legged position. He didn't bother covering himself, seemingly completely at ease with his nudity. Jenny kept her eyes resolutely on his face. It was hard.

Er, difficult. Don't think about "hard."

Her body hummed.

Stupid body.

"I didn't run away," Harry said, sounding disgruntled. Of *course* that was the part he focused on. "I was giving us both a little space."

"Uh-huh. Sure." He could believe that if he wanted to. Jenny raised her eyebrows and watched him skeptically. "And were you ever going to talk to me? Or was your big plan just to pretend we'd never had that lip-lock in the hallway?"

"Lip-lock?" There was just enough light left in the room for her to see him roll his eyes. "I would have been back in the office on Monday, you know. We would have talked. Worked things out."

"Looks like we just did that," she observed.

"Not the way I planned it," Harry said bluntly.

Ouch.

"Ah. So you were gonna give me 'the talk' and move on, huh?" she asked, trying to keep her voice light. "I get it."

"No," he said, surprising the hell out of her. "I was going to suggest we wait until after you're done temping at the police station, then see if we were both still interested. Your mother probably wouldn't like that much either, but it's better than sneaking around behind her back."

Although it was nice to hear he hadn't intended to just slam the door shut on any possibilities between them, and his thoughts had mirrored her own, what he was saying sounded so...logical. Two adults having a rational discussion. *Should we wait until two weeks after your end date to have sex or just the one?*

Logic and rationality were the exact opposite of what had just happened.

"What changed?" she asked.

Harry looked away from her. "Nothing."

"Oh, come on!" Jenny shot back. *Patience was highly overrated.* "You were out of control at the bowling alley, Harry," she said. "I have never seen you like that before. If I hadn't gotten you out of there when I did, you might have pulled that pinball machine right off the floor and scared the crap out of those kids. Not to mention anyone else who saw you."

His scowl was ferocious in the shadows. "I wasn't that bad."

"And you'd been drinking. Not drunk," she added, holding up her hand when he opened his mouth to protest, "but drinking. And not drinking beer. You don't *do* that. Something happened."

"You have no idea what I do when I'm not on the job," he retaliated, his voice harsh. "You don't hang out with me. We're not friends."

Jenny could admit that one stabbed. She'd assumed they were at least friends. Knowing he didn't feel the same way made her stomach clench. When she gave herself to someone, it was because they were in some kind of a relationship. She didn't do casual one-night stands. Ever.

Except maybe she just had.

"So did tonight happen because I was there and you were horny?" she asked, trying to push him, wanting him to be honest. She needed to know how much of an idiot she'd been.

He glared at her. "Did I say that?"

"Was I just a fuck buddy?"

"Jesus!" Raking his hands through his hair, Harry got off the bed and stalked across the room, then back.

God, he was magnificent in the low light. So tall and strong and biteable. Jenny looked away.

"Listen," he said, moving around the bed to the side where she was sitting. He dropped onto the mattress next to her and bowed his head, hands clasped between his knees. "You are not a convenience or a fuck buddy or a way to blow off steam. I was...I had...some shit happened earlier today, and it messed me up."

"Did something happen at work?"

"No, no. This was personal."

Without thinking, Jenny reached for his arm in sudden concern. "Is your grandfather okay? Your grandmother? I saw Harry Senior at the Country Time, and he looked—"

"He's fine. They're both fine." Harry covered her hand where it rested on his forearm. "It's not them. I don't want to talk about it."

"But—"

His hand tightened on hers. "It's personal," he repeated, meeting her eyes. "And I guess I'm not dealing with it as well as I thought. You're right—I drank more than I usually do, and, well, filters were off. Then you came in and...boom." With his free hand, he made the gesture of an "explosion" next to his head. "Spontaneous combustion."

Jenny smiled reluctantly.

"I guess that's one way of putting it," she acknowledged.

She wanted to know what his "personal" problem was. Everything in her wanted to ask, to prod him until he told her. But, he wasn't going to spill his secrets to her tonight. He probably never would.

Sighing, she pulled the comforter tighter.

It seemed the upshot of the situation was that Harry had been in a bad headspace, and they'd both acted impulsively. The result? Like he'd said—spontaneous combustion. Maybe they would have ended up here in his bed at some point anyway, maybe they wouldn't have. It didn't matter. All Jenny could do now was try to deal.

She had a feeling it was going to be a lot easier said than done.

"So I guess I should get out of here. You'll have to take me back to the Country Time to get my truck." A very depressing way to end what had been a spectacular evening.

Harry's frown sprang back into place.

"What are you talking about?"

"Well, play time's is over, isn't it?" she said and wanted to punch him for being dense. "This was obviously a mistake, so I should go. We'll just chalk it up to a good time and move on before things get even more difficult."

It sucked. She'd been a mistake before, and she'd sworn she'd never let it happen again. The thought that maybe she had, that maybe she'd let her pent-up desire overrule her common sense and lead her down the same path she'd walked with Stefan, well. It was hard to take.

"You think this was a mistake?" Harry growled at her.

"No," Jenny admitted before she thought better of it. "But you do."

"No, I don't."

She blinked.

"You don't?" she asked.

"Of course not!"

Jenny scrambled to regroup.

"You're not...having regrets?" She'd missed something somewhere along the way.

"No!" He sounded exasperated. "Why would I? The sex was amazing. I don't think I've come that hard since I was nineteen! Jesus, woman."

"Then why the hell are you brooding?" she demanded, throwing up her hands in frustration. The motion dislodged the comforter tucked around her body, and it slid to her waist, exposing her breasts to the cool air of the apartment. Harry's attention was immediately diverted. She couldn't see him very well, but she could *feel* him looking at her.

"Stop that!" she snapped. "We need to finish this." But she didn't pull up the comforter again.

"Sorry," he said innocently. "I'm a little distracted by your pretty tits."

"You can't even see them."

"I have excellent night vision, and there's plenty of light coming in from the street. I can see just fine."

Jenny blushed, but she put her hands on her hips and thrust out the tits in question. She felt her nipples beading, his gaze almost a touch.

"If you're not sorry about what we just did," she said, hearing the breathiness in her own voice, "then what the hell is your problem?"

His eyes flicked up to hers again.

"The fact that I don't regret what happened is my problem," he said.

She shook her head. *Well, that was a new one.*

Harry turned slightly toward her and pulled the comforter the rest of the way off before pushing her gently back on the bed. As he moved over her, she felt his renewed erection brush her naked thigh, then press against her stomach. He caged her between his arms like the predator she'd imagined him to be earlier.

Dimly, Jenny wondered if this was the true Harry—the one under the uniform and the regulations.

"I wasn't lying when I told you it was a really bad idea for us to hook up while you're working at the police station," he said.

Mesmerized as she was by the man above her, Jenny couldn't control her wince.

"Is that what this is to you? A hookup?" she asked quietly, putting a hand up to touch his hard face, feeling the roughness of his whiskers against her fingers as she tried to see the expression in his shadowed eyes.

"No." He bent and kissed her softly. "It would be easier if it was just a hookup. It's more." He hesitated. "I want it to be more."

"So do I." His honesty compelled her own.

"Puts a wrinkle in things, doesn't it?" He kissed her again, and this time he demanded a response, nipping at her bottom lip before pulling away.

Jenny ran her hands over his face and into his hair then tugged him down for a kiss of her own. She indulged in a slow, leisurely exploration of his mouth, not letting him go until they were both desperate for air.

"We should wait," she murmured and scratched her fingernails over his scalp, then down to his shoulders. "I have to stay at the police station until Suzy's back. Mom put herself on the line with Margo Truelove for me."

Now Harry winced. "Please do not bring that woman's name into my bed." He nipped her nose in punishment.

Jenny laughed. "Yeah, big boy. I saw her looking at you. But what I'm saying is that I can't quit the job without embarrassing my mother. If we're together while I'm working there, and people find out, it will make things bad for you."

"Yeah, it will. What if I don't care anymore?"

Another kiss. This one full of heat and teeth and tongue. Bracing himself on an elbow, Harry continued to torment her mouth with his own while at the same time trailing his hand down her body, palming her breast, shaping it before moving lower. Jenny felt the excitement of his touch flow through her, scored his shoulders with her nails as his hand moved to the apex of her thighs. Between them.

"Harry!" she gasped when he broke the kiss to run his lips over her cheek and down her neck.

"Do you really want to wait?" he challenged, using his

fingers to rub her most sensitive spot before slipping them into her moist heat.

"No! It's not me...it's you...you're...God!"

Jenny's brain short-circuited, her entire being focused on what he was doing with his fingers, the sensations he was giving her. The exquisite tension started building inside her again, and she moved under him. He leaned over her, his body scalding hers as he reached across her to open the nightstand drawer. This time he did dump the contents, but neither of them cared because he'd managed to snag a condom before they all fell on the floor.

She protested when he removed his hand, but he was only gone for as long as it took him to roll on the condom. Then he positioned himself at her entrance and slammed into her body with a force she hadn't expected.

They both groaned at the acute pleasure of it, the feeling of him seated deep within her.

After that, there was no thought at all, nothing but movement and demand, giving and taking, as they drove each other up, up, up... and both flew over the edge to completion.

Jenny didn't lose consciousness this time, but it was close.

For several minutes, they lay sprawled together in a boneless, panting, sweaty heap until Harry finally roused himself and got up to dispose of the condom. When he came back, he spooned against her where she lay contented and pleasure-drugged in the destroyed bedding—his front to her back, his heavy arm over her waist.

"I don't want to wait," he said against her ear.

"Hmmm?" she murmured. She wasn't entirely sure she had any working brain cells left at the moment.

"I don't want to wait until you stop working at the police station," he clarified. "Not now. Not now that..." He kissed her shoulder. "Not now. But are you willing to keep a secret from your mother?"

"I *am* an adult, you know. It's not like she watches me every minute of the day." Jenny tried to think. She wasn't used to keeping secrets from her mother. But she didn't want to wait either. And she didn't want this thing between her and Harry to end. "Are you sure?" she asked at last. He was the one who would bear the brunt of Jackie's displeasure if they were caught.

"Yes. I can handle it," he assured her.

Jenny hesitated, then made her decision. "I can keep a secret." She turned her head to look back at him and raised her eyebrows in challenge. "Can you?"

"Yes." He said it without hesitation and kissed her.

When he released her mouth, Jenny wondered about the other secrets Harry was keeping.

23

They both drifted off to sleep after that. When Jenny woke again, the bedroom was dark except for the glow of streetlights outside and the illuminated numbers of the clock on the dresser indicating that it was close to midnight. Harry shifted behind her.

"Are you awake?" he asked, pushing her hair away from her face.

"I guess," she grumbled.

"We should go get your pickup before someone notices it's still at the Country Time."

Jenny blinked as his words penetrated, then her eyes widened and she sat bolt upright, forcing him to jerk away before her head hit him in the chin.

"Holy crap!" She pushed at him when he tried to reach for her and scrambled off the bed. "You sexed me up so good, I didn't even think about someone seeing the truck!"

Harry lay on his back, laughing. "Sexed you up?"

"Yeah." She knelt next to him on the bed and kissed his smiling mouth. "And if you have any hope at all of this staying a secret, *especially* from my mother, we'd better go get my pickup before Josie gets off work and sees it in the parking lot."

Harry sat up abruptly, and this time Jenny was the one who almost got clipped.

"I forgot about Josie," he admitted.

"And Hannah. And June. They all know I'm not in the Country Time, and they'll wonder why my truck's there and what I'm doing. And *then* some helpful person will mention that we were seen together at the bowling alley, and," she waved her hands, "*voila!* Suspicion. Assumptions." She lowered her voice to a thrilling whisper. "Rumors."

"Shit."

Not turning on a lamp since the blinds were open, Jenny tried to find her clothes. Eventually she located her jeans and underwear on the floor and pulled them on while Harry retrieved and slipped into his own.

"Where's the rest of my stuff?" she asked because she honestly couldn't remember where it had all gone in those first frantic moments. She only knew everything had come off.

"Living room." Harry went to get their things, and when he returned a minute later, he handed over her bra and now sadly crumpled shirt. Tugging on her bra, she reached back to fasten it, scrunching up her nose as she did.

"I wish I could take a shower, but we need to get going."

"We can come back afterward and take one," Harry suggested, yanking on his T-shirt.

"I don't think it would be a good idea to have my pickup in the tenant parking lot or out on the street here." Jenny pulled on her shirt. Didn't look like he'd ripped anything, she thought smugly, but it had been close.

"So I'll follow you home, and we'll leave your truck there," he said, his voice muffled as he bent to tie his running shoes. He'd still been wearing the socks.

Jenny paused in the search for her own second sock and looked to him.

"Are you asking me to stay the night?" she asked carefully.

He raised his head, his face unreadable in the darkness.

"I guess I am," he said with equal caution.

Jenny was quiet for a moment. Taking off her remaining sock because she couldn't find its mate, she slid her bare feet into her shoes.

"If I come back here, you'll have to run me home in the morning," she said. "Someone might see you dropping me off."

"Oh. Right."

Jenny sighed a little. This was the first bitch-slap from reality. It was hard to be discreet in Hardy Falls.

She wasn't sure she liked being kept a secret.

Stefan had never introduced her to the other professors at the university.

But that was different, she assured herself. She'd been with Stefan for years, and he'd never really bothered to include her in his life. This time, it wouldn't be long before they didn't have to worry about it and could just act normal.

Unless Harry changed his mind and decided he never wanted her mother to know. Then they'd be sneaking around until...this ended.

That thought led to another.

What if they broke up while she was still working at the police station?

Harry straightened, and she could tell he was looking down at her.

"We'll work it out," he told her, as if he'd guessed what she was thinking.

Neither one of them wanted it to end now.

Jenny made herself smile. "I know."

Gathering up her purse from where she'd flung it in the living room, she stuffed her socks into it and followed Harry out of the apartment and down the stairs to his Jeep. When they'd first arrived at the building earlier, they'd been totally oblivious to other people. Now Jenny kept an eye out to make sure no one was around.

She felt like a secret agent looking for contraband.

Maybe *she* was the contraband.

No, she didn't like being kept a secret.

Harry opened the passenger door for her, then bent down to steal a quick kiss before she climbed in.

It was only for a little while.

They were quiet as he drove them back to the Country Time. Jenny was glad to see that the parking lot was still pretty full—it would make her little pickup truck less obvious.

"I'd better get going," she told Harry when he parked next to her truck. "Josie will probably be leaving soon, and I don't want her to see me."

"Right." He yanked her over to him and kissed her again, this time with fierce demand, teeth and tongue, opening her mouth with his own to sweep inside and plunder. "I'm following you home," he told her when he let her go.

"Um...okay..." she panted. Any of her brain cells that might have regenerated were fried again, and Jenny honestly wasn't quite sure what she was saying. She saw his quick grin when she fumbled for the door handle.

"Think you'll be okay to drive?" he asked innocently.

Jenny gave him the finger, but before she could tell him to go to hell, she heard voices. Three men, college kids from the look of them, came around the side of the building from the main entrance and climbed into a truck parked a few spaces down.

"I'd better go," she said to Harry once they'd driven away.

"I'll be following you," he repeated.

"Yeah, yeah." She climbed out and got into her truck, closing the door shut behind her, too used to the protectiveness of cops to even bother trying to argue. Soon she was pulling out of the Country Time's parking lot and onto the highway, the headlights from Harry's Jeep reflected in her rearview mirror.

"I can find my own way home," she muttered. "I know how to do that much."

But it was late, so she guessed it was nice of him to make sure she made it.

She *guessed*.

Jenny let out a heavy sigh. She was just cranky because she really *did* want to spend the rest of the night with Harry. Even though he didn't seem to want this thing between them either, he might change his mind once he started thinking. What if this was her only chance to be with him this way? What if he decided she wasn't worth the trouble he was courting.

She couldn't blame him if he decided to bail, she thought as she turned onto her street. He was right to be concerned—her mother had told her that he was up for sergeant if the town council ever got off their butts and approved the position. His entire career could be at stake if Jackie decided he was behaving inappropriately and blocked his promotion.

The thought made her even more depressed.

Jenny pulled into her driveway, parked the truck, and got out. Turning, she saw Harry's Jeep sitting at the curb. Just a friend making sure she got home safely.

She waved in acknowledgment, but he waited until she'd unlocked the front door and stepped inside. As she turned to pull the door closed behind her, she saw the Jeep drive off.

And that, Jenny thought, was that.

For a few minutes, she just stood in the living room, feeling restless and out of sorts. Then her stomach growled, and she realized she was hungry. No wonder, considering all of the energy she'd expended.

She headed to the kitchen to make herself a sandwich and wondered if Harry would call her tomorrow...no, today, since it was after midnight. Or was he expecting her to call him?

Frowning, she got out the bread and cold cuts. What was the etiquette for this kind of thing anyway? *Heyyy boo, just thought I'd touch base to see if you changed your mind after you banged me like a drum?*

And what would she do if he decided to back off after all?

"If Harry changes his mind," she said out loud, "screw him. Sideways."

Of course, she'd already done that.

Jenny's thoughts were interrupted by a sudden, sharp knocking at the front door. Startled out of her mind, she spun around, breath short, and practically dropped the jar of mustard she was holding.

What the hell?

Instinctively, she looked at the clock. Twelve thirty.

Who in the world would be at the door at twelve-thirty at night? Morning? Whatever?

"Oh, God. Please don't let it be Josie."

If Josie had seen her truck at the Country Time, Jenny wouldn't put it past her sister to track her down and demand to know what was going on.

Jenny quickly put the mustard jar on the countertop and bolted for the door, just as another knock reverberated through the house. She went to open it, then hesitated.

Don't be stupid. What if it isn't Josie? What if it's an ax murderer?

Peering through the small peephole, she saw the face of the person on her doorstep and let out a gasp. NOT an ax murderer. Or Josie. Unlocking the door, she yanked it open.

"Harry?" Jenny breathed. "What are you doing here?"

He didn't answer, just walked inside and kicked the door shut behind him. Then Jenny found herself spun around and pressed against the wall as he kissed the crap out of her. By the time he let her go, they were both panting, and Jenny was trying to wrap her body around him like a vine.

"Hi," she wheezed.

"I'm staying," he informed her. "Even though it weirds me out because this is the chief's house."

Jenny's heart felt like it was going to pound right through her chest.

"The chief is in Harrisburg," she pointed out.

"Which is why I even had the guts to cross the threshold."

"But tomorrow morning—"

"I'll leave early before anyone's up. But I'm going to be sleeping with you tonight." He kissed her. "In your bed." Kiss. "Naked."

"Sounds good to me." Jenny didn't think it would be lady-like to whimper, so she controlled it. "But what—"

"I have condoms," he interrupted her. "Grabbed a few when we left the apartment, just in case."

Jenny couldn't control her grin. "In case of what? A sex emergency?"

"You never know," he said darkly. "Isn't that what this is?"

She tightened her hold around his neck and nibbled on his earlobe until he cursed and took her mouth with his own. This time, neither of them wanted to break apart—not even to breathe.

"I'm glad you're prepared," she told him when she could, "but I was going to ask what you did with your Jeep?" It went without saying that Harry's Wrangler in her driveway would cause even more gossip than her pickup at his building.

"Left it a couple of blocks away. It'll be fine."

"Good." She hitched her legs around his waist as he pinned her even more firmly against the wall.

Yeah, baby. This sure the heck was a sex emergency.

"Want something to eat?" she asked, licking along his jaw. "A shower?"

"After," he told her. She crossed her ankles behind his back when he swung around to walk across the living. "And the only thing I want to eat is you."

Oh. My. God.

Jenny made him put her down, then grabbed his hand and practically dragged him upstairs to her bedroom.

After Harry fell with Jenny into her bed and took her again with an intensity that surprised even him—*her body gilded by the soft light of the lamp on the nightstand, her arms reaching up for him*—he was done for the night. No matter how motivated, a man had his limits. But he managed to coax her into the shower with him afterward and used his mouth on her until she couldn't stand anymore. It was the least he could do.

After they'd recovered a bit, she led him back downstairs to the kitchen, both of them pink and slightly wrinkled from the lengthy shower, and they stood companionably at the sink eating huge sandwiches. Jenny was worried because the cold cuts had been out for a while at that point, but Harry didn't give a damn. He was *starving*.

"Who cares about salmonella," he told her around a huge mouthful. "A boy's gotta eat when he's burned this many calories."

"A girl does, too," she informed him primly as she chewed and swallowed a giant mouthful. "You've got me running on empty."

True, he might have been a little demanding. He should probably feel bad about that.

But he didn't.

"I'm pretty sure little Harry is down for the count now anyway," he told her.

"Thank God. Little Harry performed above and beyond the call of duty tonight." Jenny saluted him with a cheeky grin, and Harry straightened.

Why, yes. Yes, he had.

He took another bite of his sandwich and waggled his eyebrows at her. "Benefit of a younger man with a lot of pent-up demand," he said after he'd swallowed. Little Harry had been more on-board tonight than he'd been for quite some time.

Jenny chewed contemplatively for a moment. "I forgot you were younger," she admitted. "And I don't know why your demand was pent up," she added. "Seems to me there are plenty of women in this town who'd have helped you take care of that little issue."

"A few." He was sorry he'd mentioned it. He didn't want to think about other women, and he didn't want her to know that lately he'd practically been a monk. He just hadn't been in the mood for a quick lay.

That's not what this was.

It might be dangerous to be with her like this, but so be it. Jenny Kline had tugged at him since he'd met her, and a job, no matter how great, was only a job. He'd roll the dice.

Maybe he was Junior's son after all.

The thought of his father effectively dampened his buzz. With a determined effort, he ate more of his sandwich and shoved all of those emotions back in the box where they belonged. He swallowed and put what was left of the food back on the counter. Suddenly he wasn't as hungry as he'd been a moment ago. When he looked up, he found Jenny watching him solemnly, her big blue eyes openly showing concern.

"What?" he asked.

"Something's wrong."

He shook his head. "I'm just tired."

She looked away. "Will you ever tell me what's actually going on?"

Maybe he would. Sometime. But not tonight.

"Let's go to bed," he said instead. "I have to work tomorrow."

For a minute, he thought she would push back or argue, but then she just smiled and started cleaning up the leftovers. He helped her, and once everything was away, they went upstairs to her bedroom, closed the door behind them, and locked out the world for the night. Harry set the alarm on his watch, and they dropped into bed, curled up together, and fell asleep almost immediately.

The freaking alarm went off at four-thirty—way, way too early. It took a supreme effort of will, but Harry rolled away from Jenny when all he wanted to do was pull her closer. He sat on the side of the bed and let out a yawn that almost cracked his jaw.

God, it felt like he'd only slept for an hour. Because that's basically what he'd done. Rubbing his beard-stubbled face, he grinned.

Worth it.

It wasn't like he'd never had a sleepless night before, he thought as he stumbled to his feet and started grabbing clothing from where it had been tossed in various spots around the room, pulling it on haphazardly.

Jenny woke up and threw on a T-shirt, insisting on seeing him out even though he told her he'd lock it after he left. He tried to get irritated by her stubbornness, but she just nodded and followed him to the living room anyway. When she kissed him at the front door, all warm and still drowsy, he gave up and kissed her back.

"Do you have a hangover?" she asked sympathetically, linking her hands at the back of his neck and studying his face. "I can make coffee."

The coffee sounded wonderful, but the time it would take to make it had him shaking his head even as his hands strayed down to cup her naked ass exposed when the T-shirt had ridden up.

"I'm okay."

"Are you going to call me later?" Jenny asked, her expression so placid he knew she was trying not to show any emotion.

"Of course." He kissed her again. "Not a one-night stand, remember?"

Jenny smiled. "Then I should probably give you my number, shouldn't I?"

Although he could probably have found the information himself—he *was* a police officer—Harry reluctantly let her go, pulled out his phone, and put in the number she gave him. Then he kissed her one last time and opened the front door.

It was amazing how hard it was to leave.

Jenny smiled and shook her head when he stopped on the porch and glared at her pointedly. He crossed his arms. No, he wasn't going anywhere until she had locked the door behind him.

Shaking her head again, she closed the door, and he heard the deadbolt click. Only then did he turn and start walking to where he'd left the Jeep.

The sun hadn't come up yet, so it was dark and cold, and there was some snow on the ground, but not as much as he'd expected. The chilly predawn air was bracing, waking up his fogged brain a little more. As Harry walked, he kept an eye out for people, but as expected, the streets were quiet.

He still kept to the shadows, though. All he'd need would be for Carly or Curtis to drive past on patrol and see him walking alone at this time of the morning.

Harry frowned.

He didn't like sneaking around. He didn't like lying to the chief. He didn't like keeping things a secret. What he wanted to do was just tell Jackie what was going on and let the chips fall where they may. He was still the same man he'd always been—he still had her back. He was still loyal, followed the rules, cared about the community.

What the hell did it matter if he'd also slept with the chief's adult daughter and planned to do it again?

He walked with his hands stuffed in the pockets of his jeans, head down, scowling.

It mattered because he wanted to keep working in Hardy Falls. If he and Jenny kept things out of the workplace, Jackie might not actually fire him—because they *did* have the right to their own lives—but he doubted she would ever trust him again. In a lot of ways, that would be worse.

So they'd need to be discreet.

The Jeep was waiting for him in front of a park where he'd left it. Someone might have recognized it as his and wondered why it was there, but it was his personal ride, so he doubted it had attracted too much attention.

Getting in, he drove back to the bakery, where the Knights were already hard at work making the donuts. Climbing the stairs up to his apartment, he let himself in, walked to his bedroom, and fell forward across his bed. It still smelled like sex and Jenny, a vivid reminder.

They'd only have to be careful for a little while. Then they'd see where they were.

An hour or so later, he was up again. Taking time he didn't have, he remade the bed with fresh bedding. Just in case.

But, he admitted as he shaved and got dressed in his uniform, with the chief coming home that afternoon, chances were good they wouldn't manage to see each other again today.

The thought made him frown as he headed out to the police station.

Once he'd settled into the routine of his shift at the police station, Harry quickly realized that although he might have pulled some all-nighters when he was younger—even some sexy all-nighters—he wasn't a teenager anymore. Around mid-morning, he found himself standing in the break room and trying not to shove his whole head into the luscious black depths of his millionth mug of coffee. He ached in places he'd forgotten he had, and Jenny had scratched his shoulders up good.

The memory made him smile with bone-deep satisfaction.

"Why are you grinning like that?" Bethany Clark demanded, moving beside him to pour herself a cup of coffee. She was working the shift with him again, but she'd been a little quieter than normal today. "And," she peered at his neck, "is that a hickey?"

"No. I cut myself shaving." Harry instinctively put his hand over the bruise. He couldn't remember when Jenny had marked him there, but, like with the scratches on his shoulders, he loved the fact she'd lost control like that. Too bad the hickey was just a little too high to be covered by the uniform shirt collar.

"Right." Bethany looked unconvinced. She poured her coffee and took a long time adding in the sugar. "So...who is she?"

"I don't know what you're talking about." Harry tried to sound dignified and superior.

Bethany peeked up at him, then quickly looked away as she bent to get some creamer out of the station's little mini-fridge.

"It's been quiet," she said, pouring in the creamer then placing the container back in the fridge. "Nothing's happened since I got in. Do you want to set up the cot and take a nap? I'll wake you if something comes up."

It was tempting, but Harry shook his head. He had a pretty good idea what Chief Kline would do if she came back from her trip early, checked in, and found him sleeping. He was already courting disaster—no need to speed up the trip.

"Too much to do."

"Sure." Bethany shifted uncomfortably and drank some of her coffee.

She wasn't acting...jealous, was she?

Harry's stomach took a nosedive.

Oh, fucking hell. Please do not let her be coming onto him.

There was no doubt about the fact that Bethany was a flirt, but he'd always considered her basically harmless. Still, she definitely skirted the line sometimes—and not just with him but with Tony and Curtis, too. Did it mean more than he'd thought it did? If she got pushier, he was going to have to smack her down and make sure she understood.

And wouldn't that be ironic? Him disciplining the kid would be the highest form of hypocrisy imaginable.

"What's wrong, Bethany?" he demanded. His voice was harsher than he'd intended but, fortunately, she didn't seem to notice.

She fidgeted with her mug for a minute before taking another sip. Then she put it on the counter and turned to face him, hands on her hips, chin up. Harry braced himself.

"I have to ask you a question," she said.

"Okay," he said cautiously.

"Am I a good cop or not?"

For a minute Harry didn't understand the question because what she was saying was so different from what he'd been expecting.

"Huh?"

"It's just...I keep asking the chief for more hours, and I *know* we're short-handed until Tony gets back next week, even with Curtis picking up extra time. Still. She won't let me work more than a few shifts a week. Is it because I'm not a good cop?"

Harry drank coffee to buy himself some time. This conversation might be as much of a minefield as the one he'd thought they were about to have.

The fact was, the chief *had* been careful to limit Bethany's shifts. She'd told Harry she had doubts about the girl's capabilities, and, after working with Bethany for the weekend, he could understand the concern. The kid acted like she was still in the academy and seemed quite content to wait for somebody else to give her direction. That wasn't good. This was real life, they were a small department, and they all had to be full members of the team.

But Harry saw something else now as he studied Bethany's stubborn face. The young woman was a lot more committed than either he or Jackie had realized. It was evident in the hurt she was trying so hard to hide.

"Let's go sit down," he said kindly.

Bethany seemed to deflate. "No, no. It's okay." She sounded discouraged. "You're busy and I...well, I didn't mean to bring it up. I was going to wait to ask Chief Kline after her meeting with the town council—see if I could figure out what's going on. But I thought you might know, and you're here and...sorry."

The fact that she had intended to talk to the chief herself raised his respect for her another notch.

"I've got a minute," he said and jerked his head toward the squad room. "Grab your coffee."

Bethany seemed reluctant now that she'd raised the topic, but she did as he asked and picked up her mug of coffee, then preceded him to the squad room. She was heading to her desk, but Harry pointed her to the chair next to his own.

"Sit."

She sat.

Harry dropped into his chair and sipped his coffee, studying her.

She was so young, he thought. He wondered if he'd ever been that young, that innocent. He didn't think so. She was the baby of a loving, extended family. Based on what he'd observed at town events, she was still treated as if she was the one who needed protecting, not the one who provided it. Harry had started fending for himself as soon as he could walk.

"Why did you want to be a police officer, Bethany?" he asked.

The girl's face lit up. "I've always wanted to be a cop," she said, blond hair swinging, her eyes big and blue.

They weren't as blue as Jenny's.

"Why?" Harry wasn't sure if anyone had ever actually asked Bethany why she'd wanted the job, and at the moment, that seemed like a pretty big oversight.

She'd been hired because, when there'd been an opening for a part-time officer a year ago, her grandfather had told the then-mayor that she'd be perfect. Since Ted Clark owned a lot of land around Hardy Falls, belonged to the Rotary, and had been friends with Mayor Ruffio for years, the town council, at the mayor's behest, "suggested" that Chief Kline hire the girl.

Jackie had been less than pleased, to put it mildly. But she'd done what they asked because she was afraid the council wouldn't approve funding for the position at all if she didn't.

Now Harry wondered if the chief's resentment at having been pushed into making the decision had colored the rest of her dealings with Bethany.

"When I was a kid, around six," Bethany said, "my granddad still worked on his farm behind the Country Time."

"Yeah, I've heard," Harry agreed.

Ted Clark used to have a big wheat farm on land he owned stretching behind and around both the Country Time and the bowling alley. He'd stopped working it around five years ago, so it hadn't been an active farm since before Harry moved to be with his grandparents in Hardy Falls. Apparently, the old man had sold off much of the land in the years to developers interested in the area. But he still held onto some acreage there, and he had other tracts scattered around.

Harry's own grandfather would have loved to hold onto their farm out by Friendsville, but he just hadn't been able to do it. He'd needed the money.

"It was pretty big at the time, and Granddad had a lot of people working there." Bethany's young face was shadowed, and she was looking down at her hands. "One of the workers..." she trailed off, and Harry's blood ran cold.

"Did he hurt you?" he asked, trying to keep his voice gentle.

Bethany shook her head and looked up at him.

"No. Not that. But he went after Granddad with a gun when he tried to fire him for stealing."

Harry tensed again. He hadn't heard this story.

"Did Ted get shot?"

"No. My Grammy had called the police as soon as she knew there was a problem. Chief Kline—well, she was Officer Kline then—came with her partner. They were able to sneak up on the man and get him to put down the gun. He was really, really drunk," she added. "And mad. But I don't think he would have shot anyone."

Harry sat back.

"And you saw it?"

Bethany nodded. "My little brother and I were visiting that day. My Grammy told us to hide, but we looked. I've wanted to be a police officer ever since then." She swallowed but resolutely kept her eyes on his. "I suck at it, don't I?"

It seemed like all of them—Harry included—had misjudged the girl. He'd just assumed she wanted an easy gig and had taken advantage of her grandfather's connections, and her flirting and blond good looks hadn't done anything to make him change his mind. He was surprised that Jackie hadn't clued in, though. She was normally more on top of things than that.

It didn't matter. They still had a problem.

"You don't suck," he told Bethany after a moment.

She stiffened slightly as if bracing herself. "I hear a 'but.'"

"You definitely need more training."

Now she looked offended. "I've been through the police academy," she protested. "I did pretty well there."

"I know. But the academy isn't the real world. Like what you just said about the man who threatened your grandfather being drunk, so he probably wouldn't shoot? You can't think that way. Thinking that way will get you killed."

Drunks were more likely than anyone else to shoot a gun, Harry thought. He should know.

Bethany frowned, but it was more thoughtful and less offended. "I don't know what to do about it," she said after a moment. "I already do whatever anyone tells me to do."

"You have to learn to think for yourself. Become a real member of the team." Harry made a decision. "Look, when the chief gets back, I'll talk to her. I think it would be a good idea for you to work with her for a while. Get some seasoning."

Bethany's big eyes got huge. "You think I need to work with the chief?"

"She's the best at training new officers." Even those who already had a few years under their belt and thought they knew everything. Harry had learned a lot from riding with Jackie. "Don't count on it though," he cautioned a little belatedly as he worked it through in his mind. Crap, he'd forgotten about the town council. They were so tight with money these days that they already weren't letting them hire the number of officers they needed for the size of the town. Despite Bethany's current limitations, the chief might not feel like she could pull her out of the regular rotation.

"Okay." Disappointment and relief vied for control of her features.

"But now, let's do a patrol together." He could finish paperwork tomorrow. *Always tomorrow.* "We'll go through the town, talk things over." He made a mental note to mention to Jackie that at the very least, everyone scheduled with Bethany should be more aware of her need for training.

She got to her feet, and her smile was like sunshine lighting up the room.

"That would be great. Thanks, Harry."

"Give me a few minutes to finish this, and we'll go."

Bethany went back to her desk, and Harry took a long gulp of coffee, contemplating their conversation. If she was really as committed as she seemed, then maybe they could still turn her into a real asset instead of someone they had to work around.

All they had to do was come up with a way to give her the training she needed and still cover all the shifts. Easier said than done. Even when Tony got back, they'd be stretched way too thin, and Margo's vindictiveness was making everything more difficult.

Harry rubbed his eyes and turned back to his computer so he could finish what he was working on before he and Bethany headed out.

God, he hated drama. That was why he got along so well with the chief. Jackie hated it, too.

And wouldn't the chief *really* hate it if she found out that her senior officer, the one they both expected to make sergeant if the town council finally approved the position, had indulged in wild monkey sex with her daughter several times over the last couple of hours? And that he wanted to do it again, and again. As soon as possible.

Discretion, Harry. Discretion.

"If you're going to be a few minutes, I'll head out to the bakery and pick up some donuts," Bethany said.

"That would be great." Harry dug in his pocket for money and handed it over to her, craving the sugar to go with the caffeine.

After the girl left the squad room, he grabbed his cell phone off his desk to text Jenny.

She was the other sugar he craved.

25

After Harry left, Jenny drifted back upstairs and dropped into her bed—a bed that smelled like him. She fell asleep at once and woke a few hours later, thanks to the tinkling chime of a text message notification.

Bleary-eyed, she grabbed the phone off the nightstand and checked the message.

Hi. It's Harry. Are you asleep?

He'd kept his word and contacted her.

Grinning like a fool, Jenny settled herself against the pillows and shoved her hair out of her eyes. Using her forefinger, she tapped the screen.

I'm sorry. Is this Harry Newman Sr.? Or another Harry?

She only had to wait a minute for a reply.

Smartass. This is the Harry who pounded you into the mattress several times last night.

Grin spreading, she tapped again.

Hmmm. I'm afraid I don't remember.

Oh, I think you will if you try very, VERY hard.

Jenny shivered and clutched the phone a little tighter as she answered.

It might be coming back to me.

It better be. Are you naked?

Shouldn't you be working?

I am working. Are you naked?

Oh, he was trying to be the big boss again, was he?

Feeling more than a little evil, Jenny straightened on the bed and let the sheets and bedspread fall to her waist. She stripped off the sleep shirt she'd put on when she'd followed him to the door earlier and, holding out her phone, thrust out her bare breasts and took a selfie. Before she could talk herself out of it, she sent him the photo.

This time the wait was longer. Just long enough for her to start second-guessing herself. Jenny chewed her bottom lip. What the hell was she doing?

The notification sound rang.

Witch.

Relief had her grinning again.

Well, you asked.

Yeah, but now I'm hard from looking at your sweet body. How am I supposed to go on patrol like this?

Jenny drew in a shaky breath. The things that man said. Or texted. She could almost hear him whispering to her, his deep voice soft in her ear and his hands on her.

Want me to come over and take care of that problem for you?

She giggled as she sent the text, feeling sultry and silly and sexy.

Another pause.

Shut up before I can't even walk.

Jenny giggled again.

Oh, well. If you don't need me...

I need you. As soon and as often as possible.

Jenny drew in a deep breath.

Me, too.

It was frightening how quickly it had happened. It was as

though the three years they'd known each other since he'd started working in Hardy Falls had all been moving to this point.

This time the pause was longer, and she thought he was letting the conversation drop. But when she'd started to text him to tell him to have a safe day, he sent her another message.

Bethany's on her way back. I'd better try to get something done. Wish I was there in bed with you.

That was very nice.

If you were here, you wouldn't be sleeping.

Neither would you.

The promise in the words sent arousal stirring again, deep in her belly. Jenny felt the tips of her breasts harden in the cool air of her room, and she licked her lips.

Good.

Another pause.

Shit. I have to go.

Be safe. Call me later.

I want to see you.

Go. We'll work it out.

That was going to be their freaking mantra, she thought.

She sent him a string of emojis, and, to her delight, he replied the same way. Officer Harry Newman sending silly emojis. Who knew?

Energized after the conversation, Jenny got out of bed and stretched, then winced when she felt twinges in muscles that had not been used so often or so well for longer than she cared to admit. In fact, they probably had never been used that well before.

Smirking, she headed into the bathroom and a few minutes later was sinking into a heavenly tub of hot water. There were bruises on her thighs and red razor burn between them, and she shuddered remembering how the marks had gotten there. Other light bruises and scratches adorned her torso and arms.

And she loved every one of them. Loved all of the evidence of the night she'd spent. She hadn't just been tumbled—she'd been *taken*.

Grinning widely, she tipped her head back to rest on the edge of the tub.

"God, I feel good."

Sinking further, she went under.

Jenny stayed in the bath until the water started to cool, then reluctantly climbed out and moisturized in the appropriate places. She was more than a little smug at the number of places that needed moisturizer.

After she cleaned up the bathroom and went back to her bedroom, she dressed in a simple T-shirt and old jeans and debated whether or not to strip the bed and change the sheets. Ultimately, she decided she didn't want to lose the scent of Harry in her bed quite yet, so she just made it.

She wished he trusted her enough to tell her what the "shit" was that he'd been dealing with, and why he'd been drinking more than normal.

She'd ask again later.

Sighing a little, she went downstairs, grabbed a mug of coffee, and headed out to her studio.

When she unlocked the door and walked into the former shed, the smell of the paints and oils both soothed her and fed the energy that suddenly seemed to be bubble under her skin in an almost visible wave.

Jenny hadn't felt like this in quite a while. She knew that today she had to draw. Today she had to paint. There was no choice.

Coffee mug cupped in both hands, she walked to study the partially finished landscape painting sitting on the easel. This is what she should work on—she should finish it so she could replace the one at the Country Time nobody seemed to like.

But she wasn't going to work on it today. No, she knew exactly what she wanted to do.

Putting the coffee and her phone down on a little table next to the ratty old sofa, Jenny went to the workbench and shelves where she kept her supplies. She dug out a pad of paper and pencils and took them with her back to the sofa, where she sat and flipped to a blank page in the sketch pad. She carefully studied the tip of a pencil, thinking.

Harry.

Closing her eyes, she could see him as he'd looked after they'd made love in her room. Before he'd hauled her to the shower and pleasured her out of her mind with his mouth. He'd been lying on her bed watching her, one arm flung over his head, the other hand flat on his stomach, his smile sexy and open.

Jenny began to draw quickly. She didn't sketch figures much anymore. Since she'd moved home, her paintings had been much more about the town and surrounding countryside, imagining them in new ways, breaking forms, rather than preserving them. But she wouldn't mess with Harry's form. It was too perfect the way it was—it should be celebrated, not deconstructed.

She started with studies. His eyes. His hands. His chest. One foot. The hair that ran down his rippled abdomen to swirl around his penis.

She knew she was good at retrieving mental images, often able to recall details that other people had forgotten, but she was amazed at how clear the picture of Harry was in her memory. As she worked, she knew that this particular image— him in her bed, watching her—would never fade.

The thought terrified her. Without pausing, she flipped to another page and started a full sketch. She forced her emotions into the drawing, her pencil moving faster and faster.

After a little while, she shifted from the sofa to a straight-backed chair she had set up at her workbench, impatiently clearing away the stuff on top, so she had a clean surface to work on. Time became meaningless, and she was only dimly aware of the sun moving outside the window.

Her fingers cramped, her back aching, she finally sat back and stared at what she'd done.

"Beautiful."

The image of him nude, yards of skin that would glow with color, sprawled on her bed, was a temptation even though it was composed only of pencil lines and shadows at the moment. Looking at the drawing, she saw her own fear, her own longing. His strength and vulnerability. The wariness and welcome in his eyes.

He might not tell her his secrets—not yet—but she had this much of him. She needed to paint this. She had to bring it even more fully into the world.

Shoving the chair aside, she was sorting through her assortment of blank canvases to find one she wanted to use when there was a brief knock, and the door of the studio opened.

Startled, she straightened and turned to see her mother step inside.

Now there was panic of a different sort. Jenny glanced at the sketch pad lying on the workbench and was relieved to see she'd put it face down when she'd gotten up as opposed to open to the drawing of naked Harry.

Jackie didn't come very far into the space, probably because her boots were muddy. She just closed the door against the chilly wind and leaned against the wall, arms crossed and eyebrows raised.

"Not even a 'hello'?" she asked dryly, and Jenny realized she'd been staring.

"Sorry, sorry." She put down the canvas she was holding and went to her mother, giving her a tight hug and a kiss on the cheek. "I'm just distracted. You're early."

She thought. She'd lost track of time again.

"Not that early. I wanted to get back before dark."

"Sure." Jenny could have kicked herself. If there was any way to arouse her mother's suspicion, it was to act the way she was acting. "Sorry," she repeated. "I've been working."

"Oh. Starting something new?" Jackie might not always approve of Jenny's artistic ambitions, but she knew very well how insane her daughter could get at the beginning of a project.

"Yeah."

"Well, I can't wait to see it." Jackie straightened. "I should let you get back to it, then. We'll talk later."

The guilty knowledge that Jackie was *never* going to see this particular painting, combined with the thread of disappointment she could plainly hear in her mother's voice had Jenny shaking her head.

"No, it's okay. I should take a break anyway." Now that she'd stopped, she could feel the soreness in her hands and shoulders. "I want to hear all about your visit with Uncle Bill and Aunt Noreen."

"Well, I didn't kill them, but it was close. Absence makes the heart grow fonder and all that." Jackie studied her. "Want to come in and get something to eat?"

"What time is it?" Jenny walked back to get her cell phone and check.

Jackie smiled. "It's early, but I'm starving, and I'll bet you haven't eaten all day." She opened the studio door. "Come on in and I'll tell you about Bill's new addiction to *Call of Duty* because he is apparently thirteen years old. Then you can tell me what you've been up to."

Uh...no. No, she couldn't.

"I'll be right there."

As they sat and talked at the old wooden kitchen table over spaghetti and meatballs, Jenny thought about how nice it was to just take some time to catch up with her mother. Plus, she really had been hungry.

It wasn't so nice to have to avoid talking about what she'd been doing while Jackie had been away. Talk about awkward. But she managed to steer clear for the most part by talking about painting and how people liked June's photos at the Country Time and other things her mother didn't give a shit about.

Once dinner was over, and the kitchen was cleaned up, Jenny decided to head back out to her studio.

"Since it's still early, I'm going to work for a bit," she told her mother. "If I don't see you before you go to bed, I'll see you in the morning."

"Okay. Just try not to lose track of time again," Jackie warned. "Remember, you have to get up for work."

"Right." Jenny wasn't thrilled at the thought of answering phones and working on a computer, but at least she'd see Harry again.

Back at her easel, Jenny found the wild energy she'd felt that afternoon had been dampened by her mother's return and the awkward reality of her situation. So she reluctantly put the sketches of Harry aside and went back to work on the landscape of Hardy Falls.

26

After Harry finished his text conversation with Jenny that morning at the police station, he'd felt antsy and unsatisfied. Plus, he had a hard-on that wouldn't quit thanks to a sexy picture sent by a little witch.

It took everything he had not to just say the hell with it all and go track her down. But of course he couldn't.

Closing his eyes, he concentrated on some of the deep breathing exercises he'd taught himself after he'd crashed and burned in his first year of college. His girlfriend at the time had told him he was meditating, but Harry didn't put much faith in that woo-woo shit. All he knew was that if he focused on breathing and not on thinking, he could usually get himself under control.

This time it had taken longer than normal to find his calm because he kept thinking about that picture of a naked Jenny Kline smiling like a siren in her rumpled bed, showing him her pretty breasts. Seducing him. He did not have a clue how he'd managed to keep his hands off her this long.

Harry started counting backward from one thousand.

Fortunately, he'd managed to control his body, if not his

mind, by the time Bethany came back from the bakery. Smiling like an eager puppy, she reminded him that he had to focus on the job and training her. He could not think about the woman who'd reached out for him, moaned for him, held him.

Christ.

"Let's get out of here," he told Bethany, standing and grabbing a donut at random from the bag. He shoved most of it into his mouth before they headed out to the police vehicle. As they drove around town, he tried to help the younger officer see it the way a cop had to look at it, not like someone who'd lived there her whole life.

Hardy Falls might look like a postcard, but it wasn't one. No town Harry had ever lived in was that simple. There was always darkness underneath, wasn't there?

Bethany left at the end of her shift, but Harry worked late because he really did need to clean up some paperwork. It was after six by the time he said goodbye to Bert and headed to his Jeep.

He pulled out his phone and texted Jenny as soon as he closed the driver's door.

Leaving now. Is your mother home?

The answer came almost at once.

Yes. She got back a few hours ago.

Harry had expected it, but hearing the chief was back still made him feel edgy and out of sorts for no good reason.

I wish I could see you.

There was a pause.

We'll be at work tomorrow.

Even in a text message, he could sense she was as frustrated as he was. He thought for a moment.

Maybe we can have lunch.

This time, there was a slightly longer pause before her message came.

Lunch? Or something else?

Harry smiled because Jenny was a very smart lady. With the way he was feeling, she was right to assume that *lunch* wasn't what would happen. He figured that if they were careful and there weren't any emergencies, they could easily get to his apartment from the police station without anyone noticing. And his bed.

Dangerous, his sensible side warned.

But the boy who'd lived with Junior once upon a time didn't care.

Honestly, neither did the man.

We'll see.

Yes, we will.

Yes, they would. And Harry would be seeing all of her beautiful body if he had anything to say about it.

Have a good night, sweetheart. The endearment felt natural.

She sent him some heart emojis. Then she sent an eggplant, and it made him grin.

Harry sat in his Jeep for a few more minutes. He could feel his restlessness vibrating against his skin and knew he couldn't just go home tonight—he had to *do* something.

He could go check up on his grandparents, but that was a bad idea for a lot of reasons. His grandmother might be oblivious, but his grandfather would take one look at him and know something was going on—especially if he saw the hickey. Then the old man would badger him until Harry slipped up and told him about the phone conversation with Junior or the night with Jenny. Or both.

It would be safer to go to the bowling alley. Danny and Lucio would probably be there again—the kids basically lived in the arcade on the weekends—and he felt bad about the night before. He might need to mend some fences. At the very least, he could play a few games of pinball and distract himself.

But he'd definitely stay away from the bar today.

Harry stopped by his apartment to change out of his

uniform and studied his freshly made bed, impatient because he wanted Jenny to be naked in those clean sheets with him tonight.

Tomorrow, he promised himself. It had been a while since he'd managed a nooner, but they were both clever people. They'd make it work.

Heading for the door, he grabbed his leather jacket and left.

When he pulled into the Murphy Lanes parking lot a few minutes later, he saw it was full again. Not a surprise. Pat did good business during the week with the bowling leagues, but the weekends were all about families. After he parked, he got out of the Jeep and followed a mother and two young boys through the glass entry doors into the lobby. The kids ran for the cashier at the shoe rental counter, their resigned mother lagging behind, and Harry turned to the arcade.

All of the flashing lights were bright and distracting, so it took a minute for him to see the cluster of middle school-aged kids hanging around the new pinball machine they'd all been playing the night before. Danny's red hair was easy to spot in the group, and, smiling, Harry moved toward them. If Danny was there, Lucio would be, too. Their foster mother had told Harry once that she always brought both boys to the arcade because if one came, the other whined within ten minutes, even if he hadn't initially wanted to come.

"Hey," he said as he walked up to the kids. All of the regulars were there: six boys and three girls. One of the girls, Skipper, actually loved the arcade, but he suspected the other two weren't as interested in the machines as they were in the boys. And he was sure some of the boys were only there because of the girls.

Kids.

Adults, too, he reminded himself.

"Officer Harry." Danny's smile, usually as bright as his hair, dimmed when he saw Harry. He and Lucio exchanged a glance. "Didn't expect you today."

The other kids were uncharacteristically silent, and Harry stilled. He had the feeling they'd all scatter if he tried to take another step forward. All of them were looking at him with a wariness in their faces that he hadn't seen for months.

Goddamn it.

"I promised you a rematch," he told Danny, keeping his voice easy and his stance casual, as he leaned against one of the other machines. Inside, he was anything but nonchalant, his stomach twisting at the evidence of how badly he'd screwed up.

Danny exchanged another look with Lucio. The rest of the kids shifted around but didn't say anything.

"'s okay, man," Danny said, not meeting Harry's eyes. "Don't worry about it."

"I thought you were looking forward to getting some of your own back," Harry said, pushing, trying to get the boy to talk to him.

"Changed my mind," Danny said, looking down and away and anywhere but at Harry.

"Yeah," Lucio put in. "I mean, you practically pulled out the machine because I beat you." He glanced at his friends for support, and Harry saw the tension in his thin shoulders. "You do that again, we could get kicked out for life."

"Not too much else to do around this town," One of the boys, Mickey, put in. He was small with a thin face that was the same deep, rich brown as a walnut. "What are we supposed to do if we get banned?"

"I was out of line," Harry told them. "I was acting like an asshole. It won't happen again."

He could tell that none of them believed him, and that was another blow.

"I beat you fair and square," Lucio repeated. Now that he'd

started talking, the resentment bubbled out in an uncontrolled flood, easy to hear. "I beat you, and you went fucking ballistic."

"I smelled alcohol on you, man," Danny added, his voice small. He had his arms folded over his thin chest and was trying to look belligerent instead of scared. "I didn't know you drank."

"I normally don't," Harry reassured the boy quickly. Danny was almost phobic when it came to drunks, and for a good reason. "Something happened, and I wasn't handling it right."

The kids looked at each other.

"You told us that it was stupid to drink or get high when stuff happened," Mickey said after a moment.

"Well, it wasn't smart," Harry pointed out. "Look at what happened."

The kids were quiet again, shuffling their feet and refusing to meet his eyes. It fucking killed him. He'd been working with them for so long getting them to trust him, to talk to him, to confide in him. Lucio had even started to relax around him. And now look at them, not even willing to make eye contact.

"You always told us we shouldn't care if we lose," Skipper whispered. "But then you almost tipped the machine." She was skinny, dressed in ragged jeans that looked like they'd been handed down or bought at a thrift store. Her mother had put out a restraining order on her uncle after he'd tried to shake her down for money a few months ago and then beat her up when she didn't have any to give him.

"I'm sorry for the way I acted," Harry told them. He knew some people didn't believe in apologizing to children, but he'd been a jackass. Who the hell cared if he was the adult and they were middle schoolers? Wrong was wrong. And he'd been wrong. He should never have been in their company after he'd been drinking, feeling the way he'd been feeling.

"I wasn't drunk," he said, waiting until Danny glanced up to make sure he made eye contact. "I'd had a few drinks, but I wasn't drunk. You know that."

Danny's freckles were stark, and his blue eyes were wide as they searched his face. He nodded once.

Lucio was still puffed up like a little pigeon, his dark hair a riot of curls.

"You just don't want us to tell anyone," he challenged. "If we say you were drunk, you'll get fired." This kid, a transplant from Scranton who'd lucked into the best foster home in the region, was definitely the alpha of the group. But even when Harry had first met him, he hadn't been fooled by the aggression. He could see the fear lurking underneath. He'd seen the same fear in the mirror countless times before he'd moved in with his grandparents.

"Yeah, I might get in trouble if you say something," Harry admitted honestly. Chief Kline would *not* be pleased. "But I'm not going to ask you to lie about it."

"Why not?" Lucio demanded, arms crossed and feet planted firmly on the floor.

"Because I was drinking, and I did try to toss the machine," Harry said. "If I have to take some lumps for it, I'll take them."

He would not ask these children to lie or be quiet. If they talked, they talked.

The kids didn't seem to know how to handle his candor. They shuffled their feet some more.

Danny looked at Lucio. "He's telling the truth that he wasn't drunk," he said at last. "I know he wasn't."

"He practically lifted that machine right off the floor," Lucio pointed out. "If he had, Pat would have kicked us all out forever."

"But he didn't."

"Only 'cause that chick came to get him."

"I'll never drink before I hang out with you guys again," Harry promised.

The kids' expressions were a mixture of relief and skepticism. Lucio stared at him for a long, long time, and Harry held his breath. If Lucio turned away, they all would. He'd have to start from ground zero. Probably below ground zero because this group had learned very well not to give second chances.

"Best out of three?" Lucio said, finally.

Harry's entire body sagged in relief.

"Yeah. Let's see if you can beat me again, sucker."

Lucio smirked, and it was the most beautiful thing Harry had ever seen.

"You wish, copper."

Harry stayed with them for a couple of hours playing pinball and some other games. He tried to act the way he always did, throwing himself into whatever it was the kids wanted to play.

But it was different now.

The kids laughed and cheered, but usually just each other. They didn't insult him good-naturedly the way they'd always done before. Their bodies were stiffer, their movements less relaxed. They left space around him instead of thumping into him to try to throw him off. He got the feeling they were waiting for him to snap at them or try to tilt the machine.

Even worse, he couldn't tell whether they'd agreed to let him stay with them because they wanted to, or because they didn't feel like they had a choice.

It killed him to see a gap that hadn't been there before.

After Lucio beat him at *Deadpool* pinball again—the kid really was that good—and Danny had squeaked out a win in their rematch, Harry said his goodbyes. He was very careful to keep a smile on his face the entire time.

"This isn't over," he said to Lucio, pointing his finger at the boy. "You shall not prevail."

"Oh, right, sucker!" Lucio laughed, but there was a false note in the sound that scraped Harry raw.

"I have to get out of here," he told them. "See you guys next week."

"Sure," Lucio said.

As he left, Harry wondered if they'd all be there next week. He wondered if they'd find some other place to hang out, something else to do. Lord only knew what this group would get into if they didn't feel like the bowling alley was a safe space.

"Leaving so soon, Newman?" Richie Dunlop called from his seat at the shoe counter. His rat-like face looked smug. "Sure you don't want a drink?"

Harry wanted to go over to the guy and release some of his frustration by pounding him into the floor, but that would have been supremely stupid, so he ignored him and walked out to his Jeep. Once in the driver's seat, he just sat for a moment.

His lack of control the night before had cost him dearly with those kids. Kids who needed him, whether they knew it or not. They needed an adult they could talk to, someone who understood their lives. He'd been just like them at one point.

And that crack from Richie Dunlop showed him the kids weren't the only ones who'd seen him drinking.

Harry gripped the wheel so tightly he hurt his hands. Then he started the engine and pulled out of the parking lot.

He didn't want to go home and sit alone in his tiny apartment. Not now, when the tornado inside him had started to blow again.

It wasn't until he'd parked the Jeep in the little park a few blocks away from Jenny's house that he realized where he wanted to be.

This was bad. He couldn't see her tonight, and especially not here—not at her house when the chief was home. Not now. Not like this.

He'd scared those kids. The way he'd been scared. Worse, he'd disappointed them. The way he'd been disappointed.

He got out of the Wrangler and started walking through the shadowed streets.

Dangerous, the practical side of his brain warned. *Discretion*.

He didn't care.

When he got to the Kline house, he saw the chief's big Explorer in the driveway next to Jenny's pickup truck. There were lights on inside, but the upstairs was dark.

Cursing himself for being an idiot, he walked around the house, careful to avoid the security lights, and saw the shed in the backyard where the chief had told him Jenny had her studio. Light was shining through the blinds in the single window, glowing in the darkness. More than likely, Jenny was inside.

Harry walked down the hill.

27

Jenny stepped away from the easel and brushed her hair from her face with the back of her wrist. She put down the palette and brush, and absently flexed her cramped hands as she contemplated the canvas.

The winter landscape of downtown Hardy Falls was done, she thought. Sometimes it was hard to tell, but she usually had a feeling when a painting was finished. This one looked complete and bright, the buildings on Main Street recognizable but still more impressionistic than realistic. It did *not* look like a finger painting.

She guessed she was happy with it.

Blowing out a breath, she turned to her workbench and began to clean up.

There was a tenseness in her tonight, a desire to do something—anything. If she was a runner, she would have gone out and raced through the dark streets until she didn't have any breath left, and her muscles ached.

Too bad exercising always made her feel like her intestines were going to explode.

Well, she could go to Harry's apartment and have sex. THAT exercise would relax her.

She paused, shivering at the thought, then continued with what she was doing.

It would be a bad idea and, anyway, Harry hadn't asked her to come to his place, had he? *Because,* she reminded herself impatiently, he was trying to be *careful.* She was just going to have to learn to deal with that aspect of their relationship.

Or whatever it was they were involved in.

A sudden knock on her studio door surprised the hell out of her. She jolted so violently that she almost knocked over a container of turpentine as she turned, eyes wide.

What the...?

Her mother wouldn't have knocked, and anyway, Jackie had said she was going to her bedroom to read and watch television when Jenny had come out to her studio earlier. If she wanted anything, she would have just called or sent a text. Josie probably wouldn't have knocked either. Maybe this time it really was an ax murderer.

Hands trembling, Jenny picked up her framing hammer. It was lightweight and basically worthless as a weapon, but it was the best she could do unless she wanted to douse the intruder in turpentine and set them on fire.

Probably not a good idea before she found out who it was.

"Jenny." A low masculine voice came from outside and made her freeze again. "I'm coming in. Don't hit me with anything."

"Harry?" she gasped, a new kind of tension making her weak. "Is that you?"

The door opened, and Harry slid in, closing it quickly behind him.

"My mother is right there in the house, you know," she pointed out as she went to him, although he'd probably been invisible walking across the dark yard in his black leather jacket and black jeans. "Are you insane?"

"Maybe. Probably. I don't know." He rolled his shoulders and nodded toward the old sofa. "Okay if I sit?"

Jenny didn't have a clue what was going on, but she shrugged.

"Sure."

Maneuvering through the tight space, Harry took off his jacket and threw it to the side, then dropped heavily onto the sofa. He leaned forward with his hands clasped between his knees, his khaki-colored T-shirt stretched over his broad shoulders.

"What's wrong?" she asked when he didn't say anything.

"Nothing."

Oh, that was such a load of crap.

"Harry," Jenny said, sitting next to him. "Why are you here?"

Instead of answering her question, he looked at her and then reached up to run his fingertip along her cheekbone. "You've got spots."

"What? Oh. Paint." She rubbed at her face. "Occupational hazard. I always have paint on me somewhere.

"Hmmm." His eyes took on that glow she already recognized. "Maybe I should look for more." His smile was slow and seductive. "Least I can do."

"Wait." She grabbed his hands when he shifted toward her and stopped him. He quirked his head, and she saw his surprise.

"What?" he demanded.

"Don't try to distract me. Just tell me why you changed your mind about coming here tonight."

His smile was sharp. "Why do you think?" He reached for her again. Again she pulled away.

Something was wrong, that much was clear. He was acting

strange, unsettled. Almost the same way he'd been the night before at the bowling alley, although she didn't think he'd been drinking today.

And, once again, he wasn't telling her what had happened.

Jenny drew in a breath.

He hadn't talked to her last night. He wasn't talking to her now. Although her body was already humming thanks to his proximity, she knew she couldn't let things keep going this way. She needed more than just sex from him.

He could break her heart if she let him.

"I'm not here for your convenience, Harry," she said quietly. "I'm not someone who's just going to be available whenever you decide you're ready to blow off a little steam. Find another woman, if that's what you want."

"What are you talking about?" he demanded, shoving to his feet to prowl through the small, crowded space. "You? Convenient? That's a laugh."

She refused to let that hurt her and watched him pace as she held one wrist tightly with the opposite hand so she wouldn't reach out for him.

"Your other women might not have cared if you just popped by for sex when you needed it. It might not have mattered to them if you didn't give them anything else, but that's not who I am," she told him honestly. "If that's what you want, this whole thing was a mistake." A mistake that could already devastate her, and she'd been down this road before. "And you should either sit down or leave so my mother doesn't look out and see your shadow on the blinds," she added.

His face was impassive when he glanced at the window. "There's no shadow." But to Jenny's relief, he sank back down beside her on the sofa. Instead of trying to touch her, he leaned forward again, elbows on his knees, hands clasped.

"I don't know why I came here," he admitted after another

moment. "I was driving around and before I knew it, I was heading for your house."

"Where's your Jeep?"

"Same place as last night. At that little park." He looked around her studio. "This is nice. It looks like you."

"Thanks."

She made herself wait because the next step was Harry's. He didn't look at her, focusing on his hands as the silence stretched out between them. Just when she didn't think she could take it anymore, he finally glanced her way.

"When I finished work today, I went to the bowling alley arcade to see the kids."

"Oh." In spite of how upset he obviously was, Jenny felt a weight lift because he was finally opening up to her. "I take it the kids weren't happy to see you?" she asked, prodding gently. She could have guessed that things would not go well with them. She'd had a clear view of their faces the night before, and she'd seen how they'd watched him.

Harry sighed.

"Yeah. No. I've been working with that group for over a year, trying to get them to look at me as someone they can trust, and I think I really blew it. Most of them haven't had great experiences with adults."

"Is this part of the police department's community outreach?" She wanted to stroke her hand down the line of his back to comfort him, to feel his strength through the cotton material of his shirt. But she held off, not wanting to interrupt.

"I guess it's kind of a community outreach, but it's something I do on my own time," Harry said. "I met Danny and Lucio when their school guidance counselor contacted me. The Johnsons had just brought Lucio into their foster home. Danny was already there, and the two were having a pissing contest to see who was top dog. It was turning into a real mess. I took them out and introduced them to pinball." He grinned suddenly. "I'm good at pinball, so I could beat their asses no problem. They had to band together against me."

"You didn't let them win to build up their self-esteem?" she asked.

"Nah. These kids would see right through that. Gotta earn respect. And Lucio, for one, was right on the cusp of going down a pretty dark path when the Johnsons got him out of Scranton. He was hard to crack. Danny was almost as bad. But I could relate, so I knew how to talk to them."

Jenny nodded, intrigued. "You could relate?" she asked softly, moving until her bent knee touched the hardness of his thigh.

He watched her, his eyes turbulent.

"I was exactly like them," he told her. "Once upon a time."

Jenny straightened a little in surprise.

"I can't believe Harry Senior would have put up with that," she said with certainty. She'd heard through the grapevine that Harry had been raised by his grandparents until he'd gone off to college. The old man would never have tolerated his grandson living in the conditions she knew some of those kids at the arcade had dealt with.

"Harry Senior had nothing to do with it," his grandson said. "I didn't live with my grandparents until I was eight years old. Before that, I was with my father in California." He smiled slightly, even as he watched her. "Harry Newman Jr., or Junior for short. We lack a certain amount of imagination when it comes to names in my family."

Jenny frowned. "I thought your parents were dead." She guessed that had just been an assumption on her part.

"Nope. Sadly they are alive and well but, thank Christ, still in California."

"Your mother, too?" Jenny asked.

"Oh, sure. She's out there somewhere." Harry waved that away. "I never had much to do with her—she always just came and went. Junior kept me because he knew he could use me to get money out of the old man."

Jenny sat back against the arm of the sofa, trying to wrap her mind around what he was telling her. "What does your father do in California?" she asked.

"Junior? He drinks. Some drugs." He shrugged. "Supposedly, he's still playing bass with the piece of shit heavy metal rock band he's been with for years. Mostly in LA."

"Supposedly?" That was a strange way to put it.

"Yeah, well." Harry frowned down at his hands again. "He called me yesterday looking for money. Usually he hits up my grandfather, and sometimes he can still talk Pops into coughing up some cash. I haven't heard from Junior directly since I became a cop, so it's been years." He glanced up, smile sharp. "Neither of my parents are thrilled with my career choice."

This explained a hell of a lot.

"Anyway," Harry continued, "when we were talking, he basically let it slip that the band's not around anymore. I'm not sure how long it's been since that happened. I know my grandparents think Junior is still out west chasing his dream." He looked at her again. "Pops doesn't know any of this, by the way, so keep it to yourself."

"Okay."

"I shouldn't have told you either. I don't know why I did. What the hell does it matter what my loser father does?" He ran his hands through his hair, tousling it further. "Christ."

"Well, this does answer the question of why you were drinking yesterday," Jenny said carefully.

"Yeah. Like you said, that's not normal for me. But after the phone call, I drank more than usual, and I scared those kids." He rubbed his hands roughly over his face. "Danny's father used to get drunk and beat him up before Child Protective Services stepped in, and I don't even want to know what Lucio's been through."

"Mickey's mother drinks," Jenny said quietly.

"I know. We're keeping an eye on her, but it's getting worse. And Skipper's uncle...Jesus. So me drinking and losing control at the bowling alley in front of them all was basically the worse thing I could have done."

"That's tough." Jenny reached out to smooth her hand over the rounded muscle of his shoulder. "What will you do now?"

Harry looked up and met her eyes, and suddenly she forgot her question.

"Start again," he murmured. "What else?"

"Oh."

As she stared into his shadowed face, Jenny was intensely aware of a new sense of connection between them, of a door that had been opened. And she found herself focusing on her hand on his shoulder, the flex of his muscles, and the hot male flesh under the thin T-shirt. Her breathing deepened. His eyes dropped to her breasts, and his attention was so intense that it made her nipples harden.

"Will the chief come out here tonight looking for you?" he asked.

"Probably not," she told him.

"But she *might* come out here."

"I guess there's always a chance."

"How good a chance?"

"I don't...Harry..."

"Oh, hell." He grabbed her and hauled her over and into his lap. "I know, I know. Not the time or the place, and I swear I didn't come here just for sex. I swear I don't look at you that way. I swear it. But I'm here..." he kissed her. "You're here..." he kissed her again. "I need..." Kiss.

Jenny pulled back and looked down into his face, her own slightly higher in this position.

"Not just a convenience?" she asked, wanting to be absolutely certain.

"No."

"I meant what I said, you know."

"I know." He leaned forward to run his mouth over her jawline before sitting back again. "It's hard...I don't...I normally only talk to my grandparents. I have no clue why I told you all that stuff."

It was the confusion she saw on his face that convinced her he was being truthful. Aware she'd been given a gift, she bent down to kiss him, sucking on his lips and tongue, clutching at his head to keep him in place.

She had her thighs spread on either side of his so she could feel the evidence of his growing arousal pressed intimately to her center. His hands moved over her thighs, around to her butt, and he squeezed, kneading her flesh restlessly for a moment.

She sighed into his mouth as his hand drifted to her front, moving under her loose T-shirt and the waistband of her old, baggy jeans. The feeling of his fingers, rough and hot against her stomach had her jerking her head back to suck in air, her abdomen moving in and out.

"Jenny...?" he breathed.

"Yes," she murmured.

She still didn't know what this thing was between them, but she wouldn't turn him away. Not now when he'd trusted her enough to share a piece of himself with her.

"Thank God."

He took control of the kiss, ate at her, drew her tongue in to play with his, and then pulled away.

"I think we're going to need to be clever about this thing," he murmured, and she felt him undo the button of her jeans before sliding down the zipper.

"Oh, do you?" She ran her nails down his chest and over his pectorals, enjoying the feeling of warm skin beneath the thin cloth. She paused at the top of his jeans and, mimicking his action, popped open the button to slip her hand inside.

He jerked, and she rocked against him, his hardness and her own hand pressing in between their bodies causing her to close her eyes at the pleasure of it.

"Jenny." Harry's hands were under her T-shirt, stroking up to cup her breasts through her soft, old bra. He plumped them, caressed them, and then yanked her shirt over her head. He reached back to unhook the bra.

She didn't help him, just luxuriated in the sensation of his calloused hands on her, bringing every centimeter of her skin to life.

After he tugged the straps of the bra off her shoulders, he tossed it away and cupped her breasts again, squeezing them.

"Harry," she moaned.

"What?" he murmured, pulling her nipples, then coaxing her forward so he could draw one into his mouth.

"God!" Her spine arched when he tugged that nipple with his teeth, tormented it with his tongue before letting it slip out of his mouth so he could turn to the other. She put her hands on his shoulders to brace herself, squirming on him as she tried to rub herself against him, whimpering.

"Need something, darling?" He left her breast to whisper in her ear, his voice so dark and silky it should be illegal.

"Yes, you bastard," she gasped.

"I think you have on too many clothes."

She muttered a protest, but let him urge her off his lap, and then help her quickly strip off her jeans and underwear and socks. In less than a heartbeat, she was naked. He settled back on the sofa, still fully clothed, and looked up at her, his broad chest heaving in and out with the harshness of his breathing, the bulge in his jeans impressive evidence of how much he wanted her.

"Come here." He pulled her to him to straddle his lap again, the scratch of denim against her tender, naked skin arousing beyond belief. "So beautiful."

She was glad he thought so. Rising above him, she put her hands on his shoulders as his mouth moved over her neck to suckle her breasts again—first one, then the other. He stroked his hand up her back, then down to her butt, squeezing the rounded skin before returning to the front and moving down.

Then, at last—at last—his fingers were right where she needed them, sliding through the liquid in the delicate folds to rub the bundle of nerves that was the center of her pleasure.

"Jesus!" She moved against him as he played with her, but he kept her in place with effortless strength. And she let him do whatever he wanted with her because, holy cow, the man sure knew what he was doing.

He tormented her for endless moments before pressing one finger deep inside her, his lips and tongue continuing their torment of her breasts. Jenny threw her head back, grabbed his hair, and rode the sensation—rode his hand, his thighs, his mouth. She hovered on her peak, straining towards it for a long instant. Then her orgasm shattered through her, the world breaking apart around her in shards of gold and silver while she undulated above him.

When she came back to herself, she blinked down at Harry and realized he was watching her intently, his face flushed, eyes hungry. Shuddering, he pulled back a little bit and frantically worked at unzipping his jeans.

Once Jenny's brain cells were functioning enough to understand what he was doing, she sat back on his knees and helped him drag his jeans and briefs down his hard thighs. Then she wrapped her hands around his long, thick erection, pulling up and down until he leaned his head against the sofa and groaned.

"This is...going to be over...soon if you don't...stop...," he panted, even as his hips rose to follow the tug of her hands.

Her mouth was watering with the desire to taste him, but she saw the color riding high on his cheekbones and the veins standing out in his neck and knew he was at the edge of his control.

"Condom?" she asked breathily. She was on the pill, and she trusted him, but going without protection wasn't something they'd discussed.

"Pocket."

He gripped her hips with a desperation she knew was going to leave bruises while she dug around in his jeans pocket and found the little foil package. Some women might have thought the fact that he'd come to her ready to rumble was a little presumptuous, but Jenny appreciated his preparation. She quickly unsealed the condom and rolled it on.

Her body liquid and ready, she boosted herself up and sank down on him, inch by inch...by inch. When she finally hit bottom, they both moaned.

"You're so big this way," she whispered as she leaned down to kiss him, all teeth and tongue and need. He broke away after a moment.

"Ride me, baby," he told her, his grin was wicked and wild, his eyes a rim of pure blue around the black of his dilated pupils.

So Jenny did.

Her legs and thighs were strong from years of hard work, and her motivation was just as powerful. She worked him hard until he gasped her name, wild with pleasure, his hands moving everywhere to encourage her—breasts, ass, legs. She felt his whole body tighten.

"Jenny," he warned desperately.

"I'll go when you do," she told him.

A few more strokes and he couldn't hold back any longer. He went over into his climax with a curse. And, true to her word, Jenny did too, her body spiraling out of control again for a long moment before, panting and sweaty and satisfied, she came down from the peak of pleasure and collapsed against his chest.

28

After the mind-blowing explosion of her orgasm, Jenny lay panting and disoriented, moving only when Harry eventually shifted her off his lap so he could deal with the condom. She rolled over to watch, enjoying that he looked rumpled and sexy and that she'd left marks on his skin with her teeth.

She might be feeling just a little primal.

Once he'd disposed of the used condom, he quickly adjusted his clothes and sat back beside her where she'd curled up, still naked, on the sofa. He put his large, warm hand on the bare skin of her thigh, caressing her while his eyes moved over her, glinting with appreciation.

"I forgot to tell you how much I liked that picture you texted me this morning," he said, his voice a deep and husky.

"Did you now?" She knew she sounded smug, but she couldn't help it.

"Mmmmm. The reality is better." He bent and kissed her.

Jenny longed to have him again, to take and be taken. And, *God*, she wanted to paint him.

Suddenly all of the creative energy she'd felt earlier came

roaring back to life, swamping her. While her memory was excellent, and the drawings she'd done of Harry earlier were good, they weren't enough—not nearly enough. She needed —*needed*—to capture the strength, the emotion she saw in him at this moment. Her hands twitched with the demand that she get a canvas and her brushes so she could try to hold on to this instant, this image. This man.

Driven by the necessity, Jenny pulled away. Harry smiled at her with a little confusion as he tucked a strand of hair behind her ear.

"What?"

No, she wouldn't ask him to sit while she painted, she decided. It would take too long. The moment might slip away before she caught it—she could already sense it flowing through her fingers like water.

"I have to sketch you," she told him.

His eyes widened in surprise and maybe consternation as she sprang to her feet. Snatching up her old, oversized T-shirt from where he'd thrown it, she yanked it on over her head.

"Wait," he said.

She ignored him, found the sketch pad and pencils she'd been using earlier in the day, and impatiently flipped to a blank page. Focusing her attention on his strong features, she began drawing quickly, trying to catch him in the lines. He said something else, but she didn't hear him, too immersed in what she saw in his face. The lingering heat. The expression in his eyes. His frown. He was open and closed. Vulnerable and guarded. A mystery.

Harry.

The floor lamp next to the sofa cast a soft light on his skin, created shadows in the dip beneath his mouth and the creases fanning out from his eyes. Frustrated, Jenny longed for color to show that golden skin and hair against the coarse fabric of the couch, the darkness of the protective shadows.

Maybe she could ask him to take off his clothes so she could see—

Abruptly, Harry stood and pulled the sketch pad away from her.

"What are you doing?" Jenny tried to grab it back, but he wouldn't let her.

"Stop!" he ordered.

"What?" She blinked up at him. "Why?"

"I don't want you drawing me," he said, clearly exasperated. "Which I've been trying to tell you, but you haven't been listening."

That got her attention, and she gaped at him, surprised. "Really?"

"Yes! It's kind of freaking me out to have you staring at me like I'm a...a frog you're dissecting." His voice was gruff.

For the first time, she saw that some of the lines in his face were from tension, and she realized the dull red along his cheekbones had nothing to do with passion and everything to do with embarrassment.

"Oh, God. I'm so sorry." Jenny felt horrible. It had not even occurred to her that he wouldn't be comfortable with her drawing him. Wincing, she put down the pencils and stood to face him.

"It's okay. It's just strange." He turned the sketch pad around so he could study what she'd done.

Jenny opened her mouth to tell him that she didn't let anyone see her works in progress but then closed it again immediately. After all, he was the one who owned the face she'd been sketching without permission.

"I guess this drawing's pretty good," he admitted after a moment, and she had to smile at the reluctant acknowledgment.

"What," she teased, "did you think I was drawing stick figures?"

"No, I know you're good." Before she could stop him, he started flipping through more pages. Then he froze, and she saw his eyes go huge with shock.

Shit.

Jenny sighed. She didn't even have to look—she knew Harry had just come across one of the nude sketches that she'd done of him earlier.

He looked up and pinned her with a hard glare.

"What the hell is this?" His voice was harsher than she'd ever heard it.

That wasn't good.

Jenny forced a smile. "Isn't it obvious?"

"I guess." He scowled at the sketch, then, slowly, turned a few more pages, hesitating over more than one. Finally, he met her eyes again. "When did you do these?"

"Earlier today. After we texted."

He drew himself up, suddenly all cop. "Did you take photographs of me when I wasn't looking? Is that what you used for these drawings?"

"Of course not." She scowled at him, offended. "I have a good memory."

Still not smiling, Harry closed the sketch pad. He was definitely not pleased.

Cursing herself for her stupidity and wondering if she'd ruined everything, Jenny quickly pulled on her jeans, wanting to be wearing more than just a T-shirt.

This time when she reached for the sketch pad, he let her take it.

"I guess you don't want me drawing you that way either, huh?" she asked when he didn't say anything, trying to lighten the mood. It didn't work. Harry's expression when he looked at her was blank and closed. After the open ease of a few minutes ago, it felt like a punch in the gut.

"A naked sketch of me floating around Hardy Falls, especially one that shows everything I own, is not a good thing, no," he said at last.

"I'm sorry." She took a step closer to him and was glad that he didn't move away. "I didn't even think about it," she confessed. "These drawings are just for me. I swear to you that nobody else will ever see any of them. I just...wanted to remember." She hugged the sketch pad to her chest.

Harry's stern features softened a little, and he reached out to touch her cheek with a gentle finger. "I know you wouldn't intentionally show anyone, and God knows you're talented. But, Jesus, Jenny. Honey, you drew my freaking dong! In great detail! More than once! You drew me in bed after we...and I can't take the chance someone else will come across these sketches. I can't risk anyone else seeing them. Do you understand?"

She studied him.

"You want me to rip them up, don't you?" she asked after a moment, hoping she was wrong, but it was obvious that he did.

"Yeah."

Her heart hitched. She'd be able to recreate them if she wanted to, of course. Some images just stayed with you. But it wouldn't be the same.

"All of them? Even the ones that are just studies of your face?"

He grimaced. "If I'm being honest, I'm not thrilled with them either. It's very odd to have you look at me as a...object. A thing."

It gave her some pause to hear that he felt that way. But, although a lot of people were flattered to be featured in a drawing or painting, some weren't. And it wasn't as if she'd asked how he felt about it before she'd done it.

Not giving herself a chance to think, she opened the sketch pad and ripped out all of the drawings she'd done of him. Then she tore them into pieces and threw the scraps in the can with the used condom.

Harry visibly relaxed.

"You can take the trash bag with you when you go," she told him, "so you won't have to wonder if I'll tape the pages back together after you left."

She tried to make it a joke, but it fell flat.

"Thank you." He sounded grateful, and for some reason that made her feel even worse.

She shrugged. It hurt that he didn't believe she'd never show them to anybody else. It hurt to know she didn't have this little piece of him to keep anymore. And it hurt to know that she *would* tape the sketches back together if he didn't take the scraps.

What did that say about her?

More, what did it say about how she was starting to feel about Harry? What did his reluctance to let her draw him at all —even just a sketch of his face—say about how he felt about her?

She didn't know. She was afraid to know.

Harry put his hands on her shoulders and pulled her close to him, looking down into her face, and Jenny wondered if this was it. If she'd completely blown it. *Hey, babe. Thanks for the great sex. See you at the office.*

"I love your paintings," Harry said.

She frowned up at him because that had come out of nowhere.

"Thank you?"

"I love the shapes and the colors and how they look like a place, but not quite."

"I'm glad."

"It's strange to have you drawing me, you know? But that doesn't mean I don't like what you do. I really like the one at the Country Time that looks like a sunrise," he continued. "I recognize the scene. I've been on that mountain at that time of day, and that's exactly the way it feels."

Feels. He'd said "feels," not "looks." That was exactly right.

It meant a lot to hear that he liked her art because it was an expression of the deepest part of herself. Something inside her relaxed, and she let herself lean into him as she slipped her arms around his waist.

Now that she took a minute to think about it, she guessed she could understand why Harry, a cop in a small town, wouldn't want to take the chance that someone would accidentally find nude sketches of him. It would be hard to write a traffic ticket for Mrs. Cahill if she was picturing your "dong" the whole time.

Jenny turned her head into his chest to hide her giggle, then rubbed against him like a cat until he growled and pulled her face up for a kiss.

This was no tentative kiss. It was not gentle. No, it was a hurricane of sudden need, a claiming thing with both of them striving to take. When they broke apart to breathe, Jenny was clinging to him.

"I can't," Harry said, sounding like he had rocks in his throat.

"Can't what?" she gasped.

"I can't stay any longer tonight. I'm already taking a chance being here."

Jenny gulped in some air. "I know."

He cupped her face in his palm and tilted it up for another long, slow kiss.

"But tomorrow, maybe we can have...lunch."

"At the Sunnyside?"

"I thought my apartment would be a better choice since I want to get you all naked again, and I don't want to shock Mrs. Dorinsky."

Jenny stared up into his eyes. Then she grinned.

"That sounds like an excellent plan."

Then she kissed him again.

When he gathered up the trash bag and left a few minutes later, she collapsed onto the sofa and closed her eyes.

She would paint him, Jenny thought. The sketches might be gone, but she remembered. Surely he wouldn't mind if she painted him with his clothes on. Well, most of his clothes on. Then she would always have him. Even if she was the only one who ever knew.

29

Two weeks later, Harry sat at his desk in the squad room and tried to focus on writing up a report on the attempted burglary he'd dealt with almost as soon as he'd walked in that morning to start his shift. The call had come in just before seven from the gas station and convenience store located across the highway from the Country Time. Tony, who was back from paternity leave and working nights, had still been in, so they'd both responded immediately.

Turned out, they hadn't needed to hurry. Mrs. Farrell, the sweet-looking, middle-aged woman who owned the station, had things well under control. The would-be robber, a thug from a nearby city, had thought he'd have an easy time knocking over the place. What he hadn't known was that Mrs. F. had been in the US Marines for twenty years and was well acquainted with both ends of a gun.

By the time Harry and Tony had gotten there, she'd the man hog-tied on the floor in the back room, and her husband, also a former marine, had come in from his job as an engineer to watch the cash register.

"Hopped up on meth," she'd said with a shrug when he'd asked her about the incident. "Nothing to it."

Right.

Trooper Jerold out of the Pennsylvania State Police barracks in Stroudsburg had come to pick up the guy, who apparently had a rap sheet as long as his arm and taken off with his prisoner an hour ago. Tony was long gone, happy to leave the paperwork for Harry. Jackie had gone somewhere before the trooper's arrival, and he wasn't sure when she'd be back.

But Jenny was out at the receptionist's desk.

They were alone in the station.

Knowing that wasn't helping Harry's concentration one little bit.

He sighed and leaned back in his chair, rubbing his eyes because the words on the screen were just a jumbled mess at this point. He could hear Jenny's voice as she soothed whoever it was she was talking to on the phone. As he had for the last hour, he restrained himself from going out to her.

It really shouldn't have been this hard to stick to his plan. He should have been able to treat Jenny like any other coworker when they were at the station together.

Maybe he should have known it wouldn't be easy when he couldn't stick to the original plan and keep his distance in the first damn place.

Getting up, he paced restlessly around the squad room. The buzzer rang out in the lobby, and he heard Jenny hang up the phone to go answer it.

It seemed like the more time they spent together—in bed and out of it—the harder it was for him to give off even the appearance of aloofness. It was some consolation that she was having a hard time, too. But they were going to have to be more careful, or even a blind gnat would be able to tell something was going on between them. Hell, even *Bert*, who had about the sensitivity of that blind gnat, had given him a knowing look the other day.

And the most frightening thing was that Harry couldn't seem to give a damn.

He should have been concerned about his career, his reputation, his relationship with his boss. Instead, he found himself coming up with more and more excuses to wander out to the reception area and talk to Jenny during the day, whether or not the chief was in her office.

Sometimes he would perch on the edge of Jenny's desk, look at her, and realize he was grinning like an idiot. Sometimes he had to stop himself from reaching out and touching her just because he remembered how she looked spread out naked on his bed. Sometimes he was overwhelmed with the memory of her in her studio, lying on the old sofa with paint speckled on her hands and freckles spread across her small, perfect breasts. Sometimes he just wanted to pin her up against the file cabinet where she was putting folders away and kiss the hell out of her.

A few times, when they'd been alone in the station, he'd dragged her into the file room and done it.

When they'd been alone.

At the station.

Like they were now.

Harry drew in a deep breath and paced some more.

He still felt kind of bad that he'd made her tear up the sketches she'd done of him bare-ass naked, but they'd really weirded him out. *Way* too detailed. And it had been uncomfortable to think of her looking at him so clinically. He never ever wanted Jenny to see him as a "thing," the way Junior and Daisy had. Being considered an object was definitely one of his hot buttons. Psycho maybe, but there you had it.

When Jenny had torn up her drawings—when she'd listened to what he wanted—he'd known it meant something.

Her art was important to her. It was significant that she'd been willing to sacrifice it for him.

He wasn't entirely sure how he felt about that.

Finally giving in, he walked out to the reception area.

Jenny was still at the window helping someone, but the conversation seemed to be winding down. He stayed out of sight until she'd finished the transaction, said goodbye to whoever she'd been talking to, and turned around. She spotted him at once and gave him a smile full of welcome and invitation.

"Well, hello, Mr. Harry," she said as she walked over to him, her voice smooth and warm.

"Hello, Miss Jenny." He glanced around, and once she'd gotten close enough, bent down to give her a quick kiss. It quickly morphed into more, and they were both breathing heavily, arms wrapped around each other when he lifted his head.

If somebody had told Harry a few weeks ago that he'd be acting this way in the main hub of the Hardy Falls police station, he would have called them insane. Looked like he was the crazy one.

Still holding her close, he waggled his eyebrows down at her.

"When can I see you?"

"How about now?" Her grin was basically a leer. "Mom's out, and we have a cot."

Harry groaned. "Don't tempt me." He meant it, too, because using that cot sounded awfully damned good right at the moment. "Do you think you'll be able to come to my place after work?"

Jenny frowned at him. "It's Friday, and you told the kids you'd meet them at the bowling alley. You promised them. It's important."

Fuck. He scowled, but yeah, she was right.

"Okay," he admitted reluctantly. "It *is* important." He was still trying to rebuild those bridges he'd damaged.

Jenny put her hand to his face and reached up for another quick kiss.

"Nothing to say I can't show up at the bowling alley, too," she reminded him with a smile, then sobered. "I have to try to talk to Missy anyway," she said. "It's been weeks. She'll probably be there because her women's league bowls on Friday nights. I need to try to talk to her."

Harry kissed her cheek and let his lips linger before drawing back. "You miss her."

"Yeah, I do." Her blue eyes sharpened. "So, I'll talk to her while I'm waiting for you. And then..." she trailed off meaningfully, one of her hands sliding down his chest toward his belt.

"Yes," he growled, grabbing the hand and moving it to safer territory. *She really was a witch.*

Jenny smiled again, then looked away, twisting a button on his uniform shirt before smoothing it out.

"Have you talked to your grandfather?"

Harry was confused.

"Of course I have. I talk to him all the time." Hell, last Sunday he'd even run to the grocery store for his grandparents because the old man had a cold. If dragging himself out of Jenny's warm bed—well, technically *his* bed with Jenny in it—to voluntarily enter the seventh level of hell that was the Cooper Grocery store on a weekend didn't scream dedication, he didn't know what did.

Jenny toyed with his hair, running her fingertips under the uniform collar of his shirt.

"So, you told your grandfather about getting a call from your father?" she pressed. "And you told him about...us?"

Her eyes held a gleam he didn't quite understand.

"No. Not about any of that," he admitted.

"Oh." The gleam faded. "Why not?"

"Hearing that Junior called me for money is just going to upset Pops," Harry told her, answering the simplest question first. "The old man might cave in and wire him cash after all."

Jenny nodded, not looking away from him. "And us?" It was a challenge.

Harry wasn't sure what to say. He didn't want to explain her yet, didn't want to open up that can of worms until he'd had a little time to figure out what the can of worms actually was.

"I'll tell him when it's the right time," he hedged.

He thought he sounded reasonable, but Jenny sighed and tugged back until he let her go.

"Don't you trust your grandfather?" she asked softly.

Harry frowned at her. "I trust him with my life, but I don't know if I can trust him not to tell his friends. And once more than two people know something, it's not a secret anymore."

Jenny was silent for a long moment, considering him.

"You don't trust many people, do you, Harry?" she asked at last.

He didn't know how to answer her because, no, he didn't trust a lot of people. It was something he'd learned early on. You never knew what was right under the surface.

Big hands shoving him up against a wall. Hot breath stinking of cheap whiskey. Junior shouting and then the hands were gone.

He shook his head to dispel the memory, but he could tell she'd misinterpreted the gesture when she took another step back. Before he could say anything else, they heard the beep of the lock at the employee entrance indicating that somebody had just come in from the parking lot.

Harry moved to the side just as Jackie Kline came striding down the hallway, determined as always, her dark bob of hair swinging, because, as usual, she wasn't wearing her hat. The contained energy she radiated was that of a woman twenty years her junior. She paused when she saw them standing there and scowled before walking around them to her office.

"I have some phone messages for you," Jenny called after her.

"Later." Jackie paused in the office doorway and turned, pinning Harry with the blue-eyed stare she'd passed on to both of her daughters. "Harry, I need to talk to you for a minute."

Without waiting to see his nod, she turned and went inside.

"Uh-oh," Jenny whispered.

"It will be fine," he told Jenny with a confidence he didn't feel and followed the chief. She was already lounging in the chair behind her desk when he walked in.

"Shut the door," she said, nodding toward it.

Shit.

Harry did as she asked, then sat in the chair on the other side of her desk and waited to see what would happen.

Jackie studied him for a long time. So long, in fact, that he realized he was bouncing his knee nervously and forced himself to stop fidgeting. He thought he saw some amusement flash across her face then, but she straightened and clasped both hands on the desk in front of her.

"Why don't you tell me about Bethany?" she said.

Harry kept his expression blank as he tried to hide his relief.

"Ma'am?"

"Bethany." Jackie held up some of the papers she had scattered on her desk. "You said you wanted to talk about her training."

"Yeah," he said even as he scrambled to regroup. "I do."

So they discussed the younger officer's training, or lack thereof. Harry wondered if he'd dodged a bullet, or if Jackie was just toying with him like a cat with a particularly juicy mouse.

30

Jenny was hanging up the phone after talking to Len Bisby about his latest speeding ticket when her mother's office door opened and Harry came out. Jenny tensed, waiting for the fallout. Accusations. Questions. Something.

Nothing happened. It was all pretty anticlimactic. Jackie didn't even get up from her desk.

When Harry walked past her on his way back to the squad room, the look he shot her was one of relief. A few minutes later, he sent her a text letting her know that everything was okay—the chief had just wanted to talk about Bethany.

Bullet dodged.

But it was also a warning. Jenny wasn't stupid enough to think they could keep acting the way they'd been acting and still fly under Jackie's well-honed radar. It was definitely time to start being more circumspect at the office. Any afternoon delights should probably be suspended for the foreseeable future.

Well, at least she'd get to see Harry tonight. And by "see" she meant see him in all of his glorious, naked splendor.

She *loved* it when he peeled off that stiff, buttoned-up cop's uniform.

Jenny shifted restlessly in her chair, trying to resist the sudden overwhelming urge to go back to the squad room and peel his uniform off right then and there. Thank God Mr. Looper chose that moment to call again.

Harry must have decided in favor of prudence, too, because he made himself scarce the rest of the day. But after he'd left at the end of his shift, he did send her another text to remind her to come to the bowling alley when she was done. It was nice. Jenny felt a now familiar thrum run through her body. She sent him back heart emojis.

The last hour dragged on forever, but finally she could close up her computer and lock the front door. On her way out, she stopped by her mother's office to say goodbye and found Jackie glowering darkly at her computer.

"What's wrong?" Jenny asked, propping herself up in the doorway.

"How much time did I spend planning for that damned town council meeting two weeks ago?" Jackie demanded, shifting to pin Jenny with her glare.

"Um, a lot?" Jenny honestly couldn't remember.

"Damned right it was a lot, and I don't think they freaking heard a freaking word I said." Jackie shoved back from the desk and crossed her arms over her chest. Probably so she wouldn't reach for her weapon and shoot the screen.

"What did they do?" Jenny asked.

"It's what they're *not* doing that's the problem. We need more cops. I *told* them we need more cops. I *showed* them we need more cops. But today, when I told them I need money so I can bring in someone to cover Bethany's hours because she needs more training, I get this kind of garbage." She waved her hand at the computer screen.

"They said no?" Jenny guessed.

"Of course they said no." Jackie snorted and shook her head, her cap of hair shifting. "Are you leaving?" she growled.

"I want to get out of here before Mr. Looper calls again," Jenny told her.

"I think Dazzle is pole dancing to lure over the neighbor dogs when Looper's not watching her."

"Is there ever a time when he's not watching her?"

"Good point." Jackie considered her. "Will I see you later?"

Jenny cleared her throat. "Um, I'm heading to the bowling alley after I get changed."

"You're always running around these days," Jackie said innocently.

Yeah.

"I want to try to talk to Missy, and she'll probably be there," Jenny told her.

Her mother nodded. "Good. I'm glad. It's been too long."

"I was waiting for her to come to me," Jenny protested. "*I'm* the one who got fired. *She's* the one who should be taking the first step."

Jackie smiled at her fondly. "Sometimes," she said, "you have to be the one to bridge a gap, even if you don't think it's fair. In the end, it doesn't matter whose fault it is, does it? All that matters is that you love her."

"I guess." Jenny sighed and straightened. "I'd better get going."

"Have fun," Jackie said blandly and turned back to her computer.

Jenny frowned, wondering if she'd actually heard an undertone of humor in her mother's voice or just imagined it. But she didn't ask. She just got out of the station as fast as humanly possible. Moments later, she was in her pickup truck, driving away, free for the weekend. Free...free...free...!

Too bad she was going to have to use some of that freedom on what was sure to be an awkward conversation with Missy.

But it had to be done. Her mother was right—in the end, it didn't matter who was in the wrong, did it? Righteous indignation and stubbornness wouldn't make either of them feel any better if their friendship drifted away into nothingness.

Besides, the silence between them for the last few weeks had been as much her fault as Missy's, Jenny admitted. Turning into the driveway of her house, she came to a stop at the garage and hopped out of the truck. She'd been distracted lately. *Very* distracted. Boy howdy, had she been distracted.

And she was very much looking forward to seeing her distraction again. Going home with Harry after talking to Missy would be her reward. If she got angry, she'd just take it out on him.

Grinning at the thought of wrestling Harry into submission, Jenny let herself into the house and ran upstairs to her bedroom. She changed quickly, grabbed a jacket to protect her against the chilly night air, and jogged back downstairs.

When she started the truck again, it occurred to her that she might be using the need to talk to Missy as a cover for the fact that she really wanted to spend more time with Harry. But that was okay, she assured herself as she backed out of the driveway. She really did want to talk to Missy. It wasn't a lie.

And if talking to Missy kept Jackie off her back and the other people at the bowling alley from wondering why she was there, well it was a win-win as far as she was concerned.

Still, she found herself frowning as she merged onto the highway.

Jesus, keeping everything a secret was hard work.

Jenny sighed and turned into the crowded Murphy Lanes parking lot. At least the secrecy part of the equation wouldn't last too much longer. Just another eight weeks or so and then Suzy would be back, Jenny would be sprung, and she and Harry would be able to be more open.

What if Harry didn't want them to be more open? What if he was happy with the way things were and decided he wanted to keep them a secret?

"He won't," she muttered.

But he still hadn't told his grandfather.

Jenny didn't want to think about it anymore, so she concentrated on backing her pickup into a parking space where it would be out of the way. After she turned off the engine, she shot Harry a quick text to let him know she was there then climbed out. The alert for a new message sounded before she'd gone more than a few steps. She melted when she saw he'd sent her a GIF of a face blowing kisses.

Grinning like a total fool, she shoved aside all of the doubts she'd been letting creep into her thoughts and practically skipped to the bowling alley's glass entry doors.

Of course, the first thing she did when she was inside was peek into the arcade. Harry was there, standing with his group of kids, all of them watching Lucio work the buttons and flippers of a flashing pinball machine with single-minded determination. They were all laughing, and Jenny was glad to see that everyone seemed more relaxed. She was also glad to see Teagan, Missy and Buster's son, was in the group. That should mean his mother, at least, was around somewhere.

At that moment, Harry looked up and met her eyes. The connection, in spite of the distance and the other people around them, was electric.

Jenny took a deep breath and forced herself to look away before she did something stupid like go right up to him and kiss the hell out of him.

Turning, she walked farther into the lobby where Pat Murphy sat behind the shoe counter, looming like a muscular vampire in his habitual black T-shirt and jeans. Richie Dunlop and Chet Hinkle were with him, hanging around and getting in the way. Fortunately for the people who actually wanted to bowl, a teenager she didn't know was standing at the other end of the counter and actually seemed to be working.

When Pat met her eyes, his smile faded. He knew the Klines were all tight with Hannah, so that meant Jenny was less than welcome at the bowling alley.

She ignored him and tried to see if she could spot Missy out at the bowling lanes. Other teams were competing, colorful bowling shirts blossoming like flowers against the neon lights, but she didn't see the women's league. Missy must be finished, so she was probably waiting for Teagan in the restaurant.

Still ignoring Pat and his posse, Jenny made her way to the bowling alley's newly renovated restaurant and bar, which took up a large area on the opposite side of the building from the lanes and arcade.

The bar was long and ran the length of a wall, sporting shelves crowded with bottles and more than a few beer taps. The restaurant section was comprised of a series of new, low-backed booths. The whole eating area was surrounded by a waist-high wooden wall, which meant anyone waiting for a bowler or arcade player could keep an eye on the action without actually being in the middle of it.

Everything was sparkling clean. The booths' maroon padded seats and honey gold wood gleamed, and the lighting was soft but popped with colorful accents the same way the air popped with the thunder of bowling balls, the ping of games, and the happy shouts of people. Jenny could see why families would like this place now, and why bowlers would stay here after their games. Josie had come here a few times for professional reconnaissance, and she'd told Jenny that Pat really was competition for the Country Time. She was right.

Putting that worry aside, Jenny went into the restaurant section and hesitated, looking for Missy.

"You can just sit down somewhere, and I'll be with you in a minute," a voice said from behind her.

Jenny started and turned to see Louise Weber, manager of the bowling alley's restaurant. The other woman's hair was bright red—not blond as it had been when she'd left town two or three years ago. But the expression in her brown eyes was the same combination of wary and resentful that Jenny had seen before right before she'd gone.

"Hi, Louise." Jenny gave her a professional smile.

Louise did not return the smile, and when she spoke, her voice was reserved, edging to frosty. "Hi, Jenny."

"I'm looking for Missy." As she said it, she finally saw her friend sitting alone in a booth at the back. "There she is."

"I'll be with you in a minute," Louise said, still cool, as she turned to acknowledge a summons from another customer. "I'm by myself, so I'll get there as soon as I can."

Before Jenny could tell her that she wasn't planning on eating anyway, Louise hurried off.

31

Jenny watched Louise go. She wasn't offended by the abruptness—she knew very well how hard it was when you were working alone in a place on a weekend, running around like a nut to deal with needy, irritated people. Been there, done that, bought the T-shirt. At least in the job she had now at the police station, most of the complainers weren't right there in front of her.

Shaking it off, she headed back to the booth where Missy was sitting and looking at her phone. As she approached, her friend glanced up, saw her, and straightened. She put down the phone and watched Jenny draw near, her eyes almost as wary as Louise's had been. Her red bowling shirt seemed almost incongruously cheerful.

"Hey," Jenny said when she stood at the end of the table. "How are you?"

"Fine." Missy sounded cautious.

"Did Buster come with you tonight?" Jenny asked. It would be easier to talk to the other woman if her husband wasn't there.

"He's at the bar. Why?"

Jenny looked over and saw Buster, sitting at the bar and laughing with Claude Beecher and Bernie Housemann. He looked like he'd be there a while. She turned her attention back to Missy and smiled.

"I was just wondering if you had a minute to talk, that's all."

Missy studied her another moment, then sighed.

"Sure. Sit. I told Teagan he could have another few minutes anyway, and Buster's busy trading stories."

Jenny slid onto the empty seat just as Louise came up to see what she wanted. When Jenny asked for water, the other woman scowled, then left. In a minute, she was back with a glass and practically slammed it on the table before heading off again.

"I get the feeling she doesn't want me here," Jenny said to Missy, trying to make a joke.

Missy's round cheeks creased in a smile, but she didn't laugh. "I'm getting food, so I'll make up for it. And I'm sure Buster and Teagan will want something. Lou's just having a bad day because one of the waitresses had to call out sick."

"Maybe I should see if she's hiring," Jenny said, just to be funny. The attempt at humor fell flatter than flat.

"You landed on your feet with a job at the police station," Missy said, her faint smile vanishing as if it had never existed. "I expected nothing less."

Jenny winced because there'd been more than a little acid behind those words.

"My mother took pity on me," she explained. "And she needs someone while Suzy's out on maternity leave."

"It's nice to have connections," Missy said. "That's how you get opportunities these days."

"Yes." Jenny struggled to hold on to her patience and was glad when Louise came over with Missy's food. "You should go ahead and eat," she said once they were alone again.

"It's okay. It's just a sandwich." Missy pushed the plate aside and looked at Jenny. "Why are you here?"

Jenny fiddled with the non-eco-friendly plastic straw in her water glass.

"How's Buster doing with the cleaning?" she asked. This awkward tiptoeing around each other was painful. It made her heart hurt.

"He's fine." Missy glanced over to the bar, then back. "It's just an adjustment, you know? We're working it out."

"That's good." Jenny cast around for something else to say. "Did you hear that Hannah and June are both pregnant?" she asked.

"Ms. Gregory told me." Missy's brown eyes sparkled with amusement, and for a moment she was the woman Jenny had known for the last nine years. "I can't believe it. Hannah *and* June."

"I know, right?" Jenny's laugh had as much to do with relief at finding a chink in Missy's armor as it did with humor. "I'm sure the news is all over town by now."

"It was all over town the night they announced it." Missy sobered. "Pat's not taking it well."

"Pat needs to let it go," Jenny said impatiently. "June broke up with him a long time ago, and he still hasn't bought a clue."

"Maybe he loves her." Missy's face hardened. "Most people don't give up when they're in love."

Jenny found herself bristling because that sounded like some kind of passive-aggressive bullshit to her. Like maybe Missy was implying *Jenny* had given up on the relationship with Stefan. As if *Missy* hadn't been the one to tell her to leave Stefan in the first damned place.

"So, I guess you gave Buster all of your money because you love him," she shot back before she could stop herself.

"First, it's *our* money, not mine," Missy snapped. Her pointed chin was in the air, and her arms were crossed defensively over her chest. "And, yeah, I love him. I know he's not perfect, but he's my husband and the father of my child. So, yes, sue me. I gave him all of the money."

They glared at each other for a moment.

Jenny was the first one to break eye contact. She hadn't meant to go there. And, anyway, who was the bigger idiot— Missy for giving all of her money to someone she loved, or Jenny for staying with Stefan because it was too hard to leave?

What would she do for Harry?

She'd torn up her sketches just because he asked her to.

No, she couldn't throw stones at either Pat or Missy.

"Sorry. I didn't mean to be a bitch," Jenny muttered, looking down and fiddling with the straw in her glass of water, pulling it up through the ice cubes then letting it sink down again.

Missy reached across the table and rubbed her hand, stilling the restless action.

"It's okay," she said, then hesitated. "And for what it's worth, I'm sorry about the way everything worked out. I know it screwed with you."

Jenny met her friend's warm brown eyes.

"I just wish you'd told me what was going on," she confessed. That was the part that really bothered her. "I know the thing with Mr. Foster came out of nowhere, but I wish I'd known what was going on with you and the money and all. Maybe I could have helped."

Missy shrugged and settled back. "I never hid anything from you. Maybe you just never wanted to know. You never wanted to have anything to do with the business anyway."

Jenny frowned at her. "Yes, I did." What the hell? She'd worked her ass off for Missy.

"Oh, please." Missy ran a hand through her thick hair. "Remember when I brought you on to work with me? We talked about you eventually being a real partner, not just a free-lancer. I tried to show you what I did—the books, the bills, all of the administrative stuff—but you were never interested." She shrugged. "You obviously liked being a freelancer, so I let you. Not worth fighting about it."

"But..." This time Jenny managed to swallow her angry words. "I always listened," she protested instead. "You never said anything."

"You listened when I complained, yes. But whenever I tried to get you to go further, you obviously weren't interested. That's fine. You're a terrific worker, so you more than pulled your own weight."

Jenny started to speak, then stopped again. *Was it true?*

Missy smiled, but Jenny could see tears welling up in her chocolate brown eyes. "I didn't want to let you go, Jenny, but I just didn't have a choice. I couldn't keep paying you and... I'm just trying to keep things going the best I know how. We have to keep the house. We have to keep money coming in. We *have* to."

As Jenny listened—really listened—the burden Missy had been carrying for all of these years finally started to dawn on her.

How had she missed this?

"Please tell me Buster is helping with the paperwork and money stuff now that he's working with you," she begged. Buster had been running his own business for a while. Maybe he hadn't been running it well, but he *had* been running it. Surely he knew something.

Missy's sigh was tired this time. "It's okay. I'm used to it."

Which meant she was still doing everything.

"Hey, Jenny." As if they'd conjured him, Buster's voice broke into their conversation, and he bounced up to the table, friendly as a puppy. "Why are you here?"

Jenny forced a smile. "I just wanted to talk to Missy. I missed her," she added with a look at the other woman.

He frowned, obviously puzzled. "It's only been a couple of

weeks, right?" he said, scratching his scalp through his thinning blond crewcut.

Jenny shrugged. "Still."

Buster looked like the aging high school jock he was. His muscular build was gradually softening to flab. But he was amiable enough, and Jenny liked him most of the time. He wasn't as smart as Missy by a long shot, but he was a pleasant guy who apparently didn't have a clue how to handle money.

Like she had room to talk.

Missy surreptitiously wiped her eyes before smiling up at her husband.

"Do you want something to eat, honey? I was thinking of getting food for Teagan, too. He's played enough for tonight."

Buster shrugged. "I could eat. I'll go pull the boy away from the machines before he spends all of our money." He grinned at Jenny again. "Nice to see you," he said and headed off toward the arcade.

Jenny looked at Missy.

"I'm—" she started, but Missy shook her head, chestnut-brown curls tumbling.

"It's okay, Jenny," she said. "It's all working out, right? It's going to be fine." She looked over toward the entrance to the restaurant. "Here they come already. That was quick. Teagan must be hungry."

"Okay, I'll leave you alone." Jenny got to her feet and then hesitated. "I do miss you," she said sincerely. They'd been together almost every day for years, dealt with stressful situations together, talked and laughed and cried together.

Missy shrugged and smiled faintly. "It's Hardy Falls. We'll see each other. You should come watch me bowl sometime. I got two strikes tonight. Burned Stella Bisby's ass."

"Good for you."

Then Buster and Teagan were there, so Jenny made her excuses and left.

Louise crossed her path on the way out of the restaurant and hesitated.

"Not having anything to eat?" It was a challenge.

"I'm not hungry, so I didn't want to take up the space." Jenny smiled and jerked her thumb back to Missy's table. "That crew will keep you busy, though."

"Great." Louise didn't exactly look thrilled by the prospect.

"It sucks to be alone when you're really busy, especially on a Friday night," Jenny sympathized. "I know how it goes."

"Yeah, we're busy." Louise's hackles rose immediately. "So what?"

Jenny sighed. "Forget it," she said.

Louise hurried off toward Missy, Buster, and Teagan.

As Jenny left the booth area, she came to an abrupt stop when she almost ran right into Harry walking past. That was unexpected. She'd planned to send him a text from the parking lot to see what he wanted to do.

"Oops. Sorry." Jenny held on to her professional smile with difficulty. It was a real effort not to just wrap her arms around his waist and burrow into his body.

"No problem." His smile was equally distant, but when she started to move away, disappointed, he grabbed her wrist and lowered his voice. "Wait for me outside by your truck, okay? I'll just be a minute."

Disappointment immediately morphed into something a lot stronger and more urgent.

"I'm around back," she told him, and he nodded before heading off in the direction of the men's room.

Jenny took a quick look around to see if they'd been noticed. She was glad to see that Pat, Richie, and Chet had been joined by Claude and Bernie at the shoe counter. The men were all busy talking—in fact, Claude and Pat seemed to be arguing about something. That group was usually thick as thieves, so it was a little unusual to see them fighting, but she didn't care too much. All that mattered was none of them were paying any attention to her.

Once outside, she went to her pickup but didn't get in. Instead, she moved to stand at the edge of the parking lot behind the truck, crossing her arms and staring out past the scrub trees to where Mr. Clark's dormant fields wrapped around both the Country Time and Murphy Lanes.

The darker silhouettes of deer stepped from the hedgerow in the distance, as a small herd set out to graze. In the deepening twilight, she could see wild grasses growing through lingering patches of snow—more than enough to feed the deer. Soon an abundance of wildflowers would be blooming, too. Later, Mr. Clark would get Eli Cooper, Grace's brother, to come mow the field to keep it under some control, but for now it was simply a meadow coming back to life and holding all the verdant promise of spring.

Jenny acknowledged that her conversation with Missy had shaken her. Ever since her friend had let her go, she'd assumed she was the wronged party in the whole thing, that she'd been the one blindsided. But now it looked like she had no one to blame for her situation but herself. Yes, Missy could have been clearer about what was going on, but why should she have done that when Jenny didn't seem interested?

And, honestly, the impression hadn't been wrong. Now that Jenny thought about it, she could see that whenever Missy had tried to show her anything to do with the business side of things, Jenny had figuratively—and sometimes literally—plugged her ears and run away. So why should Missy think she cared?

"Well, she still could have asked," Jenny muttered to herself.

But then again, she could have asked, too.

They both could have asked.

And neither one of them had.

Jenny wasn't willing to let the friendship go this easily, and she'd definitely seek out Missy again. But at the moment there was a sharp break between them, a distance that hadn't been there before. And Jenny also knew that sometimes friendships, even ones that had lasted a long time, fell apart, especially if the people involved didn't talk to each other. People changed, and you didn't always know it was happening.

"Hey."

She had been so deep into her own thoughts that she jumped a little at the sound of Harry's voice behind her. Turning, she saw him come striding around her truck. After making sure they were alone in this section of the parking lot, he pulled her up against him and kissed her.

"What's wrong?" she asked when he let her go because, although the kiss had been thorough and left her clinging to his leather jacket with both hands, Harry was more distracted than she'd come to expect from him when they were this close. She'd gotten used to having Harry's focus.

"I have to leave," he told her. Although there was real regret in his deep voice, she pulled back as far as he'd let her.

"Why?" she asked. "Is it because my mother said some—"

He shook his head, cutting her off. "No, no. Nothing like that. My grandfather just called. He wants me to meet him at his house. Tonight. Now."

Jenny frowned. From what she could tell, not only was it *very* unusual for Harry Senior to demand his grandson's presence like this, but he should have been at the Country Time having dinner with his friends at this time of night.

"Is he okay? Your grandmother?"

"I don't know. I have to go find out." Harry kissed her again. "Sorry."

"No, no. Go." She dropped her hands, and he stepped back. "Just maybe text me later and let me know what's going on, okay?"

"I will," he promised and smiled at her slightly before

turning and walking rapidly to his Jeep parked a few spaces away.

A minute later, he was gone, the speed with which he left the parking lot a mute testimony to his worry.

Jenny watched until she couldn't see him anymore, and then got into her pickup.

"Well, hell."

Her win-win scenario had crumbled on a whole lot of levels, hadn't it? And now she had to worry about Harry's grandparents, too.

She started up the engine and headed home.

32

I f Harry had been in the police vehicle, he would have been running hot—lights on and siren blaring. His grandfather *never* called him expecting him to just drop what he was doing and come over. The fact that he had was scary as hell.

He'd sounded older than Harry could ever remember.

"You want me to come to the house? Not the Country Time?" Harry had asked in surprise when the old man made the request. He'd thought maybe he hadn't heard correctly over the noise and clatter of the arcade machines.

"I can't leave your grandmother. Call me when you get here, so I can come out, okay?"

"Is Grandma...okay?"

"She's fine. Just upset. But I need to stick close tonight." His grandfather's voice seemed to hold the weight of the world. "I'll see you soon."

Harry had been careful not to let his emotions bleed through when he'd said goodbye to the kids—he was just starting to make progress with them again. Ditching Jenny had been harder, especially since he wanted to beg her to come with him, to stand with him against whatever it was his grandfather had to say.

That was frightening, too.

During the short drive from the bowling alley to his grandparents' neat little ranch house on the other side of town, Harry's thinking cleared up enough to realize that Junior must have called and upset them again.

"Bastard," he muttered. "Fucking bastard!"

Obviously, his father hadn't taken Harry's warning to heart when they'd talked, which meant Harry was just going to have to make sure he listened the next time. He'd contact that private detective guy who'd been trying to help Hannah find her uncle—the man worked with Sam Black's law firm, so he'd ask Sam to put him in touch.

Once Junior was located, Harry would take a field trip out to Los Angeles and deal with the man personally, no matter how his grandfather felt about the situation. He'd stood aside for long enough.

Whatever Junior had said to them must have been bad, Harry thought as he turned onto his grandparents' street. Otherwise, the old man would never have called him like this.

He pulled into the driveway, shut off the engine, and grabbed his cell phone. But before he could make the call to say he was there, the front door opened, and his grandfather's wiry form stood silhouetted against the light for an instant before he stepped out and shut the door behind him again. He must have been watching for him.

Harry leaped from the Jeep and strode quickly to the old man, meeting him on the path that curved from the house to the driveway.

"Hello, boy," his grandfather said, the glow of the lights in the windows deepening the wrinkles on his face and making it unreadable.

"What happened?" Harry asked abruptly. "Junior called, didn't he?"

His grandfather glanced at the house, then grabbed his arm and drew him back to the Jeep. As they reached it, the automatic interior lights blinked out in the vehicle, casting them into deeper darkness.

"I doubt she can hear us, but the bedroom's at the front, and I want her to try and sleep if she can. Albert, Martin, and Joe will be here in a bit, but the medication should be working by then."

Harry barely resisted the urge to grab his grandfather's scrawny shoulders and shake him. The old man sounded so sad. And defeated.

"Tell me the truth. Is she fucking okay or not?" he ground out, drowning in memories of his grandmother's soft hands and warm heart. The mittens and cap she'd knit for him. The food she tried to cook. The way she'd never—not once—resented the fact that she'd had to raise a grandson who'd been a wild, ungrateful piece of shit when he'd first come to them. If something happened to her—to either of them—Harry knew he'd lose precious parts of his life.

"She's fine." The old man sighed. "Or she will be."

"What the hell is going on?" Harry demanded, feeling like he was about to break. "What did Junior say? I know it had to be him." He tried and failed to keep the anger out of his voice, even though he knew it would only make things worse. "I don't care what you say, I am tracking him down, and I'm going to fucking deal with him."

"You won't need to do that." His grandfather looked at the ground. He seemed smaller, lighter. More fragile than before.

Oh, God.

"Please don't tell me you gave him money again," Harry pleaded. "Don't tell me you caved."

"No." The old man straightened into his habitual military

posture, his head held up, proud. "We got a call from the Los Angeles police department," he said.

Harry thought of his father's voice on the phone—the manic undertone. The desperation.

"Is he in jail?" he asked.

"No. They found him in the alley behind a bar. He'd been shot in the head several times. They think he was trying to make some kind of a drug deal, and it went bad."

Harry didn't know why he was surprised. He shouldn't have been. He knew how things could go to shit and how quickly they could go there. He'd seen it happen time and again in his years as a cop.

And yet, hearing that Junior was...gone...threw him. He hated his father, but the man had always been larger than life, always looming in the background of his world.

"I'm sorry, boy," his grandfather said, and there was a wet pain in his voice even now. Harry pulled him into a hard hug, and the old man clutched at him.

"Don't you dare be sorry, Pops," he said. "Don't you dare. Junior did this."

"It's hard," his grandfather said, and Harry heard the strain in his voice before he pushed away again and stood, straight and tall. Well, as tall as he ever was. "Maybe we weren't the best parents in the world, but—"

"You were the best parents," Harry interrupted him, not willing to listen to him talk himself down. "I should know."

His grandfather sniffed loudly, then pulled out a handkerchief and blew his nose.

"Well, thanks for that." He blew his nose again. "We were so happy when he was born, you see. We'd wanted a kid forever, but we just couldn't seem to get pregnant and stay that way. Three miscarriages. The last one...it about killed us. Your grandmother...well. But she wanted to try one more time. Insisted on it. Stubborn woman. And then there he was, all pink and perfect. A little early, but big enough. God, we loved that boy."

"Pops." It broke Harry's heart to listen, to know how his father had trampled on all of that love.

"Spoiled him," his grandfather admitted. "Albert, Martin, Joe...we weren't all living in the same town then, but we were friends from our time in the army, and they all told me that we had to stop and discipline the boy. But we just couldn't turn away. He was our miracle. Just like Deacon told me he felt about his baby. A miracle."

"I understand," Harry said, although he really didn't. "You did the best you could."

"Maybe I shouldn't have told him that I would never send him money again," the old man continued, not seeming to hear. "But we gave it all before, and his rock band never went anywhere. He never got another job. There's not much left, and we need it now."

Harry was glad he'd never told his grandfather about Junior's phone call from a few weeks ago. The old man would have only felt worse. He didn't tell him his suspicions that there hadn't been a band for quite some time and that Junior had just been playing him. Maybe it would all come out eventually, but not tonight. Not now when his grandfather sounded so old and worn. Not when his grandmother was inside the house on some kind of medication to help her sleep.

Junior Newman had done enough damage.

"You did the right thing," he said.

He told himself the same thing.

"I know." His grandfather ran the back of his hand over his eyes then faced him squarely. "The best thing we ever did was bring you into our home, Harry," he said. "At first, it was because we felt guilty for leaving things so long, for not knowing how things were for you. In the beginning, when you came to us, you were already getting...hard. No eight-year-old boy should look the way you did. And you were so skinny..." He drew in a shaky breath. "But then we got to know you, love you. You are the best thing we ever did. I hope it makes up a little bit for Junior."

"Junior was responsible for himself," Harry insisted. He tried to think of what he should say. No matter the reason, his grandparents had saved his life. They'd given him a home of stability and warmth. They'd been older, but they'd loved him with all their hearts.

They'd loved his father the same way.

"You made me the man I am today, Pops," he told his grandfather. "If you and Grandma hadn't taken me in, I would have been dead a long time ago." He swallowed and went there. "I love you, old man."

His grandfather sniffed loudly, and they hugged again, pounding each other's backs before breaking apart, both of them uncomfortable with all of the emotion.

At that moment, Albert's ancient rust-bucket of a truck pulled up to the curb in front of the house. Albert, Joe, and Martin piled out and swiftly walked up to them.

"Hello, boy," Albert said to him, grabbing his shoulder. "I'm so damned sorry about this."

"Thanks." There wasn't much else to say.

"We brought provisions," Albert said, pointing at the other men. Martin had a bottle of something clutched in each hand, while Joe carried what looked like a bag of takeout containers. "We sweet-talked Deacon into letting us buy two bottles of prime hooch to go with the food. Let's get inside and go on a real bender."

Harry followed them and waited, while his grandfather checked on his grandmother in the bedroom, then came back to say that she was indeed asleep.

"She's the one who got the phone call," he explained. "I was getting ready to go out when I heard her screaming for me. I gave her one of the pills the doctor prescribed for her, so she'll be out for a while."

"Good," Harry said, even though he knew his sweet grandma would be distraught for a long, long time. Maybe the rest of her life. No matter what Junior had done, he was still her son.

The old men ignored the food and dug into the first bottle of "hooch" that Martin had provided. It turned out to be a very nice single malt scotch. Harry drank a little bit but not enough to do much damage.

Once the old men were well into their bender, he got promises that they weren't going to drive anywhere that night and stood up to leave.

"You can't go," his grandfather said, blinking bleary eyes at him. Harry himself might not have had much to drink, but the old men had put a real dent in that first bottle.

"I have to," Harry said, and let it go at that. It was the truth. He needed to get out of there. He loved his grandfather, loved the other men, but he had to *go*. To drive. To think. Maybe go up into the mountains and scream at the moon. Try to figure out how he felt and why he was surprised and how he was going to deal with the big rock that was suddenly lifted off his chest.

A man shouldn't be glad his father was gone. The fact that Harry was felt wrong, even with everything Junior had said and done.

What if Harry had given Junior the money he'd asked for? Would his father still be alive?

Did he care?

No. Junior was better of dead.

Harry needed to go. Somewhere. Anywhere.

No, that was a lie. He knew perfectly well where he'd end up.

"Jeshh call out sick," his grandfather insisted. "Jak'll understand."

"I'm fine, Pops," he said and left as fast as he could, making assurances, and promising to call.

He had to *go*.

Finally he was back in his Jeep and, after starting the engine, reversed out of the driveway and drove down the road.

Yeah, he knew where he was going.

To Jenny.

33

Jenny went home after leaving the bowling alley to find the house dark and empty. It was seven o'clock, but she assumed her mother had worked past the end of her shift again. So, she was surprised to see she'd missed a text from Jackie that had come in earlier when she'd been at the bowling alley. Apparently, her mother had gone out to dinner with Zeke and Gen Cooper, Grace's parents, to talk about the security at their grocery store.

Although part of Jenny wished her mother had gone out to have a good time on a Friday night rather than as part of her job, the other, larger part was just happy she'd be able to avoid any questions Jackie might ask about Missy.

Sorry, didn't see this. Too much noise. Have fun.

After she'd responded to the text, Jenny ran upstairs and quickly changed into her painting clothes—baggy old jeans and an even older baggier sweatshirt—before heading out to her studio. Once she'd let herself inside and closed the door behind her, she checked her phone again.

Still nothing from Harry. She hoped everything was okay with his grandparents.

Maybe he wouldn't even remember to get in touch, she thought as she slipped out of her shoes so she wouldn't drag mud through the place. It wasn't like she had any right to information in the first place. Besides, it was almost impossible to get anything out of the man on a good day.

Still, he'd told her enough about his father and childhood for her to understand he hadn't been in the best situation before coming to live with his grandparents. She had a feeling those were subjects he never discussed. Ever. She thought that him confiding in her was a good sign.

Padding across the chilly floor in her socks, she walked around her easel and stood in front of the painting on it. The landscape that was officially her current work in progress innocently reflected a nighttime summer scene at the Hardy Falls Lake. It was going pretty well.

But she wouldn't be working on that one tonight.

Jenny moved to a stack of canvases, all paintings in various states of completion, and pulled one out. She carried it to the easel, carefully lifted down the landscape with one hand, and put the one she was holding in its place. Then she stepped back to look at it.

Harry.

She knew he didn't want her to paint him, but she hadn't been able to help herself. She hadn't done it from life because that had made him uncomfortable. She hadn't even told him about it. No, this painting had been created solely from her memories and feelings and imagination. Using thin layers of acrylic paint instead of her normal oils meant it dried quickly, so she could safely store it away after each session, keeping it hidden from prying eyes.

She tilted her head, studying it.

It wasn't quite finished yet, but the figure of Harry was well along, rounded and vital, practically leaping off the canvas. She already thought that it might turn out to be the best thing she'd ever done. But nobody else would ever see it because Harry didn't want them to.

That didn't matter—this painting was just for her. A secret that would remain here in her studio. A piece of him that she would have forever, no matter what eventually happened between them.

She wished she could paint him nude but had reluctantly come to the conclusion that he'd been right about that part, at least. She couldn't take the chance somebody in town would see it by accident. So, his image in the painting was clothed, even though Jenny felt it was a sin to cover a body that gorgeous. In the scene she depicted, he stood with his hand outstretched, shirt unbuttoned, looking at her with challenge and invitation.

Jenny reached out and touched the canvas, touched his painted skin, then drew her fingers back, and curled them into her palm. His hair needed a little touch-up, but she'd finally gotten his eyes the color they had been the last time he was with her. That had taken *forever*.

If Harry saw this, she had a feeling he wouldn't like it. There were other ways to be naked besides not wearing clothes, and somehow the expression on the face of the man in the painting had been stripped bare, open in a way Harry never was in real life. Even in this state of partial completion, she could see it. The image might have kiss-swollen lips and a sensual curve to his mouth, but there was more than the desire for sex in the eyes that were looking out of the canvas.

When he looked at her.

When she looked at him.

Oh, God.

Jenny put her hands up to her own lips and felt them tremble at a sudden, blinding revelation.

How could she have been so stupid?

This painting, what she had created, exposed her far more than it did Harry. He might be the one illustrated, but the emotions were hers. How she saw him. How she wanted him to see her. With longing. Desire.

Love.

Oh, my God.

She loved him.

Really, she should have known the first time he kissed her in the hallway at the police station.

And at that moment, Jenny knew for a fact that nobody else would ever live up to Police Officer Harry Newman III. He was *it* for her. *He* was the one. Not Stefan. Not Mat. Not anybody else. Harry.

"Goddamn it. God*damn* it!" Jenny put her hands up to her temples and tried not to cry. "How can you be such a stupid fucking idiot?"

Because Jenny might not be exactly sure how Harry felt about her, but she was pretty certain it wasn't like *that.*

Shaken, she lowered herself onto the old sofa where they'd made love so sweetly and sat for a few moments staring out the window. It was dark outside now, so all she saw was her own reflection in the glass.

"What are you doing, Jenny?" she asked. Then she got up and drew the blinds, and walked back to her easel.

She should put this painting away and work on the landscape of Hardy Falls lake.

Instead, she found herself pulling out the acrylics and brushes and turning back to the image of Harry.

The hair just needed a little more gold. But she wouldn't touch the eyes.

Time flew, as it always did, and she was working on the gleaming skin of Harry's chest where it was exposed by the unbuttoned shirt, when she heard her text message notification. Thinking it was him with news about his grandparents, she put aside her brushes and checked the phone. But it wasn't Harry—it was her mother.

Finally home. See you're in the shed. I'm heading to bed. Don't stay out there all night!

Jenny checked the time and saw that it was almost ten-thirty. Still no message from Harry.

Sleep well. I'll see you tomorrow.

She put the phone on her workbench after responding to her mother and turned back to the canvas.

Now that her concentration had been broken, Jenny realized she was tired and her back hurt from standing at the easel. Might as well clean up and go in.

She wiped her hands off on a towel and contemplated the painting and the expression on the image of Harry. She wondered why he hadn't sent her a message yet.

Maybe he'd forgotten her. He probably had.

Sighing, Jenny started putting away the paints and cleaning up the brushes, taking her time. She needed to wait for the canvas to dry sufficiently before she could hide it away again.

She was tidying up the workbench when there was a brief knock on the studio door. When she turned, startled, the door opened, and Harry stepped inside.

As soon as she saw his expression, she threw down the rag she'd been holding and jumped around the easel to get to him, grabbing his arms as soon as she was close enough.

"Your grandparents?"

"They're fine."

"Then what happened?" The fact that something *had* happened was obvious because Harry didn't look...right. His face was set and cold, while his eyes flashed with a fire she felt down to her core.

"I'm sorry. I need you," he told her, his eyes blue and blazing.

She heard the tumult of emotions in his voice—saw them in his stark expression. Whatever had happened, it had impacted him deeply.

And he'd come to her.

He'd come to her.

Smiling slightly, she took the last step to bring her body into his.

"I'm here."

It was as if she'd torn off a restraint and unleashed a whirlwind he'd been holding tight inside him.

Harry moved quickly, spinning her around until her back was up against the studio wall. Then he kissed her with almost primitive fury—all heat and teeth and tongue, overwhelming her. Jenny was helpless to do anything but respond, not just to the passion but to the urgency she felt beneath it. It was as if he'd explode if he didn't take her right then and there.

Harry's mouth left hers to bite at her jaw and neck. Then he turned her again until she was stretched out over the arm of the old sofa. He crowded into her until her ass was pressed against the rigid steel of his erection. He leaned over her, placing her hands on the cushion over her head.

"What are you doing?" she gasped, so turned on she couldn't think.

"Just stay this way," he muttered. "Please."

Jenny did as he asked. She couldn't stop herself from undulating against him as his hands came around her body, slipped under her loose sweatshirt and cupped her breasts. He molded them, shaped them, and bit the back of her neck, his teeth sharp, the small pain a shock.

"God!" Jenny clawed her fingers into the seat cushion, her head down, her body arched to fit into his. She didn't even try to disobey his orders, sensing that Harry needed to be in charge tonight. That was okay. She was extremely willing to help him work out whatever was bothering him. *Extremely willing.*

"Lift," he said, his voice harsh. For a moment she didn't understand what he was asking, but then he moved her, shifting her torso enough so he could strip off her sweatshirt and bra with quick hands. Next, he unfastened her jeans, yanking them off along with her panties. There was a ripping sound, and when Jenny turned her head slightly, she saw that her underwear hadn't survived the rough handling. That was fine.

When she was naked, he stretched her out over the sofa again, running his hands and mouth all over her. Touching. Kissing. Biting. Arousing.

"You like this, don't you," she gasped, curving up when he ran his mouth down her spine, the stubble on his chin a rough caress. "Me naked, you dressed." It wasn't really a question since the situation had happened more than once over the last few weeks.

"Yes." His breath was warm, his hands shaping her, then one of his clever, wicked hands moved between her legs to the wet heat between.

"Harry!" She couldn't keep from writhing against him, trying to increase the pressure where she needed it most. He found rubbed hard before thrusting two fingers inside her, swirling, scissoring. Her feet were barely on the floor now, and she was moaning almost constantly. It would have embarrassed her if she'd thought about it.

He withdrew his hand and his marvelous fingers.

"No!"

"Together," he growled.

She heard his zipper and the rip of the condom package, then he was back, pressing into her. It was different in this position. He was strong, insistent, as he filled her, and Jenny loved it. She crashed over the edge into orgasm, shattering around him in an explosion of sensation. *Full. She was so full.*

Harry grabbed her hips and started slamming into her, holding her where he wanted her, riding her. She felt the cotton of his jeans, the bite of his zipper, and the furnace of his body. She lost control again when he did, and that time they exploded together.

He ended up plastered over her, his front to her back while they panted for several long moments. Then he moved, slipping out of her and tying off the condom. After quickly tucking himself back into his pants, he gently tugged her until her feet touched the floor again. Jenny didn't move—she just sprawled over the arm of the sofa. Boneless. Satisfied.

"Are you okay?" Harry asked, helping her stand and running his free hand over her. "Damn it, did the sofa scratch you? I wasn't thinking—"

"I'm okay," she assured him, although, yes, she might have some fresh brush burns from the coarse fabric. She was okay with it, though. Definitely okay.

Grinning, she leaned into him, wrapping her arms around his waist and kissing the underside of his chin. "Hello, sailor."

"Jesus," he muttered and urged her to sit down on the sofa, which was now her new favorite piece of furniture. "You're cold," he said and tossed her the sweatshirt he'd ripped off her a moment before, watching while she pulled it on.

"Let me get rid of this, okay?" he said, indicating the used condom and went to the trashcan she'd put next to her easel. He threw then condom away, absently glancing at the painting on the easel as he did so. Then he froze. And stared.

When she saw the look on his face, Jenny leaped to her feet, yanking down the big sweatshirt to cover some of her nakedness.

"I know I told you I wouldn't paint you," she said quickly

because he'd shut down in a finger snap and it was freaking her the hell out, "but—"

"You knew I didn't want you to do this," he said. His voice sounded wooden, a caricature of the depth it had held. He still hadn't taken his eyes off the painting.

"It's just for me," she assured him hastily. "I promise. Nobody else will ever see it." She never wanted anyone to see it. It was hers.

His eyes flashed to hers, and she saw anger boiling in the blue-green.

"I don't believe you," he said bluntly, the words harsh. "I told you I was uncomfortable with you painting me, and I asked you not to do it. You said you wouldn't, but you did it anyway. Why should I trust anything you say?"

Hearing that hurt. And pissed her off big time.

"You asked me not to paint a *nude*, and I didn't. You said you didn't want me staring at you, and I didn't," she snapped. "Nobody else will see this, Harry. Hell, I wasn't even going to show *you*. It's just for *me*. Nobody else but me!"

"Yeah, well you didn't fucking hide it very well if I could just waltz right in and see it, did you? And why the hell do you have to paint me anyway, for Christ's sake," Harry demanded. "Why couldn't you just let it go like I asked you?"

Jenny threw her hands up in the air, her emotions so thick she couldn't see straight. "Why do you think I did it, you imbecile? Just *look* at the damned thing and see if you can figure it out!"

God, shut up already, Jenny! Just because she knew the painting proved she loved Harry didn't mean she wanted him to notice it, too.

But it didn't seem like that would be an issue because Harry wasn't looking at the image of himself now. No, he was focused on Jenny, his eyes wild and angry and completely devoid of the tenderness she'd gotten used to seeing in them.

She opened her mouth to argue some more, but he made a sharp slicing motion with his hand and moved past her to the door of the studio.

"No," he said. "I can't deal with this now. I don't even want to see you right now. I've gotta get out of here."

Then, to Jenny's utter shock, he pushed out the door and left her without a backward glance.

Jenny stared after him in disbelief. What the serious hell?

Then the moment broke, and she ran for the door. By the time she got there, the backyard was empty. Harry was gone.

Brain numb, body cold as ice, Jenny gently closed the door again. Dazed, she sank down onto the old sofa that was no longer her favorite piece of furniture.

What had just happened?

I don't even want to see you right now.

It took a little time, but Jenny eventually made herself get up and finish cleaning her studio. Moving like an automaton, she hid away the painting of Harry, put the landscape on the easel, sprayed air freshener to cover the lingering scent of sex, pulled on the rest of her clothes.

Fortunately, Jackie was nowhere to be seen when Jenny got back to the house, so she was able to run upstairs to her room without an interrogation. She wasn't sure she could have handled that at the moment.

In her bedroom, she closed the door behind her and, not bothering with the lights, walked over to the window to stare down at the empty street. At some point in the evening it had— surprise—started to rain again.

Harry had been so angry.

She still didn't know why he'd come to her, didn't know what had happened to him to make him "need" her. She didn't know anything.

Sighing, Jenny turned and went to sit on her bed and picked at a loose string on the comforter as she tried to make sense of it all. But no matter how she struggled to understand, she was still at a loss.

Why had Harry come to her? Had it just been for sex? She hadn't thought so, but maybe she'd been wrong.

Why had he gotten so angry with her when he'd seen the painting? So angry that he couldn't deal with her anymore?

What had happened tonight to make him hurt so much? What had happened at his grandparents' house?

Would he ever tell her? Or would he just show up again the next time he was horny or upset about something? Would he ever let her all the way into his life? Would he ever talk to her?

Why should I trust anything you say?

Harry kept his secrets. And that was his right. He didn't have to tell her everything.

But the problem was—Jenny didn't want to always be put in the position of begging him to include her. She didn't want to be on the outside of his life until he decided it was safe to see her. She didn't want to see him only when he wanted sex. She didn't want to be his fuck buddy or some sort of a stress-relief valve. She didn't want to be a secret. She wanted more than that.

She loved him.

Closing her eyes, she lay back on the bed, one arm over her eyes.

Maybe he had a reason to be angry about the painting, she admitted. He was right—he'd asked her not to sketch him, not to paint him, and she'd gone ahead and done it anyway. She'd never intended to show it to anyone, but she had exposed him after he'd asked her not to.

A painting or drawing, the kind of character study she'd done of Harry, was an intimate thing. She knew that—she'd just ignored it in her own need to capture his image. She'd pushed him into the intimacy without him even realizing it. It didn't matter if nobody else ever saw it, or that she'd exposed as much of herself in it as she had of him. She'd taken his vulnerability and showcased it without his permission.

Stefan had done that to her. Used her in his pieces even after she'd asked him not to because they'd made her feel exposed and vulnerable when she'd seen them. And she'd done the same thing to Harry.

How had she forgotten?

What did that make her?

Selfish?

Worse?

She didn't know.

Jenny let her arm fall and stared up at her shadowed bedroom ceiling.

So, where did that leave her?

They'd deal with it, of course they would. They were both responsible adults. He'd calm down, and so would she. She'd apologize for violating his privacy, and he'd apologize for running away. There was even a chance he'd want to keep their relationship going, even though he'd told her he couldn't trust her. Men had a tendency to ignore pesky little details like that when the sex was good. Women, too.

But Jenny couldn't do it anymore. Not now that she knew she loved him. Even if he wanted to continue their fling, she wouldn't be able to pretend. Being his secret fuck, when she knew she wanted so much more, would be unutterably painful. Maybe she could hope that if he gave her another chance, he would eventually feel the way she did. But Jenny had lived for years with that kind of expectation with Stefan. She knew she couldn't do it again.

It had to end.

The tears started.

This, she thought, was why her mother had made her stupid rules in the first place. Working at the police station now would be more than awkward. It would be hell.

Cleaning houses was so much easier.

As she turned to cry into her pillow, Jenny knew that one way or another, she was going to have to pull on her big girl panties and deal with the freaking consequences of her freaking actions.

Too bad Harry had ripped off those big girl panties a few hours ago.

34

———

Very early the next morning, Harry stood at his apartment's living room window with a glass of bourbon and watched the first light of the sun begin to strengthen over Main Street, Hardy Falls. There weren't that many people around yet—traffic wouldn't pick up until a little later. But he saw Ollie Knight, owner of the bakery on the first floor of his building, come walking up the sidewalk carrying two huge to-go cups of coffee, probably for himself and his wife, Ruth. Ruth must be making her trademark cinnamon rolls because the thick, sugary smell was wafting up into his apartment like it did most Saturdays. Any other day, Harry would have already been downstairs to see if he could talk her out of a few before the bakery opened for business. But not today.

He saw Mrs. Dorinsky, bundled in her overcoat against the cool breeze, wave at Ollie as she hurried past him on her way to the Sunnyside. It looked like she was running a little late. The diner would be open in a few minutes for the early breakfast crowd.

Just a normal Saturday morning in Hardy Falls. Nothing unusual.

Well, except that Harry's father was dead. His grandmother was inconsolable. His grandfather had gotten falling-down drunk, which he *never* did. And Harry had responded to all of that by pounding Jenny Kline into her sofa—no thought, no finesse, her body a hot, wet fist around him—before running away while she stared after him in shock because of a painting that had stripped him raw.

Harry rubbed a hand over his bare chest, his lower half clad in pajama bottoms although he hadn't slept. His mind had been too active, the bed too big and empty. He'd eventually ended up here in the living room looking out the window. He certainly didn't want anyone hurt, but he'd been almost desperate for some kind of an emergency call, some reason to get up and run, to be mindless with adrenaline. Any excuse to turn his thoughts off for one damned minute.

Naturally, the night had been deathly quiet.

He took a sip of the bourbon, and it burned all the way down to light a fire in his gut. He should drink coffee like Ollie, but hey, it was time to drink somewhere in the world, wasn't it? Hell, Junior had always thought it was okay to drink every hour of every day. Why limit yourself?

Like father, like son.

Harry stared out the window, but now he didn't notice anything happening on the sidewalk below. He was thinking about Jenny's painting.

The thing hadn't even been completely finished, but a single look at it had rocked him. Not because he was uncomfortable with her painting him, although he was. But because of the way the figure on the canvas—the figure that was supposed to be Harry—had been looking out at the viewer, hand outstretched. Looking at her.

The eyes—*his* eyes—had held no hint of restraint, just sheer intensity of emotion. Longing. Desire. Passion. The smile on the face—*his* face—had been nothing but seduction and welcome. A tease saying, "Come here and we'll have fun." A temptation.

Harry might not always be the most sensitive guy on the planet. He might not always understand women—who did?—but even *he* knew enough to guess the painting represented the way Jenny wanted him to be with her. Maybe it was even the way she saw him. He didn't know a fucking thing about art, but even *he* could see her feelings in there. No wonder she'd never intended to show it to him.

"Jesus."

What the hell was he supposed to do now?

Harry finished the drink in one swallow and walked across the open space to the kitchen area. Somehow he managed to put the glass on the countertop without filling it again, but it was hard.

He knew damn right well he wasn't the man in that painting. He was the guy who drank bourbon at six o'clock in the morning and deserted the only people who had ever loved him, leaving them with their grief just because he'd needed to *breathe*.

He was the man who ran out on a woman because he'd suddenly known—*known*—she was wrapping him up, inch by inch, tying him to her with soft and silken bonds that would be impossible to break. He was the guy who hadn't been able to deal with any of it. With his own emotions. With her.

He was the guy who had more baggage than an entire airport. The guy who never let down his guard. If Jenny had feelings for him, he'd just screw her up.

Walking back to the window, he stood staring out at the mountains in the distance. He wanted to get in his Jeep and drive to the tallest peak and shout at the top of his lungs until he lost his voice.

He wondered if Jenny was waiting for him to text and apologize for getting angry and running out on her last night. He wondered if she'd gotten any sleep, or if she'd lain awake like he had. The thought of her, soft and warm and rumpled, feeling and smelling like heaven, had Harry sinking down into his recliner and leaning forward to put his head in his hands.

She was probably furious at him, and he couldn't blame her. He'd seen the shock on her face as he'd run away like the coward he was.

He looked over to where his cell phone lay on the kitchen island but didn't move to pick it up. He'd send her a text later. After he figured out what the hell he was going to say to her.

If she was angry enough, she might not even talk to him anymore.

That would make things interesting at the station, wouldn't it? Proving Chief Kline right, yet again.

He could always ask for a shift change. Tony would probably be thrilled to be on day shift a few weeks early, and it might be a good idea to put a little distance between him and Jenny, to step back.

To run away again.

No, he assured himself. He was just trying to do the right thing for both of them. There was no way he wanted to hurt her worse than he probably already had or would. He'd let her go.

It turned out that Harry didn't have to worry whether or not he should text Jenny. An hour or so later, after talking to his grandfather and making sure he and his grandmother were okay, he had just gotten out of a much-needed shower and was pulling on his jeans when he heard the message notification "ding" on his phone.

When he picked it up, he saw it was from Jenny.

Are you asleep?

Harry drew in a deep breath.

I'm awake.

I'm downstairs. I need to talk to you for a minute.

Okay, he thought. Fine. Do it now and get it done.

I'll buzz you up.

There was a hesitation. *Want to meet somewhere else?*

It hurt his heart that she still cared about whether or not he wanted to be discrete.

No.

K

Harry hit the button to unlock the tenant's entrance door and went back to the bedroom. He quickly pulled on a T-shirt but didn't bother with socks or shoes and made it back to the living room just as there was a knock on the apartment door. When he opened it, Jenny was standing in the hallway. She was holding a large, flat rectangular package neatly wrapped in brown paper.

Harry froze. He knew what that was.

Jenny didn't seem to notice. She walked around him into the apartment and put the package on the floor, balancing it gently against the kitchen island.

When she turned to face him, he saw that she was pale, her blue eyes bloodshot. She obviously hadn't slept either.

"I know you probably don't want me to be here like this when anyone can see," Jenny said. "But I'll be quick."

"No, it's okay." He rubbed his stomach because just seeing her made his gut ache.

She took a deep breath and pointed at the package.

"That's the painting I did of you."

He knew.

"It's not finished, but I want you to have it."

He looked at the canvas covered with brown paper, then back to her. "Why?"

"Because it belongs to you, and I stole it."

Harry frowned, not understanding. "What are you talking about?"

"You asked me not to paint you, and I went ahead and did it anyway. I didn't listen to you. I just did what I wanted. If you had agreed to model, or even if I had told you what I was doing and you agreed, it would have been okay. But I went against your wishes, and I'm sorry, so it belongs to you."

"I don't—"

"You can destroy it if you want to. Or just put it away in a closet. Or whatever you want to do with it."

"Jenny, you don't have—"

"I do." She cut him off, her expression intense. "I know it pissed you off, and rightly so. When someone asks you not to do something, and you go ahead and do it anyway, it's wrong. I'm sorry I went there."

He couldn't believe they were even having this conversation. *This* was what she thought was wrong?

"Jesus Christ, Jenny! What the hell are you even talking about? It's just a painting! It's not that big a deal!"

Harry knew that he'd said the wrong thing when Jenny jerked back.

"I mean," he said, trying to be calmer, "that you don't need to apologize or beat yourself up about it. Yeah, I was pissed off, but it's not like you shot me up with drugs or something important."

Jenny's face was even paler now, her eyes stark when they met his.

"I know it's only a painting," she said quietly, "but to me, paintings are, um, important. I get that it might not be a big deal to you that I went there without your permission, but it is to me, so I wanted to try to make it up to you somehow." Her smile was a mockery of its normal self. "Just don't tell me if you decide to cut it up."

"Jenny," he said and reached out for her despite his best intentions. He dropped his hand when she took another step back. "It's okay. You don't have to give me this. You keep it."

"No." Her lips firmed, and he had the feeling she was trying not to cry. "It's yours. Just take it, okay?"

He wanted to tell her that he didn't want it—didn't want to *see* himself the way she saw him. But he couldn't hurt her again. "Thank you."

The tears she was holding back made her eyes look luminous in the morning light.

"And I don't think we should see each other anymore," she said.

"Wait...what?" To hell with the fact that he'd already decided they needed to call it quits, hearing her say it made his gut twist into a hard knot that might have been fear. "Is this because I ran out on you last night?"

"No—"

"I wasn't myself yesterday," he broke in before she could protest. "I found out my father had died and—"

"What! Your father died? Is that why your grandparents needed to see you?"

"Yeah, but that part doesn't matter—"

"Doesn't matter? How could it not matter?"

"Junior hasn't been involved in my life since I was eight, and I hated him when he was. But hearing about it, and seeing how upset my grandparents were, well, it knocked me sideways."

"Oh. And that's why you came to me?"

"I guess...yeah," he admitted reluctantly.

"I wondered why you just showed up like that." She looked away. "I'm sorry about your father, Harry. But even if that's what it was, we still need to call it off."

"Why?" he demanded. "I told you I'm not angry about the painting. I was just dealing with a lot of shit, and I took it out on you." *In more ways than one.*

Jenny gulped back a sob and shook her head before meeting his eyes again. "It doesn't matter. I can't do this anymore. I can't be with you like this anymore. I can't be your dirty little secret."

"It's only for two more months—"

"Really?" Now she looked unutterably sad.

"Of course! We just can't tell people now while you're working at the station. You know this. We've talked about this. You agreed." He was faintly surprised when he heard the desperation in his own voice.

Why? Why was he so afraid when he'd already decided to let her go?

"And you're telling me that two months from now, you won't find another reason to keep our relationship secret?"

"Of course I won't!" Of course he wouldn't. Yes, it might be a little awkward, but he would let everyone know. If he hadn't already decided to take a step back, that was.

"Harry. You haven't even told your grandfather. Why should I believe you'll ever tell anybody?"

This was surreal. "You *know* why I haven't told him. It's not for fucking ever." The panic was a shock. He felt like he was fighting for his life, but he didn't quite know why.

Jenny looked directly into his eyes, and he saw her brace herself. "Fine. And what if I said that I would talk to my mother later today and tell her I'd leave the temp job as soon as she could hire a replacement? What if I said you could tell everyone about us in a week or so? Heck, we could call your grandfather now. Would you do it?"

She had him scrambling again, trying to find his footing. Harry didn't like it.

"You told me before that you couldn't leave your job." Hell, she'd been adamant about it. "What about your mother going to bat for you with Margo? What about disappointing her?"

Jenny was studying his face closely. Whatever she was looking for there, he didn't think she found it because she sighed.

"No. You're right. I can't leave."

His temper flared.

"Then why the hell ask? Was this a trick? A test?" he demanded.

Jenny had lost her battle with tears, but she wiped them away.

"No," she said tiredly. He'd never heard that note of defeat in her voice before. "It was just a question. I wondered what you'd say."

"I don't like threats." He was bristling with anger, but it was mostly because he had the feeling he was screwing this up. Badly.

"It doesn't matter. Not now." Jenny opened the apartment door. As she stepped out into the hallway, she paused and looked back at him. Tears stained her face, but her eyes were resolute. "I don't want to be a secret, Harry. I know I agreed," she added when he would have protested, "and I do understand. But I can't. I can't always be on the outside looking in. I can't always be the one begging to be included. I'm worth more than that."

"Jenny—"

"Goodbye, Harry. I know it will be...uncomfortable...at the station, but I'll do my best to stay out of your way."

"No, wait—"

But she didn't wait. She slipped out and closed the door in his face.

35

Harry stood staring at the closed door, struggling to regroup.

He didn't want Jenny to go.

The thought sliced through his shock to hit him with the impact of a freight train. Before he knew what he was doing, he was running after her. But Jenny must have been running, too, and by the time he thundered down the stairs and flung open the door at the bottom, he was just in time to see her pickup truck pulling out of the parking lot.

Go get your keys, moron! a frantic voice in his head screamed. *Hurry! Don't let her get away!*

Instead, Harry watched the truck drive down Main Street. He was thinking clearly enough by then to realize that this was for the best, the decision he'd made earlier was right. He needed to let her go. Let them both get on with their lives before things got even more tangled up and painful between them. He was no good for her.

"Why in the world aren't you wearing shoes, Harry?"

The warm, female voice made him jump, and he turned to see Ruth Knight coming out of the back door of the bakery with a bag of trash in one hand. What she'd said puzzled him until he looked down and saw he was standing on the landing barefoot.

"Just wanted to see what the weather was like," he said lamely.

"Sure." She looked skeptical as she tossed the trash into the building's dumpster. "Well, it's not raining yet, but give it a few minutes."

Harry made himself smile. "Right. I'd better get—shit." He'd let the door shut behind him, and his keys were upstairs.

"Honestly. And you a cop." Shaking her head when she saw his dilemma, Ruth walked over and unlocked the door with a key from the big ring she had attached to the belt loop of her flour-dusted jeans. "There you go."

"Thanks, Ruth."

She shook her head again and patted his cheek in the way he imagined mothers might do with their grown sons when the sons were stupid. "Want some cinnamon rolls?"

"Not today, thanks."

A frown snapped into place on her round, weathered face as she brushed away her graying hair with the back of her hand. "Are you okay?"

"Of course."

He got inside before she could ask any more questions and ran back upstairs to his apartment. Once the world was safely locked away again, he leaned against the door and closed his eyes. Every cell in his body demanded for him to go after Jenny.

"All you'd do is hurt her," he reminded himself. "You know she has feelings for you. You *know* it." If he hadn't known it before, the painting would have sealed the deal. "Don't lead her on."

Good time for more bourbon.

He opened his eyes and started to the kitchen, but his attention snagged on the brown paper-wrapped package propped up against the island.

Why had she given him the damned painting? He didn't want it.

And yet, he found himself walking to the wrapped canvas instead of the bottle of bourbon. Picking it up, he carried the parcel over to the sofa and gingerly placed it on the seat cushion against the back. He hesitated.

He didn't want to look at it. He was just going to stuff it in a closet until he could figure out how to make her take it back, anyway.

But the next thing he knew, he was tearing off the brown paper, throwing discarded sheets on the floor. Once the painting was uncovered, the figure that Jenny thought was him looked out at the world. Smiling. Holding out his hand in welcome.

This time, Harry did go for the bourbon.

Pouring a healthy amount into the glass he'd been using earlier, he took an equally healthy sip before heading back to stand at the sofa and stare at the painting.

Oddly enough, the longer he looked at it, the more he... liked it. That was the biggest surprise of all. He *wanted* to look at Jenny this way. He was *glad* she saw him this way.

It was amazing how glad he was.

No, no, no. That wasn't good. It wasn't right for Jenny to have feelings for him.

Why not?

Well, because he wasn't the man in the painting. That person was who she obviously cared about, and it was an illusion. Harry wasn't open and caring like that. He wasn't vulnerable the way that man was. She wanted someone she could talk to about *feelings*.

Or maybe, he acknowledged slowly, remembering everything she'd said the night before, she just didn't want to be on the sideline. Maybe she wanted to be the center, not an afterthought.

He could do that. Hell, he *was* doing it. She just didn't know.

"Jesus," he muttered, and lifted the glass of bourbon again, then just put it down on a table without drinking.

Pacing over to the living room window, he stared sightlessly at the street below.

Why was he thinking this kind of insanity? He was a selfish prick for even considering that maybe he should go after her, track her down, and tell her everything she wanted to know. Tell her what she meant to him.

Why not? This time the painting seemed to be asking the question, but when he turned to face it again, it hadn't moved. It was still looking at him with its outstretched hand and soft, open eyes.

"Fuck."

He had to get out of there.

Harry strode into his bedroom, pulled on shoes and socks, then grabbed his keys and ran downstairs to his Jeep.

Every fiber of his being wanted to go to the chief's house—to Jenny—but he drove in the opposite direction instead. Out past Hardy Falls Park, past the lake with the waterfalls and the Fallside Restaurant perched above them, past Mrs. Brady's old farmhouse with the new "For Sale" sign in the front yard. Out of the town and up into the mountains.

Now that it was the middle of April, the regular trails were getting busier, even though the wet weather they'd been having had suppressed the turnout of early tourists. It was a good thing Harry knew some roads that weren't nearly as well-traveled—mostly because they were basically dirt tracks.

His Jeep was set up for off-roading, but even it had trouble handling all of the mud and ice the winter had brought. Harry welcomed the challenge, embraced it, and got farther than he'd expected before there was no way the vehicle could keep going.

He left it and started walking through lingering icy snow that soaked his socks and sneakers, and undergrowth with thorns that grabbed at his jeans and jacket. When he finally reached the clearing he'd known was there, he stepped out into the sunshine.

The snow was patchier in the meadow than it had been under the trees, but it hadn't completely melted at this higher elevation. It caught on the leaves and blades of grass, glittering like diamonds in the light.

Harry made his way to the spot where the mountain dropped away, and there was a clear view of Hardy Falls spread out in the valley below. A town that belonged on a postcard. Highways gleamed like silver ribbons from up here. You couldn't see specific buildings, couldn't see cars or people, couldn't see problems.

His grandparents loved the town they'd moved to five years ago, and Harry loved them.

You're a waste of space, boy. Waste of money.

Junior's voice.

You don't have to be a certain way. If you can breathe, you can change.

His grandfather's.

When the old man had said those words, he'd been sitting on the edge of Harry's bed in his dorm room his first year in college. His grandfather's sharp eyes always seemed to see right through him, and he'd known that Harry was on the verge of ruining his entire life.

Harry squirmed. "I wasn't doing anything different from anyone else," he protested. He'd gotten drunk, but so had everyone at the frat party. And yeah, he'd passed out on the sidewalk on the way to his car to make a beer run (he was only eighteen, but everyone knew the stores that didn't care if you were underage). At least it had happened before he'd gotten in the car, not when he was behind the wheel, right? He'd apparently thrown up, too, but he hadn't choked to death the way one of Junior's friends had.

Why the hell had the campus police called his grandfather when they'd found him out cold and smelling like his own vomit? Why had Harry agreed to go to a college close enough that the old man could drive there within an hour?

His grandfather didn't say anything, didn't shout, just sat on the side of his bed in the dorm room and watched him. Harry shifted uneasily.

"You're at the beginning of your life, boy," his grandfather said at last. "You're the one who can decide how it's gonna go. Nothing's set in stone."

"That's bullshit." Harry jumped up from the bed and paced back and forth in the tiny room, trying to burn off his furious energy. "I'm just like Junior," he spat out, wanting to hurt someone else because of the way he was hurting. "You know it, and I know it. A worthless piece of shit."

His grandfather didn't flinch, just looked worn, and Harry felt even worse than he had a moment ago. But he didn't apologize. Hell with that. If the old man couldn't handle the truth, then he could just turn around and leave. Harry would make his own way. Screw him.

"Your father is who he is," his grandfather said. "But you're not him."

"Oh, yeah?" Harry snorted in disdain. "The apple don't fall far from the tree, old man."

He was pushing now, wanting his grandfather to snap, to shout. To leave. But although Harry Senior's eyes glittered, he didn't move.

"So you think Junior is just like me then, huh?" his grandfather demanded.

"What?" Harry paused in his pacing, confused.

"If the apple don't fall far from the tree, then I'm just like him, right?"

No, that was wrong. His grandfather had integrity. Junior didn't.

His grandfather had never raised a hand to Harry, had never hurt him intentionally.

"Uh..."

"Or maybe you think he's just like your grandmother?" the old man pressed.

"No. Of course not."

"So then that tree thing is just your own whiney-ass bullshit because you want to party your way through school and do nothing with your life." Now his grandfather stood up. Even though he was shorter, he glared at Harry like the soldier he'd been. "Grow a pair," he snapped. "But don't tell me you don't have a choice."

"You send Junior money all the time," Harry accused desperately. His grandparents were the reason Junior could be the way he was.

"We did while you were with him," his grandfather agreed. "And we did until you turned eighteen a couple of months ago. We did it so he wouldn't try to take you. Now that you're of age, we'll have to stop. It doesn't matter what we did or didn't do anyway. That doesn't have anything to do with you. We made our choices. You have to make yours. You don't have to be a certain way. If you can breathe, you can change."

Then he turned and left the dorm room.

And he'd made his choice, Harry thought, looking out over Hardy Falls as the sun strengthened in the sky. He'd decided that he'd never be his father. He'd gone out of his way not to be anything like him.

So why did he still think he was?

Harry blinked.

"What?" he murmured, the thought odd and ethereal.

If he believed Junior was a lying sack of shit, if he knew his life was what it was because of the choices he'd made, if he'd gone out of his way to be a better man than his father had ever hoped to be, then why did he still accept the things Junior said about him?

He didn't. Of course he didn't believe them. He didn't really think he was worthless. He knew that was wrong.

Then why was he pushing Jenny away? Why was he telling himself he'd hurt her, telling himself she was better off without him? Telling himself he wasn't the man she saw when he *wanted* to be that man?

Mind whirling with the sudden shock of alternatives, Harry groped his way over to a boulder and collapsed against it to avoid ending up on his butt in the wet snow. At least at this time of year he probably didn't have to worry about copperheads, but at the moment he wasn't sure he would have felt the bite.

Did he have it in him to open himself up the way she obviously wanted him to?

What if he tried, and then he couldn't do it?

What if he hurt her?

What if she hurt him?

What if they hurt each other?

What if he got fired?

What if Jenny moved away? Left town? Found another man? Got married? Came home with a husband and children?

"I'd shoot the bastard," Harry muttered, and his hand actually twitched with the sudden urge to go for his gun.

Harry knew he could stay safe in his comfort zone. He could let her walk away. He could take the easy way out. Or he could roll the dice. One more time, he could roll the dice.

Roll the dice.

The possibilities spread out in front of him like the view from the mountain. He pushed himself away from the boulder and clenched his hands into fists.

Good, God. He loved her. He really, truly, madly loved Jenny Kline.

Yes.

"Roll the dice!" Harry shouted to Hardy Falls and realized he was grinning like the idiot he was, his heart pounding, and his knees somehow weak and strong at the same time.

It was just a job, for fuck's sake. It was just a town. But Jenny...well, she was more. All he had to do now was prove he knew she was worth taking a risk.

Turning, he slipped and slid and ran back to where he'd left his Jeep.

36

Harry didn't want to waste any time, but he was also wet, cold, and covered in mud after rushing and sliding back to his Jeep. Some things needed to be handled correctly, especially when you were trying to prove yourself.

So instead of following the voice that was howling at him to track Jenny down *now*, he went back to his apartment, took a shower, and changed. In the living room, he gave his portrait a wave.

"Wish me luck!"

Then he headed out again, this time driving toward his grandparents' familiar little ranch house on the other side of town. Because Jenny was right—he needed to tell his grandfather. The only way she'd believe he didn't want to hide their relationship was if he showed her.

Harry pulled the Jeep into his grandparents' driveway and turned off the engine, then sat looking at the house.

In the end, it didn't matter if Junior was alive or dead. It didn't matter what the man had thought. This place was home even though he'd never lived here because the people living here were the ones who'd raised him.

His grandfather had sounded alert when they'd spoken earlier, but Harry didn't want to wake up his grandmother if she was sleeping, so he didn't call from the driveway the way he normally did. Instead, he walked to the front door and used his spare key to unlock it and slip inside.

He should have known better. As soon as he shut the door, he turned to find his bright-eyed grandfather in the hallway, a heavy wooden baseball bat in one hand. Harry was a little surprised the old man could lift it.

"Goddamn it, boy," his grandfather said in a hoarse whisper. "Why in the hell didn't you call first? I almost beaned you."

"You always yell at me for calling first," Harry reminded him, keeping his voice low, as well.

"I meant you should knock on the damned door. I didn't think you'd just come parading on in."

"I didn't want to disturb Grandma." Harry hesitated. "How is she?"

His grandfather shrugged. "Okay. Resting." He looked at the closed bedroom door and then jerked his head toward the living room. "Come in. Sit."

Harry followed him into the room and sat in his accustomed spot on the sofa, while his grandfather settled into his recliner.

"You look better than I expected, considering your bender last night," Harry told him.

His grandfather snorted. "That wasn't no bender, boy. Just a few drinks with some good friends."

"Right." Harry felt himself jitter with nerves. "I wanted to tell you something," he began carefully. "But I should wait," he said, realizing the truth too late. "It's probably not appropriate to talk about this when Junior just died and—"

"Stop. Don't be a goddamned fool. It's a fine time. I don't blame you for not being broken up about your father," his grandfather interrupted to say. "And, honestly, I'm having a harder time with what I did or didn't do than anything else."

"I know, but still."

"Your grandmother and I are okay." The old man shrugged. "Or we will be. Maybe that's part of the problem. You shouldn't be okay when your son dies. But he wasn't much of a son, was he?"

"No," Harry said and hesitated. If Jenny needed more from him, maybe his grandparents did, too. "I shouldn't be relieved that my father's dead." He forced himself to go on, even though he felt stupid talking like this. "But he wasn't much of a father either. And I didn't need him anyway because I have real parents. I have you guys."

He thought he sounded like a jackass, but his grandfather's blue eyes got damp with tears, and he sniffed loudly.

"Well," Harry Senior said, emotion making his voice far gruffer than usual. "Well."

Harry found himself swallowing hard, too.

They quickly looked away from each other, and Harry felt an unexpected spurt of amusement.

Sometimes, he thought, the apple really didn't fall far from the tree. He'd just been looking at the wrong tree when he'd been eighteen.

"So," his grandfather cleared his throat loudly. "What did you want to tell me?"

"It really can wait," Harry said, and he wasn't sure if he was trying to be sensitive or if he was just scared. This was the moment of truth.

"Nonsense. What's on your mind, boy?"

Harry tried not to fidget.

Here we go.

"I'm seeing someone," he said, looking at his grandfather again. "Someone special," he added. "Important."

"Yeah?" The old man's smile held more than a hint of mischief. "Do tell."

Harry looked at him suspiciously. "You know?" he demanded. "How do you know?"

His grandfather laughed and held up his hand. "I know when my boy has got himself a lady friend, don't I? Not coming around without any explanation, showing up with a big, sappy grin on his face. Some interesting marks on his neck that look a lot like love bites. I'm old, son, not blind. Albert, Martin, Joe, and I started a betting pool."

Harry felt himself blush and rubbed his hand along the back of his neck. "Well, Jesus."

His grandfather laughed again. "So, who's the lucky lady? I've been waiting a long time to see that particular sparkle in your eye. I want to meet her."

"Oh, I think you know her." Harry couldn't control his smile. "Jenny Kline."

It was gratifying to see his grandfather's still-wet eyes widen. "Jenny? Really?"

Harry frowned a little. "Why are you surprised? There's nothing wrong with her." Nothing wrong at *all*.

"No, of course not. I just never thought you'd get your head out of your ass and get up the guts to finally go after her."

Now it was Harry's turn to be surprised. "You knew I liked Jenny?"

"Well, of course I did, boy! You looked at her enough."

Yeah, Harry admitted. He had.

"What can I say? I'm stupid." He shrugged. "But I got there eventually."

"Good." His grandfather chuckled. "Always liked that Jenny girl," he said. "Like Josie too, of course, but that Jenny, well, she reminds me a little bit of myself."

"Really?" Harry leaned forward. "How so?"

The older Harry shrugged. "She goes her own way. It doesn't matter what anyone else thinks, she knows her own mind."

"Not always," Harry said, thinking about her ex, Stefan.

"She just gets tripped up now and then. I know she got involved with some fella from the college and ended up coming home with her tail between her legs a few years ago. But maybe she had to go through that." His grandfather's eyes grew unfocused, as if he was looking at something that wasn't there. "Sometimes we need rites of passage," he said, quietly. "Sometimes we have to make decisions just so we know what's important." He frowned at Harry. "We can't control everything, boy. We can't always play it safe. If we do, we regret it."

"Is that why you let Junior go with his band?" Harry asked. He'd always wondered about that. His grandfather was no pushover. No matter how anybody else felt, if the old man had put his foot down, then Junior wouldn't have been allowed to run off the way he had.

The older Harry sighed. "Can't keep a baby bird in the nest forever. Your father, well, he had more wildness in him than most—and more arrogance, too. I figured he needed to get out into the world, make mistakes, figure things out." His face fell into lines that made him look every bit of his eighty-three years. "But he never learned. It was always somebody else's fault. Then there was you to worry about and keep safe."

Harry reached across to grab his grandfather's gnarled hand. "You and Grandma raised me right," he said. "I'd be nothing if it wasn't for you."

The older Harry's eyes were full of tears he refused to shed, but his smile was full. "You were always your own man," he told him. "Just as stubborn as Jenny." He grinned. "And me. You'll work it out."

"Um, there's a chance I might lose my job in Hardy Falls," Harry told him. "Just so you know."

His grandfather's smile dropped away. "Why?"

"Because the chief might kick me to the curb as soon as she finds out I've been, uh, seeing her daughter."

The old eyes sharpened. "You're going to tell her?"

Harry nodded. "I'm not going to keep it a secret anymore."

"Jenny's that important to you?"

"Yes."

"Good." His grandfather gave a pleased-sounding sigh and then shrugged. "I've never known Jackie to be vindictive."

"Jenny's her daughter."

"True." His grandfather's face turned serious. "But if a woman's worth anything, she's worth taking a chance on."

Harry looked down at his folded hands.

"But, what if I can't do it?" he asked the question he really wanted answered. "What if I can't be the person she needs?"

"Of course you can. Don't be an idiot, boy. You *are* the person she needs, no maybe about it. And what the hell are you still doing here talking to me? Go do what you need to do before she gets away from you."

Roll the dice.

Harry stood up, hugged his grandfather, and left.

37

Jenny sat on the old sofa in her studio, staring at the familiar clutter and feeling...nothing. When she'd left Harry that morning, she'd assumed that she would spend most of the day crying, but she really hadn't.

That was good, she supposed. There was no way her mother would have missed evidence of a day-long crying jag. Even though Jackie was at work now, when she came home Jenny wouldn't be able to avoid the woman.

How in the world she'd survive another two months at the office without her mother figuring out something was wrong was beyond her. Maybe she should ask Harry to change his shift. He had to be hating the thought he'd have to see her all the time anyway.

Jenny looked down at her feet and dimly realized that she'd dragged mud all through her studio because she'd forgotten to take off her shoes. Well, it didn't matter.

She wasn't quite sure what she'd expected when she'd given Harry the painting. In her fantasies, she'd thought maybe he would stop her from breaking things off, from leaving him. She might have even hoped he'd pull her into his arms and declare his undying love.

Fairy tales. Silly, little girl dreams.

The one thing she *hadn't* expected was for him to say that the painting didn't mean anything at all.

It's just a painting! It's not that big a deal!

To be fair, Harry wasn't an artist, so he probably couldn't tell that she'd slathered herself over every inch of that canvas—put quite a few of her dreams into his portrait.

Or maybe he just didn't care one way or the other.

"You need to cut him some slack," she told herself. After all, the man had just found out his father was dead. Based on what he'd told her, she got the impression he didn't exactly like the guy, but it had to be messing with his head.

It was just...she was so *tired* of always being the one to bend where Harry was concerned. She was tired of always being the one who pursued closeness.

She couldn't leave the job. If she left, her mother would be on the hook with Margo Truelove. It wasn't fair to throw Jackie under the bus when Jenny had walked into this situation with her eyes wide open.

Or thought she had anyway.

It was funny, really, because pretty much the same thing had happened to Josie last year. Her sister had gotten involved with Mat thinking it was one thing, and then found out it was more than she'd ever anticipated.

It had ended differently for Josie and Mat, of course. And when they'd been going through their hard times, Mat had chased after Jenny's sister, pounded on the front door, demanding to be let in so he could talk to her. Jenny had answered the door—because Josie had been upstairs in her bedroom crying—and the man had almost pushed her out of the way in his eagerness to get to her sister.

Harry had stared at her like he'd suddenly found a wild animal in his apartment.

Restless and tired and sad all at the same time, she pushed to her feet and wandered over to the easel. The landscape of the Hardy Falls Lake twinkled at her, bright and cheerful and looking like something a five-year-old had done with finger paints.

She wanted to get out a knife and shred it.

Even if Harry thought the portrait she'd done of him was nothing, and he couldn't see what she'd put into it, she was glad she'd given it to him. It belonged to him. Besides, now she wouldn't be tempted to pull it out and look at it all the time. Or destroy it.

She rubbed her hands up her face. "So, okay. Eight weeks. Two months. Then what?"

She'd paste on a fake smile and suffer through the two months because she had to, unless she ran across an opportunity to leave that wouldn't impact her mother. Maybe if she was rude enough, Margo would fire her again.

Jenny left the easel and walked back to the window to stare out at the backyard and the wooded park beyond. The park where Harry had often left his Jeep on his clandestine visits actually backed up to their property. He technically never needed to walk up the street and risk being seen. She should have told him before, but she'd never gotten around to it. Maybe she'd wanted him to get caught and force him out in the open.

"Selfish," she murmured.

And in love. For what that was worth.

Being in love had never been worth too much as far as Jenny was concerned. This experience had not changed her mind.

Shaking her head, Jenny turned back to face the clutter of her studio.

Her ideas of what she'd do after the temp job at the police station had been vague at best, especially after she'd gotten involved with Harry. They had involved staying here with her mother, painting with little success, and basically floating through life.

Well, no more. She might not be able to leave town this second, but she could work goddamned hard to make sure she didn't have to stay any longer than necessary. She'd get another job in the evenings, save as much money as she could, and line up something outside Hardy Falls for later. With the experience she was getting, she might even be able to work in an office with all those mythical benefits her mother kept harping on. She'd talk to Ms. Gregory about apartments. The elderly librarian didn't own many properties outside of Hardy Falls, but she had connections.

Regardless, Jenny would not be staying here. She'd make her life somewhere else.

She walked back around the easel again and touched the canvas. It was dry, so she took it off and added it to the stack of others. Then she folded the easel up and propped it in a corner.

She might paint again later. As a hobby. If she had room in her new apartment. But for now, it was time to grow up.

Jenny was at her workbench sorting through her paints to see what she could throw out when there was a quick knock on the door of the space that she now thought of as a shed. Turning, she saw Jackie come striding in.

"There you are," her mother said. "I wanted to—" she broke off abruptly and frowned. "What's wrong?"

Jenny cursed herself for losing track of time and not realizing her mother's shift was probably over. "Nothing," she said as casually as she could.

"Bullshit," Jackie told her, frown morphing into a scowl, and her hands clenched into fists on her hips. "You have your easel folded up. Your easel is *never* folded up."

Jenny cursed again, only this time at observant police offi-cers. It was clear she would have to tell her mother at least some of what was going on.

"I've been thinking," she said. *Truer words had never been spoken.*

Jackie's eyebrows lifted. "Go on," she said. It was more of an order than a suggestion.

Jenny ran her hand through her hair and then leaned back against the workbench. Probably better to just spit it out.

"I've been trying to decide what I'm going to do after this temp job is over. After all," she added, trying for some spin, "I don't work for Missy or Mr. Foster anymore."

"Right." Jackie continued to frown.

"So, uh, I'm going to get a second job at night, for now. Wait-ress probably. Maybe at one of the new places out on the high-way." She would have considered asking Louise because the other woman obviously needed help at the bowling alley, but she didn't want to hurt Hannah's feelings. "I'm going to save money." She took a deep breath because this was the hard part. "And then I'll be able to get my own apartment and get out of your hair."

Jackie did not react for a long, long minute.

"An apartment here in Hardy Falls?" she asked quietly.

Goddamn it! Why did her mother have to know her kids so well?

"Um, probably not," Jenny admitted reluctantly.

"And your painting?" Jackie persisted. "Working two jobs won't give you much time for that. I thought you were making it a priority."

"No, I know." Hiding things was fucking hard, especially when all you wanted to do was tell your mom everything. But she couldn't do that to Harry. "I think..." she stopped then started again. "I think it might be time to just give it up. I never get anywhere anyway." She looked around the shed, breathed in the air that always smelled like turpentine and oil paint, and felt a big part of herself flatten. Painting—art and the creation of it—had always come first. But painting had given her just about as much as falling in love had. Nothing.

Again, Jackie didn't respond right away, which was a surprise since Jenny had thought she'd be delighted.

"Are you involved with that Stefan asshole again?" she demanded after a moment, the words like bullets.

Jenny blinked at her.

"What? No, of course not."

"Because your sister called me about in tears saying she doesn't see you anymore and you don't even text her. She thought it was because of her and Mat, but now I'm wondering if there isn't more to it than that."

Jenny winced.

"I'm not seeing Stefan," she assured her mother.

Jackie nodded grimly. "Good. I'd hate to have to go shoot him."

Jenny wasn't sure if she was kidding.

"I'll call Josie and apologize," she told her. "I haven't been avoiding her." Not on purpose anyway. "Just had a lot on my mind."

"Thinking," her mother said.

"Yeah."

Jackie abruptly dropped her cop's stance and propped herself against the arm of the old sofa. Jenny had to work hard not to think about how Harry had bent her over that very same arm and taken her with fierce intensity last night.

If she'd been planning on using the shed again, she would have definitely needed to replace that sofa.

"I didn't know, you know," her mother said. "Not for a long time. But I did figure it out eventually."

Jenny was confused. "You didn't know what?"

"That Stefan wasn't treating you right. You'd been pulling

away more and more, so I could tell something was wrong. But you never came out and told me."

"There were problems," Jenny acknowledged. "I didn't want to bother you."

"For the record, hearing you say that pisses me off. I didn't know how he was treating you," she repeated. "If I had—"

"I didn't tell you." Jenny shrugged. Knowing how her mother would have handled the situation was one of the reasons she hadn't said anything. Well, that and embarrassment. "And I'm the one who let him treat me that way, let him get away with sleeping around behind my back. I won't make that mistake again."

"Good." Jackie tilted her head, considering her. "Just out of curiosity, why did you let him get away with it?"

Jenny struggled to find an answer. "I don't know," she said finally. "He was always so sure of himself, and he had all kinds of contacts in the art world. He just always treated me as 'less than' and I guess I thought he was right."

"Well, you should have goddamned known better."

"Really? I know I'm not as smart as Jordan or Josie. Don't have my act together the way they do, that's for sure. I'd taken the money you'd given me and wasted it on art classes, and—"

"Honey, stop." Jackie stood and walked over to her. She put her hands on Jenny's shoulders. "I had no idea you felt this way. And don't you dare say that you wasted that money."

Jenny snorted and pulled back, moving restlessly in the small space.

"Please. You've been pretty darned clear what you think about me painting. I'm sure you're delighted to hear that I'm going to walk away from it for a while." Maybe forever. "I can only imagine how you felt when I didn't go for a formal degree."

"It was an adjustment," Jackie admitted. "And, like I've said before, I wish you had more financial security in your life. But I've always been proud of your painting. Always."

Truly shocked, Jenny gaped at her. "Really?"

"Yes, really! You have so much talent, Jenny." Her mother shook her head, and there was wonder in her eyes. "I have no clue where it comes from. Certainly not from me."

Jenny didn't know what to think about that, didn't know how to process it. She never dreamed her mother would say something like that. Never.

Maybe Harry wasn't the only one who needed to talk to people more. Maybe she and Jackie needed some practice, too.

But thinking about Harry brought her back to reality and the decisions she'd made.

She still had to leave.

At that moment there was another knock on the door to the shed. No, not a knock. A pounding thump.

Without waiting for a response, Harry walked in.

38

Jenny stared at Harry, not quite sure what he was doing there. His eyes met hers for an instant, the changeable blue-green of them turbulent. Then he turned his attention to her mother.

"I need to talk to you, chief," he said abruptly.

"All right." Jackie's voice held no discernible emotion. "I'm surprised you knew I was back here."

"I tried to catch you at the station, but you'd already gone," Harry told her. "When I saw you were parked in the driveway, but nobody answered the door at the house, I took a chance that you'd be here with Jenny."

"Or I could have been in the bathroom," Jackie pointed out, mildly enough to set off all sorts of alarm bells. "Let's go outside, and you can tell me what is so important." She started to move to the door, but he shook his head.

"No, ma'am." He looked at Jenny, then back to her mother. "This is better, anyway."

Jackie raised her eyebrows and crossed her arms.

"I see." She studied him. "I don't suppose this has anything to do with the reason Jenny is talking about not painting anymore and planning on moving away from Hardy Falls?"

Jenny squeezed her eyes shut for a moment, wishing she could sink through the floor.

"What?" When she looked at Harry again, she found him scowling at her. "What the hell do you mean you're going to stop painting?" he demanded. "Why would you do something like that? You're amazing. You can't stop."

That was rich, considering he'd told her earlier that her most personal painting was nothing special. Jenny glared at him.

"I'm pretty sure you don't get to have a say in what I decide to do," she snapped.

Harry opened his mouth to reply, but her mother cut him off.

"If that's not it, what did you need?" she asked. Jenny was surprised to see Jackie was smiling a little bit, her eyes glowing with amusement instead of the earlier ice.

Harry braced himself. "I have to tell you something," he said.

Jenny tensed. *What the hell kind of game was he playing now?*

Jackie folded her arms, amusement rich in her voice. "Ah. Could it be that you want to tell me that you and my daughter have been sleeping together for the last couple of weeks?" she asked. "And that you've been sneaking around behind my back in direct violation of departmental policies? Could that be it?"

Jenny stared at her mother. *She'd known? She'd known, and she hadn't said anything? Or tried to stop them?*

Harry was standing so stiffly that he could have been a soldier in a parade.

"Yes, ma'am," he said.

Jenny's attention snapped back to him.

Wait, what? No protests? No arguments? What the hell?

"And you're here to ask me not to fire you?" Jackie asked, her voice silky.

"No, ma'am," Harry said, surprising the hell out of Jenny and, she thought, her mother. "I'm here to tell you what's going on because I'm not going to hide my relationship with Jenny anymore. We tried to keep it secret because we knew you didn't want that kind of thing happening at work, and I know you might consider it sexual misconduct. But I want everyone to know I'm with her." He glanced at Jenny. "Assuming I can convince her to forgive me."

Jenny gaped at him.

Jackie grinned. "I knew you had something to do with the painting and the moving."

"Maybe," Harry admitted. "But things will be different now." He swallowed. "I love her," he said. "I'm not going to hide it anymore."

Jenny's mouth snapped shut.

What?

Harry looked at her, and she saw him relax a little bit. The corner of his lips quirked up in a smile.

"I love you," he told her. "I want everyone to know, if you can ever forgive me for being a jackass."

Mute, she nodded.

He loved her? He *loved* her? He wanted to tell people about her?

Jackie laughed a little and straightened again. "Was that all?" she asked Harry.

"Yes, ma'am."

"I think you two must believe I am both stupid and senile if you think I didn't figure out a long time ago that this great romance was going on under my nose." She bent to kiss Jenny on the cheek. "I might have missed what was happening with Stefan, but even I'm not blind enough to miss this." She put her hands on either side of Jenny's face and pushed back her hair. "This was way too big."

Jenny sniffed back tears.

"And no, I'm not going to fire you," Jackie told Harry, turning and walking toward him. "As long as you make whatever's going on here all right again."

"I will," Harry promised, which was a little arrogant since Jenny had at least half of the say in how things would go. "Can you tell me why I'm not fired, ma'am?" he asked. "I know I've disobeyed the department rules."

Jackie raised her eyebrows. "Want me to change my mind?"

He shook his head. "Just curious."

"Because I've been waiting for this to happen for three years —ever since Jenny finally dumped the lowlife at the university," she told him as she opened the door. "You two are perfect for each other." She stopped and frowned. "Although you will have to keep it secret from everyone else in the department until Jenny leaves the temp job. I can't have the rest of them thinking they can just fraternize all over the damned place."

Harry frowned. "I don't—"

"It's okay, Harry," Jenny said hastily. She smiled at her mother. "We'll be good."

Jackie rolled her eyes. "Promises, promises."

Then she walked out, and Jenny and Harry were alone.

Jenny took a step toward him but stopped. He was watching her with eyes that had gone completely blue, burning with an inner fire. It was odd that she felt this awkward, considering she now knew that he loved her.

He loved her!

But she also had a sense that he wasn't ready for her to launch herself at him yet, so she held herself in check.

And, to be honest, maybe she wanted to see if he'd launch himself at *her*.

"The first time I remember being left alone overnight, I was four," he said, and it took a minute for her to process his words because they were so unexpected. "I think it might have happened earlier than that, but that's the first clear memory I have."

"Harry." She took another step forward, but he held up his hand to stop her.

"Please," he said. "This is hard for me to talk about already. It will be harder when I'm holding you."

He said, "when." Not "if."

"Then don't talk about it," she said. She could feel the tears that she'd battled all day rising up, yet again. But this time they weren't for her own situation. This time, they were for a little four-year-old boy alone and probably terrified.

"No, I want to tell you." He drew in a deep breath, his face as hard and angled as an ascetic. "Daisy, my mother, was gone— she had stayed with us until then, but once I turned four, she never stuck around much. I guess a toddler wasn't quite as cute as an infant doll she could dress up and play with. I had a personality at four."

"Harry—"

"I think that night Junior might have been out with his friends and forgotten me. He had a tendency to do that." He smiled faintly. "We toured with his rock band, you see. Dump to dive and back to dump. All over California. Plenty of distractions to make a guy forget about his kid back at the hotel."

Harry took a step closer to her in the small space and reached out to brush her face. That was when she was crying.

"Don't cry."

"You can't tell me what to do," she sobbed, and his smile widened.

"You're probably right about that. Anyway, long story short, we traveled with the band, my mother came and went, other women came and went, and my father drank a lot. Sometimes he did other things when he could afford them. He left me alone a lot. Always forgot to feed me. No school—we moved around too much. I grew up fierce and feral."

"Your grandparents?"

He shrugged. "They didn't know what was going on. They sent him money. When I was a kid, it made me angry because they were enabling him. But now I know they were doing it for me. And him, but mostly to try to help me. They didn't realize he took their money and bought booze with it, not cookies."

"But, you somehow ended up with them in the end."

"Yeah. When I was eight...maybe eight and a half... my mother was gone again. Aerobic instructor, I think. Anyway, one of Junior's friends started laying into me, punching me. I got slapped from time to time, but this was bad. I didn't know him, and now I think he might have wanted to...well, anyway. Junior finally sobered up enough to stop him, but some ribs and my arm were broken." He held out his left arm and looked at it.

"Oh," she gulped.

"Yeah." He smiled again at her response. "Junior was scared because I was hurt really bad, so he called the ambulance. The hospital thought it was child abuse, which of course it was, although not by Junior. He didn't hit me much, just didn't feed me and left me alone. Anyway, my grandparents got contacted somehow. My grandfather flew out the next day. And that was that."

"Your father just gave you to them?"

Harry shrugged. "I don't know the details, but he didn't really want me. He just wanted the money he got from the state and from Pops. Once my grandfather agreed to continue giving him money until I was eighteen, he was happy. I didn't find that out until later either."

Jenny couldn't stand it any longer. He might not want her to touch him, but she had to. *Had* to. Stepping into him, she wrapped her arms around his waist and buried her head against his shoulder, breathed in the clean scent of him as she nuzzled into the crisp cotton of his button-down shirt. After a second, his arms encircled her, and he held her with a strength she thought would leave bruises.

"You need to know this," he insisted. "You need to know who you're getting involved with."

"I'm already involved. And I already know."

He tugged back her head and kissed her. It wasn't gentle. It was hot and hard and full of the fire she'd seen burning in his eyes.

After several long moments they broke apart, breathing heavily.

"Let me finish," Harry told her sternly. "You're too much of a temptation."

Jenny thought she nodded. She must have looked pretty out of it because he grinned before tucking her close again.

"Once I figured out my grandparents weren't going to ship me back to Junior, I ran wild at their place," he said. "It was like they'd brought home a wolf who'd been masquerading as a puppy. I did whatever I could to push them."

"Why?"

"To see what they'd do, I guess." He shrugged. "And they just loved me. I mean, don't get me wrong, they disciplined me, but they loved me. Never hit me."

"Of course not."

Harry pulled back a little bit. "It took until I was eighteen to start to get my head out of my ass. Everything I've done since then has been to try to make my grandparents proud of me. Living up to my grandfather's name, serving and protecting, doing it here in Hardy Falls where they live—that's all huge for me."

"I—"

He put a big hand over her mouth. "I'm trying to explain

why I was so worried about what your mother would do if she found out about us," he said.

Jenny gently bit his palm to make him move it.

"I've always understood that," she insisted. "I've always known how much your job meant to you."

"It's more than a job. It's...well, it's who I want to be. Do you understand that part, too?"

"Yes."

"But I want to be the person you see, too, Jenny," he told her. "I want to be the person you painted. I want to look at you that way."

"You already do. Maybe you just didn't realize it."

"Probably." He kissed her again.

They didn't surface again until they had moved to the old sofa, which was once again her favorite piece of furniture. They ended up with Harry sprawled across it with Jenny tucked over his body, their legs intertwined. She could feel his arousal against her stomach and his rough-skinned hand stroking her back under her T-shirt.

"I wasn't the only one in that painting, was I, Jenny?" Harry asked.

It took her a minute to remember what he was talking about.

"No," she admitted. She'd put herself out there for anyone to see if they were looking. The fact that he had, that he'd recognized it, well, it made her heart sing. He might not be an artist, but he understood her.

She bent to kiss him, but he pulled back so her lips just grazed his cheek.

"Say it," he growled.

She lifted her head to blink at him innocently.

"Say what?"

"Witch." He gave her a hard, quick kiss. "I said it to your

freaking mother, the least you can do is tell me to my face. My real face, not my painted one."

Smiling, she leaned into him, and this time he let her sip at his lips. She pulled away before either of them could get distracted.

"I love you," she said.

"I love you back," he replied.

And it was perfect.

A long time later, they were still sprawled on the sofa, but they were both wearing considerably less clothing. The sun was setting over the backyard, the birds were singing, the snow was melting, and somewhere in the studio—which was a studio again and not a shed—Jenny's cell phone "dinged" with a text message notification. She reluctantly left her nest on Harry's chest and got up to find it, finally locating it in the pocket of her discarded jeans. The message was from her mother.

I refuse to think about what you two are doing in the shed, but I've made spaghetti and meatballs. I think you need carbs. I'm going out so I don't have to see either of you.

Jenny laughed and sent back a smiley-face emoji, then grinned as she looked at Harry stretched out on the sofa in naked splendor.

He certainly was...splendorous.

"How are you going to keep working with my mother," she teased, going to him and climbing back onto his body.

"Probably just avoid her until we get used to it," he admitted. He tugged at her hair, but his face was serious. "What if it doesn't work out?"

Jenny frowned and pushed his tousled hair out of his face. "She said she wasn't going to fire you."

"I'm not sure she exactly came right out and said that, but even if she doesn't, it could be too awkward. I'm not going to put people at risk just because the chief and I can't make eye contact."

"Oh." Jenny made a face. "I hadn't thought about that."

"Neither did I."

"It's because we were thinking with our body parts and not our brains."

"God bless them," he said with heartfelt appreciation, his hand squeezing the cheek of one of her body parts that he seemed to find especially attractive.

"If she fires you, what will you do?"

"Well, I guess I'll find a job in another town. My grandfather understands. I'll just try to find something close by. I mentioned the possibility when I told him about you."

Jenny's heart sang with joy.

He'd told his grandfather.

"For now, I'm going to avoid her shifts," he said. "I'm sure Tony or someone else will be thrilled to work days for a while."

Jenny frowned. "That's not fair either."

He shrugged. "It might be a good idea to put a little distance between you and me anyway, if I'm going to be pretending we're not involved. Besides, I'm used to working nights and evenings and weekends and whenever the hell. It's all part of being a cop." His face smoothed in a way she was coming to recognize. "That's not going to be a problem, is it?"

She bit his bottom lip. Hard.

"I am Jackie Kline's daughter," she informed him. "Of course it won't be a problem."

"You're Jenny," he told her. "Just Jenny." Then he kissed her again.

The spaghetti and meatballs were cold and congealed by the time they made it inside for their carbs. Neither of them cared.

EPILOGUE

Two weeks later, it was the end of April, and Jenny was sitting at the bar in the Country Time. It was only ten-thirty in the morning on a Wednesday, so she should have been answering phones at the police station. But she'd gotten a mysterious phone call from Josie the night before requesting she and Harry show up at this time, and her mother had agreed to let her go.

The bar was crowded, even though the Country Time wasn't open yet, but everyone gathered around it at the moment were employees. Well, except for Jenny. Kevin stood at the kitchen door, arms crossed, an immovable mountain. Mary Alice and Grace sat beside Drew, the new cook. The two girls who'd been hired as servers for lunch, Bev and Ashley, sat on Drew's other side. He appeared especially interested in the cute, dark-eyed Beverly.

Ah, love was in the air at the Country Time again.

Mat was in the kitchen getting set up, and Hannah, Deacon, June, and Calvin were all missing, but Jenny had been assured they were there. Jason Nguyen, who'd quit medical school and was back as the second bartender, slid her a cola across the bar. She smiled at him in thanks.

"Hey." Josie settled on the stool next to her and stole a sip of her soda.

"Hi, there," Jenny greeted her sister and gestured around the bar. "Tell me again why you called me to come in? I'm confused—this is obviously a staff meeting."

"Wait just a few more minutes," Josie said unhelpfully. "Where's Harry?"

"He'll be here soon," Jenny told her. "It's a little early for him."

Harry and Jackie had decided it would be better for everyone if he did go ahead and switch shifts. So, Harry had moved to the swing shift and was working evening/overnight hours.

Jenny was glad that her mother had agreed to let her leave the office at four o'clock, and Harry didn't have to be at the station until at least six-thirty. Plenty of time for late-afternoon delight.

She did feel bad about causing problems for Harry, though. He was the senior officer at the department, so he had to be able to work with the chief. But he'd just shrugged when she mentioned it.

"We'll get used to it," he'd told her. "It's a little weird right now, but the chief is okay with us as long as we keep things on the down-low while you're at the station." He grinned mischievously. "She thinks I'm a good influence on you."

Since at the time of this conversation, they were lying together naked in his bed after a round of "ships passing in the night sex," as Harry called it, Jenny reached over and pinched him. Difficult to do since the man was made of solid muscle.

Jenny grinned at the memory of what happened next, and of course, Josie noticed.

"Why are you smiling?" her sister demanded.

Jenny let her smile morph into a smirk.

"Oh. Harry." Josie looked around. "I hope he gets here soon."

"He will. Why?" She playfully shook her sister's shoulder. "Would you just tell me what's going on already?"

"Hannah will tell everyone," Josie said. Jenny had to stop herself from wringing her neck.

"Just tell me that she's okay."

"She's fine. And here comes your man."

Watching hunky Police Officer Harry Newman III push through the kitchen door and walk to her, all tall and strong and delicious with his light brown hair gleaming in the low lights, was enough to make Jenny's heart pound right out of her chest.

Her man.

Hers.

"Jesus, girl, would you show some dignity?" Josie laughed beside her. "You're practically drooling."

"Shut up," she told her sister.

Harry came to stand beside her. "Hi, Josie." He nodded at Josie, then smiled at her, the curve of his lips reminded her of everything they could be doing with this unexpected time. All she wanted to do was kiss him. From the way he was looking at her, Harry felt the same way.

They couldn't go there—not in public. Not yet.

But they would someday.

"I have to go get Mat," Josie said and slid off her seat. Harry took her place, his arm braced on the bar behind Jenny. It probably looked more than just friendly. She didn't much care.

"Why are we here?" he asked.

"I don't know."

Harry grinned at Jason when the young man slid him a mug of coffee. "How did you know?"

Jason smiled and shrugged. "You're a cop. It's morning. I just took a guess."

"Well, it was a good one." Harry lifted the mug and took a sip, distracting Jenny for several moments as she watched his strong throat working when he swallowed. She wanted to bite his skin and leave another hickey.

Later.

"If you don't stop looking at me like that, we're not going to find out why they called us here," Harry murmured, putting the now half-empty mug back on the bar.

"I want us to move in together now," she said, picking up a discussion they'd started the previous evening. She knew she sounded sulky and didn't much care. "I want to be able to kiss you anytime I want."

"We can't. Not yet." He put his big hand on her thigh under the bar, and her motor started revving, which made her even sulkier.

The truth was, she missed seeing him. Now that their working hours were different, they had to steal time when they could. They'd both decided that she shouldn't move in with him until after her stint at the police station was done. It would only be another six weeks, but it seemed like an eternity.

"I work this weekend," he reminded her, "so you'll have some time to paint."

Jenny patted his arm. He'd been adamant that she shouldn't give up painting, and he'd actually already gone ahead and set up a station for her by the window in his living room. Her mother had said she could keep using the shed, too.

She loved painting, would always love it. But she wasn't sure she still loved it enough to make it her career. Being with Harry was filling up some of the emptiness inside.

Maybe she didn't need to figure it all out right away. Maybe she could just see how things went.

Harry squeezed her thigh, distracting her from her thoughts, and she smiled over at him.

"Don't be sad," he whispered. "We'll work it out."

She knew they would.

At that moment, the kitchen door pushed open, and Hannah, Deacon, June, and Calvin walked into the taproom.

It was like watching a parade, Jenny thought as they marched out, single file, and came to stand shoulder to shoulder in the taproom, facing their audience at the bar.

Josie, because she was a smart-ass, clapped. Hannah shot her the finger.

"We have some freaking news," June demanded. "Do you want to hear it or not?"

She might have a rounder belly, but June was still kind of scary. They all nodded.

"Okay." Hannah cleared her throat, her hands on her own growing belly as she looked at them all. "So, Deacon and I have set a date," she told them. "For our wedding."

"We did, too," June added.

Jenny straightened and saw all of the other women do the same. Mary Alice clapped her big hands over her mouth and let out what could only be considered a squeal.

"And have you finally decided where you want this wedding to be?" Josie demanded.

"We thought we'd have a big picnic," Hannah told her, "so everyone in the town who wants to come can come. And we'd all get married."

"Okay, okay. That's a good idea," Josie muttered, and when Jenny glanced at her sister, she saw she'd pulled out a tablet computer and was making some notes. "Good publicity. Make a day of it. Where?"

"Hardy Falls Park?" Hannah suggested.

Josie frowned at her. "It would be better if it was here, like when you had the carnival. Then it's specifically tied to the Country Time."

Hannah frowned back. "This is my freaking wedding, you know. Not a marketing opportunity."

Josie waved that away. "I'll see if Mr. Clark will let us use his field again. Maybe get a few rides—"

"Josie." Hannah sounded firm. "No. These are our weddings. They will only happen once."

"I wanted to go to the freaking town hall and just get a certificate or whatever, but Calvin said everyone's going to want to see us actually do the deed or they won't believe it," June told them.

"Do the deed?" Calvin teased her gently, his dark eyes twinkling. "I had no idea you were such an exhibitionist."

"Screw you," June told him, then blushed bright red when he whispered something in her ear.

"*Any*way," Hannah continued, "we were thinking more of a town picnic. Like a potluck. Everybody brings food, sits around, and watches the ceremony. Make a day of it. That way, everyone can be invited, but the costs will be low."

Josie was scowling. "If that's what you want."

"That's what we want," Hannah told her.

Josie sighed. "Fine. I'll find the officiant."

Hannah smiled sweetly at Jenny's sister.

"I love you."

"Yeah, yeah, yeah."

Harry raised his hand. "Um, speaking as the representative for crowd control, when is this town picnic going to happen?"

"We were thinking around the middle of May."

All of the people gathered around the bar blinked at her.

"Um, the middle of May is only about two weeks away, Hannah," Mary Alice said.

"Yeah, that's not a lot of time to set up," Grace agreed.

The two women exchanged a look. They'd been there when

Hannah had pulled off a carnival in two weeks. While she'd succeeded, it hadn't been easy. Jenny remembered coming in one evening and finding Grace close to tears because the copy shop had ruined the posters she and her friends had made.

"What's to set up?" June argued. "Just need to find out if we can use the park, but that should be fine since my boo here is a town bigwig."

Calvin looked at her. "Boo?"

"Okay, my *bae* is a town bigwig. And my apartment should be done in two weeks, too, or mostly, so we'll be ready to rock."

"The weddings need to happen before the tourist season really ramps up on Memorial Day," Hannah added. "We'll close for the day. I want all of you to be there."

"Oh!" Mary Alice squealed again.

"But...but..." Jenny's mind was scrambling with all of the things that were normally found at a wedding. "What about dresses? Flowers? Cakes?"

"What kinds of dresses do you think we're going to be able to fit into?" June demanded. "We'll find something. And there are flowers every damn where. We'll pick some."

Since this year spring had mostly meant "mud," Jenny hoped there actually would be something in bloom by then.

"Since it's more of a potluck, there's not a lot to plan," Hannah said. "I thought I'd ask Mrs. Knight about cakes."

"And you guys are okay with this?" Mat asked Calvin and Deacon. "A picnic?"

"Hannah finally set a date," Deacon told him. "And I was beginning to think we'd have to hold it in Peanut's dorm room in college. I don't care when or where."

"I have to jump when June's in a good mood," Calvin agreed. "Not many opportunities."

She elbowed him.

After that, there was general chatter and lots of hugs. Josie walked away muttering to herself, and Jenny knew her sister was getting geared up to enact world domination. Or at least picnic-wedding domination. Mary Alice leaped at June and hugged her enthusiastically, much to June's obvious dismay.

"This is all great," Harry murmured into Jenny's ear, "but why am I here?"

"Or me?" Jenny agreed. "I could have heard about all of this from Josie."

"Hey, do you guys have a minute?"

Jenny turned to see Hannah had come to stand behind her and Harry.

"Congratulations," she said as she smiled at the other woman.

"Thanks." Hannah appeared uncomfortable and glanced behind the bar to where Deacon was pouring soda, as if looking for support. Jenny's blood froze.

"What's wrong?" she demanded, grabbing for Hannah's hand.

"Nothing." Hannah smiled. "Can you guys come back to my office for a minute?"

"Sure."

Really concerned now, Jenny jumped off the barstool and followed Hannah down the short hallway to her postage stamp of an office, Harry bringing up the rear. Once Hannah had sat behind the desk, and Jenny and Harry had crammed themselves in on the other side, Harry somehow managed to close the door behind them. They were effectively sitting in a closet.

"Okay. What the hell is going on?" Jenny demanded.

Hannah took a deep breath. "So, the OB says that I need to really cut back on my hours here. I had a, um, scare last week, and apparently I'm under too much stress. June is having trouble keeping up with her normal hours, too, although I'll have to kill you if you tell her I said that."

"Oh, no!" Jenny sank into the visitor's chair. "What are you going to do?"

"I'm going to ask you if you'd like to come work for me and be my...I don't know...mini-me?"

"What?" Jenny wasn't sure she'd heard her correctly.

"Well, you are kind of short," Hannah teased.

"Hannah—"

Hannah waved her free hand. "I'm not explaining it right. See, I can do some of the paperwork, at least for now. But the OB says I really should kind of be on at least partial bed rest. My blood pressure's pretty high." Her hazel eyes were wide and frightened.

"Hannah." Jenny reached across and grabbed Hannah's hand. "It's going to be okay."

"That's what Deacon said."

"Is this why the sudden rush for the wedding?"

Hannah nodded. "I wanted us to be married now, in case I couldn't have a party later. And I do want to marry Deacon, so much. I just..." she shook her head. "That's not important. Anyway, I can do some things, and Josie will set up my laptop at home, even if I end up on bedrest one hundred percent of the time. But June can't pick up for me like she always did before because she's barely keeping it together. We need somebody here who has experience, someone we can trust to run things. And, most of all, we need someone who knows the Country Time."

Jenny looked back at Harry. His expression was sympathetic, but he shrugged, telling her without words that this was her decision.

"Hannah," Jenny said gently. "I have a job, you know."

"I know." Hannah was clutching her hand, nails digging into her skin. "So, that's why I talked to your mother first."

Jenny pulled away and sat back.

"You did what?" she asked.

"Yeah. I knew you'd promised her, and Josie told me that

there were problems with Margo. So I wanted to see what she thought before I talked to you."

"I'll bet she was delighted," Harry said dryly.

Hannah bit her lip. "I'm not sure 'delighted' is right the right word, but she said she'd back you whatever you wanted to do."

Jenny put her hands up to her head because it was spinning so fast.

"She will?"

"So think about it, okay?" Hannah begged. "If you can't do it, I'll deal, but…just think, okay? I'm supposed to be backing off now, and that means we need someone as soon as possible." She drew in a deep breath. "Promise me."

"I promise," Jenny said.

"What do you think?" Jenny asked Harry later, after they'd run the gauntlet at the bar and were standing by their vehicles in the mid-morning sunshine.

"I think this is the perfect reason for you to leave the police station if you want to. Even our esteemed mayor can't badmouth Jackie if you're doing it to help Hannah."

Such an optimist. He was so cute.

"If you're not working at the police station, we could move in together. And, if you're working here, our hours will be about the same until I have to rotate shifts again."

"This job might not be permanent," Jenny reminded him. Hannah had made sure she knew that as of right now, she wasn't sure what would happen.

"But she wants it to be. Hell, she's going to need it to be. She and June are going to be insanely busy once they have rug rats to worry about. What if Josie gets pregnant, too? Or Mary Alice?"

The thought of Mary Alice pregnant was a trifle alarming. But Jenny had a feeling that the woman's boyfriend, Johnny, would be a good father.

God, it was so much to think about.

A chilly breeze blew between the cars, and Harry grabbed her hips, pulling her closer into the cradle of his body—protecting her as he always did.

"The question is," he said, "is it something you want to do?"

Was it? Well, it would be interesting, that was for sure. And she'd be able to add "manager" to her resume, which might be helpful. Most importantly, she'd be helping someone she cared about. But...

"I might not have time to paint if I do it," she murmured, and, because she could, because he was hers and always would be, she moved in closer, wrapped her arms around him, and buried her face against his neck.

"You'll paint," he assured her, more confident in her than she was in herself. She drew back to look at him.

"Yeah?"

"Yeah. It's important to you. You'll make the time." He put his hands on her face and tipped her head back to meet her eyes. "You can do it."

"I love you," she told him.

"I love you, too," he said and kissed her full on the mouth in front of anyone who happened to be driving by. No secrets. Just the two of them.

When they broke apart, Jenny took a deep breath and mentally stepped out into a new adventure.

"Let's go talk to my mother and find out how long she needs me to stay," she said. "Then I'll tell Hannah I'm game."

He kissed her again.

Whatever choices she made now, she knew it was all going to work out. She'd already made the most important one when she chose Harry.

THE END

Turn the page to read an excerpt from

Believing Love
Welcome to Hardy Falls, Book 1

BELIEVING LOVE
WELCOME TO HARDY FALLS, BOOK 1

He just needs a second chance to make things right...

June Esperanza really hates making mistakes. And if a man burns her so badly he almost destroys her, she damn well learns her lesson about letting anyone get that close again.

Too bad that Calvin Hardy, June's biggest mistake, just moved back to Hardy Falls and plans to stay.

Calvin knows how profoundly he screwed up when, young and stupid, he left his hometown and June behind. Now, years later, he can finally try to right the ultimate wrong in his life. The problem? June doesn't believe a word he says.

Simmering passion and penetrating hurt collide as June and Calvin come face to face with their past, their present, and their future. If you enjoy a wonderfully emotional romance where two people fight for, and with, their second chance at love, you'll fall for *Believing Love*.

~

Chapter One

June Esperanza was crouching behind the old wooden bar that dominated the empty taproom of the Country Time Bar and Grill putting away some napkins when she heard the tavern's front door open and quick, light, footsteps echoing across the antique planked floor.

What the hell? They were closed for another hour, and the door should have been locked. Hannah must have forgotten to secure it again when she'd gone to get some stuff for the party they were hosting later that evening.

June stood, ready to throw out the intruder, but hesitated when she saw an elderly woman standing in the middle of the room looking around with a vague expression. Her white hair was cut in a short, stylish bob, and she was clutching a large purse to her thin chest. She looked familiar, although June couldn't quite place her. She just knew she didn't belong there.

"I'm sorry, ma'am," she said, leaning her forearms on top of the bar. "We're not open."

The woman turned, chocolate brown eyes wide and confused in an oval face, and June drew in her breath.

Eva Hardy in the flesh, by God. Unofficial queen of Hardy Falls, the little, pissant, whitewashed, Pocono Mountain tourist-trap town where the Country Time was located, and where June had, for some inexplicable reason, lived for the last sixteen years or so.

"Mrs. Hardy," she said, straightening away from the bar. "What are you doing here?" Her voice was cold, but she couldn't help that. She hadn't spoken to Eva in years—hadn't even seen the woman in at least three—and could happily have gone a while longer without renewing their acquaintance.

Instead of giving her the confident, superior, smile June remembered so well, Eva appeared even more confused, her dark brows furrowed over her thin nose.

"Do I know you?"

"Yes," June said slowly, belatedly remembering that Eva had early-onset Alzheimer's disease. It had apparently gotten significantly worse over the past year, which was why Calvin had moved back to town three months ago.

Calvin Hardy. The only child of Ronald and Eva Hardy.

And an asshole.

"No, I don't. I don't know you." Eva threw back her shoulders, the habitual movement emphasizing how thin she was now. "Where's Fred? I'm looking for Fred," she demanded querulously.

Fred? Was she talking about Fred Frederickson, Hannah's father? Yeah, he used to own the Country Time, but he'd been dead for more than two years. Hannah ran things now.

"Ah, he's not here," June said, trying to think of what to do. She moved cautiously out from behind the bar and walked toward the other woman, not wanting to say or do anything to upset her more. Did people with Alzheimer's get violent? June didn't think so, but she didn't want to find out. All she'd need would be for Chief Kline to arrest her for getting into a smackdown with Ronald Hardy's fragile, little wife.

But how the hell was she going to get her out of there? Christ, was Eva still driving? If she'd driven, June would feel obligated to make sure she got home, which would be the freaking cherry on top of her freaking day.

Eva frowned. "But Fred told me to come. We made arrangements to meet here."

Interesting. June hadn't known Eva and Fred were that close.

She considered the other woman for a moment. Even with the ravages of her disease imprinted on her face, she was still lovely and had probably been quite a babe when she was younger. For his part, Fred had been one hell of a good-looking man. Heck, June had actually given some thought to the highly inappropriate proposition he'd made to her when she'd first started working for him, even though he'd been a good twenty-five years her senior.

In the end, she'd decided against it. He hadn't been married —Hannah's mother had been killed in a car crash a few years before June blew into town—but there had still been too many complications to make it worthwhile.

Fred sure hadn't liked it when she'd turned him down, though. Over the years, she'd discovered that most women came running when Fred showed interest.

Had Eva been one of them? She'd certainly been a Country Time regular back in the day, spending many an evening here at the bar talking to Fred after bowling with the leagues next door at Murphy Lanes. If June remembered correctly, Eva's husband had rarely joined in the discussions.

"I'm sorry," she said, taking another step toward the woman. Eva pulled her handbag closer to her chest, as if afraid June would steal it.

Yeah, because that's just what I would do, huh?

Stop it, June ordered herself. She doesn't mean anything. She's old and scared and confused and doesn't even realize she knows you.

"Fred isn't here now," she said, trying to be kind. She was usually better at slapping sense into a person, but she could be kind if she felt like it. Hannah would attest to that. "Do you want to sit down and wait for him? Maybe have some coffee?" If she stalled until Hannah got back, she could dump the whole situation on her. After all, she was the one who'd forgotten to lock the door.

Still clutching her purse like a security blanket, Eva glanced around the room, at the small wooden tables gleaming with polish, the stained glass lanterns hanging above them, and the flat-screen television over the bar.

"It's...nice in here," she said hesitantly, putting a hand to her forehead.

"Sit down," June said, and this time the kindness was natural. "Come on. I'll get you some coffee, and we'll talk."

"Okay." Eva sounded heartbreakingly young. She tried to pull out one of the sturdy wooden chairs at a nearby table, and June hastened forward to help when it looked like the effort might cause her to topple over.

Once seated, the older woman looked up and smiled a beautiful smile, clean and clear and bright. June blinked. Eva Hardy had never smiled at her like that before.

"You're very nice," Eva said. "Do I know you?"

June drew in a deep breath. "No," she said. "We've never met." Because she had never met this version of the woman.

"Oh." Eva beamed. "I hope we'll be friends."

June didn't know what to say to that, so she turned and went behind the bar where a massive coffee machine sat on the back counter, a full pot simmering on its burner. She got a clean mug, poured coffee, then doctored it with a couple packs of sugar and the last of the half-and-half from the open carton in the refrigerator under the bar. *Sweet and light.*

Moving with the ease of long practice, she took the mug of coffee to the other woman and put it down in front of her. Eva smiled that young smile again, then lifted it with both hands and sipped.

"It's perfect," she said, putting the mug carefully back down on the table. "You knew just how I like it."

The comment made June pause. How had she remembered that? She'd served an awful lot of coffee to an awful lot of people in the years since she'd last seen Eva.

She guessed some things just stayed with you, whether you wanted them to or not.

As if on cue, the front door slammed open, and a man came rushing in.

"Mom? Mom, are you...?" his voice trailed off, and he skidded to a halt.

Calvin. The bastard.

June had tried to prepare herself for the impact of seeing him again after fifteen years, but the reality still punched her in the gut. She stared at him—at the thick, dark hair, now liberally sprinkled with silver, the dark eyes, so like his mother's, glittering in his hard face, the broad shoulders, and the long, muscled legs.

"June," he said, his voice deep and soft, a velvet growl.

June forced herself to remain casual, arms crossed, chin up. "Calvin."

He swallowed.

"I—"

"Do I know you?" Eva asked primly from her seat at the table.

Calvin shook himself and switched his focus to his mother, allowing June to take her first deep breath since he'd burst into the room.

"Mom," he said. "I've been looking all over for you."

"I'm sorry," Eva said, folding her hands in her lap. "I don't believe we've met."

The expression on Calvin's face was easy to define—it was grief. He glanced at June quickly, as if embarrassed.

"She's been pretty bad today," he said apologetically. "Usually she recognizes my father and me."

A twinge of sympathy had June speaking more gently than she'd intended.

"She says she's looking for Fred," she told him.

"We're meeting here," Eva chimed in, smiling.

"I told her he wasn't in," June finished.

Eva frowned at her. "Did you? Do I know you?"

"Um, okay." Calvin was obviously confused, but he knelt down next to his mother, his large hand on the wooden arm of the chair. "Fred called the house, um, ma'am. He can't see you today."

"Oh." Eva's smooth face creased with dismay. "Really?"

"Yes. Why don't you come with me? I'll make sure you get back home."

"No. I don't know you." Eva looked at June. "Should I trust him?"

Not on your life. "I'm sure you can."

As if that settled the matter, Eva nodded, then finished her coffee. "How much do I owe you?" she asked June.

"On the house."

Eva let Calvin help her to her feet. "I want to go home," she told him.

"That's where we're going." Calvin looked back over his shoulder at June as he led his mother from the room. "Thank you," he mouthed.

June nodded.

Then they were gone, and she was alone again.

Calvin Hardy.

"Shit." June sank down on the chair Eva had just vacated.

She'd known she'd see him some time, she reminded herself. She'd heard he'd rejoined his old bowling league—God only knew why—and since most of the bowlers came to the Country Time to eat and drink after their scheduled matches, he was bound to show up sooner or later. It was actually kind of a miracle it had taken three months for them to run into each other.

June exhaled.

At least their first encounter was over now. She'd seen him again. They'd spoken. She'd survived. So, it would be easier next time.

Right?

Pushing herself to her feet, she went to the front door, locked it, then turned to look at the taproom. It glowed gold in the lamplight, with scattered patches of color decorating the

 Believing Love

tables and floor from the early afternoon sun shining through the old stained glass windows.

Back when she'd been twenty-two, the Country Time had seemed like just another dump. She'd never expected to stay longer than it took to save up enough money to hit the road again. No one had been more surprised than she when it had become home. No one had been more shocked that she'd stayed on in spite of everything.

Sighing, she walked back to the bar and continued with the preparations for opening. She wished to hell she hadn't come in early to help Hannah get ready for the party they were hosting that night. If she hadn't been working, she wouldn't have seen Calvin again. She wouldn't have seen Eva. And she wouldn't have seen how delicate and frail the woman was, seen the hurt in Calvin's dark eyes when she didn't recognize him.

What must that be like—to have your own mother not recognize you?

June snorted. She got a clean rag from the stack under the bar and began polishing the wooden top until it shone, rubbing hard to erase any marks or bottle rings.

Hell, in her case it would've been a miracle if her mother had known who she was in the first place. By the time June had turned three, all Leila Esperanza had cared about had been her next fix. If June's grandmother hadn't stepped in, she didn't know where she'd have ended up. Child Protective Services, probably.

Too bad Grandma Rose had decided to correct the mistakes she'd made with Leila by regimenting every moment of her granddaughter's life. June had been bound to rebel, hadn't she? Guys and bikes, cigarettes and drinking. No drugs, though. She'd seen what it had done to her mother. Leila had been a walking skeleton, her whole life plunged into her veins along with the heroin. She'd died when June had been eight, but it had hardly mattered.

It *had* mattered when Grandma Rose died of a heart attack, but June had been seventeen and not about to go into foster care, thank you very much. Instead, she'd dumped school and hit the road.

Five years and a lot of miles later, she'd ended up in Hardy Falls with Fred and Hannah.

And Calvin.

Believing Love

ALSO BY BETSY HORVATH

ABOUT THE AUTHOR

Betsy Horvath was raised on a steady diet of old MGM musicals, Nancy Drew, and Harlequin romances, so nobody should have been shocked to discover that one day she would be writing romance novels of her own. Especially not once became clear that, when given the opportunity, she could sing the entire soundtrack from the *Sound of Music*, regardless of whether or not anyone asked her to (nobody ever did), and that the only books she ever wanted to read were the ones with happy endings (which made things interesting in college).

Let's face it, Betsy is a hopeless romantic. But she's good with it.

www.BetsyHorvath.com
betsyhorvath@betsyhorvath.com